ESTHER

A STORY OF COURAGE

TRUDY MORGAN-COLE

REVIEW AND HERALD® PUBLISHING ASSOCIATION
HAGERSTOWN, MD 21740

Also by Trudy Morgan-Cole:
  Connecting

To order, call 1-800-765-6955.

Visit us at www.reviewandherald.com for information on other
Review and Herald ® products.

Copyright © 2003 by
Review and Herald® Publishing Association

The author assumes full responsibility for the accuracy of all facts
and quotations as cited in this book.

Bible texts quoted in this book are from the *Holy Bible, New International
Version*. Copyright © 1973, 1978, 1984, International Bible Society. Used by
permission of Zondervan Bible Publishers.

This book was
Edited by Penny Estes Wheeler
Cover designed by Mark O'Connor
Cover art by Robert Hunt
Electronic makeup by Shirley M. Bolivar
Typeset: 12/14 Bembo

PRINTED IN U.S.A.

07 06 05 04 03   5 4 3 2 1

R&H Cataloging Service
Morgan-Cole, Trudy J. 1965-
      Esther: A story of courage

          1. Esther, Queen of Persia.   I. Title.

                    222.9092

ISBN 0-8280-1760-3

DEDICATION

To Emma and Christopher,
who love to dress up as
Queen Esther and King Xerxes,
with all my love

ACKNOWLEDGMENTS

I am grateful to so many people for their help with this book. In the beginning Randy Fishell at *Guide* magazine got me started on the trail of Esther by inviting me to write an Esther story for *Guide*'s young readers. The research for that story sparked questions and ideas that eventually led to this book.

I'm thankful to everyone at the Review and Herald, but especially to Jeannette Johnson, for her initial excitement and steady support, Penny Estes Wheeler for her thoughtful editing and unabashed love of the book, and Gerald Wheeler for steering me toward excellent research materials.

Leona Running gave this book an extremely thorough going-over even before it reached my editor's hands, and her advice on history and language was invaluable. Many thanks to members of the Newfoundland Writers' Guild who were present and made such useful comments when I workshopped one of the more difficult chapters. Thanks are also due my online friends at Religion Debate board who listened to me "thinking out loud" about this book, especially to rashi_fan and existential_fish for attempting to answer so many obscure questions about Judaism, and to the many friendly skeptics there who drove me to explore more deeply the links and gaps between the Bible and secular history. All of these people provided me with a wealth of encouragement and guidance. The errors that remain here are, of course, entirely my own.

Last but best, many thanks to my family—my children to whom this book is dedicated, my husband, Jason, for his constant support, and my parents and Aunt Gertie for all the extra hours of child care while I rushed to finish this book in time to meet a deadline. (To be absolutely fair, I should probably also thank *Bob the Builder* and *Veggie Tales* for the occasional hour of free time they provided when no relative was available to baby-sit!) Like anything else worthwhile, this book could not have been done alone, and I'm grateful to everyone who was part of it.

PREFACE

"At that time King Xerxes reigned from his royal throne in the citadel of Susa, and in the third year of his reign he gave a banquet for all his nobles and officials. . . . He commanded the seven eunuchs who served him . . . to bring before him Queen Vashti, wearing her royal crown, in order to display her beauty to the people and nobles, for she was lovely to look at. But when the attendants delivered the king's command, Queen Vashti refused to come. Then the king became furious and burned with anger (Esther 1:2-12).

"Later when the anger of King Xerxes had subsided, he remembered Vashti and what she had done and what he had decreed about her. Then the king's personal attendants proposed, 'Let a search be made for beautiful young virgins for the king.' . . . Many girls were brought to the citadel of Susa and put under the care of Hegai. Esther also was taken to the king's palace and entrusted to Hegai, who had charge of the harem. . . . She was taken to King Xerxes in the royal residence in the tenth month, the month of Tebeth, in the seventh year of his reign. Now the king was attracted to Esther more than to any of the other women, and she won his favor and approval more than any of the other virgins. So he set a royal crown on her head and made her queen instead of Vashti" (Esther 2:1-17).

"In the twelfth year of King Xerxes" "the king took his signet ring from his finger and gave it to Haman son of Hammedatha, the Agagite, the enemy of the Jews. 'Keep the money,' the king said to Haman, 'and do with the people as you please.' . . . Then Esther sent this reply to Mordecai: 'Go, gather together all the Jews who are in Susa, and fast for me. Do not eat or drink for three days, night or day. I and my maids will fast as you do. When this is done, I will go to the king, even though it is against the law. And if I perish, I perish' " (Esther 3:7–4:16).

Between those few cryptic verses lie years of a young woman's life, lived out in a land far away and a time long ago. The story has fascinated readers—and stirred up controversy—for millennia, yet except for the barest details we know very little about this woman Esther. What happened during the unrecorded years? What emotions did she feel, whom did she love, what regrets haunted her, what hopes inspired her? Around the story's edges we see the frame of secular history, which tells of Xerxes but not of Esther or Vashti, Haman or Mordecai. How do the pieces fit together? What whole do they form?

Many writers have attempted to peer through the curtain of history into the hidden world concealed behind this short but powerful biblical book. What *really* happened? No one knows, or can know, for certain, as long as this world lasts.

What follows is just one story—one possible tale—of how it *might* have been.

CAST OF CHARACTERS

Abihail★: Esther's father, who dies when she is a small child.

Admatha★: the king's chief minister at the time of his marriage to Esther.

Amestris†: Xerxes' queen; his first and chief wife. Mother of Darius, Artaxerxes, and Amytis.

Amytis†: daughter of Xerxes and Amestris; wife of Megabyzus.

Artabazus†: commander in Xerxes' army.

Artapanos†: captain of the palace guard under Xerxes.

Artaxerxes★†: younger son of Xerxes and Amestris.

Artaynta†: daughter of Masistes and Artaynte.

Artaynte: Masistes' wife.

Artazostre†: sister of Xerxes; wife of Mardonius.

Asha: Darya's manservant.

Atossa†: King Xerxes' mother, deceased before this story begins.

Ayana: an Ethiopian girl who joins the harem shortly before Esther does; later Esther's lady-in-waiting.

Badia: an older concubine in the harem at the time Esther arrives; responsible for helping train the young girls.

Barsine†: Artabazus' wife.

Bigthan★: eunuch servant of the king accused of a plot against Xerxes' life.

Carshena★: a nobleman; one of King Xerxes' closest advisers.

Cimon†: an Athenian general.

Cosmartidine†: a Babylonian concubine in Artaxerxes' harem.

Damaspia†: daughter of Xerxes and Esther.

Darius★† (1): Darius the Great, father of Xerxes; deceased before this story begins.

Darius† (2): son of Xerxes and Amestris; heir to his father's throne.

Darya: a Persian girl; Esther's childhood friend.

Ezra★: a Jewish scribe.

Hadassah★/Esther: a Jewish girl who lives in Susa; the adopted daughter of Mordecai and Rivka.

Haman★: chief minister of Xerxes' court after the death of Admatha.

Hannah: the maid who serves Esther when she lives at home with Mordecai and Rivka.

Harbona★: eunuch who serves in the king's private chambers.

Hathakh★: young eunuch who comes to the palace about the same time Esther does; later becomes steward of Esther's household.

Hegai★: chief eunuch of King Xerxes' harem.

Hutossa: a midwife.

Hystaspes†: son of King Xerxes and Queen Parmys.

Irdabama: another queen; King Xerxes' third wife.

Kalinn: a slave girl who serves in Esther's household.

Lady Carshena: Carshena's wife.

Leila: an Arabian concubine, a few years older than Esther; joined the harem at about the same time Esther did.

Lilaios (1): poet; married to Esther's friend Roxane, the musician.

Lilaios (2): son of Roxane and Lilaios.

Mandane†: sister of Xerxes.

Manya: a concubine who arrives in the harem at about the same time Esther does; a friend of Raiya.

Mardonius†: King Xerxes' greatest general during the war with Greece.

Marsena★: a courtier on Xerxes' council.

Masistes†: King Xerxes' full brother, satrap of Bactria.

Megabyzus†: general in Xerxes' army; husband of the king's daughter Amytis.

Memucan★: a courtier and member of the king's council.

Menebar: eunuch who teaches music to girls in the harem.

Meres★: a courtier on Xerxes' council.

Meteke: an Ethiopian concubine in King Xerxes' harem.

Mordecai★: Esther's foster father; a treasury official in the palace at Susa.

Nehemiah★: a young Jew from Susa; later a servant in King Artaxerxes' household.

Parmys: King Xerxes' second wife and half-sister; mother of Hystaspes.

Pausanias†: king of Sparta who seeks an alliance with Persia.

Phratares: Xerxes' half-brother; son of Darius and a concubine, around whom a revolt forms.

Phratima: concubine who enters the harem shortly after Esther does.

Raiya: a slave-born girl who joins the harem shortly before Esther does; later serves as Queen Amestris' lady-in-waiting.

Rivka: Mordecai's wife; Esther's foster mother.

Roxane: a skilled musician who becomes Esther's good friend; wife of Lilaios.

Salabas: Persian cousin of Esther's Aunt Rivka.

Setne: an Egyptian master craftsman.

Shasgaaz★: eunuch in charge of the King's concubines.

Shethar★: a courtier on Xerxes' council.

Shirah: a Jewish girl; Esther's childhood friend.

Sofia: Damaspia's childhood nurse.

Spamitres: a eunuch who serves in King Xerxes' bedchamber.

Talia: young Babylonian girl who joins the harem a few months after Esther; later a servant in Esther's household.

Tamyris: Babylonian concubine who joins the harem at the same time Esther does.

Tarshish★: a courtier on Xerxes' council.

Teresh★: eunuch servant of the king, accused of a plot against Xerxes' life.

Tithraustes†: son of Xerxes by one of his concubines.

Vashti★: a concubine whom King Xerxes married thus elevating her to the role of queen, then divorced and banished.

Vashush†: treasurer under King Xerxes.

Xerxes★†: king of Persia (called Ahasuerus in the Bible).

Zenobia: a concubine of Xerxes' son Darius.

Zeresh★: Haman's wife.

Zethar★: eunuch who serves in the king's private chambers.

★Characters mentioned in the Bible

† Characters mentioned in historical sources outside the Bible.

Characters marked with neither of these symbols are the product of the author's imagination.

THE PALACE OF DARIUS AT SUSA

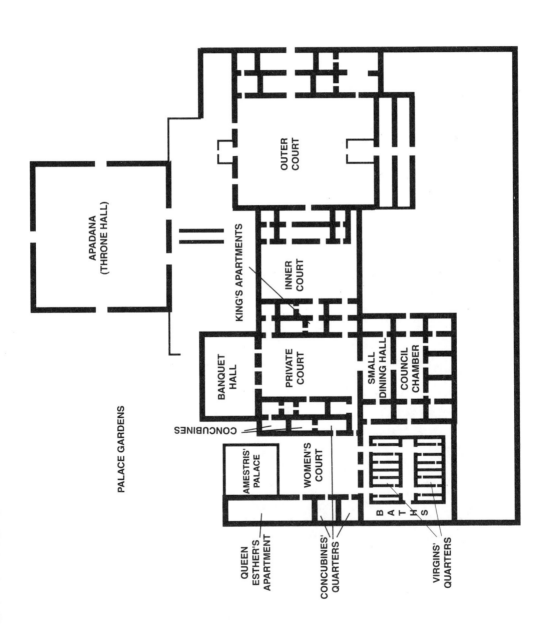

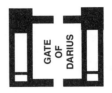

GATE OF DARIUS

APADANA (THRONE HALL)

OUTER COURT

KING'S APARTMENTS

INNER COURT

PRIVATE COURT

BANQUET HALL

CONCUBINES

SMALL DINING HALL

COUNCIL CHAMBER

PALACE GARDENS

AMESTRIS' PALACE

WOMEN'S COURT

BATHS

QUEEN ESTHER'S APARTMENT

CONCUBINES' QUARTERS

VIRGINS' QUARTERS

CHAPTER 1

The leaves of the tree formed a silvery-green curtain that shimmered between Hadassah and the outside world. The world, this moment, consisted of the courtyard of her uncle's house, the house and walls surrounding it, the distant voices of her aunt Rivka and a friend, and beyond it all the city of Susa—huge, bustling, and full of life. Hadassah bit into the peach she held and let its sweet juice trickle across her tongue.

A bird lit on a far branch. She leaned forward, molding her body to the shape of the branch, trying to see its chestnut shoulders and yellow throat, its bright knowing eyes. She stretched out her hand, slowly, slowly, willing the bird to come perch on her fingertips. It had done that before—or another sparrow of its kind had perched there, gripping her finger with its small claws, so close she could feel the tiny heartbeat almost in her palm.

The bird hopped a little closer, fixing one eye on the girl. Hadassah waited, still as the tree itself. She was so intent that she did not hear the voices of Aunt Rivka and her guest, which, like the bird, had moved closer.

The sparrow hopped once more, and landed on her finger. Delighted, Hadassah relaxed and let the half-eaten peach in her other hand slip to the ground. A sharp cry shot up from below, and the bird, startled, flew away.

"Oh no!" Hadassah cried, at the same time as her aunt called, "Hadassah! What are you doing?"

The girl peered through the leaf curtain to see the two middle-aged women, both startled, one annoyed, looking up at her bare legs, which dangled from the branch above their heads. She grinned, then hid the grin. She would be in enough trouble without Aunt Rivka knowing how much she was enjoying the whole thing.

Her aunt's voice sliced the sunny afternoon. "Come down out of there at once, girl!"

Hadassah, graceful as a bird herself, slid off the branch and dropped lightly to the ground.

"Hadassah, I am ashamed of you, but that's nothing—you should be ashamed of yourself! A girl your age, 15 years old now, climbing trees like a little boy! What would Shirah think, I wonder?" Aunt Rivka turned in despair to her friend Leah, the mother of Hadassah's best friend, Shirah. Or rather, Shirah *had* been Hadassah's best friend until she married six months before. Now Shirah seemed to think of nothing but her husband, her household, and the baby she had just found out she was expecting. She and Hadassah could find nothing to talk about anymore.

The girl did not offer any guesses as to what Shirah might think. She just stood, her head bowed submissively before her aunt, listening to the scolding, looking at her own bare feet in the jewel-bright grass. Aunt Rivka, not waiting for an answer, swept on: "Go into the house at once. Have Hannah change your clothes and bathe you. Put on something suitable for dinner—no, on second thought, don't bother! You won't be coming to dinner tonight—you will eat in your rooms. And your uncle will want to talk with you when he comes home. Go now, at once."

"Yes, ma'am," Hadassah said, walking away with as demure and ladylike a step as she could manage. If she had run, as she wanted to, she would have been too far away to hear Aunt Rivka moan, "Leah, what am I to do with that girl? Other girls her age have settled down and shown good sense long ago—like your Shirah. But Hadassah is as wild as a young kid-goat. How are we ever to make a good marriage for her?"

Shirah's mother replied with a smile in her voice, "With a face and figure like hers, Mordecai can make any match he chooses for Hadassah—as long as the bridegroom does not ask to spend too much time with her before the wedding."

"Shh!" Aunt Rivka said. Hadassah had stopped walking for a moment, interested despite herself. She heard her aunt sigh. "When Hadassah was a girl I would never let anyone speak of her looks in front of her, for fear it would make her vain. Perhaps that was a mistake. Not only is she not vain, there's not a girl in Susa who cares less for her appearance, her clothes, or her station in life. You may be right about her beauty, Leah, but that same bridegroom may have his doubts if he finds her perched in the trees above his head."

"Oh, a husband will tame her quickly enough," said Leah. The women's voices drifted away as they walked on, and Hadassah, stung by that last comment, hurried on her own way into the house. She did not want to be tamed—or married. Oh, someday, of course, when she was older. She'd just passed her fifteenth birthday and, of course, 15 was a marriageable age. But she did not feel 15, or marriageable. She felt young, and curious, and alive. There was so much to see and do, and Hadassah had no desire to be trapped and tamed just yet.

In her rooms she washed and changed with the help of her maid Hannah. As Hannah brushed out her hair, Hadassah looked critically at her own image in the small bronze looking glass on the wall before her dressing table. The words of her aunt's friend rang in her ears: *With a face and figure like hers, Mordecai can make any match he chooses for Hadassah.* Aunt Rivkah was right—Hadassah gave little thought to her looks and seldom glanced at the mirror. But she was no fool. She had caught enough admiring glances from her aunt's and uncle's guests, enough envious comments from girl friends, to know that men would find her pretty. She was taller than average for a woman, and quite slim; her face was a softly curved oval with a small straight nose, well-defined cheekbones, and light-brown eyes that gleamed almost golden under her lashes. Her mouth was perhaps a little too wide, but it was shapely and smiled easily, and her golden-brown skin was smooth and free of blemishes. Her girl friends sighed most over her thick, dark-brown hair, which fell straight and full to the middle of her back, but Hadassah found her shining tresses a bit of a nuisance; they were usually untidy and unkempt except when, as now, Hannah had just finished brushing them.

It was a relief to change into simple clothes rather than the finery she would have had to wear at dinner. It was amazing that after all these years Aunt Rivka still knew so little about her niece that she would think keeping her away from a formal dinner was a punishment. Sitting through the dinner—that would have been punishment enough, thank you! Hadassah disliked formal clothes, formal talk, formal occasions. Being penned in her rooms all evening was not ideal, but she could sit out on her balcony and enjoy the cool evening breeze and the smells of the garden flowers, play her oud, and read.

Her active outdoors nature was balanced with a sharp inquisitive mind that her uncle Mordecai had indulged more than was common in a girl. He and Rivka had no son—indeed, no children at all of their own—and orphaned Hadassah had filled all their home and hearts since she was a baby. Mordecai was actually her cousin, but so much older that she had called him Uncle and his wife Aunt for as long as she could remember. Rivka's love had taken the form of training, discipline, and sighing over a girl who would not become a proper young lady. Mordecai's had taken the form of long talks, storytelling, and tutoring, so that Hadassah could not only read well, but think about and question what she read.

Thinking of Uncle Mordecai made her feel a little guilty. Would Aunt Rivka remember her threat to send Mordecai up to lecture her? His only method of discipline was to tell Hadassah he was disappointed in her, and that cut her to the core in a way none of her aunt's lectures or punishments could ever do.

She did not want to disappoint him, and she knew that he and Rivka had pinned all their hopes on a good marriage for her and on her children, who would become their adopted grandchildren. Her fate was inevitable, and she accepted it. She just wanted to postpone it as long as possible. A year ago Uncle Mordecai had seemed to understand, and told Aunt Rivka they should not rush into marriage negotiations. Even then there had been offers. Now he too seemed to be growing impatient.

But Mordecai did not come. No doubt he was late coming home from his work at the palace and had had little time to bathe and change for the dinner. Some time later Hadassah reclined contentedly on a couch on her balcony as a kitchen servant brought a tray with lentils and barley cakes, lamb stew and fish, dates and raisins. The distant voices of her family and their guests dining in the courtyard made a pleasant background to her own meal. Beside her on the floor lay a scroll. Earlier in the day, before her disgrace, she'd asked for permission to borrow one of the precious few scrolls in her uncle's library. This one was a collection of copies of poems written by Hebrew exiles here in Persia, going back to the time before the Medo-Persian conquest, when the land was ruled by Babylon and the exiles still remembered their homeland, faraway Judah, and the famous city of Jerusalem. Their words of longing for home were poignant and beautiful. Hadassah loved to read them and think of the homeland her ancestors had left more than 100 years ago.

"By the rivers of Babylon we sat and wept
  when we remembered Zion.
  There on the poplars
  we hung our harps,
  for there our captors asked us for songs,

our tormentors demanded songs of joy;
they said, 'Sing us one of the songs of Zion!'

"How can we sing the songs of the Lord
while in a foreign land?
If I forget you, O Jerusalem,
may my right hand forget its skill.
May my tongue cling to the roof of my mouth
if I do not remember you,
if I do not consider Jerusalem
my highest joy."

Esther read the beautiful sad words aloud to the quiet evening air. She could not feel that sorrow—Jerusalem for her was only a name in a long-ago tale—but the poem enabled her to imagine it.

She did not much like the poem's harsh, violent ending:

"Remember, O Lord, what the Edomites did
on the day Jerusalem fell.
'Tear it down,' they cried,
'tear it down to its foundations!'

"O Daughter of Babylon, doomed to destruction,
happy is he who repays you
for what you have done to us—
he who seizes your infants
and dashes them against the rocks."

Could we really worship a god who wants babies dashed against the rocks? Esther thought. *Or were those Hebrew exiles only putting into words their own anger and pain, their rage against the enemies who destroyed their city?* She did not know. She felt far removed from the hurting, angry poet who had penned those words, and she felt no anger against the people of Babylon—or Persia, as the empire was called now. And she felt no real longing for Jerusalem, only a nostalgic yearning kindled by the poetry. Some of her dearest friends were Persian, and Susa was her home. She knew that Mordecai had been a young man when the decree to rebuild Jerusalem had gone out under King Cyrus. His family could have returned to Judah as many

Hebrews did. Instead, they stayed where their homes and their fortunes were, where they spoke the language and lived the culture. Their children, like Hadassah, were still taught to worship Yahweh, for in the Persian empire worship of many different gods was allowed. But truly, Hadassah felt no longing for the faraway land of her ancestors, only curiosity.

"Esther! Are you hiding here?" a light, giggling voice questioned from the garden. Hadassah rose on her couch to see her friend Darya making her way toward her. Dear Darya. The one friend who always called her by her Persian name, Esther. "I knew you must be in disgrace. What have you done now?" she asked with a giggle, perching on the end of the couch and helping herself to a handful of dates.

Hadassah laughed too. "The usual thing. Shocking my aunt with my wild behavior." She rolled the scroll carefully and dropped it at her feet. Darya had no interest in scholarship and no sympathy for the poems of Hebrew exiles. Darya was Persian, one of those great Persian friends of which Hadassah had just been thinking. In fact she had had two truly close friends in her life, Darya and Shirah, though neither was a bit like her. Shirah, the docile Jewish maiden, had always been quieter, better-behaved, and more practical. Now she'd settled into marriage with a sureness that left Hadassah feeling entirely left out. Darya, on the other hand, was a flighty bundle of giggles and vanity. She was utterly frivolous, completely consumed with gossip, clothes, make-up, and flirtations. She couldn't read and didn't care to. Her greatest interest in life was whom her parents would match her with, and when, and how handsome he would be. But Hadassah loved her for her lively and sometimes wicked wit and her boundless energy. Their families were close neighbors and often, as tonight, they were guests in one another's homes, so Hadassah was not surprised that Darya had stolen away from the after-dinner entertainment to visit with her.

As always, Darya's conversation was spiced with all the gossip of Susa. She was fascinated with the royal palace and all the comings and goings of the royal wives, concubines, children, and palace employees. Her father, like Mordecai, was a minor official at the palace gate. Unlike Mordecai, Darya's father seemed to delight in bringing home tales of palace scandal.

"Have you heard the latest?" Darya asked breathlessly. "About the king's new wife?"

"What new wife? Isn't the king still at Sardis?"

"Yes, he is, but the word has gone out: he is looking for a re-placement for Vashti." Darya eagerly bit into a fig, her eyes wide.

Hadassah had heard endless variations, from Darya and others, of the tale of Vashti. Vashti had been one of the royal wives, a minor wife in status but an exceptionally beautiful woman, rumored to be especially loved by King Xerxes who had raised her to prominence out of his vast harem of concubines. A few years before, Vashti had fallen into disgrace during one of the king's boundless and lavish banquets. The story was that the king had called her to come and dance for him and his guests—"and you know," Darya had told Hadassah, "what he meant by *dance*. She would be expected to pre-form a dance of the veils, taking off her clothing as she danced so all the men could see her loveliness."

"That sounds terrible!" Hadassah had said in disgust.

"*I* think it sounds rather exciting," Darya had replied. But Vashti had apparently thought it terrible too, and refused the king's order.

Nobody in the harem, nobody in the palace, nobody in Susa, nobody in Persia refused a direct order from Xerxes, King of Kings, the Mighty One. He was not quite considered a god but something very near to one. Vashti might have been executed, but her fate had been, in some ways, worse. She had been divorced and cast out into poverty and disgrace. Darya had shared a number of interesting ru-mors about what fate might have befallen Vashti since her disgrace, but no one knew what had truly happened to her.

Time had passed, and gossip had moved on to other matters. For more than a year and a half the king had not even been here in Susa. He had been at war with the Greeks, and news had come only a month before that his army was in retreat from Salamis after a crush-ing defeat by the Greek navy. "Although," Mordecai had told Hadassah, "they are so clever at the palace they are already thinking of ways to make it sound like we won a victory." The king had re-treated to Sardis where he was rumored to be spending the winter. The latest, most hotly reported piece of news was about the king's love affair with his brother's wife, the Princess Artaynta. Queen Amestris, his chief wife, was said to be very angry, especially as Artaynta had been seen parading around in a multicolored robe that had been a gift from Amestris to the king. What all this had to do with the long-vanished Vashti, Hadassah couldn't guess.

"I suppose his advisers think another marriage would be a good thing right now, don't they?" said Hadassah. Most royal marriages were political liaisons, either within the royal family itself or with the families of nobles, to strengthen the king's position on his throne. If the defeat at Salamis was as disastrous as rumor suggested, Xerxes' throne needed all the support it could get.

Darya tucked her feet up under her and hugged her knees in excitement. "I suppose so, but not in the way you mean. He's not marrying anyone from the noble families—in fact, he hasn't announced whom he's marrying at all. But there's going to be a huge roundup of new girls for the harem. They say there'll be hundreds of new women at the palace by the time the king returns to Susa."

"Oh, *that*." Hadassah waved her fan dismissively and gestured to her servant. "Have you finished with the figs, Darya? Take them away, Hannah, thank you. Bring us wine, and send a message down to the courtyard that Darya is here with me." As Hannah gathered the bowls and slipped away, Hadassah said, "What else could you expect after a military defeat? The king wants to fill up the harem to prove to everyone that he's a man, I suppose. It's a shame for the poor girls who get sent, but what does it have to do with him marrying again?"

"You'd know, if only you'd listen!" Darya squealed impatiently. "The King of Kings has called for new girls to be brought into his harem from all over the empire. *And* he has decreed that whichever of them is most beautiful and most pleasing to him will become a queen! He'll actually marry her, like he did Vashti—can you imagine? A concubine? Whoever she is, she'll become royalty." Darya sighed, a sigh of impossible longing.

"That does sound exciting, in a way," Hadassah admitted. "But Darya, surely you wouldn't want to be a harem girl, even for the chance of becoming queen. What a terrible, dull life it would be. And you'd never have a normal marriage or family." A little while ago Hadassah had been thinking of marriage and family as a dreadful, boring prison she was doomed to someday enter. But compared to the kind of life the king's concubines must lead, she had to admit that getting married to a good Jewish man and having children of her own wouldn't be so awful. Someday—not right now.

Darya, as usual, disagreed completely. "Esther, the women in the harem have the best of everything in Susa. The finest clothes, the richest jewels, the best food. They go to banquets, they live in the palace—and the palace is beautiful, you wouldn't believe how lovely—they have musicians come and play for them, they entertain. It's a wonderful life. And best of all, they get to see the king."

Hadassah shrugged. "I just don't think it sounds like such a wonderful life."

"That's a pity. If they took you to the harem, you'd catch the king's eye for sure." Darya studied her friend's face and hair enviously. Darya was pretty enough, but her round face would never be considered classically beautiful, and she worried constantly about getting fat and ugly before she got married.

Esther laughed. "Me, in the harem? Hardly likely, Darya! Now listen, tomorrow is a market day. Do you want to come to market with me? If I'm allowed out of the house, that is."

The next day Hadassah was, indeed, allowed out of the house to go to market with Darya. Aunt Rivka stayed home, due to a slight headache, but each girl was accompanied by her own maidservant, and Asha, a burly manservant from Darya's house, completed the group. Darya loved to search through the merchants' stands piled with silks and fine linens, jewelry and combs, fans and dyes. Before the morning was half done her servant staggered under a huge pile of fabrics and baubles Darya had selected. Hadassah was less interested in choosing finery for herself, but she loved the sights and sounds and smells.

People flocked to the bazaars on the twice-weekly market days. The vivid colors, the haggling voices of the merchants' agents and their customers, the roasted lamb on sticks that the girls bought and ate—Esther loved it all. She thought of the exiles' poems she had read the night before and felt a guilty pleasure that her ancestors had not been among those who chose to return to Jerusalem. What a hard life the Jews back there must have, rebuilding their city, struggling for their bare existence. Hadassah could not imagine life far from the riches and beauty of Susa.

"Do you see those soldiers?" Darya whispered, leaning so close Hadassah could feel her friend's warm breath against her ear.

"What soldiers? I've seen several here. The merchants usually hire some to keep order."

Darya frowned and hissed her whisper again. "Two soldiers have been watching us for more than an hour. They stop where we stop, go when we go, turn when we turn. Asha knows they're following us—he's watching them too."

Hadassah risked a glance behind her and saw two soldiers in the uniform of the palace guard some distance behind them. "You're imagining it, Darya," she said. "Perhaps you think they're captivated by your beauty."

Darya giggled. "I wish." Then, more seriously, she added, "Asha won't let us come to any harm, will he?"

"Of course not. That's why you brought him. At any rate, it's time we went home. Set aside your purchases, and when your father comes this evening he can haggle over what to trade for them—and decide to leave half of them behind, as usual."

"And what have you bought? Nothing, I suppose."

"Just one thing," Hadassah admitted. The beautiful carved and painted fan was a gift for Aunt Rivka, something of a peace offering. It wasn't Aunt Rivka's fault that she hadn't borne the kind of docile, obedient daughter she wanted. She had been good to Hadassah all these years, and Hadassah too seldom acknowledged that, saving most of her demonstrations of love for the uncle who understood her so well.

As the girls and their attendants walked through the streets to the district of merchants' and palace officials' homes where they both lived, the two soldiers continued to follow. "Asha has his hand on his sword," Darya murmured. Despite herself, Hadassah felt a thread of fear wind down her throat and into her stomach. Surely no harm could come to them on a sunny day in the streets near home. Behind her she heard the servant girls whispering nervously to each other, and with a raised hand she gestured them to silence.

When they turned the corner into the street where Mordecai's house stood, Hadassah whispered to Darya, "Are they still behind us?"

Darya nodded, her face tight with fear. This was a quiet side-street, with little traffic. The soldiers were certainly following them.

But they approached the gates of Mordecai's house with no confrontation, and one of the household servants opened the gates for Hadassah and her servant. "Go carefully," Hadassah said to Darya, squeezing her hand in farewell. "Asha will protect you."

Darya just nodded, anxious to be inside her own house.

Hadassah's heart double-tapped as she hurried up the steps toward her aunt and uncle's home. The threat, whatever it might have been, was behind her now. But just before she entered the house she looked back, and what she saw made her pulse quicken again. Darya and her servants were well down the street toward their own home now, and no one was following them. Instead, the two soldiers stood in the street outside Mordecai's house, talking quietly to each other as they looked at the house, still watching Hadassah.

CHAPTER 2

At last the soldiers in the street ambled away in the opposition direction, but the uneasy knot in Hadassah's chest stayed. Why had they followed her? Why had they watched the house? What did they want?

She couldn't think of anything she'd ever done that would arouse the interest of the king's guard. But perhaps they knew she was Mordecai's niece. Was her uncle in some kind of trouble because of his work at the palace? As one of the keepers of the king's gate he held a position of some importance, but still he was a fairly minor court official. Yet no one was too insignificant to be under suspicion. Had someone accused Mordecai of being involved in one of the thousand intricate plots that constantly swirled about the king and the royal family?

That evening Hadassah said nothing about her worries while she dined with her aunt and uncle in the courtyard. She presented Aunt Rivka with the fan she'd bought at the marketplace, which brought tears to her aunt's eyes. "How sweet of you; what a good girl you are, Hadassah," Aunt Rivka murmured over and over, apparently forgetting that the day before she had branded her niece as half-wild and unmarriageable.

Uncle Mordecai led them in prayers after the meal. They were not, perhaps, the most observant Jews in Susa—indeed, very few among the Jewish community in the city were particularly religious. Mordecai said he could just remember, from his boyhood, a time when priests and teachers of the Law had lived in Susa, when Jewish families gathered in larger homes on Shabbat to hear the Scripture read and pray together, when everyone followed the ancient laws about foods and purity. Much of that had slipped away in his lifetime, since the most devout Jews, and almost all the leaders, had returned to the homeland.

Now Esther's family, as most of the families she knew, said prayers after meals and a few extra prayers on Shabbat, but that was the extent of their worship of the God of Israel. However, tradition was important to Mordecai; being Jewish was important, and he had been careful to teach his niece about her Jewish heritage. Yet he said little in his day-to-day affairs about the God who moved behind that history—the God to whom their prayers were addressed. Hadassah wondered, sometimes, about her uncle's faith. But then, she wondered, too, about her own faith. She did not feel particularly devout, but she did feel Jewish. And that sense of belonging to her people was what Mordecai had tried to teach her, even as he had also raised her to be at home in the busy, cosmopolitan world of the Persian capital.

A servant came out to their table near the end of the meal and bowed low to Mordecai. "My lord," he said, "there are soldiers at the door who wish to speak with you."

Mordecai rose. "Soldiers? What is their business?"

"They did not say, my lord."

Mordecai dismissed the servant with a quick gesture and strode into the house. His face and bearing were calm, but Aunt Rivka turned distressed eyes to Hadassah. "Hadassah, my child, what do soldiers want with us? Why are they here? Your uncle has done nothing wrong!"

"No, of course he has not. There is no man more loyal to the king than Mordecai. I'm sure it is a small matter." On any other day Hadassah would have spoken soothing words to her always-worried aunt and meant them sincerely, but today she mouthed rehearsed lines from a recitation. Her chest and stomach churned as if they housed a swarm of angry bees. The soldiers had followed her and Darya home from the marketplace. Soldiers had stood in the street outside, watching. What was going on?

From within the house she heard the bass of men's voices blending into an incomprehensible rumble. Then three words rose above the others: "Bring her here!"

Aunt Rivka's hand fluttered to her own chest. "Bring her . . ." she mouthed in fear, but Hadassah knew better. It was not

Mordecai's wife they wanted, nor some runaway slave girl who might have stolen from her master and taken refuge with the household servants. No, the "her" they were to bring must be Hadassah. She was sure of it, though she had no idea why.

Moments later a servant stood before them, bowing nervously. "Mistress, the soldiers command me to bring the lady Hadassah to them."

"Hadassah?" If Hadassah had ever doubted her aunt's love for her, it was all there to see and hear in her voice, in that one word, in her stricken eyes. Aunt Rivka reached for her niece, gripping her upper arm. "Why do they want our little girl?"

"Come with me, Aunt Rivka," Hadassah said reassuringly. She tried to copy Uncle Mordecai's calm, confident walk as she went from the courtyard to the house, but Aunt Rivka clung to her like a fluttering moth, creeping into the entrance hall of their home as if by sheer will she could hold Hadassah back from whatever fate awaited.

In the entrance hall stood Mordecai, and she could not read his expression. The two soldiers, one on each side of him, looked menacing to her. One, she thought, was the same man she'd seen in the market; the other looked unfamiliar.

But apparently she looked familiar to them. "That's her. That's the girl," said the one she'd seen before.

The other shot a disdainful glance at Mordecai. "Why did you lie to us? You swore you had no daughter."

Mordecai barely lifted his eyebrows. "I told no lies. I have no daughter. This is my cousin's daughter, Esther." He used her Persian name, as the family usually did when speaking to Persians. "She has been fostered here in our house."

"Where are her parents?" the soldier snapped, obviously not thinking much of Mordecai's evasion of the truth.

"They are, alas, dead."

"And you are her guardian?"

"I am."

"Then she is your daughter in all but blood. Your daughter in name and in law. Not that it matters who she belongs to." Then the armed man did something Hadassah could have never imagined. He stepped forward and grabbed a handful of Hadassah's hair between his fingers, caressing it as a woman in the market would finger a bolt of silk she considered buying. Hadassah, startled, sprang away from his touch. Aunt Rivka tightened her grip on her arm, and Mordecai stepped forward as if to intervene. A collective hiss of indrawn breath went up from the household servants gathered in the hall. But the soldier, not at all deterred or shamed that he had touched a young woman of good family, reached for her again, grabbing her chin and lifting it in his hands till her eyes met his. Now he looked less like someone buying cloth than someone buying cattle.

"Indeed, this is the girl," he said, dropping her chin and stepping back. Only then did Hadassah see that the other soldier had his spear jabbed in Mordecai's ribs. The soldier who'd done all the talking laughed and nodded at his partner. "Well spotted, my friend. Yes, this one is for the harem. We can bring her along now. She needn't collect many belongings—she will have everything new when she comes to the palace."

The harem? The palace?

Suddenly Hadassah remembered Darya's talk of a new group of girls being rounded up from across all of Persia, young women for the king's harem. She felt herself sway. Black spots floated in front of her eyes. The whole conversation seemed to have taken place in another lifetime.

"Impossible! She cannot go to the harem!" Aunt Rivka protested. The soldier's spear swung in her direction.

"Do you call the commands of the king impossible?"

Rivka was silent. No one in the entire house said a word. Hadassah looked from her aunt to her uncle. Her eyes took in the stricken faces of the servants, then the walls and floors and pillars of her home. The word "harem" had struck her with shattering force, yet she could not imagine what it actually meant. The thought that she might leave her home and be forcibly taken to the palace, . . . the thought that she would live out her whole life being used for the king's pleasure like a prostitute or a child's toy was simply inconceivable.

"I beg you to give us a little more time to say our goodbyes," Mordecai said to the soldiers. His hands were clasped, almost in supplication. His voice trembled. "Tomorrow morning will surely be time enough to take her. You are right. She is our daughter in all but blood, and the only one we have. If we are to lose her forever, let us at least have this last night together as a family."

The soldiers glanced at each other. "One hour," said the one who was doing all the talking. "You may have one hour to say your goodbyes and for the girl to pack whatever things she thinks worth taking. We will stay here in the house, of course. You need not even contemplate trying to hide her or help her escape."

"Of course not," Mordecai said in a pale, thin voice not at all like his own.

"Why should she want to hide or escape?" the other soldier burst out. "It is an honor for a young woman to be taken into the king's household! She will have a life such as she could never have dreamed of—or do you, perhaps, not esteem our royal lord as highly as others do?" The accusation of disloyalty was made to Mordecai and accompanied with another swing of the spear. It pricked the fabric of his robe, and Mordecai bowed. "The wishes of the Mighty One are our commands. It is our privilege to obey."

Dazed, the room spinning around her, Hadassah could not say a word. But then, no words seemed to be required of her. The question of her future was being arranged between her uncle and the king's men. The thought skittered through her mind that if she'd let Mordecai arrange her marriage last year when he first talked of it, she would be married now and safe from this fate. Who would ever have imagined that marriage could be a haven?

While the soldiers waited in the hall, Mordecai led Hadassah to her rooms. Rivka followed as if in a dream. Reaching Hadassah's quarters, the spell of silence that held them all broke. Rivka burst into loud sobs. Mordecai raised his voice in an anguished cry that was half prayer and half curse: "God of Abraham, You do this to me? To my Hadassah, my little girl? Is this Your will, that she be the slave and toy of a heathen king?"

And Hadassah, too angry even to be amazed at her uncle's uncharacteristic storm of emotion, interrupted his prayer with her own declaration: "I *won't* do it! I *can't!* How can you let this happen?"

"How can *You* let this happen?" Mordecai echoed, his words and his glance shooting skyward. He pounded one clenched fist into the palm of his hand and, getting no answer from God, turned his attention back to Hadassah. "You saw what happened down there, Hadassah! What choice do I have? If the king wants you, he will have you no matter what we do. Would you have me fight them, and die, and you still go to the harem, with no friend or family left in the world to protect you?"

"Protect me?" Hadassah shrieked. "No one on earth can protect me once I pass those palace doors. Already . . . *already* I am the king's property!'"

Mordecai caught her by the arm. "Yes. You *are* the king's property. Not just when you go into the harem, but now, every day of your life, as we all are. Every man, woman, and child in all of Persia belongs to the king, to do with as he will. We have always accepted this reality"—his voice broke off with a strangled cough—"and now it comes home to our door. What freedom did you think you had, Hadassah? It was nothing more than an illusion. The king has summoned you. You will go."

She had no more words. He was right, but everything in her rebelled. She stood still in the middle of the floor in a silence punctuated only by her aunt's sobs, making no move to collect her belongings or do anything else that might make this nightmare real.

After a long time Mordecai spoke again. "Perhaps you spoke wrong when you said no one can protect you, child. I am angry at God right now, but I do believe He still watches you and still cares for you."

Hadassah shrugged. God seemed far away, someone to be mentioned in mealtime and Shabbat prayers, not someone who really cared for her or could do anything about her plight.

"Perhaps I have not taught you to be as good a Jew as I should have," Mordecai went on. "Perhaps I have not been as good a Jew myself. But I do believe . . . and I know you do too. And perhaps God's mercy does not depend on how good we have been. Remain a Jew—in your heart. But now I must speak of practical things, Hadassah, and I must tell you—do nothing outwardly to tell anyone you are a Jew. Use your Persian name, Esther, not Hadassah, when you go into the harem. Tell no one the name of your father's family. Use the name of your aunt Rivka's mother—they were Persians. Speak of them when anyone asks about your background."

"But why, Mordecai?" Aunt Rivka asked, speaking for the first time. "It's no shame in Susa to be a Jew. Our kings have always been good to the Jews, letting our people go back to Jerusalem, giving those of us here in Susa as good a place in the city as anyone else."

Mordecai shook his head. "All you say is true, wife, but Israel's children have learned that even the kindest hand can hold the dagger. And what do we know of the hand of King Xerxes? Kindness to people of other religions has always been the policy of the Persian kings. But look what Xerxes did in Babylon only a few years ago. The city is destroyed, their temples of Bel and Marduk desecrated. We Jews have been mistreated too often in the past to be complacent. The palace is a place of intrigue, politics, and cruelty. If our Hadassah—our Esther—is to go so close to the center of King Xerxes' power, it is better she have nothing about her that can draw attention or blame, nothing to make her stand out or be different."

Hadassah threw herself on her uncle as though she were a small, frightened child. "I still can't believe you mean for me to go," she cried.

Aunt Rivka turned to the chests of clothes and began drawing out Hadassah's finest garments, her jewelry, her sandals, laying them all in a pile on the bed. Hadassah's maid, Hannah, came from the shadows in the corner of the room, her face crisscrossed with the tracks of tears, and began to help. Each item they brought out made Hadassah's fate clearer.

Her uncle patted her head and stroked her hair. She pulled away from him and stood like a stone. She would not walk across the floor to help with the packing. That would be the same as agreeing; that would be sealing her own fate.

When her clothes and other belongings were bundled together, Aunt Rivka wordlessly handed the package to Hannah, who went to stand beside Hadassah. The girl paid no attention—her eyes were fixed on her uncle.

"I really have no choice, do I?" she said at last.

Mordecai's lips parted as though he was about to speak. He stopped himself, drew a breath, and then spoke again. "Of course you have a choice, Hadassah. We always have choices. You have no choice about obeying the king's order and going to the harem—unless you choose to take your own life, which neither God nor I will allow. But you can choose the spirit in which you go. You can choose to be crushed or to be strong. That choice is always open to you."

Hadassah wanted to say, *Then I choose to be strong,* but she couldn't open her mouth. She didn't feel at all strong, but she knew it was what her uncle wanted to hear, and she wanted to offer it to him—as a last gift. But her throat tightened. She could not say the words. Instead she reached out a hand. Mordecai took it and led her downstairs.

One soldier waited nearby to lead them back to the entrance

hall. The other still stood there, impatient. "Come, we must be going back to the palace," he said with a frown. "Take the girl."

The soldier grabbed Hadassah's arm. She reached for Hannah's hand, but the man pulled her away. "My servant," Hadassah gasped. "She has my clothes—she must come with me."

The soldier grabbed the small bundle and thrust it into Hadassah's arms. "No servants of your own," he said. "You belong to the king now, and you will be served by whoever he pleases. Nothing of your own, nothing of who you are, matters now." He pushed her toward the door, giving her only a moment for a backward glance at her foster parents, the servants, the house that had been her life and her whole world. Then they were outside, in a world that had grown suddenly unfamiliar and dangerous.

Four husky slaves waited outside with a litter, and the soldiers steered Hadassah into it, none too gently, yanking the curtains shut around her. She was glad for the privacy, though she knew it was not intended for her comfort. That impatient gesture was the first step in her new life. If she was the king's woman now, no other man should see her.

She'd ridden in a litter only rarely. The jolting, swaying ride was physically uncomfortable, but she hardly noticed it compared to the storm hammering her mind. She could not fully believe this was happening but one fact came clearly through: her future, any future she had imagined for herself, was canceled. Over. She would be locked behind the doors of the king's harem, never again to emerge. She was no better than a slave. For the past two years she'd been putting off womanhood, trying to stay in childhood because she feared losing her freedom, losing herself too soon. Now, with swift irony, fate—or God—had rushed her out of childish freedom into a womanhood she could never have imagined.

Fate—or God? She remembered Mordecai's anger at God. But at the moment, God seemed too distant even to be angry at. God, if He had ever noticed her at all, had gone away and left her.

Hadassah cried, of course, on that journey to the palace. She cried because she vowed she would not cry when she got there, not in front of the prying eyes of the king's concubines and eunuchs. She'd better do her weeping now.

She felt the lift and tilt as the men's feet climbed the hill that elevated the palace above the city. She heard their voices as they bantered with the guards and keepers at the gate about the prize they'd secured for the harem. She could not see through the curtains, but knew when they went through the gate into the open area just outside the palace itself, where she had sometimes come with Mordecai. By day it was a noisy, bustling place. By night it was quieter, but not as quiet as the city streets, for there was always business to be done in the palace.

She felt the pause as the men stopped at the palace doors, then the changes in sound as they carried the litter through the three courtyards of the palace, ever deeper into the heart of the king's world. She heard the echo of their feet as they passed through the enclosed corridors and rooms that connected the courts. Each swinging of a door, each guard's challenge answered, made Hadassah feel more trapped, more frightened. *She could never escape this place.*

She'd never been in the palace itself, but Mordecai had described it often enough for her. She knew when they entered the king's private court, the innermost court but one. Beyond that was the pillared portico that led into the women's quarters. Here, at last, the litter was set down.

Hadassah fiercely scrubbed at her eyes and face. She drew together the folds of her gown, and at the same time drew together her pride—pride in her family, in her people, in herself. No one would ever see her fear, her anger, her loneliness, she vowed, as she stepped out of the litter and felt the guard's rough hand grip her arm again.

Though it was growing dark as the guard marched her along, she could see that they were, indeed, leaving a quiet courtyard and climbing a few steps into a portico. Beyond that she saw a long corridor leading forward, away from the world of men. Hadassah knew that the guards would not be allowed into the harem itself, so she was not surprised when a smooth-cheeked man in a simple white robe—obviously a eunuch—came toward them.

"Another recruit for your army," announced the soldier still grasping her arm. He sketched a mocking salute to the eunuch as he pushed Hadassah forward.

The eunuch looked her up and down and nodded slowly. "You have a good eye," he said. "Hegai will be pleased with this one. I will take her to him now."

Then the soldiers were gone, and Hadassah, with the eunuch's much lighter touch guiding her, stepped through the pillars and into the women's quarters of Xerxes' palace.

She followed him down a narrow corridor, their progress shadowed by brightly painted figures carved in relief on the walls. By the light of flickering oil lamps she had time to notice that the reliefs showed rows of elegantly dressed courtiers lined up to pay homage to the king. Then they were at the end of the corridor, and ahead Hadassah could see a courtyard planted with shade trees and punctuated by pools and benches. Voices, music, and laughter drifted in from the courtyard. In any other circumstance Hadassah would have thought it lovely, bordered as it was by a portico of white marble pillars. Following the eunuch out of the corridor and under the portico she passed several other eunuchs as well as women whose garments proclaimed them to be anything from the lowest of slaves to the most honored of the king's concubines. Not one of them failed to stare hard at Hadassah, but she kept her eyes straight ahead.

The eunuch led her along beside the courtyard until they reached another branching corridor. Here they turned off, and paused at the door of a small room. A eunuch guard at the door nodded, and Hadassah's escort led her inside.

In the dim light of a few flickering lamps another eunuch, whose robes and jewels proclaimed him to be a man of great importance, sat at a small, elegantly carved wooden table, obviously enjoying a late-evening meal. Hadassah let her eyes quickly survey the room, avoiding the gaze of the man behind the table. It was well furnished. The red and silver tapestries on the walls depicted pastoral scenes and were as fine as those that hung in Mordecai's main hall—yet, she realized with surprise, this was the room of a mere servant of the king. Here the simple brick floors of the harem gave way to an inlaid mosaic floor. Two girls sat on the floor playing music—one playing the small harp called a chang, the other piping on a nay.

"The soldiers brought this girl just now, my lord," said the eunuch who had led Hadassah there. "She was taken here in the city, from a home in the merchant district."

The man behind the table pushed aside his plate and beckoned to Hadassah to come around the table and stand before him. He looked her up and down far more thoroughly than anyone yet had. Then he stood up and held her chin in his hand as the soldier had done, peering closely at her face. He lifted her hair and then, to her shame, he ran his hand down the length of her body, outlining her form through the thin fabric of her gown. Hadassah knew her face flushed and she knew that he saw it too, with a small hidden grin. No man had ever touched her—none ever would have, until her wedding night—but now this man who was not a man was examining her as if she were a slave or an animal, nodding and making small noises of approval to himself. When he finished he sat down again, leaving her standing.

"Your name, young lady?"

She was relieved, at least, that he used a somewhat polite form of address. At least he did not speak to her as if she were a slave, even if he looked at her and touched her like one. She almost spoke the name she was accustomed to, but caught herself and said, "Esther. My name is Esther."

"And your family."

"They are merchants, my lord. Dealers in spices." She said no more, her heart pounding a little, ready to give the name of Aunt Rivka's mother's family if asked, but he asked no further questions. Perhaps her background was no more important than a slave girl's would be.

"I am Hegai, ruler of the harem," he said. "You will be taken out to the courtyard and shown your sleeping quarters among the other virgins. If you wish something to eat or drink, you may have it. Tomorrow your training begins."

Hadassah—no, Esther, she must always think of herself as Esther now—nodded. "Thank you, my lord," she whispered, and the other eunuch led her away, out of Hegai's exalted presence. The music, which had stilled while she was presented to Hegai, grew in volume, and as she left the room she heard the chink of a goblet as Hegai continued his meal.

The courtyard was full of small groups of women, as varied in their dress and manner as the ones she'd seen on the way to Hegai's office. They were talking, eating, playing music. Esther, left alone, sank down on the ground beside a small pool. A moment later a dark-skinned girl slipped quietly up beside her and asked if she wanted anything to eat.

"No, nothing, nothing," Esther said. She looked at the girl closely, trying to see if she was a slave or an equal. The girl was simply dressed, but there was nothing servile in her manner; she carried herself like a noblewoman, and when Esther refused food, she sat down beside her. Not a slave, then. Or, no more a slave than Esther herself was.

"I am Ayana," the girl said. "I have newly come here—just a few weeks ago." She was as tall as Esther, and somehow managed to look both delicate and strong, like a slender tree that would toss in the wind but would withstand the worst of storms. Her skin gleamed the color of polished ebony. Her eyes were dark brown and fringed with black lashes. Her full-lipped mouth seemed ready with a smile and her black hair was drawn back in rows and rows of braids decorated with colored wooden beads. She said no more, but waited, perhaps to see if Esther was ready to talk.

"My name is Esther," Esther managed to say. "Where do you come from?"

"From Ethiopia," the girl said. "My father was an official there, and he gave me to the king as a tribute gift." She said it simply, without any hint of whether she was happy or sad to be given as such a gift, to be so far from her homeland. Despite herself, Esther was interested.

"You have had a long journey, then."

"Yes," Ayana said. "And you?"

"No, not a long journey." Only long enough to change her, to change everything. "I live—I lived right here in Susa."

Long minutes passed while neither girl said a word, and then Ayana asked, "Do you want me to show you our sleeping quarters?"

Esther couldn't imagine wanting to sleep anymore than wanting to eat, though she was terribly tired. How could she close her eyes in this place, knowing she would wake to a new day here, to every day of her life here? But she followed Ayana through the courtyard, past dozens of staring eyes in the dim twilight, into a warren of rooms at the south end. "These are the virgins' quarters," Ayana explained as they walked down a corridor. "Those who have been here awhile, who are going to be sent to the king, have their own rooms. The rest of us sleep together in these rooms." She gestured off to the right, and led Esther through a columned door into a large room lit by a few lamps. Esther saw rows of pallets on the red brick floor. Carved wooden benches were set against the walls between high windows. Apart from the benches and a few low stools the room held no other furniture. Small bundles or baskets of clothing and personal belongings lay next to most of the pallets.

Esther lay down on the pallet Ayana showed her, and said good night to the other girl. She could hear the others in the room: some preparing for bed, some already snoring softly, some talking quietly among themselves in a blend of accents and dialects. Esther just lay there on the hard, uncomfortable floor. She had never imagined feeling so absolutely alone. She thought of God, the God of her people. Did He really see her and care what happened to her, as her ancestors had believed? Would He really care for her?

She had never before tried to pray, outside of the formal prayers the family said at set times and occasions. She had never imagined addressing God directly as Mordecai had done in his anger only hours before. But now, moving her lips but not letting her words escape above a whisper, she said, "O God of Israel, if You hear me, if You see me, take pity on me. I don't know why I have been brought here, or what is going to happen to me, but please protect me. I need to know you are there, God of Abraham, Isaac, and Jacob."

She strained to listen as if for an answer, but beyond the hushed noises of the other women and the chirring of insects, the night was silent. A long time later she fell asleep.

CHAPTER 3

Esther sat on the stone floor of the courtyard eating what had been placed before her. It was much like her morning meal at home—a bowl of yogurt, another of dates, and barley cakes. All around her other girls sat eating too. From their talk she guessed that they were mostly, like herself, new arrivals at the palace.

One girl with hair of flaming red carried herself as though she were already a queen. "My father owned dozens of herds of goats," she was saying to the others. "One of my father's hirelings, a goatherd, was in love with me and used to tease me for kisses, but I told him he should be ashamed of himself. Imagine if he could see me now—at the king's court!"

"Raiya has been a slave all her life," a soft voice murmured in Esther's ear. Esther turned to see Ayana, the Ethiopian girl who had befriended her the night before, sitting down with her own food. Ayana nodded at the flame-haired girl whose clear voice carried loudly through the courtyard. "The other girls told me she was

bought at a slave market in Ecbatana. As a child she had been cap-
tured in lands far to the north. She tells stories of her grand family
and home—who knows, they may have been true once, for anyone
can be sold as a slave. But it would have been so long ago, Raiya
could hardly remember."

Esther looked at the loud girl with new eyes, wondering what it
must be like to grow up without home, without family, with only
your own invented stories to give you a past. For a moment she pitied
the girl. Then Raiya caught Esther's eye and leaned toward her.

"Who's your new friend, Ayana? Has she had her tongue cut out
for treachery? I don't hear a word from her."

"Not everyone needs as many words as you do to make herself
heard," Ayana said softly.

Raiya looked away from Ayana and directly at Esther. "So, are
you here because you fancy your chances of becoming the new
queen?" A few of the girls laughed, but Raiya silenced them with a
glance. "It will happen, you know. The king has sworn it, and he
will not go back on his word. One of the girls from his harem—one
of the new girls, one of us—will become his wife." She tossed back
her brilliant mane of hair. "And it won't be any dark-faced snob, nor
any little mouse who's too quiet to squeak her own name."

"The king would not want his woman to be too forward," another
girl cautioned. "Remember that Vashti was banished for defying him."

Raiya laughed. "I'd not be such a fool as to defy the king if he
asked *me* to come dance for him," she said. "Of course a woman
serves her lord, as every subject serves the king. But the king would
want a woman with spirit. Look at Queen Amestris—is she a mouse
who dares not open her mouth?"

This time nothing as bold as a laugh passed through the cluster
of girls—the sound was more like wind through grass. Amestris'
name was clearly feared here in the women's quarters, for now that
the king's mother, Atossa, was dead, his chief wife was the most
powerful woman in the harem. And from the city gossip Esther had
heard of Amestris, she was certainly no mouse.

Raiya had turned to address her group of followers in general,
but now she shot her gaze back at Esther. Her eyes, Esther saw, were
an odd color—greenish blue, a shade that must be common among
the pale-skinned, light-haired people of the northern countries.
"Well, new girl? Will the king wed a mouse?"

At that moment Esther felt more clear-headed than she had since entering the palace last night. This girl was simply a bully, and bullying could not be tolerated. "I think he would wed a mouse before he would wed a shrew," she said simply, raising one eyebrow. "And since you asked, my name is Esther."

The silence that greeted her comment and the smiles the other girls quickly covered told her she'd scored a point. She felt satisfied, but disappointed in herself, too. She had no wish to make enemies, nor to make herself outstanding in any way. And to mock another just to make herself look good was petty. Yet it felt good to have defended herself.

Raiya turned her back on Esther, obviously deciding it was better to ignore her than to cross swords with her again. But later when the girls had gathered in the southeast corner of the courtyard to meet with Hegai, the chief eunuch, Esther discovered that standing up to Raiya had given her status with the other girls. They were all eager to talk to her, to tell her the little they'd learned about life in Xerxes' harem in the few weeks they'd been there.

"The rumors about the king choosing a new queen to replace Vashti seem very great to someone like Raiya, who dreams of her own importance," an older girl told Esther and several of the other newcomers. "The truth is, even if the king were to do such a thing again—to elevate one of his concubines to royal status by marrying her—the chances are small that it would be any one of us. Hundreds of girls are being gathered into the harem under this latest edict. Most of us will never see the king."

"Never see him?" one small, very timid girl whispered hopefully.

"Of course not," the older girl replied. Esther guessed her age at 17. She had long black hair, straight and gleaming, golden-brown eyes, and olive skin. "Not every woman in the harem is the king's concubine, you know. He may be the greatest and most godlike of men, but he is only a human man, and he would hardly have the time to have hundreds of lovers, even if he had the energy!" The girls giggled and Esther blushed, though she knew far worse and more ribald things than this conversation awaited her here in her new life.

The girl who seemed to know so much went on. "The eunuchs put us through our training and beauty treatments, and during that time they evaluate each girl for her looks, her talents, and her skills.

We will all be trained in music and dancing, but some who are especially skilled will spend their lives as court musicians or dancers—not a bad fate, I think."

"That's because you dance so well, Leila," another girl chimed in.

Leila shrugged. "I come from Arabia," she said with a laugh. "All our women dance well. We come out of the womb dancing."

"Some of us will become servants to the queens or the other royal women," another girl added. "And, of course, some of us will be chosen to go to the king's bed—but most will go only once."

At once Esther had a new goal, a new ambition. *Please, God, let me never be chosen as one of the king's concubines,* she prayed. She had always enjoyed her music lessons and played several instruments well, but the oud, with its long slender neck and four strings, was her favorite. Perhaps she might become a musician. But even a life in service to some other court lady would be better than losing her maidenhood to this pagan monarch. *Surely, God, it would not honor You to have one of Your people face such a fate? You will spare me this, won't You?*

She was unsure of what God might reply, yet she felt sure He could not want her to become Xerxes' concubine. Just knowing that other fates were possible eased her mind a little. Just then the girls' conversation was interrupted as Hegai, the same man to whom Esther had been presented the night before, strode out from the portico and stood before them. At once the girls grew silent, bowing at his upright form.

Esther studied him carefully as he spoke. The common stereotype of eunuchs was that they were fat, were fond of luxury, and spoke with high fluting voices. Hegai was a large man, but not fat. His clothes and jewels were rich and tasteful—obviously expensive, but not gaudy—and his voice, while higher than that of a normal man, was rich and commanding. She could imagine him singing. He spoke with the air of someone used to power, and she had the impression, as she'd had the night before, of a man who was by no means unkind though he might waste little time on pleasantries. Improbable as it seemed, given his position and hers, Esther decided there was something in Hegai that she trusted.

The first part of his instruction was much what the older girl had just been telling them—about the fates that might befall them now that they had entered the harem. He spoke, of course, as though being brought to the royal bedchamber was the highest and most glorious achievement a woman might hope for, but Esther had already decided how she felt about that. Then he went on to detail the training they would be given: music, dance, language, deportment, beauty treatments. The beauty treatments sounded dull to Esther who could barely stand still long enough to choose a dress or have a maid brush her hair, but the other courses of study sounded interesting enough. She felt a momentary pang of loss for the scrolls in Mordecai's house. Would she ever have a chance to read here?

After Hegai finished addressing them, other eunuchs came to lead the girls to the baths. Along with women slaves, the eunuchs helped the girls undress. Esther clutched her gown a little more tightly as she watched the others being brought into the baths. It was incredible that within a few moments she would be naked in front of all these other women—and men, too. Well, eunuchs, but still—men, in some sense. She glanced at Ayana. "It is difficult the first time," Ayana said softly, "but you get used to it. As to so many other things."

"Get used to it?" Esther said incredulously. "To this—this *shame?*"

"In a little while it will not even seem like shame," said Ayana.

Perhaps not, but for today it was shame. Bathing had always been a private affair between Esther and her maid, but these baths were public, with many girls sitting around together as the slaves poured water over their heads and shoulders and washed their hair and their bodies with scented oils. When the bath was over, a slave held out a gown for Esther to put on. It was not the one she had just taken off.

"Where are my own clothes?" she asked.

"They are gone, miss," the slave said.

"They burn your clothes!" a sharp, familiar voice called from another corner of the room. It was Raiya, sitting down while a slave brushed out her glorious red hair. "They take your clothes and your jewels—anything you brought from your home—and destroy it all. We are to have no trace of our former lives."

She did not sound angry or unhappy about this. Rather, she almost sounded triumphant. Esther thought of what Ayana had said about Raiya's background and thought she understood. To the girl raised as an orphan slave, there would be some pleasure in knowing that all the others, no matter who they had once been, were reduced to the same level as she. Esther bit back the sharp retort that came to her lips, feeling sorry for the other girl. *After all,* she thought, *I am Esther—no, I am Hadassah, daughter of Abihail, foster daughter to Mordecai, child of the tribe of Benjamin, daughter of Israel, servant of the God of Israel.* She said her heritage silently to herself, a litany she must never speak but never lose. *No matter what happens here,* she thought, *no one can take my identity away from me.*

The aftermath of the bath seemed endless. Esther was dressed. Her hair was brushed. Another scented oil was combed through her hair, then elaborately arranged. An attendant massaged oil of myrrh all over her body, then followed with a cream for her hands and feet, and yet another for her face. Then she had to sit still as a stone for an hour while yet another woman painted her face with painstaking detail. Finally her gown was slipped down past her feet and another gown put on her body. It was of rich linen, wide-sleeved, with a heavy skirt pleated into dozens of broad folds, by far the finest garment Esther had ever worn. A slave put earrings in her ears and slipped bracelets on her arms and a necklace around her slim neck. There were even jingling bracelets for her ankles. Fully dressed now, Esther was brought to a mirror of polished bronze. The form and face she saw were utterly unfamiliar.

By the time her grooming was complete, Esther was mad with boredom. She longed to take some exercise, perhaps a walk in the gardens, anything to ease the cramp in her legs and the dryness in her mind. But next she was led with a group of girls into a large hall between the virgins' quarters and the concubines' area; there, she realized, one of the king's concubines was giving lessons in deportment. This involved how to speak, stand, sit, and walk with perfect decorum, as a flawless ornament to the king's court. *Oh, Rivka, if you could see me now,* Esther thought wryly, *how you would laugh at your revenge.*

But Aunt Rivka would not have laughed, of course. No matter how glad she would have been to see Esther practicing a seamless, gliding walk across the well-scrubbed brick floor, perfecting tiny smooth steps that did not cause her robe to swish—no matter how pleased Aunt Rivka would have been she would not have chosen *this* method, *this* place, to school her hoyden child. Rivka was probably still weeping.

But Esther, to her own surprise, was not. Deportment lessons were followed by music. One of the eunuchs tested her singing voice and assigned her a small oud to play, having obviously decided her voice was not lovely enough to sing the praises of Ahura Mazda. That suited Esther fine. Her music master at home felt she was particularly gifted at the oud. She decided to make the best of this lesson time by improving her skills. As she plucked out the tunes, words wove around them in her mind:

"By the rivers of Babylon we sat and wept
    when we remembered Zion.
    There on the poplars
    we hung our harps . . .
    How can we sing the songs of the Lord
    while in a foreign land?"

Surely in all the long story of the Jews' exile, no Jew had ever been more truly exiled than Esther right now, none more completely drawn into a foreign environment. She remembered Mordecai's stories of the sage Daniel who had risen to a high place in the court of a Babylonian king. But Daniel, though an exile and captive, had at least been a man. He had had some little power over his own fate, some right at least to the privacy of his own body. She, a woman, had nothing. No power, no privilege, no privacy. She was completely at the mercy of the king.

Yet here she was, playing the oud, not weeping at all. She had cried last night, and maybe she would cry again tonight when darkness fell, and she slept again on an unfamiliar mat in an unfamiliar room. But for now, she was here, and she must make the best of it, enjoying what she could. There was no point, Esther decided, in being miserable for the sake of misery. This was her life now, unless Israel's God chose some miracle to rescue her, and she had better begin living it.

"You play well," said the music teacher, a small, elderly eunuch named Menebar.

After music came dancing—finally, a chance to stretch her limbs—and then the evening meal. Esther and the other new girls sat at a table in the courtyard under the watchful eye of two eunuchs and two of the more experienced women. The meal provided another lesson, as they were lectured on the proper table manners for the king's court. Esther had little trouble behaving properly since she'd been raised in a good family right here in Susa, but she saw one dark-haired, quiet girl who tore into her food as if she were a wild beast tearing flesh from the bones, and others who, though obviously well bred, had learned their customs in other lands. The women and the eunuchs spent the most time with these girls. Esther was free to enjoy her meal—an excellent one—and to chat with her companions. Ayana, whom she already thought of as a friend, had been apart from her much of the day. Now they compared notes on their day's activities.

"You seem happier than you did last night," Ayana said. "I have seen girls cry for their entire first week here."

"I don't think I have that many tears in me," Esther said, drawing a smile from her quiet companion.

"But you have not yet experienced all the harem has to offer." A note of warning sharpened her tone.

Esther thought back over her day—the baths, the meals, the music, the dancing. She imagined each day as this one, an endless round of the same things over and over. It might be dull, but she would survive. "What else is there?" she asked carelessly.

Ayana said nothing. Then, after a long pause, she said, "There is more . . . but you will discover it as you go along. Do not take too much upon yourself at once. I should not have spoken. You are both brave and cheerful. I wish I had been as strong as you when I first came here."

"Ayana, I couldn't have survived even this first day without having met you!" Esther said. "If you hadn't made friends with me, I think I would have just crawled into a hole in the corner and hoped no one would find me." Her voice rose a little on the last words, and the eunuch nearest her gave her a sharp look. "A lady of the court never raises her voice," he said, "but speaks always in a low and pleasing tone, as befits her modesty and humility."

Esther bowed her head, taking the rebuke in silence and submission, as she knew was appropriate. Ayana, passing her a plate of bread, offered a quick smile. Esther took a piece—bread of the first quality, such as they ate only on feast days at home—wondering a little at Ayana's warning. What new challenges would she have to face tomorrow or in the days ahead?

CHAPTER 4

Esther was amazed, looking back, to discover how quickly life in the harem had become "normal," as her previous life receded more and more into the realm of memory. Sleeping in a large room with a dozen other young women, eating communal meals and bathing in groups soon seemed quite ordinary. She no longer found the baths embarrassing, but began to relax and enjoy the luxurious treatment. Long sessions of massage with oils, makeup, and hairstyling still made her impatient, but she allowed her mind to drift and soon got used to the routine.

As for her lessons, she positively enjoyed them. The music teacher had made it clear that her singing voice would never win her a place among the court singers, but she was among the best of the oud players, and she often practiced in the few private moments she could steal alone, testing herself with more complicated fingering, composing little melodies of her own.

One day she sat with her instrument in the courtyard in the cool twilight hour just after the evening meal. She had found a favorite spot, next to the pool where she had sat her first night there, under a plane tree. It was near the virgins' quarters; the tree's spreading branches blocked out the rest of the courtyard. From a distance she could hear women's voices weaving in and out of conversation, and children playing—there were children in the harem too, the children of the king's wives and concubines, and the slave children who would grow up to serve them. Tonight their laughter and cries filtered into the tune she was playing. It had begun as a song she'd learned in class but evolved into something of her own—something that tried to capture the carefree days of childhood, the laughter she had once known running with Shirah through the courtyard of Uncle Mordecai's home.

From behind her she heard someone humming. Not a woman's voice. A eunuch's voice, she decided—quite a young one. Oddly, he was humming her tune—the very notes she was making up as she went along. She turned to see a boy about her own age, maybe a year older, standing next to her tree, holding a pitcher of wine and a goblet. He stopped humming at once and blushed slightly, though not very noticeably as his skin was rather dark.

"Do you wish to have some wine, my lady?" he asked, bowing.

"No, thank you," said Esther.

"Or perhaps you would like something to eat?"

"No, I need nothing." He turned to go, and on impulse she said, "Were you singing along while I was playing?"

He turned back, and she saw again the embarrassment but beneath it a kind of confidence. He wore the garments of a slave, but did not carry himself like one. He was of medium height, a little taller than Esther, and slender, with narrow shoulders and chest; not as muscular as a boy his age who was not a eunuch would be. His black hair was cut just to the bottom of his beardless chin; his skin was a warm brown, darker than Esther's own or that of most Persians she knew, but not as dark as Ayana's. His features were fine but strong—a large, well-shaped nose and a wide mouth—and his brown eyes were lively and intelligent. Very dark, straight brows gave his face a more serious look than the bright eyes suggested. "Yes, lady. Forgive me—it was a very pretty tune. Not one I've heard before, but it caught my attention and I found myself humming along."

"I hope you haven't heard it before. I think I composed it myself."

He smiled. "Then you are a good composer, lady, as well as a good musician." He bowed again, deferentially, but the tone of his voice indicated he spoke to her as an equal. "I know a little of music myself, so that is no empty compliment."

"Thank you," said Esther. "I was beginning to be afraid that my own composition was really some well-known folk tune in your homeland."

"I think not," he said, smiling again. "But I have been long gone from my homeland, so I may not have heard all the folk tunes."

"Oh, have you been here long in the palace? I have been here only a little while myself, but I have not seen you here before."

"No, lady, I too am newly come to the king's service." He bowed again, not to her this time but at the mention of the king, and Esther inclined her head also. "I was sold when I was a boy of 8 summers. I became a eunuch and a slave that same day. I was owned by a rich man in Babylon who included me with four other eunuchs, four women, some goats, and some wine as a gift for His Majesty."

Esther said nothing. The young man's life story, so simply told and so completely without self-pity, left her with no reply. Already in the harem she had heard of many lives so troubled she felt her own existence must surely have been blessed by Israel's God. Yet this young man did not seem scarred by what had happened to him. Rather he had a security and calm she envied.

"What is your name?" she asked, adding, "I am Esther." She had an odd desire to tell her true name, but of course she did not.

"My name is Hathakh," the boy said. "Hathakh from India, once upon a time, but now Hathakh of the king's harem, I suppose. It is not a bad fate."

Esther sighed. She had begun to accept that this life was her fate, but she still longed for freedom, and she could not even imagine how she would long for it if she were as far from the land of her birth as Hathakh was from his. "I must go now," he told her, indicating the wine jug which, she supposed, he was meant to offer to other women besides herself.

"Yes, of course—but Hathakh, you said you knew a little of music. What do you play?"

"In my childhood I was taught an instrument, a kind of pipe. It was a little like the nay they play here. I played the nay at my old master's house."

"Come sometime and play with me, and perhaps we will talk more," she said.

He bowed again. "It will be my pleasure, lady Esther."

Esther sat quietly after he left, her instrument in her lap. She was beginning to get a sense of the complex relationship between the women and the eunuchs in the harem. On the one hand, the eunuchs were servants. They existed to serve the women, to meet their needs. But on the other hand, eunuchs ruled the harem. Hegai and his officials were the link between the harem women and the outside world of men, the world of real power, power that did not have to hide behind a throne. The strange tensions of that relationship led to power struggles between the women and the eunuchs, but it led also to alliances and even close friendships. And Hathakh was someone Esther could imagine having as a friend.

So far she had only one close friend, and that was Ayana. She and the Ethiopian girl ate together when they could and often talked at the end of the day. Esther admired Ayana's calm, the inner assurance that seemed to hold her together. Life in the harem, especially among the younger women, often became tense and shrill, but Ayana seemed an untroubled island in the stormiest of seas, and Esther relied on her.

Apart from Ayana—and perhaps now Hathakh—she had not grown close to anyone, though she found most of the other girls friendly. She enjoyed playing the oud with Roxane, a girl a year or two older than herself, who was easily the most skilled of the young musicians. Roxane practiced and played with the king's virgins, but she did not belong to the harem as they did. Her widowed mother had been a servant to Queen Atossa, the king's mother, so Roxane had grown up in the harem. Her musical gifts had helped her rise to a position beyond what might have been expected for the daughter of a servant. Roxanne's mother, now retired from service after the death of the elderly queen, had recently arranged a marriage for Roxane with a promising young poet named Lilaios.

Roxane, a short girl with ringlets of dark hair and dimpled cheeks, had fingers that both flew up and down the oud and teased intricate melodies from a small harp called a chang. She liked to play duets with Esther, patiently practicing over and over till Esther could master the more difficult finger work. She was fun to talk to, too, always ready with a quick grin and a witty comment.

She and Esther might have become even closer friends, but except for music classes their lives seldom intersected. Esther slightly envied Roxane both for her married status—she was quite in love with her new husband—and for her musical gifts which gave her life a sense of purpose that Esther felt her own existence lacked.

Among the harem virgins, there were constant rivalries, gossip, and petty quarrels. Just that morning, for example, two girls had quarreled loudly and viciously about a jeweled comb. Manya swore it was her own, that the eunuch who cared for the jewels had given it to her as a present because she'd performed so well the first time she danced at a court banquet. The other girl, Tamyris, had insisted it was *not* Manya's own property, but belonged to the harem and had been promised to her, Tamyris, to wear when she went in to the king.

The argument had gotten quite heated, involving slurs against Manya's dancing abilities and the likelihood of Tamyris pleasing the king when she did go in to him. Raiya, as always, had been involved. Manya was one of her close friends, and Raiya loved to stir up trouble. In fact, she seemed to be involved in most of the quarrels, though she managed to avoid being labeled a troublemaker. When one of Hegai's overseers bustled in to find out why girls in the sleeping quarters were screaming like cats, he found Manya and Tamyris, each with a good handful of the other's hair. Before he managed to separate them, Manya reached out and raked her nails down Tamyris's cheek, scarring her, thus making it unlikely she would be going to visit the king's bedchamber anytime soon—if ever.

Of course, the king had not even returned to Susa yet. He was still in Sardis, though the harem rocked with rumors of his return. The girls who'd been gathered into the harem when the decree went out after the battle of Salamis would not be ready to go to the king when he did return. A full year of training and beauty treatments were commanded before a girl was considered ready for the king's bedchamber. But the months were flying by. It had been winter when Esther was taken from her home. Now it was spring. The new girls were beginning to look beyond their present, toward the unknown future.

Esther didn't even notice that the music of her oud had quickened its pace while she remembered the quarrel, then turned haunting and sad. She thought of the nail marks down Tamyris's pretty pale cheek. Could it be that easy? Would she have the courage to scar herself in some way to avoid ever being sent to the king? She had seen the approving glances the eunuchs and the concubines gave her when she came from the baths scented, gowned, and coiffured. They were considering her, she knew. Considering her as a candidate for the king's bed.

She sighed, and pushed the problem to the back of her mind. Her natural inclination was to do her best in any situation, at anything she tried. Here in her new life that created a dilemma, but not one she was ready to deal with just now.

The next day she sat in the courtyard with several of the other girls listening to a lecture given by Hegai himself. During the winter on the days it was too cool and rainy to sit in the courtyard, their lessons were given in the inner rooms or the porticos. Now, as the temperatures again climbed toward the blistering heat of a Susian summer, life returned to the courtyard.

Hegai, busy with his tasks as chief eunuch, rarely met with the newer girls, but he took it upon himself to instruct them in the customs and manners of the court. Today Esther listened with interest, for he was talking about religion, and she was curious.

"You come from many different places, many backgrounds," he said, "and you worship many different gods. As you no doubt already know, this poses no problem here in Persia. Our religion does not require you to give up worshiping your own gods as long as they are good gods—gods whose aims and attributes are similar to those of Ahura Mazda, the great god of truth and light."

Esther heard a murmur from one of the girls behind her. It was Tamyris, no doubt, who came from ruined Babylon. Since the rebellion there, the worship of the Babylonian gods had been suppressed and the great temple of Marduk destroyed. Tamyris was eager to please the king when her time came, but angry about the destruction of her people's temples. "You should care, Esther!" she'd once said. "Your family must have been Babylonian. Surely you are named for Ishtar, our goddess."

Esther knew that both her Persian name and Mordecai's were borrowed from the gods of Babylon—her uncle's name was similar to the god Marduk—but those names had been chosen to honor friends of the same names here in Susa, not the gods themselves. Esther thought of her true name, Hadassah, which she seldom used even to herself now. To Tamyris she had said only, "It must have been a terrible thing, to see your temples destroyed." *Like the temple at Jerusalem when your Babylonian king Nebuchadnezzar took that city,* she did not add.

Hegai had not heard Tamyris's whisper, and continued lecturing about the Persian religion. "Our religion is based on the teachings of Zarathustra, which our illustrious ancestor, Cyrus, the first king of Persia, believed and followed. Ahura Mazda is the god of light, and opposed to him is Anghra Mainyu, the hostile spirit, the god of darkness and destruction."

As Hegai spoke about the teachings of Zarathustra, Esther tried to remember what she knew about the God of Israel. Religious instruction had been part of her childhood, but not a central part. More often she had simply been told about certain things: "We do this because we are Jews." She did know that Israel's God was good, like Ahura Mazda. But, too, she'd been taught that He was the only God, the One God, and that they were to worship no others.

She knew, too, that there were stories of an accuser who

sounded a little like the Anghra Mainyu that Hegai was speaking of. But surely this accuser was not a god. He did not have power equal to the God of Israel. Wasn't he only an angel, a powerful but lesser being? There was so much she didn't know. If only she could go back home and ask Mordecai. If only she could read the scrolls in her uncle's house or copies of other Jewish writings. Maybe then she would know the answers to some of her questions.

Hegai had gone to the subject of how the good god and the evil god were locked in eternal battle, and how all other gods, as well as all men and women, had to choose one side or the other. "Someday," he intoned, "one will triumph and the other be defeated. Our task, of course, is to be sure that we fight on the side of Ahura Mazda, that good and not evil eventually win."

A question occurred to Esther and she frowned, trying to puzzle it out. Hegai noticed her frown and asked, "Esther, something is not clear to you?"

She started. She hadn't even been sure Hegai knew her name.

"Pardon me, my lord. I was only—wondering."

"Wondering about what?"

"I would not be so rude, my lord, as to interrupt your teaching with a question." She bowed her head, hoping he would move on. The question that had occurred to her was so complicated she could hardly find words for it, much less trouble the chief eunuch with it.

"Very well," Hegai went on smoothly. "I am sure this talk of religion is dull to many of you young ladies. We will continue in our next session with the history of the Achaemenid royal house from the time of Cyrus. You may be dismissed now." The girls rose to leave in a rustle of soft skirts, each one bowing respectfully to Hegai before she made her exit. Esther was half way to the door when she heard the chief eunuch's voice. "Esther, wait a moment."

Esther waited, hoping she was not to be reprimanded for daring to have a question. She had not, after all, voiced it, only allowed it to show on her face. Yet how often had she been told that even when the women of the court were unveiled their faces must still be as calm and still as if they wore veils, so that no emotion should trouble the serenity of that surface. She stood, head bowed and hands crossed in front of her, waiting for Hegai to speak.

"What was the question?" he asked, not at all angrily.

"My lord?"

"The question you thought of, but did not ask."

"Oh, it is probably a very foolish question, my lord. I only wondered . . . Ahura Mazda and Anghra Mainyu are both equal in power, are they not?"

"Yes, that is what we are taught."

"Neither is superior to the other? Neither came first?"

"No, they have always been, as light and dark have always been."

"Then, my lord, how do we know one is good and one is evil? I mean—" She saw his confusion. As she had feared, her question made no sense. "How can we say one god is good, if both have always been? Where do our ideas of good and evil come from if they are in perfect balance and there is no higher law to tell us right from wrong?"

Hegai was silent. Into the silence Esther finally said, "Forgive me. It was a foolish question, as I said."

"No, not foolish. Perhaps a very wise question. I do not know the answer. I suppose the magi might, but then they might not think of such things. The world is as it has always been, good and evil, light and dark."

"Yes, my lord."

"But, Esther"—he took her chin in his hands as he had done that first night and gave her his searching glance, but now it did not shame her—"you are a very intelligent girl."

"Thank you, my lord, but I am nothing."

"It is odd that you, out of girls from so many lands, would be the one to raise a question. You were raised here in Susa. Surely you would understand our religion."

Esther felt her chest tighten. Was her duplicity about to be revealed? What harm would it be to admit she was Jewish? Yet Mordecai had been so certain she must keep it secret.

"My lord, as you said yourself, the priests do not talk of such things. Even in the heart of a daughter of this land, questions may arise."

"Questions arise in the minds of the intelligent," Hegai said, still holding her face in his hand. "And you are intelligent, Esther. Talented, too, your music master informs me. Peaceable and modest, your keepers here in the sleeping quarters say. And with all this, strikingly beautiful."

"I thank you, my lord." She had glanced up briefly into his face and seen the cool appraising glance—detached, but not unkind.

"I believe it is time for the next stage in your education, Esther.

What are you appointed to do this afternoon?"

"Baths and an oil massage, my lord."

"I will give instructions you are not to be massaged today. After the bath you will be brought directly to the concubines' quarters, where you will receive further instruction."

Further instruction? In what? But she had been impertinent enough for one day. Astonishingly, it seemed to have brought her nothing but praise—and privilege, perhaps? Esther wasn't sure. Hegai dismissed her, and she went to meet Ayana for the noon meal.

"I see Hegai has taken notice of you," Ayana said with her gentle smile. She grasped Esther's hand and swung it as they walked to the tables.

Esther recounted the conversation as they sat down and waited to be served. "Ayana, what did he mean? What 'next stage in my education'? What is going to happen to me this afternoon?"

Ayana's dark face grew sober. She dipped her flatbread in yogurt and nibbled the edge of the bread. "Do you remember your first day here when you were ashamed to go in the baths, and I told you that far worse than that would happen to you here?"

"Yes." Esther's heart seemed to jump in her chest.

"Hegai has decided that you are marked out for the king's bedchamber. You will be one of those presented to the king. Before that happens, you must have some—lessons."

"Lessons?"

Ayana looked away. She seemed embarrassed. "They're what is called the . . . it's what they call here the arts of love. You will be taught how to please a man. You must remain a virgin when you go to the king, of course, but not an innocent, unknowing virgin. Harem women are expected to be skilled in such arts."

Ayana spoke calmly, but her eyes would not meet her friend's. Esther laid down the date cake she'd been eating. "Ayana, is this true? Did you have to do this, too?"

The girl nodded. "Yes." She stopped, trying to gather her thoughts. "At the time I first spoke to you this was something I'd only heard of from the other girls. But some weeks ago I was called to begin these lessons. I'm sorry. You will be ashamed at first—very much so. Any modest young woman would be. But after a time it will not seem so bad. You will get used to it."

"Get used to it!"

This was impossible. She'd never get used to it. The very idea made her feel as hot as a fish dropped into the scalding water of a cooking pot. Fear and disgust rose in Esther's throat, and she pushed away her plate. Her appetite was gone. This was terrible. It was beyond her most desperate fears. But the reality was infinitely worse.

A slave women took her straight from the baths to a private suite of quarters in the concubines' wing. Here the rooms and corridors were a little more spacious, the walls covered with intricate and expensive hangings. She was led directly into a well-appointed bedchamber where she found Hegai talking with one of the older concubines, a woman of perhaps 30 named Badia. A younger eunuch sat silently on a couch.

Hegai and Badia were deep in conversation when Esther appeared but quickly turned their attention to her. "Ah, here she is now," Hegai said, and Badia looked up and nodded. "Yes, I have seen this one before. She is as you said . . . " The woman stood and walked toward Esther, circling her slowly. Esther, accustomed by now to being examined like a prize heifer, stood still, her eyes toward the floor. "Very beautiful," Badia murmured, almost to herself. "Perfect skin, fine bones, good hair, excellent carriage. . . ."

Badia continued enumerating Esther's beauties, growing more and more intimate. "Yes, she's a fine choice," she told Hegai approvingly. "I will do my part to prepare her."

"Good. Do your work." Hegai gave a dismissive gesture and left the room. Esther was alone with Badia, the young eunuch, and the slave who had brought her there.

For as long as she lived Esther never forgot the next hour. She'd thought she knew something of shame, something of humiliation, when she'd been snatched from her family and brought like a slave to the harem, but she had never imagined an hour like this. Badia touched her body like a fruit vendor handling melons. Inwardly Esther writhed, but she willed herself to show no sign of the anguish twisting her belly.

To begin, Badia called the young eunuch and the slave girl over and, using their bodies as if they were dressmakers' models she demonstrated what happened when a man and woman were alone in bed. Just once Esther met the girl's eyes; the eunuch's twice. Both times she looked away as quickly as possible, not wanting to make their shame, or her own, any worse. All three were locked in a bizarre tableau against their will, making a mockery of what must once have been intended as love between a man and a woman.

Nothing was required of Esther that day except to watch and listen. But Badia made it quite clear that the lessons would become more intimate, more intrusive, until Esther had learned everything a harem girl should know in order to be of service to her king.

When the hour was over, Esther was dismissed. She went alone, with no one to guide her, back to her quarters. She was glad to be alone. She felt numb. She stumbled out into the courtyard, away from the area she was familiar with, past the concubines' quarters, and past the more imposing apartments where the king's wives, sisters, and daughters lived. Esther looked neither at the buildings nor at the women she passed. She hurried along, her eyes on the ground, glad to be lost, to be away from any familiar face or place. If she could not escape this horrible prison altogether, perhaps she could get lost inside it.

She hardly even noticed when she passed through the entrance that led out of the women's quarters into the gardens beyond. She heard the deep voices of men, and her mind vaguely registered that they must be guards, not eunuchs, but they were not particularly interested in one rambling harem girl. At last she stopped beneath a cluster of small trees. She stood leaning against a tree, trying to catch her breath. Her stomach hurt, and bile splashed into her throat. She heard footsteps and voices a little distance away and thought vaguely that some of the other harem women must be out for a stroll in the gardens.

Esther dropped to the ground and drew herself into a small knot, arms hugging knees, desperately hoping not to be seen. When the voices faded away, she put her head on her knees and wept. She had no idea how long she cried, letting her anger and pain and shame flood out with the tears that seemed to have no end.

CHAPTER 5

Ayana asked Esther nothing about her lessons with Badia. That first night Esther recovered enough of her dignity to return to the courtyard and go to her sleeping quarters with the other girls, though she stayed in the palace gardens during the evening meal. She could not have eaten, anyway. And as it happened she couldn't sleep either. She lay awake long after the last whispers had quieted down, listening to the stirring through the room as dozens of girls breathed softly in and out, each locked in her private dreamworld. *What are they dreaming?* Esther wondered. She couldn't stand to close her eyes, for behind her eyelids was stamped the images of the afternoon's training. She felt spoiled, like a piece of overripe fruit that had begun to ooze and turn soft and brown. She felt that never again would she feel whole, sound, or good.

She lay on her back, her hands clenched at her waist, and tears pooled in her eyes. The worst of it was that tomorrow there'd be another session. And the day after, and . . . The tears dripped down the sides of her face and into her hair. Her hair. Her mind shifted past her weeks in the harem, back to her bedroom at home and to Hannah brushing her long, thick hair.

Who was that carefree girl, anyway? What had happened to her? Where had she gone, and who was this bruised and damaged young woman who'd taken her place?

At some point Esther's eyes closed and did not open again until she heard the sounds of her roommates awakening. Tears filled her eyes as she jerked back to reality. It was time to face another day.

The hour spent with Badia and another faceless couple seemed interminable. And the next day, and the next . . . and another and another. Badia grew amused with Esther's shyness; apparently most girls got over it sooner. The cast of characters varied little—always there was Esther and Badia, one or two slave girls, and one or two young eunuchs. Never the same slaves or eunuchs. They were always young and good-looking and seemed bored and detached.

Detached. That's the key, Esther thought. *Let my body go through the motions and keep my mind somewhere else.* She knew that she could not refuse to participate forever. Badia would report her to Hegai.

Around and between the hated lessons the rest of her life went on as usual. Esther continued to both practice the oud and play for her own enjoyment. She ate meals and went to the baths with Ayana and some of the other girls. They talked about inconsequential things, and Esther managed to have a fairly pleasant time. But she had stopped praying, or even trying to pray. Any thought of God in

connection with the world she now lived seemed unreal. The idea
that God had been interested in her life, that she might have been
able to talk to Him, now seemed ridiculous. She was alone here,
making the best she could out of her life.

Then suddenly the harem was consumed with the news that the
king was on his way back to Susa. Reports that he had left Sardis and
was on his way home flew around and were as quickly discredited.
Finally Hegai told them that it was officially true—Xerxes was returning to Susa. "When he arrives, there will be a great banquet to
celebrate our mighty lord's victories in Greece," Hegai told the girls.

"Victories?" Esther whispered to Ayana afterward. "Everyone
knows by now that the stories are true—our army was sent running
from Greece like a dog with its tail between its legs."

"Hush!" Ayana hissed, trying hard not to smile. "The great victory was the land battle at Thermopylae last summer. They don't
talk much about the sea battle at Salamis. And besides, we have a
large army left in Greece still. The war is not over, and the king's
greatest general, Mardonius, will conquer Greece this summer."
Esther's eyebrows raised nearly to her hairline, while she slowly
nodded her head.

"Or so they tell me," Ayana added with a laugh.

"I think if our great king were not so anxious to be a copy of his
great father, we might not have to bother going to Greece at all,"
Esther said. They'd spent several history lessons learning about the
achievements of Darius, and Esther had begun to understand why
Xerxes was so driven to conquer Greece. King Darius would have
been a hard parent to live up to.

After music class a few days later Menebar asked several of the
best musicians to stay afterward for a few moments. Esther was
among them.

"I have been asked to have some of the young women provide
music for a royal banquet," he told them. "As you know, His
Majesty the king soon returns to Susa, and there will be a great banquet to honor his return. I will be assembling musicians, singers, and
dancers to perform in his presence on each night of the feast, and I
have chosen each of you to play along with the more experienced
musicians. We will, of course, have additional practices between
now and the time of the banquet."

Esther felt almost faint with gratitude and relief. She craved the extra practices, something more to fill her hours and fill her mind; something to keep her hands and head busy so she could not dwell so much on those other lessons. And perhaps—just perhaps—if she continued to perform well enough, her music master might recommend to Hegai that hers was a talent too great to lose. She might become part of the permanent group of harem musicians and never have to become a concubine. For a moment her spirits soared. She might never be sent to the king. She would be quite happy never seeing more of Xerxes than she saw at a public banquet.

In the courtyard that night she sat alone beneath the plane tree, practicing one of her new pieces on the oud. The bubbling water of a nearby pool played a counterpart to her tune, and she paused momentarily to enjoy its music. The fingering on the new piece was difficult, and she played certain sections over and over, struggling to master it. So intent was she on her practice that she did not notice someone come near until she heard a few piped notes joining her own.

She looked up. Hathakh, the young eunuch she'd enjoyed such a friendly talk with a few weeks before, stood before her playing a small cane flute. Esther smiled. "You brought your nay!" she said happily. "Sit down, please, and play with me."

"Thank you, lady."

A smile teased her lips at his solemn charm. He seemed to know the piece she was playing and joined in with a dancing melody of his own that complemented her music. The two tunes wove in and out through each other like two lines of dancers, and for a while they played together without talking, just enjoying the music.

Finally Esther laid down the oud. "My fingers need a rest," she insisted. "You must either play for me or talk to me." She'd met Hathakh only a few times since their first talk, and he was always pleasant, but this was the first chance they'd had to sit together and have a conversation.

Hathakh laid down his nay on a stone bench. "The truth is, lady Esther, I came looking for you for more than just music. I have a message to deliver to you."

"A message? From whom?"

"Do you know a man named Mordecai?"

Esther's world spun. Mordecai was looking for her? But of course he and Aunt Rivka would be worrying, wondering about her. Yet he had said she must conceal all evidence of her Jewish background.

"I know him," she said carefully. "He is a friend of my father's family."

Hathakh nodded. "Yes, that is what he said. He is an officer at the gate, I think. I met him in the private courtyard near the entrance to the women's quarters, and he asked me if I knew a girl named Esther. He asked if she was well."

"Please, if you see him again, tell him I am very well and ask him to give my best wishes to any of my family he may see."

"I will," said Hathakh, standing up to go. "And if he has other messages for you, I will bring them; shall I?"

"Yes, please do." She clasped her hands in excitement. What news! She should have known her uncle would find a way to contact her.

Hathakh had turned and was striding away. She called him back. "Hathakh! I haven't had the chance to tell you—I have had great news today!"

"What news?" he asked, his voice a little sharp.

"I will be playing with the other musicians at the king's banquet. Isn't that exciting! That's why I was practicing just now."

A smile replaced the hard lines that momentarily framed his mouth. "That is good news. I'm sure you will do well. And they say the king's banquets are dazzling. You must tell me all about it." His voice was warm, but he seemed in a hurry. "I must go now, my lady, but I am at your service as ever." He bowed and was gone.

Life in the virgins' quarters became more difficult after the announcement about the banquet, because Raiya, who quite fancied her skill as a dancer, had not been chosen as one of the performers. She was angry, and Raiya never missed the opportunity to turn her anger outward, especially on those she saw as weaker than herself.

Her latest target was a frail new girl named Talia. Talia, who came from Babylon, looked hardly more than 12. Thin and fragile, she was so racked by homesickness that she cried aloud every night in her bed. Most of the older girls were gentle and protective toward her, but Raiya looked for opportunities to make her life miserable.

One morning as the girls made their way into the baths Raiya laughed aloud as a slave lifted Talia's robe from her shoulders. "Careful when you go in to the king, Talia," she called in a voice loud enough to be heard throughout the baths. "You'll slip down between the bed and wall, and the king will never find you."

Talia hugged herself and stared up with her huge wide eyes. She was a pretty child, but so frightened that she seemed almost stupid, and a few of the girls laughed. Esther felt her own anger flare, like the first spark of a fire that might someday blaze out of control. As a child she'd often flown into rages when Aunt Rivka laid down rules or gave punishments that seemed unfair. It was odd to remember that now, so deeply ingrained was the habit of hiding her feelings, keeping an outward calm. Now she remembered what anger felt like, not on her own behalf, but on someone else's.

"Hold your tongue, Raiya," she said quietly.

Raiya turned on her, perhaps glad to have a livelier target than Talia. "What business is it of yours? Is she your little sister? Or do you want her for your own bed?" There were always rumors of that sort in the harem—women who had unnatural relations with other women. Esther didn't know if they were true or not, but in this place where everything was unnatural, nothing would surprise her.

Ignoring Raiya's jibe, she said only, "To pick on the youngest and weakest girl here does you no honor, Raiya. Do you lack the wit to spar with your equals? Or have you no equals?"

"Not in this place, no," Raiya said defiantly, and spat on the ground. The other girls were quiet now, watching, straining to hear the confrontation, which was by no means loud, but which had attracted attention by its very intensity.

Esther felt that flame-tongue flicker inside again, but she stilled it. Maybe someday there would come a time to be angry, but the time was not now. She looked the red-haired girl up and down slowly. "You say no one in here is equal to you, Raiya? I think you are right." Slowly, deliberately, she turned her back and went to her own bath, leaving Raiya to find the sting in that compliment.

She knew Raiya would not let that lie. There would be a reckoning sometime. But at least poor little Talia had been allowed to get on with her bath without further scorn from Raiya. Esther made a point of sitting by Talia at the noon meal and sharing some food with her, since the child never seemed to have enough to eat.

Ayana soon joined them, bringing cheese and bread with honey. Forgetting decorum for a moment she plunked down beside Esther. "Are you excited about playing for the king's banquet?" she asked.

"Very. Have you ever been to one of the banquets?"

Ayana shook her head. "Not yet. But I'll go to this one, as you will. I've been asked to sing with the choir."

"Ayana, that's wonderful! We can both go—that makes it even better. I admit I can't wait to see the banquet hall. I've heard so many tales of it. The gold plates, the golden goblets, the lords in all their fine clothes. . . ."

"I used to see banquets in my father's great banqueting hall," Talia said in a soft, dreamy voice. The older girls looked at her, as surprised as if a flower had spoken.

"Was your father a great prince?" Esther asked.

"Yes, he was a brother to Shamash-eriba, our prince," Talia said, her voice hardly more than a whisper. "But when King Xerxes put down the rebellion in Babylon, we lost our wealth and our palace. I was just a child then. I stayed there with my family for awhile. I was betrothed already—to my cousin Mardion. He was my best friend. We used to play together . . ." Her voice trailed off.

The girls sat in silence, not even eating. "What happened?" Ayana finally asked.

Talia blinked, as if waking up. "One day the soldiers got word that my father and some other men were planning another uprising to take back their land and their power. I don't know if it was true. The soldiers came and killed all the adults in our house . . . my mother and my father . . . I saw them killed." Her voice dropped even lower and the girls leaned forward, straining to hear. "Mardion was 13. Almost a man. They would have killed him, I guess, but they gelded him instead. Made him a eunuch. They forced me to watch that, too. Then the soldiers . . ." Her eyes were dark pools of pain. Esther leaned forward, holding her breath.

Talia's voice was feathery soft, her lips hardly moving. "The soldiers . . . they got to me next. They were careful because they knew I had to be sent to the harem. But they didn't mind hurting me as long as I remained a virgin. They made Mardion watch, too. Then we were both sent away. I don't know where they took him. But they brought me here."

Surely, Esther thought, *the girl should be crying by now.* But her huge wide eyes were dry. Perhaps there was a point beyond which tears didn't matter anymore, a time when tears meant nothing. Perhaps after you'd absorbed enough pain, it failed to have any impact. No wonder Talia seemed impervious to Raiya's taunts and jests. Ayana slipped an arm around her, and Esther took her hand. They sat still and quiet like that for quite a while. Talia neither cried nor smiled nor spoke, but when she got up to leave she whispered, "Thank you."

Esther and Ayana sat looking at each other, both too full of thoughts to speak.

After that strange and warm encounter it seemed doubly unreal to walk across the courtyard, past the baths to the concubines' rooms, knowing what awaited her there. Esther prided herself that she'd gotten quite good at separating her mind from her body, going through the motions of this pretend lovemaking while keeping her mind as well insulated as possible. Sometimes she wondered if her mind would be as far away from her body if she was in the king's bedchamber . . . and would he notice, or care?

Today something was different. The bed, the couch, the pillows on the floor were all artfully arranged as usual. Two female slaves stood with downcast eyes. And as usual, a handsome young eunuch was there too.

No! It was Hathakh. Her friend Hathakh was the eunuch with whom she was supposed to practice these shameful acts.

For a heartbeat Hathakh's eyes met hers in mute apology, then both looked away.

"Esther, good. You are here," said Badia in her usual businesslike tone. "Take off your robe. We will continue with what we talked about yesterday."

"Wait! Stop!" Esther cried.

She so rarely said even a word during these sessions that Badia whipped around in surprise. "What did you say?"

"I said, 'Stop.' I will not do this."

"What is wrong with you, girl? Of course you will do this. This is what you are here for."

"Not—not today. Not like this." She caught Hathakh's eye again and saw there a gleam of hope that her feeble attempt to assert herself might work. But it would not work with Badia.

"Please. I need to speak to Hegai."

"Don't be a fool, girl. The lord Hegai cannot be called from his duties by the likes of you."

"I assure you," said Esther, drawing herself up to her full height and pulling her robe around her as if Badia might rip it off, "this lesson will proceed no further until I am permitted to speak with the lord Hegai. Please take me to him."

Badia fussed a little more, but Esther would not be moved. At last one of the slaves was dispatched to lead her to Hegai's private office.

Esther bowed low before the chief eunuch. "What is the matter?" he said. It was rare for any of the girls to approach him directly.

"My lord Hegai, you will think me very foolish, but I have a small request to ask of you. It is no great thing, and perhaps I am acting as a child, but today, when I came to your quarters to be schooled by Badia, the eunuch who was present for our lesson is one Hathakh."

"I know him. What of it?" asked Hegai impatiently.

"My lord, Hathakh is . . . he is a friend of mine. We have become friendly. We play music together. I . . . I trust him, my lord. It would shame me to perform these acts with him. I could not, I would not, behave as I should, my lord."

Hegai frowned. "Are you telling me there is some kind of attachment between you and this boy Hathakh? Something improper?"

"No, my lord. How could it be? He is a eunuch, and I am set aside for the king. Who could dream of such a thing!" Her shock was genuine. Among the lurid tales of harem were stories of eunuchs who had not lost all their manhood, who still took lovers—of a sort—among the harem girls. But such a thing had never occurred to Esther. She had enjoyed Hathakh's friendship and their mutual love of music. She'd never even thought of Hathakh as a man.

The brutal change that had been forced upon him at such a young age moved him irrevocably into another category. Indeed, for months now Esther had not seen any man who was not a eunuch. *Is that one reason the young women are kept in the harem with only the eunuchs around them, that they might forget about other men and come to think of the king as the one and only true man?* The thought flitted across her mind in an eyeblink, but she had no time to pursue it.

"You know, Esther, it is sometimes unwise to form close friendships in a place such as this," Hegai said thoughtfully. "We exist—all of us here—for only one purpose." He paused, raised up on his tiptoes and leaned toward her, his fingertips together. "And what is that purpose?"

Esther dropped her head and bowed. "The king's pleasure."

"Exactly. And anything—even a friendship—that stands in the way of that single goal must be put aside."

"I know that, my lord," Esther said. Her mind flew down several tracks at once. The truth was that even though she was learning to think as everyone else in the harem did, in her heart she truly didn't much care about the king's pleasure. But of course it was no use telling that to Hegai.

"Yet are there not times, my lord, when a true friendship may be an asset in achieving that goal? I am the king's loyal servant, as is Hathakh, and each of us wishes nothing more than to serve the king. My lord, I do not wish to speak indelicately, but I cannot learn what Badia would teach me if I am embarrassed or—restrained. With a stranger it is different." Her cheeks were hot, and her measured words spoke only a fraction of the resentment raging in her heart, but Hegai nodded slowly.

"I will speak to Badia. Hathakh will not return. For today you may be dismissed to your other duties. I understand you have music to practice."

"Thank you, my lord." Esther bowed almost to the ground and left the eunuch's office without glancing up. She had never dared to hope it would be so easy.

Outside, she leaned against one of the pillars that bordered the courtyard. Her forehead was cold with a thin sheen of sweat. Her heart was racing. It was odd to remember she had once thought of herself as strong-willed, independent, even a little rebellious. That girl—Hadassah—seemed very far away. She had unleashed a little of her own nature today, losing her temper with Raiya. It had felt surprisingly sweet, but dangerous. She knew there were women here—Raiya seemed to be becoming one of them—who were ruled by their passions, but she did not admire them or wish to live as they did. Rather, she had inscribed a small circle of safety around herself, bounded by caution and control, and had discovered in her confrontation with Hegai how dangerous it was to step outside that circle.

Esther practiced in the music room for the rest of that afternoon, first alone, then with other musicians. She tried to lose herself in the music, in the flow of the strings beneath her fingers. She loved the way the melodies created a world of their own, causing the complex world of the harem to drop away.

Later that evening the musicians practiced first with the dancers, then with the singers. It was late when Esther got to bed and fell asleep. For the first time in a long time she slept soundly.

The next few days were so busy she had time for little else beyond her beauty treatments and music practices. She saw her friends briefly at meals. She did not see Badia at all, nor was she summoned to her. Once Hathakh passed her in a corridor. For a moment, both uneasy, they averted their eyes, then Hathakh paused for an instant and bowed.

"My lady, I saw your friend Mordecai again outside the courtyard."

A smile lit Esther's eyes. "Did you? Did he have messages for me?"

"He said that your family hopes you are well, and they are well too. And that Shirah had a baby boy."

Shirah. For a moment the name meant nothing, then it dropped into place like a stone. Shirah, her closest friend in childhood. Shirah had had her baby. Her life—the normal, settled life Esther had chafed against but always expected—was in full motion now. And Esther's was suspended in a strange half-world where even a friend could not be a friend.

"Thank you for the message, Hathakh," she said.

He bowed his head again. "Thank you, my lady."

"For—?"

"For the other day. I had no wish to see you shamed, but I had no power to stop it."

"I know," Esther said after a pause. "I thought I had no power either, but—I appealed to Hegai."

Hathakh raised an eyebrow. "You do not realize how great your power is. The eunuchs speak very highly of you. Hegai thinks well of you." He sketched a brief bow again. "I will think of you as you play for the banquet tonight. May it go well."

Because the banquet was to begin in a few hours, Esther went early to the baths, along with the other musicians, dancers, and singers. Every detail of their appearance must be perfect. They were to be ornaments for the eye as well as the ear, and in all her months in the harem Esther had never been bathed, massaged, perfumed, made up, and dressed as she was that afternoon. Her gown was white, richly embroidered about the hem and collar with silken thread. She would have rather spent the time in another practice, but the music master that decreed there would be no more practices before the performance. Further practice would only confuse them and make them nervous, he said.

Late in the afternoon, for the first time since entering the world of the palace, Esther left the women's quarters. Holding her oud, she walked in a long double row with the other musicians. All were white-robed and veiled. Through the veil's diaphanous fabric she could see the porticos as she passed under them, and the corridor that led out of the harem and into the king's private court. She wished she could push aside her veil for a better look, but now that she'd entered the king's harem she could rarely, if ever again, look upon the outside world except through a veil. No man must ever feast his eyes on what belonged to the king alone.

Yet even through a veil, the private court was beautiful with its glazed-brick panels decorated with winged griffins. To the north lay the greatest of the banquet halls, a pavilion open to the courtyard on the south and the gardens on the north. The east and west walls were decorated with almost life-size relief carvings of the Persian kings and their victories—the artists had just completed a new carving honoring the victory at Thermopylae—and hung with gorgeously woven tapestries. Walking across a mosaic pavement of alabaster, turquoise, and white and black marble, Esther took her place among the other musicians seated on a small raised platform in a corner of the hall near the gardens. Behind them stood the singers. The dancers sat on either side, awaiting the time when they would go to the open space in the center of the hall to perform.

Despite a persistent ache in her heart for the life she'd given up, and despite everything she'd experienced in recent weeks, Esther could not help being excited about performing in this banquet hall. Its beauty defied anything she'd ever seen or dreamed. With care she pushed aside her veil and let her eyes drink in the silver curtain rods and rich blue and white curtains fastened with cords of purple. Her eyes traveled to the couches of gold and silver drawn up to the tables. She had never imagined such splendor.

No one was in the hall yet but the servants. Everything from the wine to the musicians must already be in place before the honored guests entered. And so Esther watched the intricate dance of detail necessary to make one of Xerxes' famous banquets appear seamless and perfect. Two young boys struggled in with a platter bearing a roasted pig larger than either of them. A eunuch put finishing touches to an enormous replica of the king's royal carriage made entirely of fruit. Several women scurried about checking the placement of plates and goblets. And the dishes were, indeed, made of gold and silver.

Finally the lesser servants retreated to their invisible positions, while the greater servants waited at the edges of the room. The music master signaled the first notes to begin. These first pieces did not matter much, since no one was there yet to hear them, but Esther's heart pounded nervously until she was caught up in the flow of the music and carried beyond the point of worry.

Everything went beautifully. The noblemen began to arrive, progressing staidly in from the courtyard. Most were accompanied by their wives. Esther was surprised to see this, for many banquets were men-only affairs. But at some such as this one, the women came at the beginning and later withdrew to the women's quarters when the drinking began in earnest. The music took a great deal of her attention, but not so much that she could not admire the gorgeous robes and jewels on the lords and ladies who glided across the mosaic floor to take their places at the tables.

Not far from where the musicians sat was a raised dais, and here the higher nobility—members of the royal family—soon entered and took their places. Esther recognized the king's brothers, half-brothers, and their wives by description. Most of the men had been commanders of the army in Greece. Finally Menebar directed them to strike up the music for the royal entrance, and everyone stood as Xerxes entered the hall.

Esther fiercely concentrated on her music even as she strained to get a good look at the king. He was a tall man who moved slowly, with the regal stride one would expect in a king. *Indeed,* Esther thought, remembering her own lessons in deportment, *by now he probably knows no other way to walk.* His purple robe, his jewels, even his crown were clearly visible, but two attendants walked on either side with fans held a few feet before his face. The fans acted as screens, for it was considered improper to look directly on the king's face. Mounting the steps to the dais, he walked past the table where his brothers were seated and on up to an even higher platform where a single small table, curtained on three sides from public view, was set with the royal dishes. Even at his own royal banquet, the king would not allow his subjects to gaze on his face.

Behind him came Queen Amestris. She was his chief wife and mother of his two sons, Darius and Artaxerxes, both of whom followed her into the hall. The queen was veiled, as were most of the women. Esther had never yet seen her, but her tall, proud carriage and the elaborate headdress above her veil spoke of a woman of pride and command. Behind her, the two young princes looked immensely pleased to be attending their father's royal banquet. Darius, 11 years old and teetering on the brink of young manhood, walked with a perfect imitation of his father's stately dignity. Little Artaxerxes, just 6, grinned at everyone he passed. He had not yet mastered the royal reserve.

The evening winged by, measured for Esther and her companions by the transition from one piece of music to the next. While the guests ate, the music was soft and subtle—and accented by hunger pangs of the musicians, for they could not taste any of the rich dishes being carried to and from the tables. Martial strains of music were produced to accent the many long speeches congratulating the king on his victories and looking forward to the news that Greece would soon fall to the Persian army. When the women rose to go in procession behind the queen, recessional music escorted them. Then the music became livelier. The hymns gave way to songs of passion, and the dancers took center stage.

The central core of the dance troupe were girls whom the eunuchs had already decided were not destined for the king's bedchamber. That left them free to be unveiled and thus openly display their charms for the men of the court. As the evening progressed they grew increasingly unclothed as well. Though Esther loved playing the complicated fingering of these later pieces, she tried to avert her eyes as the dancers whirled and spun. She felt embarrassed for them. Many of the men, quite drunk by now, banged their fists on the table and shouted lewd suggestions at the girls who dipped and twirled just out of their reach.

She knew that the king watched from behind his curtain. If he took a fancy to a certain dancer he could have her, even though she was not actually one of his concubines. She knew that now and then it happened. And on the other hand, if a woman who had already known the pleasures of the royal bedchamber was called upon to dance for the king and his cohorts, she was required to oblige. *Even if she were a queen,* Esther thought in dismay, remembering the legendary Vashti. How could she have defied the king? Even defying Hegai on one small point had almost taken more courage than Esther possessed.

The musicians played until the early hours of morning when the king departed with great ceremony, his face still hidden though his feet, Esther noticed, were a little unsteady. Only then were the exhausted guests led by servants back to their bedchambers.

Esther's fingers were sore, her back ached. She was starving and desperate for sleep. And this was only the first night of a week-long banquet.

The whole week had an air of unreality to it, with the days and nights turned topsy-turvy. The royal musicians performed almost all night, slept most of the day, and arose just in time to eat, have their makeup applied, slip into a new gown, and have a short practice before returning to the banquet hall. Oddly, exhausted as she was, Esther liked it. For that short week her life had a shape and purpose, unlike the usual long, aimless days in the harem. Not for the first time she wished she might be chosen permanently to be a musician. Then, even though she'd live out her life in this gilded trap, at least she would have work and a purpose.

On the last day of the banquet, reality again raised its ugly head. She never figured out a rationale for the scheduling of it, but she was brought to Badia's quarters for another of the hateful lessons. Exhausted as she was, Esther had no energy to resist what was happening to her. She simply let her mind drift, hardly aware of where she was or what went on around her. The music she'd been playing all week hummed a counterpoint in her mind as pictures floated unbidden to her inner vision. She thought of her home—of the man she might have married, though she did not know his face or name. As a bride, she would have been led proudly into Mordecai's hall. After a brief ceremony she would place her hand in her husband's and that night would have gone joyfully to her husband's bed, loving and being loved. Suddenly she felt warm and content, even happy.

Then she opened her eyes. She was in Badia's room with a strange man—no, a half-man—touching her with mechanical precision. And once again, Esther's mind snapped shut and she wasn't there at all.

The strangeness of that moment stayed with her, though, as she returned to her quarters, put on a soft, rustling gown, then sat and idly plucked the strings of her oud. The summons to go to the banquet would come any minute.

"Are you as tired as I am?" Ayana asked, her back to Esther as she adjusted the combs in her hair. The hairdressers had undone Ayana's elegant braids and now struggled to keep her thick, glorious hair controlled with heavy combs. "I should not be talking to you," she added. "The choirmaster has told us not to talk at all, for most of us are losing our voices." She turned, curious at her friend's silence. "Are you all right, Esther?"

"Not really. I had to go to Badia today for another lesson—a lesson in love." She spit out the words with a short, unhappy laugh. Badia called it that sometimes.

Ayana sank gracefully to the floor. "You still find those difficult?"

Esther nodded. "It seems . . ." she swallowed the bitterness that rose to her throat. "It seems *wrong* to me, in some way. My religion—the religion of my family, the customs we were taught—says that a young woman should remain . . . pure until she is married."

Ayana shrugged. "Most religions teach that. But our case is different, Esther. We belong to the king. Surely even the kings of your people have concubines."

Esther nodded. She knew little of the history of her people, in truth, but she had heard of King Solomon, who had 300 wives and 700 concubines. "Still . . . it seems wrong to me."

Ayana shrugged. "I don't know much about right and wrong in a place like this. I would have been happy to have stayed in my homeland, married a man there, had children and a household of my own. But that did not happen, and here I am. If the truth be known, I do not want to be the king's bedmate. I do not like the fact that my body does not belong to me, and if I could find a way to avoid becoming his concubine, I would do it. But this is my lot and I take what is given me, as we all must. Good and bad. Such as the pleasure of singing in the choir—which I will ruin if I keep talking." She held out her hand to Esther, giving it a little squeeze. "Come, it's time for us to go."

"Thank you, Ayana." Esther followed her friend out into the courtyard, wondering why this afternoon's encounter still haunted her. Then she remembered her half dream of her marriage, of the husband she might have had. To know that kind of intimacy with someone who truly loved you, someone who would be there always and not just when his whim ordered you to his bed—that was what she had lost. Until now she had never realized exactly what she'd been forced to give up. Freedom, yes, but so much more than that. Esther felt tears welling up in her eyes. For the first time since arriving in the harem, she mourned the life she could have lived.

But the life she actually was living flowed on, and she could not be late for the banquet. For the final time that week she joined the long procession of women heading for the banquet hall. Again the same scene unfolded: the servants, the exotic foods, the costly dishes. The parade of guests. The entrance of the king. And through it all she had the music, healing and soothing her, giving her something to hold onto. *I take what is given me,* Ayana had said. And this had been given her, this music. So Esther took it, and took comfort in it so completely that when she stood and stepped forward to play her solo, she played with a passion never reached before, a passion that mourned all her losses and expressed all her confusion, and was even, perhaps, a prayer to the God she had almost managed to ignore.

This final banquet stayed in full swing until that darkest hour before dawn, when the sun is holding its breath to rise. Esther drifted back to the sleeping quarters as if in a dream. There she found a slave was waiting for her with a summons to Hegai's quarters.

She had no idea what Hegai might want with her in this hour when the common people still slept. She sleepily hoped it was nothing to do with Badia, no more humiliation or shame, though she was almost too tired now to care. But Hegai was alone when she entered his private office—alone, and smiling.

"You have done well, Esther," he said, in a voice that sounded not at all tired. "Before he left the banquet hall tonight, His Majesty asked one of his officials the name of the girl who played the solo. He said he had particularly liked the music. You will remember that after your solo the women began to dance, and how they were applauded. Yet after all that, the king remembered your solo. You are gifted, Esther."

Here it was, then. Her reprieve. She was going to be a musician, and free forever from the complexities of the bedchamber. Perhaps, after all, God was still watching over her.

"Menebar asked that you be assigned permanently to the musicians. He is impressed by your talent." Hegai clasped and unclasped his hands. "I wonder if that would please you, Esther? I think so. But I told him he could not have you."

She gasped. "What? I mean, I beg your pardon, my lord?"

Hegai allowed himself a small smile. "I have watched you, Esther. I watch all the girls, but I have especially watched you. You excel in everything you do. Your music pleases the king. Who is to tell in how many other ways you will please him? When you came here you were an uncut stone, an untrained girl, and even so your beauty was arresting. Now—with all the best the king's palace has to offer—you are matchless. You will go in to the king, Esther, and if I were a betting man I would wager you will not go once only."

Esther stood silent. In this barrage of compliments she could sort out only one thing—she would have no reprieve.

"You have been here five months, Esther, almost half a year, and it is time you for you to move beyond the confines of the newcomers. You will be assigned quarters of your own with your own servants, as are our more promising girls once they've been here awhile and shown their potential. I have very nice quarters picked out for you, and I have been giving thought to your servants as well. If there is anyone you would particularly choose to serve you, tell me within the next day or so, and I will see if I can arrange it."

He smiled again, a warmer smile than before. For the first time she noticed his crooked, overlapping teeth. "Go to bed, get some rest," he said, clearly seeing that she was still dazed. "Tomorrow a new stage in your life begins. And we want nothing but the best for you."

CHAPTER 6

Esther awoke in midmorning and found herself alone in the girls' sleeping quarters. She looked around at the empty beds and thought that soon she'd be waking up in quarters of her own, in a private room. She'd forgotten how much she longed for privacy. Slipping her hands behind her head she closed her eyes and let herself spend a quiet minute thinking of home. She saw her own bedroom and balcony, her aunt bustling in with news or a reprimand. Esther laughed out loud even as tears filled her eyes. Even a private room wasn't as good as freedom, but freedom would never be hers again. Shaking her head as if the motion would chase away both memories and emotion, she got up. Freedom, it seemed, would never again be within her grasp.

She felt lazy this morning, as if the last week's excitement and missed sleep had literally added weights to her arms and legs. So she dressed slowly, called a slave to bring her some bread and cheese, and pondered what she should tell Hegai about her choice of servants. Some of the slaves here in the virgins' quarters were excellent. Could she have any of those? Perhaps she should ask advice of one of the older girls who already had her own rooms and her own staff. Or maybe the best thing would simply be to let Hegai choose for her.

After last week's hectic pace, life seemed curiously suspended. Esther had not attended her regular lessons for the past several days and wondered where in the court she was supposed to be. Deciding to head to the baths, she was surprised to meet Ayana on the way.

"It is odd, isn't it, to have a moment to ourselves again?"said Ayana. Her voice was rough and husky from the hours of singing she'd done in the last week. "Before this banquet I thought that I'd like to join the choir permanently, but now I'm not so sure. I would be exhausted."

Esther sighed. "I thought I wanted to be a musician," she told her friend, "and I wish that was how things had fallen out. But Hegai spoke to me last night. He has decided for certain, it seems, that I am to be sent in to the king. He said that he's going to transfer me into my own quarters and that I'll have my own servants."

Ayana raised an eyebrow. "Very impressive. Not surprising, but very impressive. Most of the girls aren't given their own quarters until they've been here at least three-quarters of a year."

"Why do you say it's not surprising?" Esther said with some shock. "I was certainly surprised."

They were entering the bathhouse as they talked, and two of the attendants came forward to slip off their clothes and lead them to benches, where they sat awaiting to have water poured over their bodies. Ayana did not reply till they were both settled and the attendant had poured deliciously cool water over their shoulders, making Esther shiver. The heat of Susa kept everyone sweating and even a clean loose-fitting robe soon stuck to the skin. The cool, cleansing water felt wonderful.

Ayana turned to study her friend. "Everyone knows Hegai thinks well of you," she said, finally answering her question. "He believes he has already chosen His Majesty's next wife."

"What!"

"Don't be so shocked, Esther. It is common talk that any girl Hegai favors is destined to become a favorite of the king. Either Hegai knows the king's taste uncommonly well or he exercises a great deal of influence over him. Either could be true, of course."

Esther knew how great Hegai's power was within the confines of the harem, but she had not realized his choices held so much sway with the king himself. "But you are being foolish, Ayana, to speak about the king's choice of a wife. I'm sure that out of all the young women brought to the palace, Hegai has several 'favorites.' He must! Any one of them might end up marrying the king."

"Perhaps," Ayana mused, leaning back to allow the servant to rub oils into her hair and massage her scalp. "But Esther, there is much talk of you, how well he speaks of you. Don't you know that's why Raiya hates you so? She's very jealous."

"Well, she need not be." Esther was so impatient she almost stamped her foot. "I don't even want to be queen!" She lowered her voice to a hiss, knowing perfectly well that the slaves could hear her and that she was supposed to ignore their presence yet maintain some illusion of privacy.

Ayana warned her with a glance that the rest of their conversation must wait until they were alone. "Of course, you mean that the idea of being a queen is frightening," she said clearly, "because it is such a great honor. And you are right. The king will choose whomever he chooses. But you should be pleased that Hegai thinks so well of you."

"Of course I am," Esther agreed. This was all so frustrating, not even to be able to have a conversation without being forced to remember the slaves' listening ears.

After the baths came the massages, as the skilled masseuses rubbed oil of myrrh into their skin. Then came the usual process of being made up and dressed. Only then were Esther and Ayana free to sit together in the courtyard and talk.

Esther's mind was still untangling the confused feelings that had been awakened by Ayana's comment. Was it true that Hegai's obvious approval of her was a good indicator of the king's approval, too? She had never seriously allowed herself to consider what might happen if the king actually chose to marry her. She had only considered the possible alternatives of becoming a concubine or somehow avoiding that fate. Nothing beyond that had entered her mind.

She bent down to pick a leaf off the floor of the courtyard, first lightly rubbing it against her face, then tracing its fine veins with a finger. *A queen! A queen? What would that mean for me, anyway? Would it be good, or bad, or . . . What would it require of me?* She did not realize that she had sighed, a deep intake of breath that came from her very soul. *What happened to that carefree girl who'd teased her uncle into postponing a match and her marriage?* Esther had no answer, only knew that she was gone forever.

"Esther!" Ayana's voice pierced her thoughts. Laughingly Ayana took the leaf from Esther's hand and used it to tickle her nose. "Esther, wake up! Has Hegai chosen your maids for you?"

Now it was Esther's turn to laugh as she snatched back the leaf and twirled it between her fingers. "No, he told me I could recommend someone if I wished. Can you think of anyone I ought to ask for?"

"Me," said Ayana.

"What? You? But you are—how could you be my servant? That would be impossible!"

Ayana shook her head. "Not impossible at all," she said. "Many girls who don't become concubines become servants to those who do, or to other royal women."

"But you are going to be a concubine," Esther protested. "You've been prepared for it."

"But I don't want it."

"Neither do I."

"You say you don't, Esther, yet you're willing to accept it. Maybe if it were the other way around, maybe if I were the one rising fast in Hegai's favor, and he asked me to choose women to enter my service, you'd be begging me to let you serve me." Her voice was matter-of-fact, holding no jealousy at all. "But this is how it is," she continued. "This is what has happened, and, Esther, I would be so honored to be your lady-in-waiting."

Esther shook her head in protest. "You are of far better birth and lineage than I am."

"That may give Hegai pause, but not if he knows I am willing and he sees it is for the best. What does our birth matter here, anyway? You and I are equal, for you and I both are the king's property. I only fear that Hegai will not let me turn aside from going in to the king. I've thought this out, and my fear is that he will see it as robbing the king of something. However, the king knows nothing of me. I've attracted no special attention, so perhaps Hegai will not care." She looked up with a mischievous smile. "Of course, in honor of my noble birth, I would expect to be *chief* among your ladies."

"Of course!" Esther agreed. The two sat in silence, both thinking.

"You could ask for Talia, too," Ayana suggested. "She is so frail—both in her body and in her spirit. She has suffered too much. She will not fare well here; in fact, I sometimes fear she will not survive at all. She certainly is not the sort of girl who will be chosen to go before the king, and what will become of her then?"

"I will ask Hegai," Esther said decisively, "for both you and Talia."

To her surprise, when she spoke to Hegai he agreed to all she suggested. "Ayana will be a fine choice as chief among your maids, and she is not of such a proud spirit that she will be offended by a servant's position. Only you must be careful of your friendships, Esther. Remember that these women will now be your servants, and while we may be very close to our servants, they are not equals. Be cautious. As for the little girl Talia. Yes, that is a good choice. I can see you wish to be her protector; so be it. She needs one. Have you any other suggestions? I think seven maids would be appropriate for your new rooms."

"For the others, sir, whatever you think is best."

"Fine, very good. And a eunuch? You are entitled to one, as your manservant."

Esther hesitated. She very much wanted to ask for Hathakh to serve her, though she had not spoken to him about this. Would he, like Ayana, be willing to be her servant after having been a friend? But she needed his loyalty, his friendship, and not least, his connection to Mordecai. Hathakh had already served her well. Yet having spoken about him once to Hegai, she was reluctant to speak again for fear Hegai would think she was too attached to Hathakh. He had already warned her twice about close friendships.

But this time he was ahead of her. "What about Hathakh? I do recall you think highly of him, don't you? He is a very able young man, and if, in time, you have a larger household, he may be able to serve as your steward. I would like to see him in such a position myself, if you are agreeable."

Esther bowed. "My lord, I could have chosen no better myself. If I may have Ayana, Talia, and Hathakh in my household with whatever other servants you choose, I know I will be well served."

Word spread quickly that Esther was going to be moved into her own quarters and given her own staff well ahead of the time when such an honor would normally be granted. Some of the girls wished her well. Others were openly jealous. Raiya, of course, was the leader of the latter camp.

"So, you're leaving us, are you, Esther?" she said that night in the sleeping quarters. "I hear it's a very fine place Hegai's got set aside for you, the corner rooms down near the baths. Aren't you the privileged one. Now what did you have to do to earn such favor from Hegai?" She looked Esther up and down critically. "As he's a eunuch, it can't have been the obvious. Do you perhaps have rich relatives on the outside? Is someone feathering Hegai's nest so that he can feather yours? I wonder. You don't talk much about your family, do you, Esther?"

"No more than you do about yours," Esther said as mildly as she could.

Raiya's version of her background changed almost daily, depending on the point she hoped to make. "Well, everyone knows my people are humble and simple," she said. "Far too poor to pay off the chief eunuch so that I can have all kinds of advantages and luxuries in here. No, whatever I achieve in the palace I will have to do on my own merits alone." She shook back her radiant fall of bright hair, turned in profile to display her figure to best advantage, and went out into the courtyard.

Esther went out too, a little later, not to find Raiya, but to be alone for a few moments. She drifted down to the area where her new rooms would be. Raiya was right. It was a nice location, fronting on the courtyard and quite close to the baths. She was being treated well, there was no doubt. Why? She wasn't sure. Raiya's theory was impossible—no one would or could bribe Hegai to treat her well. Ayana's theory was plausible, yet she shied away from thinking of its implications. And then . . . then there was God.

She looked up. Silver stars hung suspended in the black sky. "God, this is Esther, daughter of Abihail, here in the harem of Xerxes the king. Do You know me? Do You remember me? Are You the one responsible for showing me favor? And if You are, could you tell me why?"

Silence. Music and voices drifted out of the rooms. Insects chirruped and the wind blew softly, but the God of Israel was silent. Yet for the first time in a long time Esther did not feel that He was absent. Rather, she felt Him close, as close as He had been when she first entered the harem and reached out in faith toward Him. Perhaps in the intervening months, God had never really gone away. Perhaps she had just turned her back, refusing to see Him.

ChAPTeR 7

Esther lay in bed feeling the sun's warmth spilling across the room and over her skin. Months after moving into her private quarters, she still relished the luxury of being able to rise in privacy on her own schedule, break her fast, and begin her day alone. Communal living had never really suited her. Now that the babble of high-pitched girlish voices had been replaced by the stillness of her own rooms, the distant sounds from the courtyard, and the hushed noises of her own servants beginning the day, she felt much more at peace.

Still, she was not a late sleeper, and now as sunlight flooded the room she rose and pulled a light wrap from the bed to throw around her shoulders. Her sleeping room was a tiny compartment on the second floor. Ayana had an even smaller room adjacent to it, and from that room a stairwell descended to a common room below where Esther's other servants slept.

Brushing back her hair and tying it away from her face with a leather thong, Esther stepped out onto the tiny balcony outside her sleeping room. There she sat, overlooking the courtyard, watching day begin in the harem. Below her, slaves scuttled back and forth carrying basins of water, baskets of flatbread, pitchers of wine, piles of clothes for the laundry. They moved in the almost noiseless and invisible way all the slaves seemed to have perfected, hardly noticeable as they skirted the edges of the courtyard doing the tasks everyone needed done but no one wanted to see or know about. Behind her, Esther could hear that her own chambermaid, a slave girl named Kalinn, had entered her bedroom and was making up the bed and laying out water and towels for Esther to use. A scorpion had fallen onto the bed, and Kalinn scurried to remove it. Esther shuddered, glad it hadn't fallen on her while she slept—something that had more than once disturbed everyone's sleep in the virgins' quarters when an unfortunate girl woke to find a scorpion on her arm or leg.

Above the almost soundless movement of the slaves in the courtyard came drifting that same girlish chatter Esther was so relieved to be removed from. At this distance, though, it seemed a pleasant remote music, as the newer and younger harem girls came pouring sleepily out of the buildings to sit in the courtyard in twos, threes, and fours eating and drinking.

Beyond the baths, the courtyard angled and Esther could see clearly the bank of apartments that formed the western border of the harem court. These were some of the quarters set aside for the concubines. These older, more experienced women were also rising for the day in solitude, as Esther herself was doing. She saw two women walking to the baths, their heads bent toward one another as they talked; other women sat outside their own rooms, as she was, taking their morning meals.

Closer to her own quarters she could see signs of life in the quarters of the other virgins who had the privilege of private rooms. Phratima was out on her balcony, too, and lifted a hand in quiet salute. Raiya, who liked rising late, had not yet appeared. Esther often saw Raiya going to and from the baths, but they rarely exchanged greetings. Another benefit of privacy was that her and Raiya's path crossed far less frequently than before.

"Good morning, my lady," came a soft low voice from behind her. Esther turned to see Ayana gliding across the stone floor with a goblet of wine and a bowl of figs—Esther's favorite.

"Good morning, Ayana." Among the many changes she'd adapted to these past months was having Ayana, her elder by a year and her mentor when she first entered the harem, address her as a superior. At first Esther had chafed against Ayana's deferential words and manner, thinking them foolish. Ironically, it was Ayana herself who had to take her to task as they talked late one night.

"Esther, as your lady in waiting I set the tone for the other servants. They must see me treating you as the mistress. You must think of yourself as the mistress, always. You know and I know I am no slave girl. You know and I know we will always be the best of friends. But our friendship must be different now, and this is how it will be." Ayana had been, as always, completely serious and wise, and Esther had trusted her. And now it no longer seemed strange to have her closest friend say "My lady" and wait to be invited before she sat down next to her.

"What do we have planned for today?" Esther asked.

"After your morning meal, the baths, a massage, the cosmetics, and of course the hairdresser," Ayana said with a wry smile. When she had entered Esther's service, Ayana had carefully rebraided her hair after the fashion of her own people. She looked more herself again, less a product of the harem's hairdressers. "A full morning. In the afternoon, a lesson in etiquette and deportment with Hegai, and a music class."

"Quite a day," Esther said. She intended irony. Though her new quarters were comfortable, and she felt she had adjusted to harem life as well as any girl might be expected to do, she still found the inactivity confining. There was, essentially, nothing to do, except pose like a doll for beauty treatments.

Lessons in deportment and in court manners—and lessons of the other, more private sort—continued. The only thing in her whole day that Esther found truly appealing was her music lessons. She no longer attended the general classes; once a girl had been set aside for the king's bedchamber, she received no additional training in music or dance for her role would not be to entertain at court functions. Girls were encouraged, however, to keep up their musical skills in case the king should ever require them to play for him. For someone like Esther who truly loved music, it also provided a welcome diversion in the ennui of harem life. So she continued private lessons with her old music master. She had also, over the past weeks, fallen into the role of music teacher for a handful of harem children—sons and daughters of the king's concubines—who wanted to learn to play but were considered too young or too unimportant for formal lessons. Today the children—a half dozen of them—would come to her quarters for their lesson, which gave her one thing to look forward to.

"And for dinner?"

"We dine in the courtyard tonight with the other young ladies, unless you would wish to dine privately."

"No, that is well. I would like to give a dinner, though, perhaps tomorrow night or the night after. Is tomorrow too soon? I only want to invite a few people."

"Tomorrow should not be too soon. I will speak to Hathakh," Ayana said. "Whom do you wish to invite?"

"Ah, Tamyris, Leila, and Phratima, I think."

Ayana smiled. "Leila will have a tale to tell."

"Will she? I knew Tamyris would, but is it Leila's turn?"

"Tonight, from what they say."

"She goes to the king tonight! What has she chosen to bring with her?" Esther's eyes darted toward Leila's balcony a short distance away and lowered her voice as she spoke. Among the women who, like herself, were nearing or had reached the end of their year of training, the greatest topic of conversation was who had gone to the king and how she had fared, who was about to go and how she was preparing for the event. Tamyris and Leila had moved into apartments of their own about the same time as Esther, and the three often visited in each others' rooms or went together to the baths. Phratima had come to the harem several months after Esther did, and Esther had not known her well until recently, when she moved into the nearest apartment.

A fortnight ago Tamyris had gone to the king and the next morning, as the custom was, had been removed to the eastern block of concubines' apartments. Esther had not had the opportunity to talk with her since. Leila and Phratima were, like Esther herself, still awaiting their turn. And now Leila's had apparently come.

"Ah, you know Leila, she is very fond of display," said Ayana. "She has asked for that very large set of gold and lapis. You know, the set with the collar, the earrings, and four bracelets. And she will wear a blue robe to match the lapis—a new one she had made for the occasion. Rumor has it that before she goes she will be anointed with a potion certain to win the love of any man who touches her skin."

Esther laughed. "Is Leila really silly enough to believe in potions? If potions could secure a man's love, the first girl who went in to the king's chamber would be the last, for he would be hopelessly in love with her forever."

"Well, if you have Leila to dinner tomorrow night, you can ask her how successful it was."

"If she goes tonight, tomorrow is too soon. Make it the next night, and issue the invitations."

"As you wish," Ayana said formally, rising to go. "The morning meal is laid in your room. After you wash and eat, Talia will escort you to the baths. I must go now and talk to Hathakh about this dinner of yours."

Leaving the baths at noon, Esther paused before a huge, polished bronze mirror—the largest and clearest mirror in this part of the harem. Usually she didn't bother to glance in it as she passed by, but today she stopped and looked.

She had been in the palace almost a year. She carried in her mind a vivid picture of herself, Hadassah, as she had been the day before her capture. A pretty girl—far more girl than woman—tall and slender with untidy dark hair and skin bronzed by too much sun. A girl who was always in a hurry, eager for what came next.

She stared at herself now, a year later. Today was her sixteenth birthday, though she had not chosen to tell any of her friends or her household that. Sixteen years old, and the product of a year of the most intensive training in womanhood Persia could provide. She knew that none of her family, none of her old friends, would know her if they saw her today. She was dressed and ornamented as a princess. Beneath her elaborate makeup—eye paint, lip color, rouge—her face looked serene and composed, not because she always felt serene, but because she'd been trained to make it so. Her wild dark fall of hair was tamed, curled, styled elegantly atop her head. She walked with small even steps so that she seemed to glide rather than pace across a floor. More than once she had been commended for her grace. That would have shocked Aunt Rivka, had she ever heard of it.

Esther smiled at herself in the mirror at the thought of Aunt Rivka seeing her now. It was not the practiced court-lady smile she'd been taught but a genuine smile from her heart. In some ways, Aunt Rivka would have been pleased with what had become of her little foster child. In other ways she would be shocked. For Esther was a Persian courtesan now, not a good Jewish girl, and soon she would go to meet the test for which she had been preparing for 12 whole months.

The king was calling for new girls almost every night now, ever since word had arrived of the terrible slaughter at Plataea, the utter defeat of the Persian army, and the death of Mardonius, the king's brother-in-law and one of his closest advisors. Xerxes' hope for a conquest of Greece was completely crushed, and countless thousands of lives had been lost. Many in the palace and the city were in mourning, and there was much criticism of the king, who now seemed to have thrown away thousands of lives on a foolish quest for glory.

"If our army had won they would have been singing his praises in the streets. They would have called him as great a conqueror as Cyrus or Darius," Hegai pointed out to one of the girls who asked about the criticism of the king. Even in the sheltered world of the harem the young women heard rumors of the talk going on in the outside world. "That is the working of fate, ladies. Any man, even a king, may be on top of the world at one moment—and then, through no fault of his own, through a turn of fate's wheel—he finds himself at the bottom. Those who judge our king harshly must beware, for the wheel may turn on them at any moment. Any man—or any woman. Fate is fickle."

While the city mourned, the king, it was reported, did not. No great banquets were held, of course—that would have been clearly inappropriate—but the dancers and musicians reported that they were called almost every night to small parties in the king's chamber, where he and his nobles caroused late into the night. Concubines, too, were needed in unusual numbers. "The king is nearly always drunk, and nearly always has a girl with him," one of the dancers had whispered to a cluster of virgins one morning in the baths. "They say he has decided to drown his sorrows in wine and to bury them in bed." All in all, it did not make an attractive picture. Esther could only hope that the king's grief and anger would have spent themselves before her turn came.

On her way back from her lesson in deportment, Hathakh found her. He was now the steward of her small household, responsible for the everyday management of her affairs. She had found him to be as loyal and efficient as she had imagined he would be, not to mention the fact that his friendship, like Ayana's, gave her life a solid foundation she could not imagine living without.

"My lady," he said, bowing. "Will you accompany me? There is something I would speak to you about."

"Certainly, Hathakh." She knew she had an hour or more before the children arrived for their music lesson. She had planned to spend that time playing some music on her own in the courtyard, but walking with Hathakh was just as pleasant a diversion. "Is it about the dinner? Ayana has spoken to you, has she not?"

"Yes, she has spoken to me. The dinner will not be a problem. I have to request extra wine from the storerooms, and I have reported to the keeper of stores which women will be coming to your dinner so that he can supply the additional food and drink from their allotments. Herta has already written the invitations, and Talia has been sent to deliver them."

This was considerably more information than either Hathakh or Ayana usually gave her about household matters. Esther trusted both of them completely to take care of such details on their own. But she noticed that as they talked, Hathakh was leading her away from the virgins' quarters at the south end of the harem, past the concubines' quarters to the east, toward the porticos that led out of the women's quarters, to the king's private court, the outside world.

"Hathakh, where are you taking me?" she asked.

His dark eyes lit up with a smile. "There is someone I want you to see."

Esther wondered who it could be, but she allowed herself to be led through the porticos and the corridor, even though her heart quickened its pace. Here where the corridor opened into the private court there was some mingling between the harem women, the eunuchs, and officials from the rest of the palace. The women were almost always veiled if they had reason to come out here, and the young virgins, such as Esther, never came here at all. Except for the few times she'd played with the orchestra at official court functions, Esther had not been outside the harem since the day of her arrival.

She touched her face. "I have no veil."

Hathakh smiled again. "The person you are going to see does not wish to see you veiled," he said, steering her toward the small groups of people talking as slaves hurried back and forth on their business. There, standing near a pillar, obviously waiting for her, was Mordecai.

"My lord, Mordecai," Hathakh said, bowing. Mordecai turned to meet Hathakh's greeting, and saw Esther. His eyes widened. He hesitated, then reached forward a hand.

Eagerly Esther grasped his outstretched hand. "Mordecai," she said, hardly above a whisper. "All this time—sending messages through Hathakh—I thought I might never see your face again."

"Nor I yours." His eyes searched her up and down, seeing the changes. "But Hathakh has been telling me, and I have seen myself, that it is not unheard of for the women to meet with outsiders here in the private court now and then. He also tells me that soon your time will come to go to the king, and after that it you may not have as much liberty to move freely. After that," he said solemnly, "there may be far more interest in your friendships and family connections. So today I decided to come. To honor your birthday."

He had remembered. For the first time in almost a year Esther felt connected to something and someone, rooted in the soil she'd grown up in, rather than feeling like a feather drifting on the wind. "Thank you," she said as tears sprang to her eyes. Her voice was hardly more than a whisper. More than anything she wanted to rush to Mordecai's arms, to feel his fatherly embrace as she had when she was a little girl. She could not do that now, of course. She turned to look for Hathakh, but he had withdrawn a discreet distance. His alert gaze made it clear he was both watching over her and watching for anyone who might notice and wonder about this encounter. But he had moved beyond hearing range, allowing her a few private moments.

"Aunt Rivka—is she well?"

"She is well. All our relatives and friends, they are well, and they ask always what news I have of you. Shirah's baby—Hathakh told you about Shirah's baby?—he is a fine little fellow. He laughs—oh, how he laughs—and he's learning to sit up. Oh, Esther, we miss you so much. We pray for you, Esther."

"I—I pray too, Uncle. For you, and for myself." The words were pitifully inadequate to express the depth of her search for God, the questions, the doubts and the certainties that had filled her heart since coming here. There was so much she wanted to ask him—not about neighborhood gossip but about the God of Israel, about his own faith—but she would not have the opportunity. Even now she realized that she still held his hand and that would look odd to a passerby. She dropped her hand and stepped back a little.

"Are you truly well, Hadassah?"

He spoke her name, her true name, in a gentle breath. "I fear for you in this place, yet Hathakh tells me you are blossoming, that you are winning favor and privilege. You have a good and loyal friend and servant there," he added, nodding toward the young man.

"I know it. I have been blessed, yes, Uncle. Highly favored. And it is true, I will go in to the king soon. What happens after that, I can't know."

Mordecai's voice was tender. "Yet my child, Hathakh tells me you are highly favored to the be one who wins the king's heart and his hand in marriage. He says the oddsmakers have you marked out as a favorite."

"People bet on such things?" Esther asked, incredulous. Familiar as she had become with the closeted world of the harem, its intrigues and gossip, she had thought little about how the rest of the palace viewed that world, how eagerly they followed the rise and fall of the favorites.

"So he says. You know I have no time for such folly," Mordecai said emphatically, and Esther laughed. He sounded just like his old self.

"Have you remembered my words about keeping your nationality a secret?" he asked her.

"Of course I have, though I confess I do not see why."

"Neither do I, yet I strongly feel you must do this. Rivka's mother's family know of this. They are prepared to say you are one of them if anyone comes to question your lineage."

"I do not think that will happen, Uncle."

"If you become queen, it will."

That possibility, voiced for the second time, silenced Esther. It was a void beyond which she could imagine nothing. Her vision of the future simply did not—could not—stretch beyond the night she would go in to the king's bedchamber. Who or what she might be when she came out the next morning was in other hands than hers—the king's hands, or the hands of fate. Or of God, if He cared for such details.

"I'm afraid that I must go, Uncle Mordecai. It will seem suspicious if I stand long talking to you like this."

"Yes, of course. My story is still that I am a neighbor, a friend of your family, carrying you their good wishes. As I do."

"And carry my good wishes back to them," she said. "Tell them I am well. Kiss Aunt Rivka for me. When the king has seen me and I know something of my fate, I will get word to you."

"Goodbye, my daughter." Again the words were a whisper, as was her reply: "Goodbye, my father." And Mordecai was gone.

She stood alone for a moment, feeling again like a feather blown about the busy courtyard, or a leaf carried on a fast-flowing stream. Then Hathakh was by her side, leading her back into her own protected world.

"Thank you for doing that, Hathakh. That meant a great deal to me, especially today."

He nodded, and did not ask any questions. "It meant a great deal to Mordecai too."

A thought occurred to her, and after wrestling with whether or not to speak aloud, she did. "Hathakh, you must know by now that Mordecai is not just a friend of my family, don't you?"

Hathakh's eyes gave away nothing. "He has never said so to me, my lady. But I can see and hear his concern for you every time we talk. It is greater, I think, than the love of an old family friend."

"He is not my family's friend. He *is* my family. He and his wife, and their people. He was my father's nephew, my cousin, and when my parents died, he and his wife raised me. They have no other children, and I have no other family." She found it hard to speak. She was on the verge of tears.

"It must have cost them a great deal to let you go," said Hathakh.

"They had little choice." Esther could not keep the edge of bitterness from her voice.

As she entered the harem, instead of turning toward her quarters Esther turned right through the courtyard, passing the residences of the royal women, going toward the palace gardens. Hathakh followed her. She drew her cloak a little more closely around her shoulders. After sweltering through Susa's oppressive summer heat, she welcomed the cooler airs of late autumn. They passed small groups of women in these courts; Esther had learned to recognize Queen Parmys, Princess Amytis, Princess Mandane, and others, though she had never spoken with them. The most imposing quarters of all, taking up most of the north end of the court, belonged to the chief wife, Queen Amestris, who was not in residence at the moment. Passing through the gate beside Amestris' apartments, Esther and Hathakh went out into the gardens.

When Esther stopped at a fountain pool in a small grove of trees and sat down on the low stone wall surrounding it, Hathakh stood beside her until she motioned to him to sit, too. Silent tears ran down her cheeks and as the minutes passed she longed to share this sorrow, to not bear it alone any longer.

He sat in silence for a while, then said, "My lady. Esther, perhaps I should not have brought you to Mordecai? I hate to see you suffer so."

"Oh no, Hathakh, I am so glad I saw him! This loneliness is always with me, but only today—only because I saw him—I can let it out. Don't you know how that feels? You are much farther from your home than I am."

She saw his face tighten, the firm clean line of his jaw clench. "Yes, but I was very young. I do not—no, that is a lie to say I do not remember. I do not remember everything, but what I remember never leaves me." Hathakh very rarely spoke of himself—all the more rarely since he had become her servant rather than just her friend—and as she watched him and waited she sensed that for him, as for her, a well-maintained dam had burst inside, letting loose a flood of memory and regret.

"I remember my mother going down to the river in the morning to bathe. I rode on her hip. How small must I have been, to remember that." As he spoke, Hathakh's voice took on a different lilt, as though he were tumbling back into the past when another language had shaped his tongue. "I remember the sunshine there, different from the sunshine here, and the voices of the women at the river. I can still see our shrine at home where my family worshipped our gods. Going to work in the fields with my father. I was just old enough to go into the fields with him when the famine came." He spoke no more, but Esther knew from the little he had said before that his parents had died when starvation struck his village, and Hathakh's surviving relatives had sold him into slavery.

She laid a hand on his arm. "I feel like a fool for pitying myself. You have lost so much more."

Hathakh's laugh was short and brittle, and he gestured at the gardens around them and the women's court beyond. It was humming with activity as women, children, and eunuchs went about the business of their secluded lives. "Who here cannot say as much as I can? Think of Talia, or Ayana, or even Raiya, for all her harshness. So many have lost their homes, families, gods, lives."

"You have lost more, though. You and the other—men—the other eunuchs." She did not want to be indelicate, but in this place such things were discussed freely in a way she could never have imagined in the world outside.

Again the sharp laugh. "Yes. I was not even a man when I lost my manhood. But that makes it easier, they say." He picked up a loose stone and threw it expertly into the bushes. "When I hear other men talk—that is when I do see other men who are still men, which is not often—when I hear them talk about women, about lust, about desire, I don't even know what they mean. That part of my life is missing, but it is not as if it were taken from me. It is as if it had never been. Rather like someone born blind, I think, rather than someone who has lost their sight."

"So you don't—feel that loss?"

Hathakh looked at her for a long moment, the longest and straightest gaze he had given her since he had come to work for her. The deferential servant's glance was utterly gone. "Not in that way, no. They say that the boys who are made eunuchs when they are older—13 or 14—suffer more in that way. But then they often do not survive the cutting. In the days afterward many become quite ill. And many die."

Esther shuddered, but Hathakh held her gaze. "But of course I feel a loss. My body may not be as other men's, but my heart is no different. I could love a woman, could fall in love, could wish to marry and have children with her. That—could happen to me." There was such wistfulness in his voice that Esther thought he meant to say, *That has happened to me.* "But I would not be able to do anything about it. That—yes, that is quite a loss."

Then he looked away, tossed another stone. "But it is no worse than the losses anyone else here has suffered, including you, do you see? Everyone here has lost their chance at a normal life. For some of us, that normal life might have been far worse than what we have here. I was a slave. I could have ended up in far worse places. I fill my life with—other things . . . work . . . music . . . friendship. I like beauty, and I like music."

"Yes," Esther said. "Music and friendship, for me, anyway. I have no work. I wish I did. Sometimes I'm so bored. But you're right, self-pity is foolish here. Only sometimes, Hathakh, sometimes I'm afraid."

Now it was his turn to touch her, very lightly on the hand. "Of course you are. In a few weeks you will go to the king." He closed his eyes and took a long breath, then went on. "And of course you wonder, What will happen next?"

"Exactly. If the king doesn't like me, then I live out the rest of my days with the other unwanted concubines, with no occupation, no meaning, no purpose at all. No future. And if he *does* like me, if I'm the one chosen to be a royal wife . . . I suppose everyone would think it foolish of me to be scared of that, but—I am."

"Of course," said Hathakh again. "You would have wealth, position, honor beyond your dreams. And you would be married to a man you hardly know. You will bear children who will grow up to be playing pieces in their father's political games, and you will share your husband with dozens of other women—not least with Queen Amestris, who hates all rivals. I tell you, Esther, when I hear the other girls talking of their chances with the king, I think that if you are the only one who is frightened, then you are the only one who is not half-witted!"

"Oh, thank you, Hathakh. You are so good to me." Impulsively she squeezed his hand, then jumped up. "I've almost forgotten. The children will be coming for their music lesson, and I'm going to be late if I don't hurry. Will you bring your flute and play with us today? They always enjoy that."

Hathakh stood up and fell quickly into step beside her. When he replied, Esther noted that the earlier tension in his voice had been replaced with a note of amusement. "I have a thousand things to do to arrange for this dinner party of yours, my lady. But for you, my lady, anything." The words were light, but she felt a weight behind them. It was almost as if he really meant it.

Two nights later Esther's guests clustered at her apartments for dinner. The girls who had been given their own quarters were encouraged to arrange small parties. For the women who rose high in the king's favor, entertaining would be an important part of their future role and this was considered good training. Of course, with only seven maids and one eunuch, a girl could not be expected to staff a proper household. The living quarters did not have their own kitchens. Food was prepared in and carried from the communal kitchen in the virgins' wing.

Because it was autumn there were few fresh fruits and vegetables, but that did not affect the quality of the meal. The feast began with a soup with a base of barley flour. Onions, lentils, and mutton fat made it rich and nourishing—a meal in a bowl. The next course was fish garnished with garlic, vinegar, and winter greens, and served with sharp cheese and soured milk. Bread—fine, slightly sweet loaves—especially made from flour to which sesame oil, fruit juice, and dried cherries and apricots were added rounded out that course. Bowls of almonds, pistachios, and dates finished the meal.

Esther's servants had laid two tables in the courtyard immediately outside her quarters. One was for Esther, Tamyris, Phratima, and Leila. The other table was for their four ladies-in-waiting and four eunuchs, the upper servants who were privileged to eat with their mistresses in this small, informal setting. Ayana and Hathakh had worked very hard behind the scenes to make this feast possible. Now they sat and allowed the maids to serve them, though Esther noticed several urgent queries being directed to both of them by the maids as they dined.

There was a clear divide at Esther's table—herself and Phratima, still awaiting their summons to go to the king, seemed to be in a different world from Tamyris and Leila who had been moved to the concubine's quarters and had an air of worldly-wise sophistication.

Tamyris was bubbly and full of talk about the king. Leila was quieter, but allowed herself to be drawn in.

"One thing I *must* tell you," Tamyris said, "when your time comes, *insist* on bringing love potions. Oh, you laugh, Esther," she said, her own laughter like the jingle of silver bells on anklets. "I know you're a skeptic, but let me tell you, I anointed myself with a potion Badia recommended, and the results were—well, quite impressive, let me tell you. Isn't that so, Leila? You used the same thing?"

"Oh, yes, and it worked very well indeed," said Leila, rousing herself out of a thoughtful daze.

Esther giggled. "But how do you know, ladies, if all we have is your report and both of you used the potion? How do we know it's effective? Perhaps your potion made the king ardent—or perhaps he merely *is* ardent, potion or no? Surely His Majesty is the most virile man in the kingdom?"

"Indeed he is. No other can compare to him," Tamyris said devoutly. Esther wondered how she could judge since all the girls were known to be virgins before coming to the harem, and none had seen any men but eunuchs since. But all the other girls chimed agreement.

"And handsome," Leila added. "He is like a god."

"Like one of the gods of the Greeks—Adonis!" Tamyris said with a wink.

"But how does he treat a woman?" Phratima wanted to know. "Is he gentle, or fierce? Is he a good lover? Is he kind?"

Esther caught the split second glance that passed between the two concubines before Leila said, "He is very kind. He was most gracious to me."

"No one could be more attentive to a woman's needs than my lord the king," said Tamyris.

Esther realized that the chatter at the other table had hushed. The maids—some of them such as Ayana, girls who had not been given a chance at the king's bedchamber—were wildly curious. *As are we all,* Esther thought, especially those who still had to go into the king. What was this man, this center of their world, this being so powerful that even his face could not be seen—what was he really like in the privacy of his own chambers? So far, Leila's and Tamyris's stories had been exactly like that of all the other concubines she'd spoken with. The king was handsome, passionate, virile, and considerate beyond description. If it was all true, he was, indeed, a paragon.

But later in the night, when the four girls had withdrawn in private to the balcony outside Esther's private chamber, when the maids and eunuchs had gone to their beds, and the wine now flowed freely, Leila reached forward to fill her goblet again, and Esther saw a faint dark circling of bruises on her arms. She told herself not to say anything, to ignore it, but something made her lean forward and put a hand on the other girl's arm.

"Someone has hurt you," Esther said.

Leila looked confused, then scared. Her eyes sought Tamyris's, questioning.

"In the height of his passion the king sometimes becomes—forceful," Tamyris said, her voice low. "No one would expect less of such a great ruler, of course. And we *are* his servants."

"And we would not complain," Leila whispered.

"He is a very great man. Almost a god," Tamyris said. "He is not cruel—only thoughtless, I think. Even a common man may be so, how much more a king."

"Do not defy him," Leila whispered. "It is said he likes women with spirit, but that spirit must not be directed against him."

"It has been worse since Plataea," Tamyris said. "The king grieves for the loss of his army, the loss of Mardonius . . ."

Esther nodded. Somehow, that she understood. "The loss of his dream," she said.

"Yes. And sometimes it is a woman's role to . . . to bear that burden for him. He is angry sometimes."

Their voices were hushed. Twilight had come and darkness crept over their faces. Wine and dusk made the girls talk more freely. Old stories, harem gossip.

"You do know what happened to Vashti," Phratima said. "Sometimes I think it would be better not to be the king's favorite."

"He was tired of Vashti by then," said Leila. "He tires of women quickly."

"What about his wives?"

"Even his wives. Irdabama has not been called before the king in almost two years, they say."

"He never loved her. His marriages are political matches."

"Perhaps he has never loved anyone. Except himself." That was

Esther, the clarity and firmness of her words startling everyone, even in their half-tipsy state.

"Hush, Esther," Tamyris commanded, glancing around, back into the chambers and down into the courtyard.

"There is no one around."

"There is always someone around," Leila said with a sigh, and then they were silent. This was the harem, and Leila's words were true.

CHAPTER 8

Esther stood in the hall outside Hegai's office. He had asked to see her, just as he requested an audience with all the women before they went to the king. His servant opened the door, announced her, and gestured for her to come in. Hegai stood as she entered, something he had certainly never done before.

He eyed her as a sculptor might eye his final masterpiece just moments after laying down mallet and chisel, and in his eyes she saw nothing but approval and pride.

"You are perfect, Esther," he said at last. "Perfect. I could not suggest one thing more."

She bowed gracefully. In fact, Hegai himself had suggested everything. When word had come a few days before that on this night Esther would be sent to the king, she had been given her choice of wardrobe, jewels, cosmetics, and even love potions from the harem's stores. Ayana, the other maids, and her friends had plenty of suggestions, but Esther felt curiously detached from the whole process. For a long time she'd felt that her destiny was out of her hands. She was still mostly afraid, but she no longer knew for certain what she wanted the outcome to be. Destiny, or God, or maybe just Hegai, was preparing her for something, and Esther had begun to feel it would be foolhardy to try to influence the course of events—especially when she herself didn't even know what she truly wanted.

So she'd asked Hegai to choose for her. She knew immediately from his reaction that she had pleased him. Daily he had girls coming to him, asking for this gown or that necklace, whatever trinket or toy they believed would win the king's heart. Hegai was delighted to have a girl so pliable, so willing to be molded. He chose everything—her dress, her jewels, her cosmetics. And he gave her no love potions.

"I don't believe in them," he had said, "and I think His Majesty, the king, would be insulted to know that half the women in the harem believe he needs a love potion to make love to them. Although perhaps it is themselves they are insulting. You need little to heighten your allure, Esther. Only the simplest, the finest, the best."

That was two days ago. Now he looked at her fresh from being bathed, dressed, and made up, and nodded judiciously.

"You know that tomorrow morning you will pass out of my direct care," he told her. "Tomorrow, when you leave the king's chambers you will be taken to the concubines' quarters where Shasgaaz will . . . will see to your needs."

He'd hesitated a moment. Esther wasn't sure why. Not everything she had heard about Shasgaaz, the eunuch in charge of concubines, was good, but he was hardly the man who concerned her most at the moment. She wondered if Hegai would have anything at all to say about the king. She was too nervous to ask anything.

Hegai came around the table, placed his hand in the small of her back, and gently propelled her out of his chambers and down the wide hall. "You will please our lord, Esther. I know you will. He is—not always easily pleased these days. He can be difficult. Great matters occupy his mind. But you will be good for him. Be yourself."

He paused, looking into her face. He cleared his throat. "Be as the gods have made you, and you cannot fail to please the king."

Be yourself. Be as the gods have made you. The refrain drummed in Esther's head as she took her leave of Hegai and, accompanied by Ayana, began the long walk through the women's quarters, into the king's private court, and across the court to his chambers. No one gave much notice of their progress. Young women went in to the king almost every night. The evening meal had ended, darkness was falling over Susa and over Xerxes' great palace.

Be as the gods have made you. Earlier Esther had thought that God, or destiny, or even Hegai himself had taken control of her life. She chose to believe it was God even though believing in her God, in Israel's God, was not easy in a world where He was silent and absent, where no one else worshiped Him, and when she herself hardly knew how to serve Him. It was a choice, an act of hope, to believe that the

same God who had called Abraham to be the father of His called people, the God who had parted the Red Sea and led Israel into and out
of captivity here in Persia—that that same God was somehow leading
and acting in her life. If it was true, what a strange role for God to
play—leading a girl into the bedchamber of a lustful pagan king.

Ayana remained quiet throughout the long walk. She would wait
outside the king's chambers till Esther had gone in, then she would return to Esther's quarters and oversee the removal of her belongings and
her staff to their new home in the concubines' wing. In the morning,
early, she would return to escort Esther back to the harem. Neither of
them would sleep much tonight.

One of the harem eunuchs strode before them, speaking to the
guards who kept the entrance to the king's living quarters. Ayana
pressed a little tighter on Esther's arm as they passed through that portal, and caught her eye with a quick half smile. Esther's heart pounded,
and her throat felt so tight she couldn't have spoken even if there had
been anything to say.

From the king's quarters came the sounds of male voices, laughter,
and quiet background music. Esther had known, of course, that the
king generally had musicians playing in his private chambers, and that
these were almost always women from the harem. However, she had
not given any thought to the fact that they would be women whom
she knew, that girls she'd sat next to in music classes and played with
at banquets would be strumming their ouds or playing their pipes as she
bedded with the king. It was all very strange.

On the threshold of the bedchamber she and Ayana paused. The
eunuch went ahead to inform His Majesty that the virgin had arrived.
Ayana squeezed Esther's hand. "May your own gods bless you," she
whispered. "All will be as it is supposed to be."

"Thank you," Esther murmured. The eunuch stood in the doorway and gestured to Esther to enter. She stepped across the threshold.

It was, as befitted a king's most private chamber, a busy, noisy
place, and for a moment no one even noticed her. That gave her time
to look at the walls, crowded with the usual painted carvings and embroidered hangings. She saw the bed with its lightweight multicolored
tapestries and the small raised platform where four or five musicians sat.
They were, indeed, all girls whom she knew. One was her friend
Roxane, but she did not meet Roxane's eyes. She noted the elaborate
chairs where a half dozen noblemen sat with a half dozen servants

hovering behind them. Two more girls were there, too—but she did not recognize them. They were likely slave girls or prostitutes from the city who sat, half uncovered, one on the lap and the other at the feet of two of the richly dressed nobles who attended the king.

It was one of those men who first saw Esther and widened his eyes with appreciation. "Your Majesty!" he said. "Your prize has arrived."

"Hegai has outdone himself this time," a quieter man murmured, but Esther did not see who spoke. Her eyes were riveted to the man whom the other had addressed as "Your Majesty," the man who'd been busy holding his wine cup to be refilled when she entered and who now turned to look full at her as she sank slowly to the ground in a complete obeisance, then straightened up, as she had been taught, to kneel before him.

King Xerxes sat in a straight-backed wooden chair, but he lounged as if he were reclining at a table, his long legs stretched out before him, one arm hooked indolently over the chair's back. His face—which she'd never seen full-on except in carvings which caught only the barest outlines—was long and slender, strong-featured, with high cheekbones and dark shining eyes that fixed hers eagerly, glancing briefly at her face before they traveled down her body.

The gown Hegai had chosen for her was revealing but not tawdry. Her makeup was only a light-green ointment on her eyelids, a high-light of gold upon her cheeks, and red pigment on her lips. Hegai did not wish her to look like a woman of the street, but like a woman whom the king would want to know better. And the gown—or something—seemed to have been a good choice, for the king smiled a slow, languid smile, took a deep drink from his cup, and held out his hand to Esther.

She reached forward to touch the tips of his fingers, and arose. He took another long look at her then said, "Very fine. Very fine indeed."

He turned to his friends. "Do you envy me, gentlemen? What one of you could ever purchase a woman so fine? Yet I have hundreds!" He laughed; they laughed. Esther remained unmoving before him, waiting for him to tell her where to go, what to do.

Suddenly he reached out and pulled her down on his lap. She gasped. She had not expected to be so close to him so quickly. He smelled of wine and his own perfumes and faintly, but not unpleasantly, of sweat. His hands quickly and expertly explored her body as he talked with his friends, neither glancing at her nor addressing any further comments to her. She willed herself to relax at his touch and gradually the warm flush that had reddened her face when he pulled her down faded away.

She sat in that rather uncomfortable posture for perhaps a quarter of an hour while the king and his companions traded ribald jests. Then the king told the two men who had girls with them to go away, and they left with their slave girls in tow. The king called for more wine, and gestured to Esther to move from his lap to the stool at his feet. He asked if she wanted any wine. She did by now, but she also wanted to keep her head very, very clear, so she sipped it slowly.

Xerxes continued talking to the few men who remained. The conversation had shifted from bawdy humor to military talk. "When will Artabazus be here?" the king demanded, peering at the other men as if either of them would hide the answer. "Dispatches after dispatches I receive from him, yet he's dragging his heels all the way back from Sardis. Does he think I'll whip him for running away? Perhaps I will!" Artabazus, one of the army commanders, had been the only one to extract his forces almost intact from the disastrous battle at Plataea earlier in the fall, and he and his men had been reported to be making their way gradually back to Susa.

Esther wondered if the king had forgotten her altogether. She had plenty of time, now, to study him. There had been little in what she'd heard of the great Xerxes to put her mind at rest about this encounter, but she had to admit that talk of his handsomeness was something more than just the flattery always given to royalty. He was a striking man in his late 30s, the prime of life. He stirred with restless activity as he talked, his slim hands working through his dark, curled beard or through his shining, shoulder-length hair. His eyes flickered from one face to another. He drank steadily, but seemed sharp-eyed and sharp-tongued, none the worse for wine.

Finally the conversation lagged and his restless eyes stopped for a moment on Esther. "Come, my friends," he said, "you must leave me soon, but before you leave shall we see what my newest possession can do? Stand up, girl."

Esther stood. What did he mean—see what she could do? In front of these men?

The king gestured to the musicians. "I want music for a dance. You know the ones I like." Esther heard the hurried flutter of the musicians' whispers as they chose a song and moved seamlessly into it. The king eyed her expectantly as the light notes crescendoed into a complicated beat. "So dance, girl," he said.

Dancing was not Esther's strongest talent. She had been told she danced better than she sang, but played the oud far better than either. But neither singing nor oud playing was likely to suit the king's mood just now, and she'd been told that he often asked girls to dance for him. The dancing teacher had taught each of them some particularly attractive numbers to perform if asked to give a private performance. Esther had prepared herself to do such a thing for the king alone, but to her surprise the other two men remained seated, watching expectantly.

She felt self-conscious as she began to sway to the music's rhythm. She closed her eyes to shut out everything else, allowed herself to listen only to the music, and began to sway in response. She let her feet and hands fall into the patterns she'd been taught, trusting the music to bring the dance to life. At last, opening her eyes she looked only at the king, looked straight into his eyes—a daring thing to do, but a woman about to spend the night with the king might dare things that others did not. He leaned just slightly forward. He approved.

Her heart pounded and her olive skin was flushed by the time the music fluttered to its end. Xerxes dismissed his men with a quick hand gesture that had them rising from their chairs and bowing as they backed out of the room. All but two of the servants left also. The musicians remained, but their music became quieter and more intense.

The king stepped forward, placed his hands on either side of Esther's waist and looked at her with delight. "A very fine specimen indeed," he said. "I must remember to compliment Hegai." Then drawing her toward him her gathered her into an embrace.

His mouth was strong, his kiss forceful. She tasted wine on his tongue and smelled the sharp, spicy scent of his perfume. She was still a little frightened, but she no longer felt awkward or ashamed. Rather she felt completely present in her body as the king, still kissing her lips and face, lifted her in his arms.

Inside the royal bed, with the hangings closed, they were as private as a monarch could ever be. Esther had imagined that she would be remembering those hateful lessons with Badia, trying to imitate the things she'd been taught, but those lessons must have burned deep enough into her blood that she could remember without thinking. She thought only about the king as he lay down beside her.

It seemed a long time that they lay together in the dim, curtained cave. The room was warm. Shadows from the flames of the oil lamps played across the light fabric encircling the bed. Xerxes was a handsome man, and he was not unkind. Esther could feel her pulse hammering in her throat. Unexpectedly, she realized that amid her stormy emotions she felt excitement and anticipation, though it was sharpened by her fear of this Persian monarch and the strangeness of this situation.

At that moment they heard a rude rapping on the chamber door.

Xerxes rose up on one elbow and smiled down at her. "Pay no attention, my love. They know it is death to disturb me."

Faintly she heard one of the servants answering the door and a hurried, urgent conversation. The king kissed her again, but she could tell he was distracted; half of him was trying to listen to the conversation going on outside. Esther expected to hear the door close as the intruder was turned away, but it did not. The voices continued, and she heard one—a eunuch's voice—insisting, "His Majesty cannot be disturbed!"

With a sharp, irritated sigh, the king sat upright, pulled his robe around him, and parted the bed curtains, swinging his long legs outside the bed and looking out into the room. "Who is there, Harbona?"

The eunuch's voice again: "My lord, it is the Prince Masistes."

"What?" Esther's heart jumped at his tone. "Send him in!"

Xerxes stood up, and was gone from Esther's view. The curtains fell back, enclosing her in the silken, dimly lit world of the bed. But as Prince Masistes, the king's brother, strode into the room, the level of their voice rose to the point where she would have heard them even with her hands over her ears.

"My lord king," the prince said in a dismissive tone, lacking the awed respect with which people generally spoke to and of the king. "Have I interrupted you? I am surprised to find you alone so early. Have your companions all gone? But perhaps you are not quite alone."

"Not quite alone, no, my brother. But nothing so important I cannot tear myself away to speak with you, at any hour of day or night." Esther was surprised to hear the edge in Xerxes' voice. Earlier in the evening, surrounded by his servants and his lords, he had spoken with the careless, assured command she thought quite proper for a supreme ruler. Now he seemed on the defensive. She sat up, her arms locked around her knees, listening.

"I bear important tidings. Artabazus is in the city. My sources say he will seek audience with you tomorrow."

"Tomorrow?" Esther heard a shuffling noise of servants, a clink of glasses and pitcher, and the king asked, "Wine?"

Prince Masistes gave a short, unpleasant snort. "I suppose so—abstinence is hardly seemly in *this* chamber, is it?"

"Peace, brother." Xerxes' voice was a low growl. "I am king in Susa yet. Do not taunt me."

"No, my lord. Still, I have some leeway, have I not? Another of the king's brothers dead? That would hardly look good at this point, would it?"

"My other brothers died honorably on the field of battle!"

"While you and I escaped. Ironic, isn't it?" Masistes paused, to sip his wine, Esther supposed.

"Is that all you have to say to me? That Artabazus is coming?"

"Is that not enough? It is what you have waited for."

"I knew he would come eventually. It is no great surprise."

"Of course not. And it does not disturb you, I can see. The people in the city are hailing Artabazus as a hero—the only hero of Greece, they say. Though they call Mardonius a hero, too—or a martyr. Sacrificed to his king's glory, while his king sits in Susa with his eunuchs and concubines."

"Get this man out of here!" the king roared as his anger burst like a fireball. Esther jumped, and found herself trembling. She heard the scuffling of the servants' feet; the musicians had stopped playing. What she did not hear was any sound that would indicate Masistes leaving the chamber.

She held her breath in the silence. At last the king shouted, "Get out!"

"As you wish, my lord." The tone was a combination of sarcasm and indolence. "Your command *is* supreme. I will attend upon you tomorrow, as it is your pleasure, Your Majesty." Esther heard the swish of his bow, then his slow footsteps out of the room.

There was another long silence.

"Get you gone. All of you!" Xerxes bellowed—he must have been talking to the servants and musicians. She heard them scuttling for the door, punctuated by one more roar: "You! Leave that! And bring me another!"

She had little doubt what "that" was, for the next thing she heard was the king pouring himself another cup of wine. She sat still, knowing it was not her place to move or to speak. No doubt he had forgotten her very existence.

Suddenly a shattering crash split the silence, followed by an inartic-
ulate cry of anger and pain. She guessed that the king had hurled his
silver wine goblet across the room, to clatter on the stones. He was pacing the room now, and she wondered if he had remembered her after
all, or if he thought he was alone, for he began to talk.

"Darius lost at Marathon, do none of them remember that? No! All
they recall are his victories; all they see are my losses! Masistes! He
would have had the throne from me when Darius died. I should have
killed him then, not rewarded him with power and position. Impudent
ass. How dare he taunt me? How dare he mock me for Salamis and
Plataea? He will suffer for this!" The pacing stopped; she heard him sit
down. There must have been another goblet on his table, for she heard
him pour and drink again.

For the second time that night, time seemed suspended. Esther
had no idea how long she sat alone in the king's bed, listening to
the man outside drinking and occasionally talking to himself.
There were no more loud outbursts, but he muttered to himself,
long passages of discontent from which only names sprang out to
her ears—Artabazus, Masistes, Mardonius—spoken with pain—
and Darius—spoken in anger.

Then, quite unexpectedly, he did speak directly to her. "You
there. Girl! Are you still awake?"

"Yes, my lord, I am."

"Come out of there. No, wait, I'll come in." He laughed. Esther's
heart lurched for his words were slurred. He was quite drunk. She
could see that when he parted the curtains, threw off his gown, and
stumbled onto the bed toward her. Fear beat in her temples. She knew
that some men became violent with drink. She remembered the bruises
on Leila's arms, and shivered.

"Ah, yes, I remember you. The pretty one. All pretty, of course,
all of them. Why should you be any different?" He reached an unsteady hand toward her face, touched it clumsily, stroked her hair.
"Come to me, pretty one. It's time for you to serve your king."

This time it was quite different. The scent of wine that had been a
heady perfume before was now an overwhelming miasma. Xerxes groped
and fumbled for her, but his touch brought only fear and confusion. He
did not seem inclined to be violent, but he was clumsy and rough. She
shut her eyes tightly, hoping the ordeal would soon be over.

It was a while before she realized what was wrong. Badia had warned her about this. She'd warned all the girls, Esther had discovered when they talked among themselves. Sometimes, for any number of reasons—and excessive drink was often one—a man was unable to respond normally. "But no matter what the cause," Badia had said, "be sure of one thing. He will always blame you. It will be your fault. I speak now of a common man, but—" she had lowered her voice, "this thing can happen even to a king, and a king, even more than a common man, cannot believe such a thing could be his own fault. It will be you he faults, for not being attractive enough, alluring enough. If you are lucky, he will dismiss you. If you are unlucky, he may beat you badly."

Badia had, of course, taught the girls a number of tricks to perform to hopefully arouse a fading king, but Esther could not imagine trying any of them now. The man beside her in the bed was drunk, exhausted, angry, and sad. Whatever he needed, whatever would save her, it was not some courtesan's practiced teases. Esther decided to gamble on speaking. She was better at that anyway, though he might not want to hear her. She ran a number of possible comments through her mind as he sat up and turned away from her in disgust.

She took a deep breath, then moistened her dry lips. "My lord, it was a cruel chance that your brother the prince came to interrupt us when he did," she said softly.

Xerxes laughed. "A cruel chance, indeed. It is one of his little games to come striding into my bedchamber. My bedchamber! A better king would have had him put to death by now."

Esther relaxed just the tiniest bit. He was at least allowing her to speak. She sat up, too, and tentatively laid her hands on his back. "My lord, there could surely be no better king."

"A better king would've had him put to death years ago. I was too soft. He wanted to fight me for the throne. You know that, don't you? When our father died. When Darius died. Darius the *Great.*"

Esther teased hands up and down his back. All the girls were taught the rudiments of massage. Her fingers worked lightly at the knots of tension in his neck and shoulders, not enough to cause him discomfort, of course. "Your royal father was a great king, my lord. Yet not even he subdued Egypt as you did." That was because Darius had died before putting down the rebellion in Egypt. Xerxes had inherited the task, but she guessed correctly that he would not be particular about details just now.

"That's right, isn't it?" Xerxes threw his head back and groaned softly—whether out of pleasure at her touch or out of his own despair, she did not try to guess. "And he lost Marathon," he told her. "They never say that, but he lost at Marathon. He couldn't conquer Greece, and I can't either."

"Your reign is but young yet, my lord." That was a risky thing to say, because everyone she had ever heard talk about it said Xerxes would be mad to ever risk attacking the Greeks again but, as before, she was fairly confident his critical faculties were not at their peak at the moment.

Indeed, his mind seemed to have wandered in another direction altogether. He lay back and stared at the rich purple and white bed-hangings above him. She shifted her caresses to his chest. She worked on the tension in the muscles girding his shoulders. Her touch was soothing, almost putting him to sleep.

"I was his favorite, you know," he said dreamily. "Never any doubt he wanted me to rule. Never any doubt. Mother's favorite, too. The golden boy. Could do no wrong—that's why Masistes hated me."

"But he honors you, my lord, as all must do. You are his king."

"That's right, isn't it? His king. I'm the king, when all's said and done." He sat up abruptly. "Wine! Is anyone out there?"

"I believe your servants have all gone, my lord, except the guards at the chamber door. Do you wish me to serve you?"

"Get me more wine." He collapsed back on the pillows.

Esther slipped from the bed and found the wine jug and goblet. She felt confused and a little fearful. It was a shame to pour more wine for a man so obviously a slave to drink, but she dared not dream of refusing to do so. She hesitated for a heartbeat, pondering, then decided that at this point it might well put him to sleep.

"Lie here beside me," he commanded as she gave him the goblet. He was leaning up on one elbow. "Keep touching me just like you were doing." And he was lost in his thoughts again, spilling it all out to her in increasingly slurred words—his father, his failures, his dreams, his power. Twice more she refilled his glass at his command. And at last he slept.

Esther lay beside him all night, never closing her eyes. She looked at his sleeping face, the face that had looked so proud and handsome when she first saw it hours ago. In drunkenness and sleep its fine lines relaxed. It was still a handsome face, but softer, more dissolute. It was the face he might wear in five or 10 years if no more victories came his way, if the shadows of Salamis and Plataea, of Darius, continued to hang over him, and he sought comfort only in wine.

She had begun the day feeling nothing for this man except a subject's proper awe of her king and a deep-rooted fear. Neither of those things was gone or even much lessened, but they had been joined by a tangle of other feelings, feelings she pulled out and examined as she lay beside him throughout the night. Not all were pleasant, by any means, but all were important. From this night on, her life was bound up with the king's. As indeed it had been all this past year, for she was his property. But now she felt that bond inside her, where before she had always felt free.

She'd been told the king would not go to sleep in the presence of a concubine unless she was a very well-known and trusted woman. He dared not trust a concubine, for even a concubine might be an assassin, though she'd been checked for weapons before entering his quarters. A woman might, Esther supposed, smother him with a pillow. Before the king was fully asleep she heard his guards reenter the chamber and take up their positions. The king and his woman were never fully alone. But she felt alone, here in this curtained world while the king slept.

At last their dim world began to lighten a little, and a shaft of sunlight from one of the small windows fell and bent upon the curtained wall. The king stirred, opened his eyes, and looked across at Esther. He smiled the same smile of appreciation and pleasure he'd had upon first seeing her.

"Well, aren't you the pretty one," he said. "What's your name?"

"Esther, my lord."

"Esther." He leaned up on one elbow and winced. "I've a headache straight from Anghra Mainyu himself, Esther. I suppose I've been drinking. Have you been here long?"

"All night, my lord."

Now his dark, bright eyes focused on her again. She had no idea what he remembered of the past hours, but she had a clear idea what would happen next.

CHAPTER 9

"Imagine, all this time we thought the concubines lived in such luxury," Esther said, looking around at the tiny room where she sat with Ayana. The virgins' quarters were so incredibly cramped—even the private apartments—that it was common to fantasize about the spacious accommodations the king's concubines must enjoy. Now that she'd actually moved into her new apartments on the west side of the women's court, Esther had to admit they were larger—by a hair's breadth. But they were still far from spacious.

"And the concubines envy the royal women," Ayana said. "Everyone must have someone to envy."

"I suppose the other wives envy Amestris," Esther said. "I wonder who she envies? At any rate, we will need to find more linens—it's ridiculous we haven't enough bed coverings for the servants. Ayana, can you see about that? And Hegai assured me that after I moved to the concubines' wing we would have another eunuch. I don't care so much for myself, but Hathakh"—she glanced over to catch his eye—"if you need more assistance, and it's our due, we should have another man. Can you speak to Shaashgaz about that?"

"I will, my lady, but it will take time. As will the linens if Shaashgaz keeps dragging his heels," Hathakh added, making a note on the clay tablet he carried. "You ought to have a scribe, too, but that may take months."

"Why? Is Shaashgaz so disorganized? I visited Leila's quarters, and things seem to run smoothly there."

There was a brief silence as Ayana and Hathakh exchanged glances. Ayana was the one who finally spoke: "Leila has not been called to the king again since her first night with him."

"And I . . . " Esther's voice trailed off. She had first been brought to the king a fortnight ago. He had called for her again tonight—the seventh or possibly eighth time since. She had spent nearly every other night in his chambers as Ayana and Hathakh—and the rest of the harem—knew very well. "But what does that have to do with Shaashgaz?"

Another pause. "My lady, it is very clear you are becoming a favorite," Ayana said. "First Hegai's favor and now the king's obvious pleasure in your company make it very likely that if the king does follow through with his plan of taking another wife, it may well be you." Esther started to protest, but Ayana put up her hand for silence—one of those rare commanding gestures that showed Ayana would never truly be a servant at heart. "Whether that happens or not, you are on your way to becoming a favorite. And Shaashgaz does not like favorites."

"What? Why would he not?" Esther was puzzled. Shaashgaz was the eunuch in charge of concubines. His job was to see to the needs of the king's women. Why on earth would he be prejudiced against one of the king's favorites? "Wouldn't he want to treat a favorite especially well, to get further into the king's good graces?"

"Shaashgaz has a royal patron already," Hathakh put in, glancing casually around the room to be sure no one was eavesdropping. "It is not the king's favor he curries, but the queen's."

"The queen's? Shaashgaz is Amestris' man?"

"To the core," Hathakh confirmed.

"And of course Amestris resents any privileges shown to the king's favorites or to the other wives, so Shaashgaz makes it his business to make their lives as difficult as possible," Ayana added.

"He also spies for her, of course," Hathakh added. "In fact, we could have had our second eunuch by now—Shaashgaz suggested a man to me just the other day. But I made an excuse to refuse him. The reason I say it will take a long time is that I have been trying to arrange for someone I know and approve of to come into the household. I have had to work through Hegai, and that is awkward, for Shaashgaz hotly defends his territory."

Esther raised her eyebrows. "The man Shaashgaz suggested would have been a spy?"

"Absolutely," Ayana said. "Eventually he will have a spy in your household, my lady. If he cannot force us to employ one of his people, he will bribe one of ours. But if we are vigilant, we can protect you to some extent."

"I had no idea," Esther said. She had known for a year that the harem was a hotbed of politics and power struggles, but till now she had lived on the periphery of that world. Now she was drawn inexorably into its center.

Hathakh rose and bowed. "If you will excuse me, my lady, I have an opportunity to go now and speak with Shaashgaz. I will try to obtain some of the things we need." Esther nodded her dismissal; Hathakh bowed again, and left.

She watched for a moment as he left. "Perhaps this business with Shaashgaz is the reason Hathakh has been acting so odd lately. Had you noticed?" She turned back to Ayana. "Whenever he speaks to me, he seems so distant and preoccupied—not relaxed and comfortable as you are, and as he usually is. I wondered what was troubling him. Is it Shaashgaz, or do you know of anything else?"

Ayana opened her mouth as if to speak, paused, then said, "The change in your station has meant a great upheaval for us all, my lady. It will take all the staff some time to adjust." Esther had the clear impression that wasn't what Ayana had been going to say at first, but she trusted Ayana's judgment and wouldn't pressure her to divulge things she thought should be kept private.

Anyway, Esther had more on her mind right now that Hathakh's moods, or the supply of bed linens, or Shaashgaz's alliance with Amestris. All those things touched on her life, of course, but none came close to the core, the center, the tangled knot of feelings she could only acknowledge and examine when she was alone. After Ayana went to see to the maids, Esther also left the tiny living quarters and walked out, through the courtyard and into the gardens beyond. The portion of the palace gardens nearest the harem was reserved for the women's use. She found the stone-walled fountain where she and Hathakh had come on her birthday, the day Mordecai met her in the private courtyard. Just a few weeks ago. It seemed a lifetime had passed since then.

Esther sat on the edge of the fountain. Over the past year, she had gradually grown accustomed to the once-strange world of the harem, till its rituals and routines had come to seem commonplace. Now, all that had shifted. The daily round of beauty treatments and lessons had ended. She was free to go to the baths, to have her hair and makeup done whenever she chose. She was no longer required to attend any classes, for there was nothing left for her to learn. The purpose of those long months of waiting and training had been accomplished—she had gone to the king.

Her greatest fear, over those long months, was that after that fateful night was over, she would return to the harem and spend the rest of her life in a kind of limbo with nothing to do and nothing to live for. Instead, something different had happened. The king was pleased with her. She had been called repeatedly back to his presence. And her life had taken on a new shape, around a new center—King Xerxes.

Esther leaned back a little and looked up at the bright-blue sky arching above the delicate leaves of the trees. No one was around to hear, so she said softly, "God of Israel, this is Esther, daughter of Abihail, in Xerxes' harem. You know where I am and what I am doing, don't You? I have begun to believe again that You are watching me, that You care what happens. But I don't understand, my God. What do You expect of me? What is required of Your servant in such a situation? Surely everyone would say the gods are favoring me—which means You are showing me favor. But why? Will I bring honor to your name by hiding the fact that I am a Jew, by marrying this king—if that is his choice? Is it Your choice? Is there some good I can do here? Some good I can do for the king?"

She was searching out loud for answers, using her conversation with God to explore the feelings and questions that plagued her. No one, of course, had asked what she felt toward the king though a few of her friends among the concubines such as Leila and Tamyris were curious about her frequent visits to his chambers. But no one wanted to know if she, Esther, cared for this man in whose arms she laid and in whose bed she slept. The question would have been considered ridiculous. He was the king. Just to be one of his concubines, much less a favorite, was the highest honor a girl could dream of. Naturally, she would be thrilled.

Am I? Esther asked herself. She hardly knew the answer. Xerxes fascinated her. She felt the powerful pull of his strong personality. And yes, their times alone behind the tapestried bed curtains were exciting. Even with her training the first experience—that morning when he had awakened to find her in his bed—had been a shock. But after the first time, things had gotten better. The king, when sober, was a strong, virile man, and if his interest in his lover's pleasure was only peripheral, that was to be expected. He was forceful but never rough with her. Esther had no bruises on her arms.

But perhaps that was because when his dark moods came on him—and they did come, often quite rapidly—she did not try to entice him to make love, but instead followed the pattern that had worked well that first evening. She encouraged him to talk. He loved to lie in the privacy of the bed with his head in her lap, talking about himself, his dreams, his family, his frustrations. Of course, despite the brilliant and strong-willed women he had known—his mother, his chief wife Amestris, the queen Artemesia of Halicarnassus who had been his ally in the Greek war—he clung to the belief that a woman could not really grasp matters of statecraft. Just two nights ago he had talked to her for an hour about his most perplexing current problem—what to do with the Greek Pausanias, king of Sparta, who, after having whipped the Persian army at Plataea, was now secretly seeking an alliance with Xerxes. Then he had quite suddenly pulled her toward him, kissed her, and said, "My pretty little Esther, how bored you must be. I might as well be speaking Greek to you, hadn't I? Forgive my prattling, and come here to me."

In fact, Esther had been rather interested in the whole problem, but of course she didn't tell him that, any more than she told him that if he had been speaking Greek, she would have been able to understand at least a few words, for Mordecai had taught her a little Greek when she was a child. That was not what Xerxes wanted to hear from her. Indeed, he wanted to hear very little from her at all. When she did talk, it was always about him, never about herself, which was as it was supposed to be.

He still called her to his presence when his few close companions were eating and drinking with him, but he never again asked her to dance before them. Indeed, he kept her veiled and allowed her to retain her modesty in front of them. This was not the case with all the concubines; Esther had heard stories of shameful things he had required other women to do when men were present. For Esther he seemed to have developed a kind of tenderness, almost respect.

And she for him? Yes, there was tenderness, she discovered. She was fond, in a way, of this powerful man who was yet so in need of approval and affection, even from a concubine who was worth little more than a slave to him. There were things to admire in him, things to despise, even things to pity. She noticed after that first night that he drank wine to celebrate when he was merry, and took refuge in wine when he was angry or sad. He drank far more than was good for him, but after that first night she had not seen him incapacitated by wine. Yes, she had to admit, she was already beginning to care what happened to him. She worried what a man such as he might become if he won no more victories, if his one great loss shadowed the rest of his life, and he constantly sought comfort in the wine bottle.

But that was looking too far ahead. Esther's perspective had narrowed in the same way that a horse wearing blinders can only see straight ahead. She found it difficult, just now, to think what might happen in the future—to Xerxes, to herself, to anyone. She lived from moment to moment, day to day, nothing more. Only her God held the future and so far, though she felt comforted by the sense of His presence, He had given her no clues of what His plans might be.

The sound of footsteps in the grass snapped her attention back to the present moment. She saw Hathakh coming toward her. He bowed as he drew near. "My lady, I have word for you."

"Come, Hathakh, and don't be so formal. Is something wrong?" she added impulsively. Perhaps Ayana was right and it was only the strain of moving the household to new quarters, but she could not help remembering the ease with which she and Hathakh had talked, sitting by this same fountain just a few weeks ago.

"No, my lady. Nothing is wrong. But I have messages for you. I have just seen your kinsman Mordecai, and he greatly wishes to see you."

"Really?" Esther stood, smiling. It would be wonderful to see Mordecai again. "Take me to him."

"No, he is not there just now. I warned him it might be dangerous for you to be seen talking to him and asked him to wait a while. Forgive me, but I had your best interests at heart."

"Of course, of course." Esther sat down again and motioned for Hathakh to sit beside her, but he remained standing. "Why would it be dangerous for me to see Mordecai now?"

In the moment's silence before Hathakh spoke, the sun slid behind a rare cloud, and they both looked up, surprised. "You must be very careful right now, my lady," he said. "This is a crucial time. When you were still one of the king's virgins, little attention was paid to you. If you had gone only once to the king and were merely another of the concubines, people still might care very little what you did or whom you spoke to. And if—if the king does marry you, or even if you become a favorite, you will have certain privileges, such as entertaining guests from outside the harem. But as it is now—you are what they call a rising star. Many eyes are on you. Any hint of scandal, even anything that arouses curiosity, could be dangerous."

Esther sighed. "I didn't know. I feel like I'm walking across a battlefield without armor, Hathakh. I never guessed there was such danger in being the king's favorite."

"Life in the harem is never simple, my lady," Hathakh said. "I can carry a message to Mordecai for you, if you wish."

"Yes, please do." What Esther really wanted was a chance to sit down and truly pour out her heart—all her questions—to her foster father, but that could not be. What could she say in a brief message, passed through Hathakh, that would fill some of her need for connection with her family?

"I will think about it and tell you later what message you may bring him. That I am well—that much, of course."

"Of course."

She smiled. "So, I am a rising star, am I?"

He smiled too, at last. "Fitting, I suppose. After all you were named for Ishtar, the goddess of the evening star. But it's not only for your name. It is fitting. You deserve to rise in the king's favor." At last his strange distance dropped away, and he looked like her friend and servant Hathakh again, capable of feelings, even if he seldom showed them. "If the king is a man at all and not a complete fool, what other choice could he make?"

"You are flattering me," Esther laughed, standing up as she spoke. "And if I have learned one thing since coming to the harem, it is that flatterers inevitably want something. What can I do for you? Shall I see about having your grain rations increased? It is time you got fat—you're too thin for a proper eunuch." She lowered her voice. "You should be as fat as Shaashgaz. Though I suppose with Shaashgaz in charge it will be hard for me to increase anyone's portions at this point."

"There are ways," Hathakh said, falling into step beside her as she walked back through the gardens toward the harem court. Yellow butterflies rose and dipped among the flowers, and the two paused to watch their dance. "I am learning . . . it will take a little time, but we will find ways to manage our household without too much interference," he went on. "But no, I do not think I want to be as fat as the honorable Shaashgaz, . . . and I don't need or want anything. Nothing anyone could give me," he added, his voice wistful.

They'd arrived back in the harem court where pairs and small groups of women strolled about or sat on the ground, and small children ran and played. "But you are making me forget that I had another message for you, an important one. You are summoned to the king's private dining hall tonight at the hour of the evening meal. You will dine with him and his guests, and you should be veiled."

"Oh—really?" Esther felt unsettled. She had not been invited to take a meal with the king before. "What does this mean?"

No question took Hathakh by surprise. "I have been making inquiries. I believe it means that the king is more serious about you. Being asked to dine with him in company raises your status."

Esther had been walking away from her own quarters, now she headed back toward the apartments. "I suppose I'd better talk to Ayana about what to wear tonight."

Hathakh shot her a quick glance. "You are nervous."

"A little, yes. No, a lot. I still don't know—there's so much I *don't* know. Where all this is leading. What's expected of me. What I really want."

Hathakh only nodded, and they walked back to the apartment in a silence that was once again companionable. Esther still didn't understand what had caused Hathakh to become so remote and distant, or why he seemed relaxed and friendly again, but she was glad for the change. He and Ayana were her closest friends in the world, the two pillars on which she leaned, and she could not imagine losing either their faithful service or their friendship.

Ayana spent the rest of the day with her, going to the baths and helping her choose a gown and jewelry for the evening. Appearing as the king's companion, even at a small private dinner, was a very different matter than going to his bedchamber at night, and required quite a different mode of dress. "You must appear modest, serene, and tasteful," Ayana said firmly, holding out a heavy gown the color of cream, with a richly embroidered collar.

"And say nothing, of course," Esther added, remembering her deportment lessons with Hegai.

Later that evening in the king's dining hall, she remembered those words and smiled behind her veil. She had hardly needed that particular lesson. Speaking out of turn in this setting would have been as alien to her as flying. The dining hall, though much smaller than the great banquet hall on the opposite side of the courtyard, was still very formal. There were eight other guests besides herself and the king. Since this was a private meal among friends and family rather than a public banquet, Xerxes did not sit behind a screen, but he did recline at a separate table placed on a small platform. At the main table Esther reclined on a rather hard but beautifully carved couch surrounded by seven men she'd never seen before and the only other woman in the group. Xerxes' brother, Prince Masistes, had brought along his wife, Artaynte, who was also veiled. Esther wondered if the princess was concentrating as much as she had to on the challenging task of eating while veiled.

Perhaps it was a skill royal women mastered early in life. It was hard not to stare at Artaynte and wonder if Artaynte was staring at her. It was difficult to forget that this woman had been the king's last great love affair, less than a year ago. The other guests were men she recognized as highly-placed courtiers, most of them veterans of the Greek war. She had seen a few of them in the king's chambers late at night.

There was one newcomer—a short, stocky man with blunt, unattractive features and grizzling curly hair, who ate with much gusto and little refinement, and spoke loudly and freely. Before anyone had addressed him by name Esther had guessed he was Artabazus, the commander who had remained behind in Greece along with ill-fated Mardonius, and had survived to bring his army back to Susa. He was at once a hero and a constant source of worry to Xerxes. She had heard much about him but had not seen him before this.

The men were all talking about Pausanias, the Spartan king who wanted to form an alliance and marry a Persian princess. "It's quite clear, Your Majesty," Masistes was saying smoothly, "that the Spartans see us as the victors despite the fact that some of them claim we lost at Salamis and at Plataea. Why would their king want an alliance with us if we were the losers? They fear us, my lord. They fear us greatly."

Murmurs of agreement swept round the table. Esther had noticed even in the informal evening conclaves that Xerxes' men spent a good deal of time reassuring him that he was respected, honored, and feared, and that, despite all appearances, he had won a great victory in Greece. Prince Masistes fawned over the king in public in a way that totally denied the angry tension of the one private conclave Esther had witnessed between the two royal brothers.

"The Greeks know they cannot stand forever against the might of the Persian Empire and its king, my lord," said another.

"Indeed!" Xerxes said. "So, what princess shall we give them? How old is your little girl now, Masistes? Is she 6? Maybe 7. Ready to be betrothed to a Greek?"

Esther recognized the taunting note in his voice, and she noted the swiftness with which both Masistes and Artaynte turned to stare at the king. It was commonly believed that little Artaynta, named for her mother, would be married to her cousin, the crown prince Darius. Even to suggest she be given to an uncouth Greek to seal an alliance was a calculated insult to the prince and his family.

Into the shocked silence Artabazus' rough voice fell like a bucket of bricks. "What none of you seem to see," he said, ignoring the comment about the princess, "is that there's no one great monster out there called 'Greece.' You ought to know it—you who fought out there"—he waved his knife, a chunk of lamb speared on the end of it, at Masistes and the other men—"but you keep talking as if we fought against something called Greece, and Greece defeated us, and now Greece wants to make peace, and Greece is still afraid of us. There is no Greece. It's a place, not a government. Don't you remember what it's like? They have no king, no emperor."

He inclined his head sideways toward Xerxes, a gesture that might—if the viewer were feeling kindly toward Artabazus—be taken as a very slight bow. "They have no center. They're just a collection of city-states, at war with each other as often as they are with us or anyone else. Sparta is one of them, and King Pausanias doesn't want an alliance with us because he's scared of Persia." He dipped the last bite of lamb into a dark sauce then snapped it into his mouth. "Nobody's scared of Persia after Plataea, no matter what you all want to think. He wants our gold so he can conquer some other Greek king, maybe make himself emperor over them all. I tell you, if he succeeds, if any of them do—if the Greeks ever stop fighting each other and find a *real* king, we'll be the ones who'll have to be afraid. *We'll* be the ones protecting our borders." His meaty fist thumped on the tabletop, and the gold-plated dishes jumped and shivered.

The room fell silent. The guests studied their food or their forks. No one looked at the king. What Artabazus had said was as shocking in its way as what the king had said about Masistes' daughter. Artabazus' words were shocking because everyone knew they were true, but they were the kind of truth no one said, at least not in the hearing of the king. The silence stretched on. Nervous glances darted toward the high table where Xerxes sat chewing a piece of bread, staring fixedly at Artabazus.

Then a huge roar of laughter from King Xerxes split the table. "You have your nerve, Artabazus! But if anyone has earned the right to talk about the Greeks, you have. Would any man here dispute that right?" His eyes swept the table; of course no one answered.

"More wine!" the king shouted to his cupbearer who hovered nearby. "Bring wine for myself and for Artabazus, my most loyal rebel. And for all these, my good friends. Let us drink to the Greeks—long may they quarrel among themselves, and never find a king."

Uneasy laughter followed as cups were filled, raised, emptied, and refilled, and gradually the talk grew more relaxed. Artabazus continued to say audacious things—though none quite as audacious—while talking with his mouth full of food and stabbing his knife in the air like a pointer. Esther watched him closely. She wondered if anyone else had noticed how deftly this seemingly blunt, uncouth man had stepped in to deflect the tension between the king and Masistes; how fearlessly he had drawn the king's anger onto himself instead. Everyone knew that of the many small fires waiting to burn out of control in Susa, the king's relationship with his second brother was the most dangerous. Artabazus seemed willing to walk across coals to prevent a flare-up, with little concern for his own scorched feet.

When the food was finished and the dancers had come in, Xerxes stepped down from the high table. He motioned the servants to bring him a high-backed chair to sit in just behind the couch where Esther reclined. The dancers began slowly, sensuously. Though she could not see Xerxes, Esther was aware of his presence. She felt his eyes were on her. Several times she saw Artaynte watching them. She wondered what Artaynte felt for her husband's brother now. Had their short affair been as passionate as gossip had had it? Had Artaynte been willing, or had she been compelled because her lover was the king? Had her husband forgiven her, or was he burning with stifled jealousy still? Was Artaynte herself jealous when she watched Xerxes with his other women, his wives, and favorites?

I am the king's property. The words burned through Esther's mind. She never forgot that. She had no choice about going to his bedchamber, but, she'd reasoned, she did have a choice in how she felt about him. It was dangerous. She knew that allowing the slightest particle of her feelings to attach to him was to be drawn into a complex and deadly spider's web of intrigue and jealousies. Yet, even knowing that, shivers ran down her spine as she remained aware of his body an arm's length from her, aware of the sound of his breathing under the music, and aware of his eyes on the back of her long, slender neck.

The dancers ended with dramatic whirls then parted to reveal the next performer—a poet. It was Lilaios, the husband of Roxane the musician, and, in fact, Roxane was accompanying him on the oud. A few appreciative murmurs went around the table as the couple came forward to perform. Lilaios was new as a court poet, but was already much acclaimed.

Tonight he bowed low and announced, "Your gracious and glorious majesty, princes of the realm, honored lords and ladies, tonight, at the request of our lord and our master the king, I will present to you the tale of Zariadres and Odatis."

Esther comfortably settled back on her couch. This was the first part of the evening she expected to truly enjoy. She loved hearing poetry, and this familiar love story was always good. Tonight it was better than good; it was great. Lilaios's voice was a brilliant instrument, weaving in and out the crafted words of the ancient story more gracefully than any troupe of dancers. Roxane's fingers flew on the oud, creating haunting melodies that vividly set off the words. Esther was caught in the magical story of the two lovers who had never met, yet had each dreamed of the other and fallen hopelessly in love.

The story rose to its climactic scene in which Odatis stood at the banquet holding the golden cup. Her father, who had refused Zariadres' offer of marriage, told her to offer the cup to any man in the hall she wished to marry. Esther could feel Odatis' confusion and sorrow as she looked at the roomful of nobles and princes, none of whom she loved, not knowing that Zariadres had left his army and driven all across the land in his chariot, then walked in disguise, right to the very banqueting hall. Lilaios let his words hang in the air for a moment. The tension built as Roxane plucked low notes on the oud. Then came the climax as the lovers' eyes fell on each other, each recognizing the face they had seen and loved in dreams, and the disguised Zariadres swept Odatis up and carried her off to his chariot, where they escaped into the night.

A collective sigh went up as the poem and music finished. The performance was as satisfying in its way as the meal had been. The king called, "Bring wine for this fine artist," and a servant scurried to Lilaios's side bearing a goblet. It was easy to see how both Lilaios and Roxane flushed with pride and delight. Xerxes leaned forward and said in Esther's ear, "Do you know who that fellow is? And the oud player? Find out about them for me, and we'll think of some reward for them. They deserve to be better known." And Esther, too, flushed a little with pleasure, not only at the honour for Roxane and her husband, but for the way in which the king had spoken to her, pulling her into his confidence, making her his ally. It was just a little matter, but she felt that it marked—as this whole evening did—a change in their relationship.

But a greater change was coming. The king stood to his feet, his own goblet raised. Immediately everyone else in the room stood too.

"My honored and noble guests," he began. His voice was rich and clear; he was still quite sober and very much in command. "What a pleasure this evening has been. What a joy it is to dine with you all, to welcome again our old friend Artabazus, so deservedly honored for his incomparable bravery. I have taken great pleasure in our conversation, in your company, in the fine entertainment."

He stepped forward so that he stood beside Esther, and took her hand in his. His palm was smooth and cool, his fingers firm. Lifting her hand, he continued, "And I take this moment to introduce to you one in whom I also take great pleasure, the lady Esther of Susa. She is the delight of my eyes, and I hope you will all know her better in days to come."

Esther modestly bowed her head. She knew they could not see her veiled face, yet she needed to hide even more from the piercing stares that she could quite well see. They would know her better. Now that they knew she had some importance, they would be watching her like eagles watching their prey.

"And now, let wine be poured out without measure," the king commanded. "Be merry! Bring back the dancers!"

He sat down on Esther's own couch, pulled her down beside him, and put a glass in her hand. "Drink, my love," he whispered as the music began again. "I want you, of all of us, to be merry tonight."

Later that night, alone in his chambers, he took her in his arms. He'd had a lot to drink, but he spoke clearly, though with a certain headlong abandon that Esther recognized as one of the last pleasant stages of his drunkenness. Even knowing this, tonight of all nights she felt drawn into the spell of his happiness. He placed a hand on either side of her face and gently pulled her to him, kissing her eyes and forehead.

"Did I please you tonight, Esther? I wanted to please you." She heard a note of small-boy pleading in his voice. "I want to honor you, to make you the proudest and finest woman in all of Persia. I am intoxicated with your beauty, my love. I am as Zariadres—I saw you in my dreams for years before I ever saw your face. You are my Odatis and you will be my bride." He picked her up and swung her around, even as he kissed her again. "Esther, my Esther, I want to make you my wife." He asked for no response, just led her toward the bed and drew her again into his arms.

Hours later Esther awakened to the morning's light filtering through the bed hangings. She lay alone. The king had risen already. She had an odd feeling in her stomach, as though something momentous had happened. The slit of sunlight widened and deepened, and she remembered: the king had said he wanted to marry her.

It *was* momentous, yet she felt oddly detached, as she had so often since coming to the harem. Detached from her own life. Detached from the real world. The king had decided; no decision was required of her. Her mind was cobwebbed with conflicting emotions, yet did it really matter at all what she felt? She was going to be the king's bride.

The chamber was quiet, but when Esther peeked her head outside the bed a servant scurried over. "Lady Esther, His Majesty has asked that you remain here until he returns. May I bring you food and drink?"

Esther pulled one of the linen bedsheets around her for a robe. It would be foolish to dress in the elaborate gown she had worn the night before. When the servant returned with bread, a bowl of yogurt, and dates she asked him to send someone to her own quarters for clothes. Until now, she had always returned to her own apartment in the morning. This was the first time the king had asked her to stay.

Xerxes returned as she finished dressing and glanced at her clothes. "I suppose I should have left clearer instructions," he said, kissing her lightly. "We ride to the hunt today, so you will need clothes suitable for riding. And a warm cloak. It will be cool."

Esther had heard mention last night of today's hunt but had not expected to be included, though she knew that concubines often went on hunts with the king. She'd spent little time on horseback and was not a good rider by any means. "My lord, I can return to my own rooms and change. When do you leave on the hunt?"

"Shortly—less than an hour. My servants are preparing now. No, do not go back—send someone. I want you here with me." He took her hand and pulled her down to sit beside him on the couch, kissing her again. "We have spent many nights together, but this will be our first day and I do not wish you out of my sight—not yet. Today I will hunt the stag, but you will be my true quarry, my Odatis."

Esther returned his kisses, but even as she enjoyed them, inside she was nervous. The king had hardly had time to drink much this morning, yet his protests of love were every bit as intense as last night's had been. A new phase in her life seemed to have begun more swiftly and decisively than she'd thought possible. And amid all that turmoil, she was going to have to ride to the hunt along with the king's lords and ladies, all strangers to her and no doubt all suspicious and curious about her.

Worse yet, she discovered an hour later, as the royal party rode through the palace gardens and into the king's hunting forest beyond, Xerxes' declaration that he did not intend to let her out of his sight did not apply once the hunt began. A dedicated hunter, he was soon at the front of the pack, leaving Esther behind to struggle to keep her seat on the horse and aware of the critical stares of the other hunters. They were mostly the same guests as at last night's dinner, though Prince Masistes and Artaynte were absent, and there were several other women—wives or concubines of the king's nobles. Silently she worried that she needed to know who they were, learn their names, and what was important about each one. Some of these women might well be enemies or allies in her new life. But right now she was more concerned with staying on her horse, not looking like a fool, and finding one person to talk to in this strange situation.

Her ally turned out not to be one of the ladies at all, but Artabazus, that plain-spoken soldier. He rode up beside her and trotted his horse alongside hers for a little ways. Finally he said abruptly, "City-bred. Merchant family."

"Who—me? Yes," Esther gasped, surprised.

"Thought so. That's what gossip says about you, but I'd know anyway—city people can never sit on a horse. Don't hunch down; sit up straighter. You feel like you'll fall, but you won't. Grip it with your knees." He stared critically at Esther for a moment. "Suppose you've been told all this by riding masters before, and you still feel like you're going to fall off, don't you?"

Esther allowed herself a tiny giggle. The few times she'd previously been on a horse she'd received exactly the same advice. "You're right," she confessed.

"Ignore me, then. Practice—that's the only thing that will make you feel comfortable. And you'll get plenty with His Majesty—loves to hunt. Loves to bring his women hunting. And riding. You'll get used to it."

Esther risked a tiny revelation. "It seems I have a great deal to get used to."

Artabazus grunted. "Like the horse, my lady, it all comes with practice. Some girls don't last long enough to ever get comfortable, but I've a feeling you will. Last awhile, that is."

"Is that so?"

This time the grunt sounded like a laugh. "Didn't expect an old soldier to be full of gossip about the king's bedmates, did you? But you look like you could use some reassurance, and I have my reasons for wanting you reassured. Fact is, I think you're good for the king, and I hope he keeps you a good while."

Esther couldn't help being both amused by his manner and intrigued by his opinions. "What makes you say so?"

"My lady, I've known King Xerxes my entire life—and his. Since we were boys. He has his passions—power, of course, like any king, and proving he's as good a man as his father was. Hunting, of course—and wine, also of course, and perhaps too much. And women. He liked that poem last night, didn't he? Zariadres! He's been thinking he's Zariadres twice a week since he was 13." Artabazus shot her a sidelong glance as the horses picked their way down a gentle slope. Esther squeezed her knees into her mount's sides, praying to stay upright. "Time for me to shut up yet?"

"Ahhh—no," Esther told him as they regained solid ground. "No. I'm not offended. I'm interested. Do go on."

Artabazus grinned. "Of course, no man's in a better position to go falling in love every few months—a king with hundreds of women in his harem! And you'll know by now he doesn't always confine himself to his own. Witness the lovely princess Artaynte. Is it any wonder the Prince Masistes looks like he's drinking gall whenever he raises a glass of wine with his brother the king? I wasn't there when he was fooling with Artaynte—I was still in Greece, same as poor old Masistes. But I know what the king was like—nervous, tense, pacing like a cat in a cage. I've seen it. Right back to Amestris, when he was just a boy."

"The queen? But I thought—"

"Oh yes, it was a political match, of course. But it didn't take King Xerxes—he wasn't king then, of course—long to decide she was his sun, moon, and stars. And it didn't take long for her to see she could lead him around like a lapdog as long as he thought that way. And Vashti! What an idea—marrying a girl from his harem, no political connections, a love match. Only king Xerxes could have thought of that one. But he thought Vashti was a goddess walking the earth. Whenever it happens, he's cross and preoccupied and makes foolhardy decisions—until the fever passes and he comes back to earth." Artabazus looked around to see if anyone was listening, but the trail was narrow enough for only two to ride abreast, and the others were well in front of and behind them.

"Now he says he's going to do it again—another Vashti, another love match. The smart money's on this girl Esther, did you know that?" Artabazus shot her a shrewd glance but didn't seem to expect an answer. "That's who my money's on too. I don't know the girl, but I think she's good for the king. He's different this time. More settled. Happier instead of troubled. And the gods know that's what he needs right now."

"Because of Greece?" Esther ventured. The horse picked up a little speed and she lurched in her seat, but Artabazus put out a hand to steady her.

"Because of Greece. I love my king, lady, but after Plataea, if he doesn't find something else to do besides drive himself mad because he couldn't conquer Greece, then he's either going to stumble into some fool love affair that will spark a civil war, or drink himself into an early grave—or both. He's my friend, you know. As well as my king. I want what's good for him. And what's good for him is good for Persia. And I'm starting to think you're good for everyone."

"But—Lord Artabazus—you flatter me. And you don't even know me. If it is as you say—the king falls passionately in love for a while, then moves on—any influence I can have on him will be fleeting. What difference will it truly make in the end?"

He looked straight at her and nodded, as if she'd scored a point, and risen in his estimation. "You're right. I don't expect him to be in love with you forever, though women seem to have fool notions about such things. I'm hoping that while he's in love with you, he'll be sane enough to find something else. Not someone else—not another woman. Another passion. Not warfare, or conquest, or Greece. He has to leave that behind if he's to survive—if the land is to survive. We cannot go to Greece again."

"I believe the king knows that," Esther said, thinking of the darkest of the nights she had sat with him in his chamber listening to his despair and torment.

"He knows it," Artabazus agrees. "But knowing it will destroy him unless he finds something else to do. Something to put his energy into. Something else that will make him believe he's as great a king as Darius."

And Esther, straight from a Jewish exile's home to the harem and now plunged into the court, was supposed to help the greatest king on earth find out what to do next? Perhaps Artabazus was mad. Aloud she said, "But what could that be? I don't know."

"Well, *I* certainly don't. I'm a soldier. I don't know anything but fighting. But there must be something else a king can do. There's supposed to be more to being a king than fighting wars, isn't there? King Xerxes just has to figure out what that is. I'm hoping you can keep him from destroying himself until he works that out. That's all." He nodded curtly, spurred his horse on, and left her behind, to be surrounded a few moments later by the lord Carshena and his wife, who politely introduced themselves and rode along beside her for the next little while.

Esther made polite conversation with them, but her talk with Artabazus churned in her head. She knew why he'd left her so abruptly. Any man would be a fool to be seen talking too long or too intimately to the king's new favorite concubine. But delivering that message had obviously been important to him and reassuring to her, in a strange way. Knowing that the king fell passionately in love on a regular basis—which fitted well with what gossip had always said of him, anyway—made her feel better, rather than worse. She had never imagined herself to be his only love, but she was intrigued that Artabazus felt the king seemed to be reacting differently this time. Could she really be good for him, in some way she couldn't understand?

The king himself returned to her side once the stag was down and the party was making ready to stop on the riverbank for the midday meal. "I have neglected you shamefully," he said, not sounding particularly contrite, "but Artabazus tells me you are not used to riding. As you become more accustomed to it, you'll be able to ride at the front with me. This afternoon I'll ride with you and make up for my rudeness."

He kept his word, riding with Esther and telling her stories of other hunts he'd been on and of things that had happened on campaign, riding to Egypt and to Babylon and to Greece—though he spoke little of Greece, for which Esther was glad. He was in high spirits and kept interrupting his stories to give her riding lessons, some of which were actually quite helpful. Once she was riding more easily, Esther turned her attention to her surroundings—the trees shading her path, the murmur of the river not far off, the sharp tang of cool, crisp air. She breathed deeply. She'd been caged within the harem walls for so long she'd almost forgotten what it felt like to be outdoors.

By the end of the day Esther felt almost comfortable on horseback—until she dismounted back at the palace and discovered how excruciatingly uncomfortable her body could feel. She had only time to go to the baths before she was expected to appear at dinner. Ayana met her there, bringing clothes and jewelry. "I can't believe I have to sit through another banquet, and then, no doubt, be expected to return to the king's chambers for another night of passion!" Esther told Ayana as her hair was being washed. "I feel I can barely sit at all, I'm so sore from riding all day. Oh, before I forget, I need to get a message to Hathakh. I won't have time before I go to dinner, and I want to do it today. You know Roxane, the musician?"

"Married to the poet Lilaios? Yes, didn't they perform last night?" Ayana said, taking the comb to style Esther's hair herself.

"They did, and brilliantly. The king was pleased. He told me that they should be rewarded, and again today when we were riding he told me to see to it that they received honors for their performance. He gave it to me as a commission—so I suppose it's my first real opportunity to be someone's patron—on the king's behalf, of course. Hathakh needs to see about getting a gift for them. What would be suitable?"

"Something from the royal treasury, some jewel for Roxane, I suppose. You'll have the authority to do that. And an increase in their food and wine rations," said Ayana, who, as always, seemed to know everything. "And an invitation to perform at the next large banquet or function, though that may be outside of your control, but Hathakh can have a word with the right people. He can talk to Hegai—there's no need to involve Shaashgaz. It's not his business. Don't worry, we'll see to it. And you should arrange to meet with Roxane and her husband yourself to give them the gift and tell them about their portions. That way you can tell them the king is pleased with them, but they will look to you as their patron, and be loyal to you."

"Loyalty," Esther echoed. "It all comes down to loyalty, doesn't it? Everything here. Who is loyal to whom, whose loyalty can be bought or swayed." She sighed as Ayana drew the comb through her long hair. "I feel as if I'm learning some very complicated new game with rules that are always changing, and the stakes are . . . " She sighed, wordless.

"The stakes are everything," said Ayana simply. "Life or death. Misery or contentment. You are playing a game, my lady, and do you know what?" She dropped to her knees beside Esther as she applied her makeup, giving her an excuse to lower her voice to a whisper so the slaves and attendants could not hear. "I am grateful to my gods every day that Hegai chose you as fit for the king's bedchamber, and allowed me to be your servant. Half the women here would kill to be in your shoes, but I would not change places with you for all the jewels in the king's treasury." She squeezed Esther's hands tightly. "But you are where you are meant to me. Your own gods will smile on you—no, you have only one God, haven't you? Then He is smiling. You are where you are meant to be."

Later that night Esther remembered Ayana's words and prayed they were true. After the dinner, after the singing and dancing, King Xerxes stood up among his guests and announced that the competition he had set in motion more than a year before was at an end. He had chosen the maiden who would become his next wife, his newest queen. Her name was Esther of Susa, and he planned to marry her within a month. The small group of guests—the same nobles and women who'd been on the hunt—bowed, not only before the king but before Esther, and she swallowed hard to keep back panic. Aware as she was of Xerxes at her side, holding her arm, she was just as aware of Artabazus on his knees, his steady eyes watching her, counting on her to do something she was not sure she could do.

CHAPTER 10

Esther stood on a footstool in the main hall of her new apartment, an island in a swirling sea of activity. The seamstress knelt at her feet measuring the hem of the new gown, while two assistants circled them both. Servants came and went carrying bundles of clothing, furniture, dishes, and vessels. Esther's household had only the day before been assigned to these new quarters and it was as if her life had been turned upside.

Music wove a background to the hubbub for Roxane sat curled on a floor cushion cradling her chang, trying out various melodies and asking Esther's opinion on what would be most suitable to play at the wedding banquet. Through it all Hathakh and Ayana glided like twin swans floating on troubled waters, speaking words of instruction or calming the flustered slaves, creating order out of the chaos of Esther's new life.

The day after tomorrow Esther would marry the king. That night, after the wedding ceremony, the feasting would begin, continuing for 28 days. Twenty-eight days and nights of banquets, music, dancing, hunting, new gowns—28 days of staggering work for the servants and headaches for the palace administrators. And the weight of the celebration was made even heavier by the fact that only three weeks had passed since the king had announced his intention to make Esther his wife.

"Why so soon?" she had asked—not asked the king, of course; that would have been foolhardy. The question was asked of Ayana once Esther was safely back in her own chambers after the whirlwind two days in which Xerxes had declared, first to Esther and then to his court, that he intended to marry her.

"We have all been asking the same question," Ayana had said, brushing out Esther's hair as she spoke. "I think the king wishes your marriage and the following celebration to take place here in Susa. And if it's to be in Susa the month-long celebration must be over a fair while before the preparations for the move to Parsa begin."

"And I suppose we will be going to Parsa too, this year?" A note of weariness flattened Esther's tone. In the spring the royal wives and many of the concubines generally removed to Parsa along with the king and most of his household, often finishing the summer in the palace at Ecbatana.

"Oh, yes, and the move requires a great deal of preparation."

"I would be happy to wait, myself, until we arrive in Parsa to be married. We'll be there till summer. Isn't that plenty of time for a wedding?"

Ayana had frowned. "There is a problem with Parsa. The king's birthday is celebrated at the beginning of Simanu, two months after the New Year's ceremony. There is always a great banquet, and some feel there would not be time to celebrate the New Year, a wedding, and then the king's birthday in only two months. Others say he wants to avoid unpleasantness with Amestris."

"Oh." Amestris again. She seemed to lurk around every corner.

"Amestris has interesting ideas," Ayana had continued, lowering her voice as they always did when speaking of the queen. "The custom is that at the birthday feast anyone may ask the king to grant any request, and he must give it. Many people ask for trivial things so that the king has an opportunity to show how generous he is. But if Queen Amestris is angry, she has been known to make requests that will hurt someone or shame the king. And this year she is very angry."

"Because of me."

"At least in part," Ayana concurred.

Just after that conversation, word had come that Esther was to move her household to spacious new quarters in the northwestern corner of the harem court. The other wives, Parmys and Irdabama, had their apartments there as well, though Irdabama spent most of her time on her private estates in the country. Esther's new apartment was large, beautifully decorated, and well-appointed. Unfortunately, it was also right in the shadow of the large building which housed Queen Amestris' private quarters, a palace within the harem itself that took up most of the north side of the court. Esther couldn't imagine why the harem had been designed so that all the king's wives and favorites were so close together—it seemed like a poor design, one only a man could have created.

Within a matter of hours after the king's announcement Esther was at the center of a whirlwind, moving her household and preparing for her wedding. In reality few of the actual preparations fell to her or her servants. The king's eunuchs had, after all, managed three previous royal weddings. Esther's job was to choose and be fitted for not only her wedding gown but an entire wardrobe of far greater variety and luxury than anything she'd ever owned.

The seamstress' fittings, along with the deliberations over fabrics and styles, took by far the largest amount of time. Esther had learned to have a little more patience with such business, but she still found it tedious, and she longed for the wedding to be over so that life might, if not return to normal, at least settle into a new pattern.

And suddenly the wedding was just one day away, and that day could not possibly have enough hours in it for all she had to do. One task seemed impossible to fit in—yet she could not imagine going to her wedding without it. She had spoken to Hathakh a week ago, asking if he could get word to Mordecai, somehow arrange for her to see him. Hathakh, who was busier than anyone else in the household except perhaps Ayana, had not even hesitated. "I will do all I can," he assured her.

But he had not returned with any word of Mordecai, and Esther was troubled. She hated to ask again, but she could not face what lay ahead without seeing her foster father at least once more, asking for his blessing—and the blessing of his God.

The morning before the wedding day, Hathakh finally came to her. "My lady, I have found Mordecai. He says he will come to the king's private courtyard near the harem entrance at noon today, if you can meet him there."

"Would it be—do you think it would be all right if I spoke with him for a few minutes?" Esther pleaded. "I know that all eyes are on me, never more than now, but Hathakh—I must see him. I must speak with him."

"You will certainly call attention to yourself if you have a conversation with an unknown man in the courtyard the day before you are wed to the king," Hathakh said bluntly. "I do not want trouble for you." He paused, looking with narrowed eyes at Esther's face. He seemed to be weighing the problems, then he spoke. "I can see this is very important."

"What if I went veiled? Heavily veiled—so that no one would recognize me?"

"If I were with you, or if any of our people were with you, most anyone in the harem would still know it was you." He stopped, tilting his head in a posture Esther recognized as typical when he was searching his mind for a solution to a problem. "You could take one of the girls—not Ayana, but one who's seldom seen in public—if she were veiled also. People would be curious, but if it were a very brief meeting you might escape notice."

Esther chose Talia—quiet, loyal little Talia—to accompany her to the courtyard at noon. She had a thousand appointments and commitments, but this was more important. She hoped she didn't stand out too much. Most of the women wore veils when they had occasion to go to the private courtyard, but usually they were brief or partial veils. Esther and Talia were both more heavily veiled than usual, but Ayana had agreed with Hathakh that she should take no chances.

Esther knew that the king's officials had already made inquiries in Susa about her family. Aunt Rivka's Persian relatives had apparently been able to satisfy the officials that Esther was actually their daughter, for no further questions had been asked of her. She hated the deceit that was necessary. She would have been proud to acknowledge her family as her own, but Mordecai's conviction that her Jewish background must be kept secret had been unshakable, and she trusted his instinct. It would be disastrous if, on the eve of her wedding, something were to happen to alert the king that she had lied about her family, that she had something to hide. Almost any kind of immorality seemed to be tolerable in the palace, but lying was spoken of as an unpardonable sin. After all, Ahura Mazda was the god of Truth.

Now she saw Mordecai standing near a pillar, looking toward the two veiled women coming toward him. His face was impassive. He did not allow a light of welcome or joy to touch anything but his eyes. It had been only a few months since she'd last seen him, but all the world had changed, and was about to change even more.

"Mordecai," she whispered as she drew close, not daring to call him Uncle.

"Hadassah," he said. "Tomorrow is the day?"

"Yes."

"We were overwhelmed when we heard. Rivka cried. She said she did not know if they were tears of joy or sorrow. We are proud of you. We pray for the best."

"Please do that. Please pray," she said, her control breaking for just a moment. He could not see her face or her eyes, but he must hear the need in her voice. "I want our God to guide me. I do not know what my future holds. This palace can be—a dangerous place."

"I know it," said Mordecai. "Hadassah, I hear rumors. No, not of you—of things that touch the king. If I learn anything that the king must know, can I bring it to you? Through your servant, Hathakh?"

"Of course," Esther said, wondering what sort of things he could be thinking of. "When I am . . . when I am in my new position, I will do whatever I can to help you. You know that."

Mordecai shook his head slightly. "Do not think of me. And do not give away your secret. We have all lied for you already, may God forgive us. But I know this is best."

"Do you? Do you know"—a stifled sob broke her voice, which dropped even softer—"if this is where I'm meant to be? Does our God have a plan in all this? I'm so afraid . . . "

"Are you not happy, my Hadassah?"

"Happy? I—the king is kind to me. I think he cares for me. But nothing is safe here, nothing is secure. I am happy now, but I am afraid. And I must go, for Hathakh says we will surely be noticed if we talk too long."

"Yes. He is a good servant, your Hathakh. I wish I could embrace you, Hadassah. Know that I'm holding you in my heart. And as for God's plan—I cannot guess. But I believe He has one. Since you were taken from us, God seems closer, not farther away. I think He has a purpose for you."

"Thank you." She wanted to take his hand, to touch in some way, but knew she could not. She could only turn and go, leaving Talia to follow in her wake and leaving Mordecai to watch as she disappeared into the bustle of women and servants.

Wedding preparations continued without end. Two slaves staggered into the central hall of her apartment with a large bronze mirror to set up on the sofreh, the marriage table. Two ornate golden candlesticks came next, straight out of the royal treasury, flanking the mirror on either side. Other servants were arranging the flowers, fruit, herbs, spices, rice, and rose petals that would adorn the sofreh and be used in the ceremony.

Ayana hurried in. "Lady Esther! The seamstress is here with the wedding gown. This is the final fitting. Hurry!"

Roxane was on Esther's other side. "You are sure, quite sure, my lady, that you want *Zariadres and Odatis* for the first night's banquet? Lilaios is learning a new love poem, very moving. I think the king would like it."

"No, it must be Zariadres," Esther called over her shoulder as she trailed behind Ayana. It was the king's favorite poem, the one Lilaios had recited on the night Xerxes said he wanted to marry her. "But tell him he must prepare the other poem as well. He may be asked to give an encore, and if not, he can do it one of the other nights of the feast." The young poet and his musician wife were being thrust into the spotlight as dizzyingly and unexpectedly as Esther herself, since she had declared herself their patron and begun showering honors upon them—most importantly, the honor of performing at the wedding-night feast.

Hathakh waylaid her on the way into her bedchamber for the fitting. "One moment only," he promised Ayana, who was fuming with impatience. "My lady, you saw him?" he whispered.

"I did. Thank you, Hathakh. It was very brief."

"I know. I watched." His face wrinkled in a sudden grin. "I just had to be sure all went well."

"Thank you," she said again. Hathakh was, after all, the only person who knew that Mordecai was her foster father, knew how badly she wanted her own family to be present at her wedding. Lavish gifts had been sent to her supposed family, Mordecai's in-laws, and she felt certain they'd passed the gifts on to Mordecai and Rivka, but as the family was not nobility they were not invited to the king's feast.

The fitting went well. The gown was finally finished down to the last tiny star embroidered on the creamy white skirt. Esther took a long look at herself in the bronze mirror. The gown's bodice fit snugly across her bosom, its slightly scooped neckline showing off her smooth shoulders. The bell-shaped skirt was edged with tiny rings where it met a pleated ruffle that just swept the floor.

Incredibly, by evening almost everything was ready. Even Esther herself. She spent her last night apart from the king, as tradition dictated. Her maidservants and a few women friends from the harem crowded into her private chamber to drink to her future happiness. As a soon-to-be queen, Esther lived in quarters set apart, and she had the privilege of reserving the communal baths so that she could bathe at a time when the other women would not be there. She usually took advantage of that privilege, enjoying the greater privacy, but sometimes she missed the noisy female intimacy she'd grown accustomed to, and the friends who had filled her old life as a harem girl.

"Esther, so many of the girls are jealous of you," Leila declared late in the evening when she had drunk a little too much, "but I know the king made the right choice."

Everyone murmured polite agreement, but Leila raised her voice. "No, I'm not saying it just because it's Esther I'm talking to. Everyone says it, Esther. He treats you differently. You have—a good effect on the king, I think," she added, unconsciously echoing Artabazus.

"I've been told that before," said Esther, "not least by the king himself. I think he believes I am sent from Ahura Mazda to help him find a way out of his troubles. But I am also told that he thinks that of every woman he falls in love with. It will not last forever."

"It will not, but when it's over, you'll still be a queen," Tamyris said, with a transparent envy that was completely free of bitterness. "No one can take that from you."

"Except the king himself," Ayana said softly.

"Oh, as he did with Vashti?" Leila asked. "But Esther will not be foolish enough to refuse him or defy him, will she?"

"I cannot imagine it," Esther confessed. She was still in awe of the king, overwhelmed by his power and his forceful personality despite the weaknesses she knew so well, that she could not imagine pitting her will against his, and certainly not in public as Vashti had done.

The hour grew late, and Ayana shooed the girls away, reminding them that Esther's day was going to be quite full on the morrow. When they were gone and Esther was dressed for bed, Ayana took up her lamp to go to her own adjoining chamber.

"No, don't leave me tonight, Ayana," Esther said. "Stay here with me. I don't want to be alone."

Ayana smiled and placed the lamp on a table. "I am here, Esther," she said.

Morning came at last. Toward dawn Esther had slept briefly, when her tired mind finally stopped churning. She ate little at the morning meal. Ayana accompanied her to the baths and stayed with her while her hair and makeup were done. The makeup artist accented her dark eyes with a light ointment spread with a carved ivory pin, then brushed a rosy pigment over her cheeks. Back in Esther's own rooms, her servants arrived to dress her in her gown and drape a flower garland around her neck.

Her apartment's main room had been transformed with the sofreh table as its centerpiece. Fresh flowers filled it with color and perfume. Esther caught a quick glimpse of it as she hurried to her own chamber, but she would not enter the room until after the king had arrived.

At noon the musicians struck up their music in the outside courtyard. Esther stood, fully dressed and ready, in the center of her bedchamber, but her servant girls peeked at the windows for glimpses of the king as he arrived. When he had come, they led Esther out through the apartment's back entrance so that she could arrive in through the front doors, accompanied by the pounding drumbeats that signaled the bride's arrival.

In the room, amid a handful of guests, her servants, and the priests, sat King Xerxes at the sofreh, also clad in white with a flower garland around his neck. He sat with his back to her as she entered. As tradition dictated, she caught sight of his face in the mirror. Bronze could not accurately reflect the look in a man's eyes, but when she was led to her place on his left side, she saw the brightness, the sheer pleasure with which he looked at her.

The marriage witnesses were usually close friends or family. In a royal wedding the choice of witnesses was political as well as personal. Prince Masistes stood as the king's witness and ironically his wife, Artaynte, was Esther's witness. Presently she was the highest ranking woman at court, except of course for Queen Amestris and the other queens, none of whom could be expected to stand witness for their husband's newest wife. Esther tried to catch Artaynte's eye as she sat down. She wished she had a sister or friend beside her today rather than her soon-to-be sister-in-law, her husband's former lover. But Artaynte's serene expression revealed nothing of what the princess was feeling.

Artaynte and Masistes held the white silk cloth over the heads of Esther and the king as the pagan priest asked them each three times if it was their desire to marry each other. Esther, as she had been instructed, kept silent after the first two questions, so as not to indicate an unseemly eagerness. The third time she clearly answered, "Yes, I do."

Throughout the prayers and the recitations Esther sat with her hand in the king's, knotted together by the threads they had tied. She felt strength in his hand, and even some comfort. Now and then his fingers caressed her skin, and somehow she was reassured by that small, secret gesture. Whenever the magus spoke of Ahura Mazda, she silently substituted, *Lord God of Israel, God of Abraham, Isaac, and Jacob.* That was the God whose blessing she needed today, whose guidance she longed for.

Then the ceremony, the aghd, was over, and Esther and the king stood as the guests showered them with rice, flower petals, and coins for good luck and fertility. Together they drank the sweet wine flavored with honey. "May your lives together be sweet!" cried a robust voice, and Esther turned in surprise to see that Artabazus was among the guests, flinging a handful of crushed rose petals in her direction.

King Xerxes raised his glass. "Indeed, my friends and my subjects, our lives together will be sweet, for how else could they be with such a sweet and beautiful woman by my side? Ahura Mazda and all the gods have smiled on me today. Come with us, friends, to our marriage feast."

The procession spilled out of Esther's apartments into the harem courtyard. It was lined with spectators who waved and tossed rice and flowers as the couple made their way out into the palace gardens and through them toward the grand banquet hall.

This banquet hall was used only on the greatest of occasions. As they entered, Esther thought that the last time she was here she had played as a musician with the other harem girls. Now she entered the hall as queen—the only queen present, for Amestris, Irdabama, and Parmys were not invited to this celebration though they would appear later during the many days and nights of feasting. But this night was Esther's own—Queen Esther's banquet, the king called it.

And tonight only she joined him at his private table, hidden behind the decorated screen. As his new bride, she was especially honored. King Xerxes was very much the attentive bridegroom, tracing the curve of her face with one finger, caressing and touching her constantly as they reclined at the table. He took delight in feeding her from his own plate and made private toasts to their future together.

As the banquet ended the king, still hidden behind his screen, arose and addressed his guests. He thanked them for coming to honor his marriage. He spoke in praise of Esther. Then he announced, "To my new bride, in honor of our wedding day, I offer a gift—whatever she chooses. Ask for whatever you wish, Queen Esther, and it will be given you—even up to half of my kingdom!"

Esther was prepared for this moment. Hegai, still her mentor, had told her it was customary for the king to make this lavish and entirely meaningless offer. "Your response is important, of course," he'd explained. "If you ask for too much, you look presumptuous and grasping. But if you ask for nothing at all, it is as if you are denying the king's generosity—a great insult to his honor. You must ask for something large and significant, but not extravagant, and not selfish. Oh, and ask for nothing for your own family. Courtiers would see that as a sign that you want your own people to begin holding influence at court, though that is hardly likely in the case of your family, as they are commoners."

Together they had discussed what gifts she should request. Now Esther now rose to make her carefully prepared speech. She asked for increased rations and gifts for all her household servants, particularly those who'd served her from the beginning, and especially Ayana and Hathakh. The king agreed, and seemed pleased. Hegai, as always, had schooled her well.

It was almost dawn when they were alone again in the king's bed-chamber. Everything was different tonight. For one thing, despite the extended feasting and celebration, Xerxes was quite sober. His happiness had a different source, and Esther felt happy too. It was as if for the very first time she was with the man himself—as he was meant to be.

"They say queens are never happy," Xerxes mused as they lay together in their bed. "I don't know if any of my other queens are happy. Irdabama is in her own way, I think, because she has her own life and her own interests, but I couldn't say she is particularly happy with me. And I don't believe Parmys has the temperament for happiness. She wouldn't know what to do with it."

He mentioned neither Amestris nor Vashti, but the little silence that followed was enough to call both their names to memory. "But you, my Esther—I want you to be happy. I want you to be more than my queen. I want you to be my wife and my lover. Can you be those things? Can I be a man and a husband, not just a king, to you?"

"I don't know, my lord," she said softly, risking complete honesty with him for the first time. She traced her finger down the strong clear line of his jaw beneath the curling of his beard. "You are so very much the king. I do not know if I will ever feel for you what the peasant's bride must feel for her husband. I don't even know if it would be right for me to feel that."

He smiled. "Not, perhaps, the peasant. But you could feel the love of a wife to an ordinary man, a man who is not a king." Suddenly despite his smile he grew serious, and the hand that had circled her wrist gripped her so tightly it almost hurt. "I want to be loved that way, Esther—as a man, not a king. Can you give me that?"

She could have said yes, obeying a king's command, but that was not what he wanted. So she gave him the truth again. "I can try, my lord. I will try."

It must have been good enough. He took her in his arms and kissed her.

Throughout the 28 days of feasting, Esther and the king were rarely apart. Except for the few days when her monthly courses kept her from his bed, she slept in his bedchamber every night. But even those days she spent at his side. Daytimes were generally filled with riding and hunting parties. During the celebration Xerxes spent the absolute minimum amount of time on the business of ruling. He made a brief appearance in his audience hall every few days, and even there he often asked Esther to attend him. On a few occasions he invited her to play her oud there along with Roxane, which seemed to entertain him, although Esther felt that being on display as the king's new wife was nerve-wracking enough without having her musical talents on display as well.

On the whole, however, those were the happiest days Esther had known since coming to the palace. She grew more at ease in the small circle of the king's intimate friends and counselors and their wives. Most of all, she became more at ease with the king, with her husband. Their hours together were far more peaceful than the nights they'd spent together before their marriage. At that time Esther had felt like what she was—a concubine, a paid bedmate who could be called and dismissed at the king's will. They'd drawn close during those nights, but it was a strange kind of intimacy, a distant closeness.

Now they had hours free to talk while they rode together in the daytime or lay in each other's arms at night. Lovemaking became something more than physical; something more, too, than Esther healing the wounded pride of a despairing king. For Xerxes was happy, too—everyone saw it, and everyone commented on it.

Most commented behind her back, of course, but one person was blunt enough to say anything he thought to her face. One evening halfway through the marriage celebrations, Artabazus approached her in the garden as the king mingled with his guests before dinner.

"You look well," he said approvingly, lifting his glass to Esther.

"Thank you, sir," she said, smiling.

"And you're not the only one." Artabazus jerked his head toward the king who was laughing loudly at a jest one of the lords was telling. "He glows. He looks like a cat who's swallowed cream."

"Or like a child with a new toy?" Esther probed, raising an eyebrow.

Artabazus glanced back at her. "You're a sharp one. Yes, that, I suppose, too. Bound to feel a bit that way, for the woman, I suppose. Still, you're doing a good job."

"I still don't know what my job is supposed to be, although you seem to have a number of ideas on the subject."

"Don't get bristly with me, now, my lady. I'm telling you I approve. Notice something?" he added.

Esther laughed aloud. The king heard her laughter and caught her eye, smiling at her. He began to disentangle himself from the group around him, to gradually make his way toward his bride. "I notice many things, Lord Artabazus. What, in particular, were you thinking of?"

"Your husband, the king. Always the first to raise his glass and lead in the cheer, as always. But I haven't seen him drunk—good and drunk—in, oh, a fortnight, now." The king was almost close enough to hear them. Artabazus gave Esther a quick nod, like a salute. "As I said, you're doing your job well."

He turned toward the king and said, "I've been congratulating your wife on her excellent taste in kings. Now I suppose it's time to congratulate you on your taste in wives. And now that the flowery talk is done, I'll go get myself a drink, if you don't mind, Your Majesty."

"No need to go. We can summon wine for you," the king told him, gesturing vaguely in the air, a movement which sent four servants running from four different directions. "I hope you have not been boring my queen with talk of horses and cavalry and chariots, have you?" Artabazus' current task was overseeing the rebuilding of the army which had been so decimated by the losses in Greece.

"Must you assume I'd be bored?" Esther put in quickly. "You know my great love of horses, my lord." Both men burst out laughing. Esther's riding skills had improved greatly in the past weeks, but she still had much to learn.

Much later that night it was the king who chose to speak to her about Artabazus. "What do you think of him?" he asked. They were sitting together in a tiny interior garden tucked between the king's bed-chamber and his retiring room, wearing as light and scanty clothing as decent because of the heat of the spring night. Esther sat in the cradle of her husband's arms and legs, leaning against his well-muscled chest, both their bodies filmed lightly with perspiration.

"Of Artabazus?" She thought a moment. She was still testing the waters when it came to expressing her opinions to Xerxes. She knew he liked women with intelligence and spirit, but also that he expected those qualities to be kept under strict control, subservient to his own opinions.

"I like him," she ventured at last with a nod. "He's very forthright—certainly he's no diplomat—but I think you can trust a man like that."

"H'mm." The word *trust* was a risky one. Kings, she knew, trusted no one. Betrayal, even from those nearest and dearest, was a constant threat for royalty. "I can't decide about Artabazus. I need to send him to his new satrapy in Phrygia to deal with this Spartan king, and I need to know I can rely on him. I'm still not sure whether he's my bravest warrior for getting his army out of Greece when he did, or a craven coward for turning tail and running away from certain death."

"I don't know about that," Esther said thoughtfully. "I think . . . perhaps women see these things differently. Men are scornful of some-one who runs from a fight, but I think there is a time to run. Anyway, Artabazus did not run from a fight. He simply escaped successfully after one, isn't that so?" When Xerxes murmured agreement, she went on, "At any rate, I am sure he is loyal to you. I have spoken little to him, but that little has convinced me he has your best interests at heart."

"We have been friends a long time," Xerxes said, "though that doesn't matter as much as one might wish, with some people. What did my old friend say to my new love to convince you he is looking out for my best interests?"

Esther paused, wondering how much to dare. There was little about her conversations with Artabazus she would want Xerxes to hear, but she did risk saying, "He congratulated me. He thinks I am responsible for the fact that you have not been—that you drink less wine than usual."

After one of those brief pauses in which Esther wondered if the king was about to laugh or pronounce a death sentence, he laughed. "Does he think he can get you to badger me about drinking too much, instead of doing it himself? The old fool!"

Then, swift as lightning, his mood changed. He touched his lips to the back of Esther's neck, and she shivered. "But my old soldier is right about one thing, my love. These nights I have not needed wine. I have been drunk on love. I've been drunk on Esther." He ran his hands through her hair and tipped her head back so he could reach down and kiss her lips. And Esther let go, for a moment, of the worries and thoughts that troubled her. He was drunk with love, and like all drunkenness, it would pass, and he would someday be sober. These moments were fleeting. She gave herself up to the pleasure of his touch, and the relentless power of his desire for her.

In all that month of feasting and celebration that followed her marriage Esther had only one truly unpleasant day. That was the day that, as tradition dictated, she had to host a dinner for the other royal women in her quarters. The royal women currently living in the palace were the queens Irdabama and Parmys, the king's second and third wives; Princess Artaynte; the king's daughter, Princess Amytis, married to the general Megabyzus, and two of the king's sisters, Princess Artazostre, the widow of Mardonius, and Princess Mandane. Queen Amestris had been away at her own estates since Xerxes had announced his intention to marry Esther. That was a relief, though Esther supposed it was only delaying an inevitable confrontation. Hosting the other royal women was already daunting enough; some of them she had been only briefly introduced to before now.

Ayana and Hathakh oversaw the details of the dinner. It was a great event for them too, since it was by far the largest banquet ever hosted in Esther's own household. It would not be the last. She would do a great deal of entertaining in her new position, and her steward and lady-in-waiting were kept busy learning the protocols involved in such a feast. Esther herself was left free to fret about how she was going to make conversation with her husband's two other wives, his daughter, his sisters, and his last lover.

In fact, the evening went far better than she could have imagined. This was because of Queen Irdabama, Xerxes' third wife, who was an excellent conversationalist. Esther had met the other two wives only briefly before now. Harem gossip said that Xerxes was known to like a woman with beauty and wit, and in Parmys and Irdabama he'd gotten two halves—enough to make up one whole woman. Neither, of course, had been a love match. His marriage to Irdabama was a political marriage into an important noble family, while Parmys was his own half-sister. Both women had borne him children, but Irdabama had only daughters surviving, so she was considered unimportant politically. Parmys' son was between Amestris' sons Darius and Artaxerxes in age, and might give trouble someday, but it was unlikely. Certainly he would have no iron-willed mother to back any attempt he might make at the throne.

Queen Parmys was still a strikingly pretty woman, though nearing 30 now, but she was so quiet and dreamy that she seemed almost tongue-tied. Queen Irdabama, on the other hand, was certainly no beauty. She was a hefty woman of almost staggering plainness, but she had a quick wit, high spirits, and seemed to know a great deal on almost every subject without ever making her knowledge sound heavy-handed or superior. She was kind, too, Esther realized partway through the evening when she deflected a comment from Artaynte that was certainly intended to be resentful, perhaps hurtful, toward Esther.

"I used to be considered quite a fine dancer when I was younger," Princess Mandane was saying. "But, of course, I haven't danced in years." She sighed. She was in mourning for her three young sons, who had all been killed fighting in Greece.

"Did you never even dance before your husband?" Princess Amytis suggested. She was a very pretty, spirited girl of Esther's own age with fair skin, a long slender white neck, and black hair piled atop her head. Her large eyes were so light they looked almost golden, and bright makeup accentuated their vividness. Amytis was said to look almost exactly like her mother, though Esther had never seen Queen Amestris up close and unveiled. Princess Amytis already had quite a reputation of her own. While her husband was fighting with the king in Greece, she had had an affair with one of the royal guard—while only 14 years old—and had been severely reprimanded by her father on his return. But her husband had agreed to take her back.

Mandane laughed at Amytis' suggestion. "My husband is much more businesslike than that. He does not expect his wife to dance for him."

"Your brother, the king, expects it of his women," Artaynte said, dropping her eyelids with a small smile. "Or so it is said. Perhaps Esther could tell us more. Or—perhaps poor Vashti could have."

Into the small awkward silence Irdabama said, "Actually, this may amaze you, but I once won a prize for dancing. As a girl. You wouldn't think it to look at me now—they say fat women can't dance—but that's not true at all, I assure you. I still have the urge to get on my feet when I hear a lovely tune. That's a particularly fine oud player you have there, Queen Esther. Didn't she play at one of the wedding banquets?"

"Yes," Esther said, quick to grab the change of subject. "Roxane accompanies her husband, Lilaios, who has just recently received a commission as a court poet. They are both very gifted."

Gratefully, the other princesses latched onto the topic of musicians and poets, which kept everyone—except Parmys—talking animatedly until the last dishes were cleared from the table. At the end of the evening, Irdabama lingered for a few moments after the other women had gone.

"It's all very new and sudden to you, isn't it?" she said to Esther, who nodded gratefully. They were sitting on a bench in the courtyard just outside the entrance to Esther's apartments.

"It was a shock to me, too, though I was born into the nobility, used to palaces and all the ceremony. To you it must seem even more dizzying. Raising queens up from the harem is not a common practice here in Persia, though Xerxes seems to think it's quite appropriate. You don't mind if I mention poor Vashti, do you?"

"No, not at all. It seems her name is not to be spoken, yet everyone must be thinking of her," Esther confessed. "I am, in a way, her replacement."

"Yes, but her better in every way, I think," Irdabama said, looking Esther up and down. "Not that she was a bad girl, just unsuited to the role. And of course, she was passionately in love with the king. A terrible mistake in any marriage, but especially in a royal marriage." She did not look at Esther now as she spoke, but out at the gardens. The warning in her tone and words was clear enough without glances. "Now Xerxes and I, we've been wed seven years—since just after he took the throne—and we get along fine. I have my own concerns, with my private estates and my children, and he knows I don't like court life much. It's sort of a business partnership with us, but a very amiable one, of course. Parmys, now, she's not choosy, and she's certainly no romantic. Actually I've never known what she wants, although she's probably got

ambitions for her boy, Hystaspes. And that will put her afoul of
Amestris, which is not somewhere I've ever wanted to be, no matter
how badly every woman wants to bear her husband sons. Any wife, any
concubine the king is fond of, is Amestris' enemy—but the wife or concubine with a boy child is an enemy she'll track into the ground.
Nothing is going to stand between young Darius and the throne.
Amestris is certain of that."

"So their marriage—Amestris and Xerxes—is that a business
partnership, too?" Esther asked, marveling at how easy she felt with
this woman.

"Good question. It used to be, certainly. They were partners in the
business of Persia, of the Achaemenid dynasty, and that looked like it
had a chance of being a long and successful partnership. But things have
gone wrong these past few years. The king's love affairs, and Greece of
course. Amestris isn't interested in backing a loser. Of course, the greatest trouble with them was that it wasn't *strictly* business. They were in
love once, too. A great mistake, as I said. These days they're more like
two opposing heads of state. Xerxes rules Persia, but Amestris strives to
rule the palace, which can sometimes be more important. You'll be
careful of her, of course."

Weakness seemed to nail Esther to her seat. "It seems I'll have to
be," she said.

Finally the days of feasting and celebration were over, and almost at
once the royal household began to prepare for the move to Parsa. Esther
had grown up with Susa's oppressive summertime heat. When possible,
Mordecai and Rivka had tried to take her away to relatives in the
mountains for a little relief during the hottest weeks. Last summer,
trapped here in the harem, had been the worst. Now she would be
going to Parsa to escape the heat. It would be the longest journey of her
young life, and she was excited. Her servants, on the other hand, were
in upheaval over having to pack again so soon after their last move.

One morning a few weeks before the planned departure, Esther
was in her rooms meeting with Hathakh. Now that the wedding festivities were over, she still spent most nights in the king's chambers, but
usually returned to her own quarters in the morning. She had gotten
into the habit of meeting first with Ayana and then with Hathakh, for
a little while each morning to discuss plans for the day and any needs
the household might have. She was very grateful for the administrative
skills of her two chief servants. At least a dozen new people had been

added to her household in the preceding weeks and she had not even met some of them yet.

This morning she expected to discuss some of the details of the move to Parsa with Hathakh, but he had something else on his mind. "I saw Mordecai again yesterday," he said. "He is very anxious to speak with you again. I warned him that this might not be a good time, but he said it was a matter of great importance."

Esther grew serious. "I wonder if someone in the family is ill. I hope it's not Aunt Rivka. Is there some way I can see him, if only for a little while? Surely my position is more secure now than before I was married."

Hathakh nodded. "It is. In fact, there is no reason you could not now invite your family quite openly to visit you here in the palace—except that, for some reason, you and Mordecai don't want anyone to know that he is your family." Hathakh knew that much. He was not the sort to press for explanations.

But he deserved one, Esther thought, for all the intrigues she had involved him in. She paused, weighing what she was about to reveal, then took a deep breath. She got up and looked beyond her doorway, before sitting down on the carved bench next to him. "There is a reason, Hathakh, even though it doesn't make sense to me sometimes either. You see, we are not Persians. My family—Mordecai's and mine—we are Jews, exiles from the land of Judah."

Hathakh's brow wrinkled. He came from the other end of Xerxes' far-flung empire, from India in the east. He probably had never ever heard of Jews or of Judah or Jerusalem. "What of that?" he said. "Did Mordecai think your chances of becoming queen would be less if you were known not to be of Persian blood? The kings usually marry Persian noblewomen, it's true—indeed, they often marry within their own family—but surely the king made it clear that he was considering women from all over the empire for his new bride."

Esther nodded. "I don't think that's the reason," she said. "It's something to do with our religion, with our people. We were taken into captivity by the Babylonian kings before the Persians conquered Babylon. I mean, our ancestors were. Since then, many of them have gone back to our homeland, under King Cyrus, I think. The Persian kings have treated our people well, but Mordecai is afraid. He thinks the tide of opinion might yet turn against us again. Our people—well, our religion, I suppose, is peculiar. Different, even here in Persia, where there are so many different cultures and peoples." She didn't know how else to explain it when she herself understood so little. "I don't really know why," she concluded lamely, "but Mordecai believed strongly that I should not reveal that I am a Jew. Many people know him as a Jew, so if it were known that he was my cousin, my secret would be out in the open. And now, of course, that would mean trouble, for the king would know I had lied about my family."

"It's not so much that you've lied," Hathakh said. "Your parents are dead, are they not?"

"Since I was a baby."

"And Mordecai and his wife fostered you? And these people—Mordecai's in-laws—the Persian family who claimed you were theirs? They are really relatives, people you knew, isn't that right? So in a way it's as if they're adopting you now, just as Mordecai did once. Your real parents are dead in any case, so I suppose any relative, Persian or Jewish, might claim you as their own."

Esther hadn't thought of it this way. She could see Hathakh was producing this possibility just to stop her from worrying, which was very sweet of him, but it didn't help the immediate problem. "If Mordecai says it's important and he can't pass a message through you, then I really must see him," she reminded Hathakh.

Hathakh thought a moment. "I'll arrange for you to meet him in the gardens. That will attract less attention, I think, than if he came here. Go lightly veiled, as the women do in the gardens. We can try to make it seem very casual, almost a chance meeting. But again, you won't be able to talk for long."

When Esther and Hathakh went to the palace gardens the next day, Mordecai was already there. Esther was careful to keep her face and demeanor neutral, as if it were indeed a chance meeting with a casual acquaintance, but her voice betrayed her concern. "What's the matter, Mordecai? Is anyone ill, or in trouble?"

"No, no. Anyone at home, you mean? No," Mordecai said. "We are all well. Esther, do you remember when I saw you last, I told you I had heard rumors of unrest? I hear a great many things in my position. I suppose I am highly placed enough to be near the people with power, but unimportant enough that people may sometimes talk carelessly in front of me. I have heard something more definite this time. I am almost certain there is a plot to assassinate the king."

"What?" Esther's hand flew to her mouth. Quickly she tried to rearrange her shocked features into a mask of calm. "What—when—how?"

Mordecai's smile was tense. "Too many questions. I can tell you this—there are two eunuchs involved, Bigthan and Teresh." Esther knew the names. They were highly placed within the king's household. "I don't know if they're working for anyone else. No doubt they are, and we could all make guesses, but these are the two names I know. And I know that the attempt is planned for the time when the court leaves for Parsa. I'm not sure what's planned—an accident of some kind, something that won't be detected in the confusion of the journey. You must warn the king, or someone close to him."

"Thank you, Mordecai. I will. I must go—give my love to Aunt Rivka, to everyone, please."

On the way back to her own quarters she struggled with whether to confide in Hathakh. By the time they reached the apartment she knew she would. There was no one, except perhaps Ayana, that she trusted more. Since Hathakh already knew there was a secret, he was the logical person to talk to.

He listened carefully to the few details Mordecai had confided. "It makes sense," he said. "The journey to Parsa is a time when everyone is on the move. An assassin would be very difficult to trace. These two men—Bigthan and Teresh—are very close to the king, but I know that Bigthan, at least, is also close to the king's brother, Prince Masistes. And I think Teresh has ties to the family of Mardonius. You know many of them blame the king for Mardonius' defeat and death. He has many enemies."

"So, what must I do? Go directly to the king with this?"

Hathakh was silent. "Seek counsel from someone else first, someone who knows the king and the palace well. We are new at these games, Esther—my lady. Whom can we trust?"

Esther's first thought was of Artabazus, but he was gone to Phrygia. Anyway, he was a military man, not a courtier. "We need someone who understands the business of palace intrigue. And only one person comes to mind."

"The same person who comes to my mind, I'll wager," Hathakh said with a smile, and together they both said, "Hegai."

Esther had not had many opportunities to speak with the chief eunuch since she'd left the virgins' section of the harem, save for meeting with him just before her wedding to discuss matters of protocol. He bowed deeply and then smiled warmly as she entered his office. "My lady queen," he said. He smiled. "Here you are, the woman who has left me almost unemployed."

"Unemployed? How is that?"

"You know that while I oversee the whole harem, my main duty is the training and preparation of the virgins. Now I find that because one was trained and prepared so very well a great many others are superfluous. I have dozens of girls on my hands who were all awaiting their chance to go to the king, to see if one would be chosen as his new wife. Now their lives, and mine, are almost without purpose."

Esther laughed. It was amazing how much easier and more confident she felt in Hegai's presence now than when she had been a newcomer here. Hegai had once seemed powerful and imposing. That was before she had met Xerxes. "Keep the girls on hand, Hegai. I am not so naive as to think the king will never require their services again." It made her solemn for a moment, to think that some night the king would not call for her, would request a newer concubine instead. But that was the way of men. No wife, especially a royal wife, would expect anything different.

Hegai sobered too. "I am not naive either, Your Highness," he said. "But all my sources tell me the king is enchanted with his new bride—and rightly so. I would wager you have a good chance of keeping his attention at least until you are carrying his child. Then, of course, you will be forbidden his bed, and he will find someone else to warm it for a while. But"—he looked at her tenderly—"if you give him a son, you will have a key to his heart."

"And a lifelong enemy in Queen Amestris," Esther said softly.

Hegai's eyes darted around the room. "You learn quickly, my lady," he said. Esther had noticed that no one in the palace ever spoke of Amestris without that quick, cautious glance. Her spies must truly be everywhere.

"But I did not come to talk of myself," she said quickly and even more quietly. "I have received information the king should know, but I do not know how best to inform him. A man I know—an officer at the king's gate named Mordecai—is an old friend of my family. He met me recently in the gardens and told me he has heard of a plot to assassinate the king during the move from here to Parsa. The men involved are Bigthan and Teresh."

Hegai frowned. "I have heard nothing of this," he said in disbelief.

Esther knew why he was surprised. Hegai had an extremely good network of sources himself. "I know little about this Mordecai—you are sure you trust him? He is not a fool, someone seeking to stir up trouble?"

"He is no fool, and I would trust him with my life."

Hegai nodded. "Then I will look into it. Discreetly but thoroughly. If we make an accusation outright, they will deny it, and we will know nothing. The king could still have them put to death, but he could just as easily decide your friend is making trouble for nothing, especially as these two eunuchs are highly placed and your friend holds a minor position. Without evidence, he may not believe the story. But if it is true, we will find evidence. Leave it with me, my lady." He rose as she stood up, and bowed to her again.

Esther repeated the conversation to Hathakh, and asked him to get a message to Mordecai if possible. For the next two days she and her household were busy with preparations for their departure. The king spent many additional hours in his audience chamber, meeting with his councillors, dealing with affairs that needed to be cared for before leaving Susa. It was necessary to make up for time lost during the wedding celebrations On the second night the king called for Esther to come to his chambers, but they had only a few hours together before the sun rose and the king once again went about his business.

Hathakh came to Esther's chambers in the hours after the evening meal. "I had word from Hegai a few hours ago," he told her.

"You did? What news?"

"One of the two eunuchs—Bigthan—was caught bribing the groom who looks after the king's carriage. He and his accomplice had made arrangements with one of the groomsmen to disable the carriage—loosen the wheels or some such thing. The plan was to stage an accident at a particularly dangerous turn in the road a few hours out from Susa. The carriage would fall apart and plunge down a cliff, and the king and anyone riding with him would be killed."

Esther was speechless for a moment. Clasping her hands together to still their shaking, she said, "Quite a complex plan."

"Yes. It was elaborately designed to make it look like an accident, but unfortunately the planners had to involve quite a few people. Bigthan and Teresh and everyone they bribed or coerced have been arrested."

A shudder ran through Esther's body. "They'll be put to death, of course."

"Yes, but Bigthan and Teresh will be tortured first. It's assumed they were working for someone higher up, someone with a grudge against the king or someone who could benefit from his death. They may reveal that under torture."

"So the king knows about it now?"

"Yes. He was told this evening."

Esther did not hear from the king that night or the next morning, but in the afternoon a summons came to attend him privately over the evening meal in his chambers.

It was a pleasant change, dining alone with her husband, rather than in the midst of a royal retinue. Only a few of his most intimate servants remained to serve them, and they kept a discreet distance as Esther and Xerxes ate in the interior garden within his quarters.

Xerxes raised his glass to her as the meal ended. "Yet again, a toast to my wife. I understand that I owe you a great debt."

"Which debt is that, my lord?"

He smiled. "Ah yes, there are so many. But I was referring particularly to information you gave Hegai about a planned attempt on my life."

"It turned out to be true, then?"

"It is true, and the plotters are being dealt with." He took a sip from his glass, set it down, and looked at her with serious eyes. "Assassination attempts are nothing new to a king—at least not in our royal house. Perhaps there are lands elsewhere where kings can sleep in peace, but not in Persia. My father killed a king to win his throne. Some upstart may do the same to me someday. I have brought you into a dangerous world, my Esther, and already you have saved me once."

"It was not my own doing, my lord," she said. "As Hegai no doubt told you, I received the information through my steward, from a man who is a friend of my family. He is one of the keepers of the palace gate."

"Yes, of course. What was his name again?"

"Mordecai, my lord."

"Mordecai." Xerxes frowned. It was obvious he didn't remember the name of every minor official in the palace. "I will see to it, of course, that he is rewarded. As for you—you might just as easily have disregarded his news, thinking it untrue. Or perhaps—how should I know?—you might have kept quiet because you might not be sorry to see me dead, and you a free woman again." He spoke soberly, but a smile quirked the corner of his mouth. She could not tell how earnestly he meant that. Probably he found it hard to imagine that any woman could hate him, yet the evidence was clear that many people did. Perhaps he just needed reassurance.

It was easy to give, in that moment. "Not in the least, my lord. I am very pleased to have you alive."

Xerxes' face grew stern. "I am no fool, Esther, though many take me for one. I know many women who come to a king's harem come looking for riches and an easy life—and in spite of that, many others do not come willingly. I meant it when I said I had brought you into a dangerous world, out of whatever world, whatever life, you knew before. You had no choice in coming here, or indeed in marrying me—I know that. But you do have choices. You had the choice to speak or remain silent, and you almost certainly saved my life by speaking."

He reached down to the ground below the table and brought up a small carved wooden chest, just slightly larger than the palm of his hand, and passed it across the table to Esther.

Inside she found a jeweled silver collar set with brilliant turquoise. She had received beautiful, costly jewelry upon her marriage, but this was special and lovely—a personal gift rather than a state treasure.

"Thank you," she said, reaching back to place it around her neck. "I will treasure this."

"Lift up your hair and I will fix the clasp for you," the king said. "And thank you."

Three days later they were on the road, Esther riding with the king in the very carriage originally slated for demolition. People lined the streets of Susa to see the royal party pass by. Once they were out in the country, Xerxes grew restless, wanting to get out and ride. Naturally, he expected Esther to ride with him.

The entourage was huge. Along with the king himself and his personal staff, almost all the noble families at court and their servants were moving to the summer palace. A large number of the palace administrators were going, too. And from the harem, both Irdabama and Parmys with their children and their households, along with most of the concubines, the musicians, and dancers, were traveling as well. A huge contingent of royal guardsmen in their special attire accompanied the travelers. Queen Amestris would be at Parsa, too, but she was traveling separately. She had spent the past several months on her own lands far to the west in Cappadocia near the place where her late father had been satrap.

"One of the disadvantages of being king," Xerxes said, waving his hand at the huge procession of caravans, carriages, and horses. "Very difficult ever to go anywhere quickly."

"Or without attracting attention."

"Indeed."

After a few hours of riding, Esther was happy to return to the carriage, but as the roads grew rougher over the next few days, she realized she had a choice between having her bones ground together on a jolting carriage ride or straining her muscles with hours on horseback. Xerxes still wanted her company almost all the time, so she alternated between one form of discomfort and another at his whim.

The spring weather was far enough advanced that they took the mountain route to Parsa, traveling by day over rugged narrow roads that climbed ever higher into the hills where bare rock was dotted with sparse trees. Esther's servants began to mutter about the danger of bandits, but Ayana set them straight. "Don't you know the king himself pays tribute to the brigands to leave his caravans alone while he passes through?"

"You mean there are brigands here so powerful that even the king must pay tribute to them?" Esther asked in surprise. "For some reason that doesn't make me feel much safer."

By night they camped, the king in a tent almost as lavish as the great command tent he took on his military campaigns. It was not quite as big, but still larger than many houses Esther had been in. Each night servants rolled out the carpets, set up the royal bed, laid out the gold and silver plates and goblets. Each night Esther left the rutted, uncomfortable road and joined the king in a miniature traveling palace. Her people, like all the other servants and retainers, had far less comfortable accommodations. Some slept in simpler tents, and some slept out in the open under the great endless blue expanse of mountain sky.

Finally, after several weeks of traveling, they came down into the foothills and saw Parsa below. The palace dominated the city, spread out before them in the slanting rays of the late-afternoon sun.

"It's beautiful," said Esther, riding beside the king, looking at the white palaces and pillars, gates and walls, shooting up to the sky.

"It's unfinished," Xerxes said, reining in his horse and gesturing to her to do the same so they could enjoy the view. "All palaces are unfinished, of course—there's always more to build, more to do. But this one, particularly, has possibilities. I had grand plans for it, but for the past few years I have always been away on campaign. Seeking glory in the field, when perhaps I should have been carving it in stone."

"Stone sometimes lasts longer," Esther said. "Palaces often out-live kings and even kingdoms. Think of Egypt, of the pyramids. What a monument!"

Xerxes was silent a moment, looking thoughtfully at his palace. Then he turned to his queen. "This summer I will hire architects and artisans," he declared. "This field has lain fallow too long. It is time to plant in stone and reap a palace. You will help me."

His gaze swept across the sweet spring grasses, up to the copper sky. "Esther, I want your advice, your good taste, and your opinions. I already know you can choose well in musicians and poets—now we will see how you do when you are given stone and paint as your tools. Help me create a palace that will outlive us both." He turned to her, a light of excitement glowing in his eyes, something she'd never before seen except when he took her in his arms and talked of love. She remembered Artabazus' words: *There must be more to being a king than fighting wars. Help him find something else . . . something to make him believe he's as great a king as Darius.*

Looking down at Parsa glowing in the golden light, she thought, *Perhaps Xerxes has found that special something.*

ChAPTER 11

Very good! Good music, all of you," Esther called to the assortment of children as they finished playing their simple tune.

Roxane, helping one small boy with his chang, clapped her hands for the others as the music ended. "Time to go now," she added, and most of the children quickly scampered away.

Since coming to Parsa, Esther had revived her former practice of giving music lessons to some of the concubines' children, with help from Roxane who loved to teach. Every few days a group of six or eight small children gathered in the courtyard in front of Esther's apartment to play the oud, the chang, and the nay. Most were children Esther knew well from the harem at Susa, but the last two times a slender, serious, dark-haired boy had joined them. He did not offer his name, but of course Esther and Roxane knew quite well who he was. Eight-year-old Artaxerxes, the king's second son by Queen Amestris, was a familiar face in the palace. He was a quiet boy who seemed content in the shadow of his older brother, Darius, the heir. But he played the oud extremely well and seemed to enjoy the music lessons. Perhaps it gave him an opportunity to shine in an area his brother had no interest in. Esther wondered, though, if Amestris knew where he went or who his teacher was. Probably not—royal children were generally in the care of their nursemaids, and Amestris was not known to be a doting mother, except in her passionate desire to someday see young Darius on his father's throne.

Artaxerxes remained after the last child had scampered on to other things. He sat cradling his oud well after the others were gone. "You play very well, Prince Artaxerxes," Esther ventured. She had not addressed him directly before.

He looked up, unsurprised. "It's my hands," he said, holding them up for her to see. The boy did have unusually long, graceful hands with long, slim tapered fingers. "My brother says I should have been born into a family of oud players or weavers." He didn't seem to find the comment offensive, but Esther had encountered young Darius a few times before and was quite sure those words were intended to sting. The longer Artaxerxes remained unaware of that, though, the better.

He got up to go then. "Day after tomorrow?" he asked solemnly.

"Yes, I believe so." Esther quickly scanned her mind for appointments. She could be called away at any moment at the king's bidding, but she usually had several free hours each day when he was in his audience chamber or meeting with his councillors.

With the courtyard clear Esther and Roxane sat quietly together on the benches, their fingers busy at their instruments, plaiting a background of soft music for the clear, bright summer day. Esther had no trouble appreciating why the royal family chose to spend spring and summer at Parsa and at Ecbatana. The air at Parsa had a clean, fresh quality entirely lacking in the oppressive summer heat of Susa. She found herself loving the place already.

Ayana came out from the apartment carrying a tray with fruit and drink. She brought it over to the bench where the two women sat, set it down, and waited a moment till Esther gestured for her to sit and join them.

"Word came from the king this morning, my lady," Ayana said as she bit into a ripe pomegranate. "He wishes you to attend him this afternoon. He will be looking at the sculptors' sketches for the new gateway."

Esther laughed. When she had first entertained the idea that building his palace might become the king's new passion, replacing his desire for conquest, she could not have imagined how firmly the idea would take hold of him. In the month since their arrival at Parsa he'd become obsessed with architects, builders, masons, sculptors, and painters, as his grand vision of what the palace could become grew ever more elaborate. Esther didn't mind. Besides being glad he was occupied with matters other than military ones, she enjoyed the work itself. The idea of constructing something beautiful, something future generations could see and touch, appealed to her, too.

"I envy sculptors," Roxane said suddenly.

"Why? You have a secret desire to carry chisels and ruin your fingernails chipping away at stone?" Esther asked playfully.

"No!" Roxane giggled, flicking a pomegranate seed at the queen. "I envy them because, like musicians, they create something beautiful with their art—but unlike musicians, they create something that will last forever. Or for hundreds of years anyway. When I play a beautiful air for the king, it pleases him for a few moments; then it is forgotten. If Lilaios recites a wonderful poem, the words may linger in memory for an evening, but soon they are gone. But the relief carvings Setne is doing on the stairs—men will look at them for a thousand years and remember the glory of King Xerxes' reign, the beauty of Parsa—and the craft of Setne the Egyptian, even if his name is forgotten."

"You're right," Esther said after pondering this for a moment. "It does seem unfair."

"Unfair or not, it is how things are," Ayana said. "You could not be other than what you are. The gods made you a musician, and Lilaios a poet; they choose other men to be artists. And growing up in my country, I heard songs that my mother told me had been sung for a thousand years. Perhaps in the end, song can last as long as stone. A few songs, anyway."

"That's the trouble—never knowing which are the few," Roxane said. "I know Lilaios would love to compose a poem—a work of his own—that would be recited and remembered forever. But who can say what will endure and what will be forgotten? It's in the hands of the gods. Or of the God, as you would say, my lady," she added, nodding at Esther.

"Yes," Esther said. Her closest friends knew that she worshipped only one God, the God she believed was the Creator of everything and King over all other gods. She had never tried very hard to explain. "Our God is like Ahura Mazda," she told them once, "but different. More. Not just one great God among many smaller ones. My people do not even believe that the smaller gods are real." At that she'd stopped, hoping that her friends were not offended. She understood the Jewish faith so little herself that she felt unable to teach anyone else about it.

"Not that I have much to complain of," Roxane added, "even if my name and my music is forgotten by history. Ahura Mazda has smiled on me, for certain." She reached for an apple and a handful of almonds and smiled contentedly. One hand rested lightly on her belly. Her baby was due in four months' time. In a few short months she and her husband had been elevated from unknown artists to Xerxes' most honored court musician and poet, able to raise their child in more wealth and comfort than they would have been able to imagine when the baby was conceived.

Esther wondered if this was the time to share her own news. Ayana knew, of course, but no one else did, not even the king himself. The midwife knew, too, of course. She'd examined her, asked her a number of questions, and confirmed that she was probably about two months with child. Her baby would probably be born sometime after midwinter. Esther wanted to share the news with Roxane, to be able to talk freely about her excitement, but although she exchanged a quick glace with Ayana, Esther held her tongue. It was not right to tell others before she told Xerxes himself. Perhaps tonight would be the time to tell him.

In the week since she'd seen the midwife, she'd certainly had no shortage of opportunities to talk to her husband. Though all four of his wives and dozens of concubines were in residence at Parsa, the king still chose to spend almost all his time with his newest and best-loved wife. Esther was his consort at public banquets where she sat with the other honored guests at the high table, leaving the king alone at his private table, screened from view. She dined with him at private dinners on nights when there was no banquet. She rode out with him to the hunt and on riding excursions to the surrounding countryside. She spent hours with him most days reviewing his plans for the expansion of the palace, and then there were the nights. Almost every night she was with him in his bedchamber, making love and talking till the early-morning hours.

They were good nights, and good days. Esther was even happier than she'd been at Susa in the month after her marriage. Back then she'd worried about the future. Now, that concern seemed to have lifted. The holiday atmosphere of the summer court, the pleasure of working with the king on his great project, and above all the growing certainty that she was carrying his child—all that made her content. Xerxes was content too; she could see that. He took obvious delight in her company, he was seldom if ever drunk, and he did not fly into fits of rage or sink into despair. They had been married three months, and still he showed no signs of tiring of her. For a man with Xerxes' reputation, that was remarkable—or so the harem gossip said.

She joined the king a few hours later in the large room where he interviewed architects and artisans. The room was simply furnished with one large, heavy wooden table and a few wooden chairs. Its only decorations were the large broad-silled windows in the white walls, windows that spilled Parsa's golden sunlight freely onto the polished brick floor. King Xerxes was sitting on the edge of the table holding a small stone carving in the palm of his hand. Wordlessly he held it out to her.

Esther took the statue. It was a bull with great upward-curving wings and a human head, bearded and crowned. The detail was beautiful, lovingly crafted, giving a clear impression of strength and power. "Is this Setne's work?" she asked.

"This is his model for the statues he wants to place on either side of the Gateway of All Lands," said Xerxes, taking the sculpture back from her. "Imagine it, Esther—two of these towering creatures, 20 times the height of a man. Above them I will have carved: *I Am Xerxes the Great, King of Kings.*"

Esther could, indeed, visualize the awesome effect of the finished gateway. "It will be majestic. You've told him you approve?"

"Approve?" Xerxes laid the carving carefully down and took Esther in his arms, sweeping her around the room. "I am delighted," he sang into her ear. "I am thrilled. Esther, he is more than a craftsman, more than an artist. He is a genius. New ideas sprout from his head like stone flowers in a stone garden. If I had all the wealth in all the world and Setne lived 500 years, we could never exhaust all his ideas for this palace. It will be magnificent—the greatest palace anywhere in the world. And it will stand forever, Esther—as long as the world lasts."

Esther touched the king's face as if she could somehow engrave on her fingers the memory of his smile and his joy. She wished that his joy would, too, last forever. Now was the moment to tell him, she decided.

"I have news for you, my lord," she said slightly pulling back from him so she could look into his face. "Something else new, though not as enduring as stone, perhaps."

"What is it?"

"A child, my lord. I have seen the midwife, and she says I will bear you a child in midwinter."

For a moment Xerxes was silent, and she thought that this news, so amazing to her, was nothing to him. He had six children by his wives and many more by his concubines. But then light broke over his face and once again he embraced her, tenderly this time. "My Esther! But that is wonderful news, wonderful! And far more enduring than stone. What better monument does a king have, after all, than his sons? And a child by you—by my love—this will be wonderful! We must consult with the magi about his stars. Get the midwife to tell you as closely as possible the date of his birth, and the magi will begin studying the heavens to tell us what secrets they hold for our son's future."

Esther was elated with her husband's happiness. She would never have told him her own doubts about the magi and their star predictions. Certainly everyone she knew believed the stars were the key to determining human destiny, and that those skilled in reading the heavens—the magi—could predict what the future might hold. Even among her own Jewish kin there were traces of that belief, yet she had often heard Mordecai speak scornfully of stars and destiny. "It is not the heavens, but the God who made the heavens, that knows our future," she remembered him saying. Not for the first time she wished she could talk to Mordecai, and perhaps even more, that she could look again at the Jewish scrolls he had and the others he'd told her of. Even if she could not raise her child—Xerxes' child—in the faith of her own forefathers, she felt she needed to know that faith for herself. Already thinking of herself as a mother, she felt a strong need to be grounded in a belief that went deeper than the shifting cycles of the skies, before she could hope to raise a little Persian prince—or princess—to adulthood.

She said nothing of this to the king, of course, but accompanied him, a few days later, to hear the magus predict their child's future based on his date of birth. She stood by Xerxes' side as he offered a sacrifice to the gods for the safe delivery of the child. Here at Parsa, religion played a far greater role in their lives than it did back in Susa, for Parsa was the heart of the Zarathustran religion, the center of the magi's learning and craft, and the place of sacrifice.

After the sacrifices she saw Xerxes join the priests in a ritual she'd never seen before, the drinking of *haoma*. That was considered a sacred drink that enabled the worshiper to see things unseen and know what was beyond human knowledge. Esther found it eerie. As a woman she was not included in the rite, and was glad, but it was strange to watch her husband under the influence of *haoma*. It was nothing like when he was drunk with wine. He became neither merry nor despairing; not angry, but merely distant, as though he really was looking through a door into a room she could not even guess. She was glad when its effects abated and they had left the temple, glad to be back in air and light and everyday things.

One of those everyday things included yet another visit from her seamstress for the fitting of a new gown to be worn at the great banquet coming up in a few weeks' time. The king's birthday feast was one of the most lavish events of the summer court, all the more so since this was his fortieth. Yet underneath the excitement of the festival ran an undercurrent of suspicion, for rumors of Queen Amestris' plans for the birthday feast ran rampant in the harem.

"She's plotting something, that's certain," Irdabama said quietly to Esther, raising her eyebrows. She was sitting on a couch in Esther's private chamber stabbing with her needle at a piece of needlework. Ayana sat nearby, also doing needlework, but watching the progress of Esther's gown with a critical eye at the same time. Roxane, whose pregnancy was beginning to show, sat on the floor cradling her oud, playing a soft counterpoint of music to their conversation.

"That is what everyone says, my lady," Ayana agreed. Queen Irdabama was now enough of an intimate in Esther's household to know that Ayana and Roxane were to be trusted completely, and one could speak freely in front of them. The seamstress was Irdabama's own servant, one she had recommended to Esther. "Candidly, my dear, if she can dress me and make me look presentable, she'll make you look ravishing," Irdabama had told Esther. Apparently Irdabama felt that the seamstress, too, was discreet enough to talk in front of, for she continued, "The only question is, what has she planned? Everyone I've heard speak of it agrees it's nothing pleasant."

"Does she know about . . . ?" Ayana glanced toward Esther and her voice trailed off a little. Discretion was still an ingrained habit, since everyone there knew of Esther's pregnancy. The seamstress had already been enlisted to make fuller, looser gowns she could wear later in the summer. But outside Esther's private circle of friends and servants, only the king knew that she was expecting a child.

"If she does, she will be angrier than ever. There's nothing Amestris hates more than a rival, unless it's a fertile rival," Irdabama said.

"Is this all about *me?*" Esther asked. She had been silent for most of the conversation. She found it hard to speak without moving, and the seamstress was very strict about keeping still. Also she felt nervous whenever Amestris was mentioned in conjunction with the king's birthday. "Is she planning something terrible because she's jealous of me?"

"I'd imagine you've a great deal to do with it," Irdabama said placidly, "but don't fret, my dear. If it wasn't you it would be someone else. She's the kind of woman that always has to be scheming against someone. And she won't do anything against you directly. You're too close to the king right now for her to dare that. But watch her, my lady; watch her closely."

"I will," Esther promised. "There, are we done? I think that looks fine." She turned to Ayana for her approval of the gown. Ayana stood up, wrinkled her brow, walked all around and then nodded. "It's a very good fit. Very becoming," she said, not to Esther but to the seamstress. Esther still thought it was ironic that her new life included such extended sessions in the baths, having her hair and face done, and being fitted for dresses—all of which had been her least favorite activities when she was a girl. She still took little interest in them. Having a new gown made was largely a transaction between Ayana and the seamstress, with Esther standing in for fittings.

The golden summer days slipped by. Esther, with the midwife's approval, continued to ride almost every day with the king, though she was spared the rigors of the hunt. She felt well, though tired. A warm, lazy lethargy seeped like honey into her bones, making her sleep late into the morning and keeping her yawning at dinnertime.

The palace buzzed with activity as builders and laborers worked on the new sections. At the Gate of All Lands, Setne and his workmen had already begun work on the two huge blocks of stone that would someday be the great winged bulls. "It will take years," Xerxes said as he rode out with Esther by his side to inspect the huge, shapeless masses.

"But I can see them there, with my name above them. And someday I will cut an inscription to go below my father's." Esther had seen Darius' famous inscription describing himself and his kingship. He set a high standard for any son of his to follow: *I was not a Lie-follower, I was not a doer of wrong. According to righteousness I conducted myself. Neither to the weak or to the powerful did I do wrong . . .* it read in part.

It was, of course, conventional for a king to claim that he was virtuous as well as powerful. Esther knew Xerxes well enough by now to understand that he took his father's claims seriously in all things. But surely he must know that Darius was no paragon of virtue, anymore than he was himself. Yet he constantly measured himself against the words of his father's inscription rather than against the real man and his real life. Here at Parsa, where the words were carved in stone, Esther had come to think that Xerxes was like a man dashing himself against that stone, determined to make an impression on it with the weight of his own body. Would he, like such a man, be broken at last by the attempt?

She pushed the thought out of her mind. It was a sunny day with glorious blue skies arching above, and she was enjoying her ride. She had actually come to like riding, now that she had learned not to fall off. A pity she would soon have to give it up till after the child was born. All the more reason to enjoy today's ride. And tomorrow began the celebration of the king's birthday.

The feast lasted seven days, with his giving lavish gifts to all his guests each night at dinner. Esther received some beautiful jewelry and exquisitely carved dishes. She sat at the royal table night after night surrounded by the other wives, the princes and princesses, with the king, of course, secluded from view. The meals were excellent, the entertainment superb—Lilaios performed twice, once with an ode he had composed himself—and, despite everyone's apprehensions, nothing sinister happened at all.

It happened on the last night of the feast. As usual the king made his offer. Coming down from his private table to stand before his guests, he proclaimed that anyone present might ask any boon they craved, and he would grant it, even to half the kingdom. An uneasy silence spread across the room, broken when Queen Amestris rose to her feet and bowed before the king.

"My friends and servants," Xerxes said in ringing tones as he raised her to her feet. "My wife Amestris, my great queen, and the mother of my son and heir, Darius, has something to ask of me." Darius, at his mother's right hand, sat up a little straighter, his face a solemn mask. "What would you have, my lady? Whatever it is, it shall be given you."

Esther watched King Xerxes' face carefully. She knew he was worried about this. He had said little to her, but hinted that the empty formality of offering up to half his kingdom might not be as trite as it usually was. Amestris wanted something from him—rumor made that clear. And whatever it was, it was likely to cause trouble. That was her nature.

At a gesture from the king she began a smooth, careful speech in which she told everyone how greatly honored she was to celebrate the king's birthday feast with them all, and paid many lavish compliments to her husband. Women very rarely had the opportunity to speak in public, and Amestris, who had a good voice and was supremely confident, took full advantage of her chance. Nearly a quarter of an hour passed before she finally reached the heart of her request.

"My lord king, mighty Xerxes, King of Kings, I have but one request to ask you. I do not ask for half your kingdom, for none could rule it better than you. I do not ask for gold or for riches, for the woman who is your wife is rich already. I do not ask for armies to command, for you are the supreme commander, and we ask for no other. I ask only one thing: that you give me another woman as my gift, that she may serve me however I see fit."

Gasps ran around the room and were as quickly stifled. Esther saw a moment of panic on the king's composed face and despite the assurance that Amestris would dare not harm her personally she felt a quick clutch of fear at her chest. But as Amestris' gaze swept down the royal table she did not even pause at Queen Esther. Instead, her eyes came to rest on the woman sitting next to Prince Masistes—his wife, Artaynte.

"My lord, mighty king, I beg of you that you give me this woman Artaynte as my servant—or my prisoner. I ask nothing else of you."

The room was as silent as any tomb. The musicians had stopped playing in midnote. No one whispered. No goblets clinked. Even the air seemed still. The unseasonable rain that began falling that afternoon had quickened to a downpour, but even that seemed hushed in that strained moment. The guests looked from Amestris to Artaynte, whose face had gone white as marble; then every eye was pulled back to Xerxes' face.

Esther felt her own heart pounding under her gown. It was as if she felt the king's pain as a physical stab in her chest. It was a long time before he spoke.

"My lady wife," he said at last in a voice that sounded as if he were choking. People unconsciously leaned forward, for his words were too quiet for anyone more than a few tables away to hear. "I beg you to reconsider your request. The princess Artaynte is the wife of my brother. Surely you would not distress and dishonor the prince Masistes so?"

He paused. Amestris said nothing, only kept her eyes on him. She looked splendid tonight in a gown of scarlet and blue. Her dark hair was dressed high, and her eyes, bright in her unveiled face, were lavishly made up to accentuate their golden splendor. Just down from Esther, Amestris' daughter Amytis sat upright on her couch, her eyes fixed on her mother. Her dress and her hair were very like her mother's. Her long white throat was ringed with a brilliant jeweled collar presented by her father at the previous night's feast. Her bright eyes were avid. Esther saw in them how much Amytis admired her mother and wanted her to emerge victorious from this contest.

Faced with silence, the king tried again. "My queen, I will give you anything you ask. If you wish slaves, I will fill your palace with eunuchs and women slaves from the farthest reaches of my empire. Only I ask that you do not do this thing. It does not befit you as a queen to take another woman of noble birth and use her as your slave. It is a disgrace to our house."

Amestris never even blinked. A minute passed, then another. The king stood as a statue, willing his wife to give in.

"My lord king, Mighty One," she broke the silence, "you have said you will give me anything I ask. I want no slaves but this one. I want no eunuchs, no gold, no land, no power—only power over this one small thing—this one woman. You have given your word."

It was true, and everyone in the hall knew it. Xerxes was in an impossible position. He had given his word to grant Amestris anything she asked, and could not without shame deny her. Yet to hand over his brother's wife, his own former lover, to a woman who hated her and intended her evil—the shame of that was, if anything, even greater than the shame of breaking his word.

The silence continued. Esther wanted to look down at Artaynte and Masistes, but dared not. She kept her eyes fixed on Amestris and the king. Finally Xerxes spoke, anguish etched on every line of his face. "It shall be done," he breathed in a whisper, then turned away.

That was not enough for Amestris. "I beg your pardon, my lord," she said haughtily. "I did not hear your reply."

Xerxes turned back, his eyes filled with rage. Esther shuddered to imagine how it must feel to be the butt of that anger, but Amestris held her ground. "I said, 'It shall be done'!" the king repeated in a voice that shook the pillars of the banqueting pavilion. "The woman is yours." He spun around and, with heavy steps, climbed the stairs to his private table behind the screen.

With the king gone, Amestris addressed the empty air, "I thank you, my lord. I will call for her at my will." Then she sat down, picked up her wine goblet, and drained it.

Esther's hands and feet, her whole body, felt as cold as ice. Gradually, slowly, the hall came to life again, but it was a horrified kind of life, whispers and glances darting around the room, no one daring to speak aloud. From the far end of the table Esther heard tight, strained voices and turned to see what everyone else was watching. Masistes had risen to his feet and was starting up the steps toward the king's table. Someone stepped forward and grabbed his arm. Esther saw with surprise that it was Artabazus, who'd arrived at Parsa only in the past day or two. Yet why be surprised? Who else would dare throw himself between the king and his brother?

Masistes shook off Artabazus' grip and started forward again, his hand on the hilt of the dagger he wore at his waist. Artabazus stood in front of him, blocking him with his bulk. There was a short, whispered argument. Everyone in the hall knew what Artabazus must be saying, for Masistes was courting death, not only for his wife but for himself, by approaching the king uninvited at such a moment. After a long minute, Masistes turned on his heel and stalked out of the hall. Artaynte still sat alone. She looked as if she had been drinking the haoma, as if her body sat at the table while her soul had been spirited off to another world.

Lord Admatha, the king's chief minister, had been summoned to the king's table a few moments before. Now he stepped forward into the quiet chaos. "My lords and ladies," his thin but loud voice crackled across the room, "in the name of the King of Kings, you are thanked for your presence here tonight and bidden to go to your own places. This feast is done."

Esther stood up with the others at the royal table. There would clearly be no processional music, no formal parades. This terrible night everyone was eager to return to their own rooms as quickly as possible to prepare for whatever might come. As Esther took a step forward she found herself face to face with the princess Amytis. Large, gorgeous golden eyes, exactly like her mother's, caught and held Esther's eyes for a moment.

"Artaynte may have been married to a prince, but she was nothing but a concubine—my father's prostitute," the girl hissed for Esther's ears alone. "My mother is a true queen, her blood as noble as my father's, and she *will* have what she wants. Now, and always." She could have said, *Beware,* but she didn't need to.

Esther felt blind as she stumbled out of the hall. Most nights after dinner—including most of the nights of the feast—she was given word to come to the king's chambers. Tonight she prayed that no one would speak to her. She could not imagine what Xerxes might want from her, from anyone, tonight. And yet—surely he would not want to be alone? It seemed beyond thought, beyond imagination. She felt that a palatable force of evil had been unleashed, a force that changed everything.

Reaching the perimeter of the pavilion, she heard a commotion behind her. Royal guards were seizing Artaynte, who struggled and cried out. Esther stood as transfixed as everyone else, watching this elegant noblewoman twist and writhe in the grip of two armed men. Artaynte's voice, shrill and desperate, cut the air. "My lord! My husband! Masistes!" And when no answer came, she tried again: "My lord king! My lord king!"

No one answered. No one came to her rescue. Under Amestris' impassive eye she was carried screaming from the hall.

In the darkness outside, Esther started across the grass and stopped, rain-soaked. She had forgotten it was raining. Rain at Parsa in midsummer was as strange as unicorns prancing down from the hills. Yet tonight it was raining. She felt confused, disoriented, and frightened. One of her servant girls had accompanied her to the banquet and was supposed to wait until she was ready to leave, or had need of service. Esther couldn't even remember who her attendant had been, yet no member of the royal family would walk back to their apartments without an escort. Tonight, of all nights, Esther did not want to walk alone.

A hand touched her arm—not the timid touch of a maidservant, but the firm touch of someone who knew her need and was there to take care of her. She turned, grateful, knowing she was safe even before she saw that it was Hathakh, ready to take her home.

"I came as soon as I heard," he said.

Esther shivered. The night was hot, but the rain was cool on her skin. Perhaps that was why she shivered. Perhaps not. Hathakh had one of her cloaks over his arm and now placed it around her shoulders.

Esther said nothing until they were well away from the pavilion, from the other departing guests. She found that despite the cloak she was shaking. "Oh, Hathakh, it was terrible. She is so—so *evil.*" Her voice dropped to a whisper on the last word. "And the king—I always thought he was strong. I know he has his weaknesses, but in public, in his court, in his kingdom, he has always reigned supreme. Yet she made him look a fool and a weakling. And surely, Hathakh, surely she's not still angry at Artaynte for being the king's lover two years ago?"

Inside her own apartment now, she let her voice slightly rise, but Hathakh put his finger to his lips. "It's me she's sending a warning to. I mean, it's horrible, of course, for Artaynte and horrible for the king, because now all his troubles with Masistes will come to a head. But oh, Hathakh, I'm frightened. Frightened for myself."

Her steward stood in front of her, less than an arm's breadth away. She stumbled forward. Hathakh put his hands on her shoulders to steady her, and Esther fell closer, seeking comfort, letting him place his arms around her and hold her as if she were a crying child. For a heartbeat she felt safe again. The world was still a huge and terrifying place, but she had this one place of comfort, of refuge, of friendship.

Then Ayana was there, adding her own embrace to Hathakh's, drawing Esther into a circle of protection. "It must have been terrible, terrible to see, Esther," she said. Neither she nor Hathakh said, "my lady." They were not deferential but protective, caring for her as Mordecai and Rivka must have done when she came to them as an orphaned child. Esther felt a sudden longing for the simple, safe world of her childhood home, a longing so acute it made her throat ache.

"Come sit down. I have Talia bringing some spiced wine," Ayana said, leading Esther out of the central hall toward her own bedchamber. Hathakh followed. He generally did not come into Esther's private rooms, but tonight he seemed reluctant to let her out of his sight.

Voices echoed throughout the courtyards. Beyond them rumbled voices all over the palace—shouts and cries, angry confrontations. Esther still half expected to receive a summons to the king. She did not know whether to be relieved or disappointed when none came. She had no desire to sleep, and she sat up telling Ayana and Hathakh the story of what had happened at the banquet over and over.

After a few hours, Hathakh went out to see what news he could find. It was near dawn when he returned.

"Nobody knows what has happened to Artaynte," he said, "except that she is taken into Queen Amestris' custody. But Prince Masistes has fled, and with him many of his own men at arms, and other nobles who support him."

"Where is he going?" Ayana asked.

"To Bactria," Esther replied without thought. Bactria was Masistes' own satrapy. There he would be able to raise support.

"He will rebel against the king?" Ayana said.

"What else can he do?" Esther replied. "He was in the field against Greece when the king took his wife as a lover. Taking her back after that must have galled him, but now to have her handed over for torture and maybe death?" She shuddered. "He hates the king anyway, and has needed only an excuse to rebel. Others would not have supported him for mere jealousy, but this touches his honor far more. He will have supporters, and there will be a revolt."

Nobody spoke. There seemed nothing more to say. Gray dawn light spilled into the chambers. Outside, the rain still beat against the walls.

At last Esther slept. She awoke at about noon, and soon afterward Ayana came up with a tray of food.

"Is there any news?" Esther said.

Ayana nodded. "The king is preparing a force to march toward Bactria and try to put down Masistes' revolt before it even starts. They expect to leave tomorrow morning. Megabyzus will ride with the king to command the force. Artabazus will stay here to keep order in the palace. Amestris is still holding Artaynte in her quarters. Nobody knows what has happened to her, though messengers from the king have already gone there. Some think he's requesting Artaynte's release, but no one knows for sure. And this morning two new eunuchs came here from the king. He has assigned them to be your personal bodyguard."

"He thinks I need a bodyguard?"

"I think you do," Ayana said, "and I'm glad the king agrees. Queen Amestris did this to show her power, my lady. She wants to send a clear message to any rivals—past, present, or future—that no matter where the king's affections may lie, she is the great queen, and no one will take her power or authority away from her."

"Or her son's right to the throne," Esther said, involuntarily laying a hand over her womb.

"Exactly," Ayana said.

That day dragged by, gray and threatening another storm. Esther stayed in her quarters, not eager to venture out into the rest of the palace. The lethargy that had dogged her throughout her pregnancy had a tighter grip on her now. She wanted only to sleep, to retreat from this strange world in which even a princess—even, perhaps, a queen— was not safe from a vengeful, powerful woman. Day blurred into night. She heard the next morning that the king and his troops had marched out from Parsa at dawn, heading toward Bactria, hoping to intercept Masistes before he could raise enough support for a revolt. He had left without sending any word to her, except the gift of two bodyguards.

Esther had little need of bodyguards in the days that followed, for she rarely left her quarters. That same strange lethargy seemed to cloak her. She slept for hours at a time, even in the day. "Are you worried about me?" she asked Ayana, who came herself to bring food up to Esther when she did not want to eat.

"I was," Ayana said. "But not anymore."

"No? Why not?"

"I talked to Hutossa," Ayana said. Hutossa was the midwife. "She said that it's common when women are with child and they experience something, or see something, that frightens them. It's as if their bodies turn inward, knowing that the most important thing is to protect the child within."

"I wish she'd told me that," Esther said, taking a piece of bread spread with cheese. "I wouldn't have thought I was going mad or falling into despair. But I think she's right. I didn't know it, not in words, but I am frightened for the baby. And I think my body is try- ing to make me rest, to care for the child and protect it."

Ayana was silent. "What is it?" Esther pressed. "Is there news?"

For several days she'd not asked for palace news. She didn't have the courage to know. But a look at Ayana's face told her she'd guessed right— something had happened. "Tell me," she insisted. "There is news?"

"There is news."

"Is it the king? Has he met Masistes?"

"No, not the king."

"Artaynte, then?"

Ayana nodded.

"Tell me, Ayana. What has Amestris done to her? Is she dead?"

Ayana shook her head slowly, speaking as if the words were being pulled from her throat. "No, not dead, though I'm certain she is begging the gods to die. Amestris' soldiers tortured and mutilated her, then put her on display outside Amestris' quarters so that all could see. After an hour or two Artazabazus ordered that she be taken back inside—out of sight. I'm still not sure how he compelled Amestris to agree."

"He can be very persuasive," Esther mused. She studied her hands, then placed them across her belly. "Ayana," she whispered, "what was done to her?"

"You don't want to know."

"No, I don't want to know. . . . But I think I should."

Ayana sighed heavily, set down her plate of food, and quietly told her.

"She is a monster, Ayana," Esther whispered.

"Then the world is full of monsters, my lady. She may be worse than many, but people will do very cruel things in the name of power, or revenge—or even love."

"Ayana, I wish I'd never been taken to the harem," said Esther as tears filled her eyes. She sat up on the bed, hugging her knees like a little girl.

"Hush now, hush," Ayana whispered, rubbing Esther's back with firm, sure strokes. "You cannot say that. What has happened has happened. Your god has led you here. This is your life as it is, as it was meant to be."

"It frightens me."

Ayana said nothing, but began to sing, an eerie high-pitched lullaby of her homeland. Esther left the rest of her meal untouched and lay down on the bed, letting Ayana rub her aching back and sing to her until she fell asleep.

Over the days and weeks that followed, conflicting reports filtered back to the harem from the world outside. Artaynte was dead. No, she was alive, but still Amestris' prisoner. Then finally, what turned out to be the truth, and perhaps the cruelest of all—Amestris had sent Artaynte back, under guard, to the palace she shared with Masistes near Ecbatana. Some said that Masistes had gone there himself and seen what had been done to his wife, and sworn vengeance on the king. Others said that, all unaware of her fate, he had gone ahead into Bactria to raise an army for revolt.

Finally, one hot, sultry midsummer day, Artabazus himself came to call. Esther, feeling stronger, was sitting in the courtyard outside her

rooms, sewing with Ayana and Roxane. Artabazus, flanked by two soldiers, came toward them. Here at Parsa the women's quarters were less
secluded than the harem at Susa. Men sometimes passed through the
women's court on their way from Xerxes' new palace to the royal trea-
suries, so the sight of a man in the courtyard did not arouse the same
amazement it would have done at Susa.

Artabazus bowed before Esther. "My lady queen," he said.

"Good day, Artabazus." She had not spoken to him since his arrival back at Parsa, just before the ill-fated birthday feast, but she
heard of him everywhere. Only his iron hand seemed to be keeping order in a palace rife with rumor, discontent, and even rebellion. He had simultaneously controled Queen Amestris from
flaunting her vengeance on Artaynte, and protected Amestris from
those supporters of Masistes who had sworn to see her punished. He
looked like he had aged five years in the past weeks, and Esther was
not surprised.

"I have news for you, my lady," he said. Roxane quickly stood up
and asked to be excused. Ayana glanced at Esther, but Esther said, "My
maid may stay. I trust her as myself."

"Very well."

"Will you sit, Lord Artabazus?"

"No, my lady, I'm more comfortable on my feet. We have news
from the king, my lady. Not gossip—he has sent a courier."

"Truly? What has happened?"

"He met his brother's force near the border of Bactria. Prince
Masistes had a few hundred men joined with him, but the king's force
easily defeated them. Prince Masistes was killed, and his army slaughtered or scattered. The king will be returning to Parsa."

That was it, then—a handful of words, and the sordid business
was finished. As was the long-smoldering rivalry between the brothers. All neatly tidied away with nothing but a pile of dead bodies to
show for it all.

"You are sure this news is reliable?"

"Yes, my lady. But that is not all. A courier came this morning
from Susa. You will remember the two eunuchs who plotted to kill the
king, before we came to Parsa? One died quickly; the other has been
kept in chains and tortured ever since. He finally revealed that he was
in the pay of Prince Masistes."

Esther tried to grasp what this might mean. "So the prince was plotting against the king? But no one could have known this before . . . before . . ."

"Before Queen Amestris acted," Artabazus said. "It puts a different complexion on things, though, doesn't it? I must go. I came to you first, after Lord Admatha, of course." The old councillor still wielded nominal power in the palace and the land, even though Artabazus was clearly the real ruler in Xerxes' absence. "I must deliver this news to the other queens, including Queen Amestris, though I do not think she will welcome a visit from me." He smiled wryly. "It is my hope, though, that it will be of most interest to you, for it is to you that the king will turn when he returns."

"Is that what you know, or what you hope, Lord Artabazus?"

"What I hope, my lady. As you know. Now, if you will excuse me please, I must go."

Esther rose with him as he turned to walk away, and fell into step with him until they were out of hearing of Ayana or the guards. "Artabazus, you pin too many hopes on my supposed influence with the king. I could do nothing to prevent this terrible tragedy."

Artabazus frowned, creasing his already-wrinkled brow further. "Queen Esther, nothing and no one but Ahura Mazda could have prevented this, and he chose not to. We do not question. But the king will come back broken and devastated. I know him. He loves his honor— and he loved his brother, once. And neither have survived this conflict. He will have need of you."

Esther caught his eyes a moment, wondering what it was she needed to say. Then she found words. "I will try, my lord. Only—do not hate me if I fail."

He took her hand and kissed it, a courtly gesture by a man with few courtly graces. He seemed awkward doing it, but there was nothing awkward in his eyes or voice as he said, "I could not hate you, my lady, or blame you if you fail to do the impossible. But I love my king, as you do. Only try."

"I will try."

Soon the news of the king's victory and his return was all over the harem. No one was surprised when Queen Amestris departed suddenly for her own properties. Irdabama, too, went to her own lands, and Parmys returned to Susa. Even the king's lesser wives, it seemed, did not want to be present for his return. Except Esther. Esther stayed at Parsa, in her quarters. She lay in bed at night with a hand over her belly. Hutossa had told her that soon, now, she would be able to feel the babe quicken to life inside her womb. She waited.

One night, very late, Esther awakened from a dream of noise and confusion. She didn't even realize her hand lay on her belly until she felt something like the fluttering of a bird trapped beneath her skin. She held her breath. It came again.

"Ayana! Ayana!" she called.

Ayana hurried from the adjoining chamber. "Put your hand here," Esther said. "Feel it? Can you feel him?"

A slow smile lit Ayana's dark face. "Your prince is knocking at the doors of his palace," she said, and held Esther's hand.

Ayana returned to bed. Esther lay feeling the baby move until, finally, he must have gone to sleep, and she did too.

She awoke a second time to a commotion outside her doors—not imagined this time, but real. Talia, who slept at the foot of Esther's bed, flew up, lit an oil lamp, and rushed out to the main hall. Esther heard voices.

Talia returned a moment later, wide-eyed. "My lady queen, the king has returned."

Esther sat up, struggling for a wrap to throw around her shoulders. "And has he summoned me?"

"No. No, my lady. He is here, right now. He is hurrying up to your chamber." The girl quivered like a frightened rabbit.

"He is the king, Talia. He may go where he wants." Esther's heart pounded in her throat as she dismissed the servant girl. She could hear a man's heavy tread in the corridor outside. It was an unfamiliar sound to her, for the eunuchs moved as noiselessly as women. A loud, familiar voice barked orders as he passed her servants' quarters. She could hear, prominent among them, the demand for wine.

Then he was in her bedroom, tall and commanding, but swaying slightly. He had come to her first of all, she saw, for he was in his riding clothes, and he smelled of horses as well as of wine. "Were you waiting for me, Esther?" he asked, his voice harsh as a dull knife blade.

"My lord, I have been waiting for you ever since you went away."

He stripped off his clothes as he spoke. His boots, cloak, swordbelt, and tunic fell to the ground. "So you know, then, of my great victory? How I faced down my brother and slew him for the terrible crime of daring to defend his wife? How I boldly stood up for the right of my own wife, my great Queen Amestris, to torture and mutilate and kill anyone she desires?" Here was one person at least who did not whisper when he spoke Amestris' name; he almost shouted it.

A servant appeared in the doorway with a jug of wine and two goblets. Xerxes took a filled goblet, tilting it up and swallowing in a frantic motion, then threw the vessel across the room. Esther sat on the bed feeling oddly calm, even detached, as he raged. He came and sat beside her, towering over her. She had never guessed that love, fear, and pity could be so entwined.

"Are you proud of me, my wife? Have I not bravely defended my honor? I am Xerxes the Great, King of Kings! Neither to the weak nor the powerful did I do wrong." His laughter was without humor, almost turning into a sob at the end.

"The Prince Masistes was plotting revolt against you, my lord. We know that for certain now. Even if his wife had not been—dishonored—you would still have had to fight him."

"How wise, how very wise. And how true. He was a fool, Esther."

Xerxes was on his feet again, pacing, his restless energy looking for an outlet. "He wanted an excuse to fight me. He had wanted it for years. He and all his followers who called me a weak king, a king in defeat. But they never dreamed of an excuse like this! Perhaps he never truly mourned her. I thought of that. Perhaps he was glad—glad to see her sacrificed for his own ambition. Poor Artaynte—everyone's pawn. Even mine. *Even mine, Esther.* You women are such fools!"

He gripped a tapestried wall hanging and ripped at it. It tore and fell, and he grabbed another and another. He was very drunk and very angry. Esther watched as his rage spent itself on her wall hangings and bed hangings, goblets and vases. Then he turned to the bed, to her, and she saw that his anger was not spent at all. He gripped her upper arms with his powerful hands. She remembered the bruises she'd seen long ago on a concubine's arms. She remembered, too, her promise to Artabazus, that she would try to heal the king's wounds. But at what cost to herself?

Late, very late that night, Xerxes the Great, King of Kings, fell asleep across the bed of Esther, his wife. Later still, Esther slept too. Once she awoke to find his head buried against her chest. She thought he was sleeping until he turned toward her and said, "I killed him with my own sword, you know. By my own hand. My brother. It happens all the time in royal houses, but I've never done it before. My own brother." He turned his face away, and she felt rather than saw his tears.

The sun was well into the sky before the king left that morning. Within an hour after he departed, Esther began to bleed. Ayana sent for Hutossa the midwife, who stayed by her through that day and the night that followed, until it was all over. Hutossa and Ayana sat beside her through the long hours, through the fear and the hope and the pain and the loss, till the baby who had so briefly quickened to life was gone from her body, gone from this world, gone to whatever gods there were.

CHAPTER 12

Esther sat by her window, looking out at the rain. Autumn was drawing to a close. Soon her birthday would come, then winter. Soon it would be one year since she had first gone to the king.

The court was back at Susa now. She knew Hathakh and Ayana had hoped she would be happier back at Susa. It was her home, after all; the place she knew best. She thought she would never grow to love Parsa now, or even want to return there. It was too haunted with dark memories. But that didn't mean she was happy in the palace at Susa. Happiness seemed as elusive as a bird fluttering on a far-off branch. She remembered, in childhood, coaxing wary birds to come perch on her finger. If happiness could be coaxed like that, she would, if only to ease her friends' worry. But she had lost the knack of coaxing happiness.

Despair had shadowed her like a faithful lapdog ever since she'd lost her baby. She found that the lethargy and tiredness she'd experienced during pregnancy only increased now that her baby had died. She could sleep through the morning and awaken still tired. She no longer wanted to pick up the oud or to walk, or talk, or ride. She found that she could sit for hours simply staring, thinking about nothing, feeling almost nothing.

Only when a summons came from the king did she make an effort. She put on a cheerful demeanor even as she put on cosmetics and fine clothes, all masks to hide her true self. For King Xerxes she attempted to be charming, attractive, seductive. She knew he wasn't fooled. They made love when he requested her, but they no longer talked together or laughed together. Since Parsa, since Masistes' death, he was wrapped in his own troubles. He needed a woman who could draw him out of his gloom, not a woman who carried her own darkness within her.

Anyway, she had been called very rarely these past months. Once or twice each month, no more than that. The harem was back in business again. Concubines and new virgins were again being summoned nightly to the king's quarters. Sooner or later, Esther supposed, he would find a new favorite. Candidates were already said to be jockeying for position.

She couldn't have found the subject less interesting.

Talia came into the room carrying a tray of fruit and set it down beside her. She waited a moment. Esther glanced and nodded thanks, and Talia left. Esther looked at the fruit without interest. She was still staring at it moments later when Ayana came into the room.

Ayana stood for a moment, then sat down without being invited. She reached forward to help herself to a polished apple from Esther's platter. Ayana's deferential demeanor was wearing very thin these days. "Hathakh and I have just come from the storehouses," she began.

Esther said nothing.

"It took a long time," Ayana went on, "because we had to find Shasgaaz himself and argue with him. He's trying to have your household rations cut. We pointed out that the household had not decreased any, but he says your circumstances have changed. I can't imagine what he meant by that, but at any rate, we prevailed—eventually. He's going to continue giving trouble."

"You know what he meant," Esther said dully. "He meant that I am no longer a favorite with the king. A decrease in rations shows a decrease in status."

"That command would have to come from the king himself, I would think," Ayana said. Her voice was livelier. She was obviously encouraged to hear Esther reply at all. "But it's a good sign that Shasgaaz is trying to make your life difficult. It must mean that Amestris still sees you as a threat."

"I can't think why."

"She knows the king still cares for you, I suppose." Ayana paused, allowing time for any personal revelations Esther chose to make, but none were forthcoming. "Although it is true there are rumors of a new favorite."

Esther looked up, surprised. She wasn't surprised that the king had a new favorite, not at all. She was surprised that Ayana would share the information with her. Her servants and friends tiptoed around her these days, speaking in low voices, trying to keep upsetting news from her. But Ayana had always been forthright. Perhaps she had decided plain speaking was the best thing.

"Who is it?" Esther finally asked.

"Manya," Ayana said. "You remember Manya?"

Esther remembered Manya. She had entered the harem about the same time they both had. She was a pretty, small, spiteful girl who had been good friends with Raiya. Raiya, always so concerned about her chances of becoming queen, had actually never gone in to the king. Instead, after Esther's rise in favor, Raiya went into the service of Queen Amestris. Her friend Manya had also waited in vain for a call to the king's bedchamber. By the time her turn had come around, Esther was already betrothed to the king, and newer virgins were left to wait. But now, apparently, Manya's turn had come.

"I heard she is summoned to him again tonight," Ayana said, watching Esther's face closely as she spoke. "It is the third time this week."

"She must be quite talented," Esther said sharply. She knew Ayana was wondering what she felt about this. Esther wasn't sure herself. She had thought little about the new procession of girls going to her husband's chambers. It wasn't as if she had ever expected to be his only lover. He had other wives; he had concubines. He was a king. But the thought of a new favorite, a new Odatis, did hurt a little. In some way, Esther had grown close to this man with whom it was impossible to be truly close. She had not really understood their relationship, but she had valued it. Yet she didn't feel she had the energy to care very much, certainly not to launch an attack to win back her royal husband's attention, which was clearly what Ayana was hoping for.

"I can't see that there's anything I can do about it, anyway," she said aloud. "I don't want to hear about Manya—or the king. Isn't there any more news?"

"Well . . ." Ayana hesitated. With the first flash of real spirit she'd shown in months, Esther said, "Come on, girl. Surely you can find one bit of palace gossip that isn't going to make me burst into tears."

Ayana smiled. "There is news, but I am afraid it might make you cry indeed. Roxane has had her baby."

At that a flood of emotion came rushing up in Esther's heart. She loved Roxane, and was glad for her happiness. But she had held herself aloof from her friend these past months. The sight of Roxane's growing belly, her husband's tender pride, Roxane's glowing skin and shining eyes, simply hurt too much. She did not summon Roxane to play for her. She had Ayana send gifts of food and clothes instead.

Now the baby had been born. Once, Esther had imagined her own child and Roxane's playing together. She felt a sudden, visceral longing to see, touch, and hold this new baby; yet to do so, knowing it was Roxane's and not her own, would break her heart.

"Is it healthy? And Roxane? Is she well?"

"Yes, a healthy boy. And Roxane is well."

"Send a gift," Esther said. "You'll know best what they need. And send my congratulations. See about having their rations increased."

"Is that all?" Ayana said.

"That's all," said Esther.

But it wasn't. She lay awake that night, sleepless for the first time in weeks, letting her thoughts wander from Manya in the king's bedchamber to her friend Roxane in her bedchamber, holding her sleeping baby. The picture tormented her. She knew it would hurt, but she wanted to be with her friend, to see her, to congratulate her. She wanted to hold the baby even though she would have to give it back.

Three days later she asked Ayana to take her to Roxane's and Lilaios' quarters to see the baby.

They lived in the palace, in the warren of apartments adjoining the outer court where upper servants and minor functionaries such as court musicians and poets stayed. There Esther found Roxane reclining on a couch, nursing her baby boy. She was still in the middle of her 40 days of seclusion, but an exception could be made for a visitor such as the queen, if the mother was willing—and Roxane was willing.

Roxane looked wonderful, lying on a long upholstered couch in her son's nursery. *She's far prettier than she's ever been,* Esther thought as Roxanne returned her smile. Roxanne's skin glowed, her dark eyes sparkled, and she and the child together seemed bathed in a brilliant light. Her smile was radiant. "Thank you for coming, my lady," she said. "I know it must have been difficult for you. I dreamed of you and your baby visiting me and mine, one day."

She was the first person who had been so bluntly honest, and it felt right. "Do you want to hold him?" Roxane asked as the baby fell asleep after nursing. She handed the small wrapped bundle to Esther.

"We've got another slave girl to be a nursemaid, but we couldn't afford a wet nurse and I didn't want one anyway. I like nursing him."

"Are you sure?" Esther asked, adjusting the baby comfortably in her arms. "I can pay, if you want a wet nurse."

"No, no, it's very kind of you, but no. Perhaps later, when I begin playing at court again. Not now. All I want to do is hold him and feed him. I could look at his little face all day long. It's very lazy, but I like it."

Esther looked down at the solemn tiny face, very red and unattractive, peeking out from between the wraps. She thought of her own child and felt a physical pain in her stomach, as if just now the baby had been ripped from her womb. But this was not her child—it was Roxane's. Roxane's and Lilaios', the child they would love and care for and raise. Esther felt tears spill down her cheeks before she knew she was crying. With the tears came sobs, and her body shook, but she still held the small warm bundle of life. The baby didn't stir or awaken, and neither Roxane nor Ayana spoke or did anything to break the spell as Esther finally grieved for her lost child.

After that, she visited often. She found the visits with Roxane and the baby healing rather than hurtful. Lilaios was often there, too. Men were not supposed to be very interested in babies, but Lilaios doted on his infant son and was already composing an ode to him. It was a very private ode, of course—one that would never be performed, but one that Lilaios saw as his greatest work. Esther found she could indeed bear seeing the little family together. Some days their happiness was the only thing that seemed right in the world.

While Roxane nursed the baby and sometimes fell asleep with him in her arms, Esther talked to Lilaios about poetry. He was well educated and well read, and it seemed ages since she had talked to anyone who knew that world—the world of words and ideas. For so long her life had been bounded by harem gossip and, while she was with the king, politics and palace building. When Lilaios talked to her about epics and ballads, about the great religious hymns of the Avestas, Esther felt her interest in the outside world beginning to awaken for the first time.

One day she had an idea. "Lilaios," she asked, "could you find me copies of some tablets or scrolls? some poems? I want to read the Avestas."

"Yes, Your Highness," Lilaios said, a little surprised.

"I was taught to read as a girl," Esther told him.

"Very commendable of your father. More women should be educated," said Lilaios, which in turn surprised her. "I can find tablets or scrolls for you."

"And do you know where to find the scrolls of—other peoples, other religions? I would like to compare them. When I was young, our—our family had friends who were Jewish. You know of the Jews? I would like to read their writings. And perhaps . . . I am interested in the gods, in what people believe. Maybe you could suggest something else I could read."

Lilaios bowed slightly. "I will search for you, my lady, and see what I can find."

A few weeks later he visited her apartment bearing a collection of tablets and scrolls. She had given him her personal seal to obtain permission to borrow them, and he had done well. He laid before her a copy of the Avestas, a translation of some passages from the Indian holy books, the Vedas, and—the thing she really wanted—a large scroll owned by a Jewish scribe which contained several portions from the Jewish Law.

"How can I thank you, Lilaios? This is wonderful!" Esther caressed the scrolls in her hands. It had been so long since she'd read anything except Hathakh's endless lists inscribed on clay tablets.

"If there is anything there you have difficulty with, my lady, I would be honored to read to you," Lilaios offered.

"Thank you again. That's very kind." And useful, because Esther wasn't sure her education was equal to everything these scrolls contained.

"The Jewish one, particularly, is difficult, as it's written in their Hebrew tongue. I have difficulty with it, but I know a little and can learn more if you want me to read it for you," Lilaios added.

Esther was about to reply that that was the one scroll she was sure she could read. Mordecai had taught her the rudiments of reading and writing in Aramaic, the language they spoke, and a little of the Persian script, used for ceremonies and formal writing. But he had taught her to read fairly well in Hebrew, "because every Jew should know the language of our Law," he had explained. "I have no son to teach it to, so I will teach you."

But telling Lilaios that would certainly give away that she was a Jew, and so far only her most intimate friends—Ayana and Hathakh—knew of her background. She wanted to include Lilaios and Roxane in that circle, but Mordecai's warnings rang in her ears.

As spring grew out of winter during the next few weeks, she spent some time puzzling over the scrolls herself. The court was preparing for another move to Parsa. The queens Amestris, Parmys, and Irdabama planned to travel separately to their own estates for at least part of the spring before coming to Parsa. But Esther, who had no private estates, had orders to accompany the king, so her household was preparing to move. In the midst of the chaos and confusion of packing and planning, Esther sat in her chamber, no longer staring dully out at the gardens but avidly reading the Hebrew scroll Lilaios had found for her.

It was one of the Books of Moses, the Books of the Law, the most sacred writings, Mordecai had told her. She had heard him read some passages from the Law, and recite others, at Passover and other important occasions, but she herself had read only a few short passages. Most of what she now read was new to her.

It told the story of humanity from the creation of the world up to the point where the people of Abraham, the people who would become Jews, were marked as God's chosen people and brought into Egypt, and saved from famine. Esther knew many of the stories, but reading the words herself for the first time gave her the feeling of opening a door into the past—the world's past and the past of her people. She read about Adam and Eve's choice to disobey God and fall into sin, about the great flood, about God's call to a man named Abram and the promise that Abram's son would become the ancestor of a great nation of people who would bless all the world.

Shivers ran down Esther's spine as she read that. She was sitting on her bed late at night, reading by the flickering light of two oil lamps. She read in private, while in public, Lilaios came to her hall along with Roxane and the baby and read from the Persian Avestas or the Indian Vedas. Esther's servants and sometimes a visiting friend gathered to hear these readings. To Lilaios, Esther pretended she was not very interested in hearing the Hebrew scroll read. In secret she devoured it, feeling the strange sense of being marked out by a God who had, inexplicably, chosen her people for His own. For the first time in her life she felt truly a part of a people, a people with a history, a past and a future. Whatever else she was, Esther realized, she was a Jew. What God had chosen her for, she still didn't know, but she *was* chosen. It was in her blood.

Knowing that made a difference, though not at first in her outward life. It made a difference inside where she had felt hollow and empty, discarded by God and by her king. It made a difference when they rode down to Parsa, Esther in her closed carriage with Ayana and her other maids, the king in front as always—this year with Manya traveling in his carriage, and Manya riding beside him on horseback when he chose to ride.

Just as Esther had ridden, last year.

"Soon I suppose we'll hear she's carrying his child," Esther speculated to Ayana one day on the journey as the carriage rocked and swayed them down the rutted road.

Ayana looked surprised. "No, I do not think we will hear that."

"No? Why not?"

Again Ayana raised her eyebrows. "I often forget how little you hear," she said. "A servant has far more freedom than a queen, though a queen can have her sources of information, too, if she cares. You have not cared much of late, have you?"

"For a while I cared about nothing," Esther admitted. "Now I am starting to care again. But I don't know how much I care about Manya bearing the king a child. After all, I have no child of my own for whom I can hope for a throne or power." Even those words—I have no child—did not sting as they once had.

"It is good to see you caring again," Ayana said. "And I think you are right not to become too obsessed about Manya and the king. That is exactly what Amestris hopes you will do, I think."

"Amestris? Why should she care? Am I any threat to her any longer?"

"Of course you are. You are not a mere concubine. The king has married you. When you do have a child, that child will have status, perhaps even be a contender for the throne. She wants to eliminate any threat to Darius. Queen Amestris has never cared about keeping the king's love. She's not a sentimental woman. You should know that. Power is what she cares for. Another queen is a threat to her power."

"So you think she actually wants Manya to be the king's favorite right now?"

Ayana leaned forward, her voice just above a whisper even though all the girls in the carriage were Esther's, all trusted and known. "Of course. As long as Manya supplants you, that's good in Amestris' eyes. Remember, Manya is a friend of Raiya, and Raiya is now high in the queen's favor. Raiya is in a position not only to promote Manya, but to know the crucial thing about her."

"The crucial thing?"

"Manya may be pretty, or a good dancer, or good in bed," Ayana said. "Those things might interest the king. But none of them would make Amestris support and promote her. Manya's one invaluable gift is her infirmity—she is unable to bear children."

"What? Really?"

Ayana nodded. "Since her girlhood she has never had her monthly courses. The court physicians, when she was a virgin in the harem, suspected that something was wrong with her inside, something that would prevent her ever carrying or bearing a child. She is barren."

Esther could see how that made sense. Amestris would never encourage a rival who might bear a child to rival hers, but a pretty, barren young girl to draw the king's attention away from the beloved new wife who might well bear him children—that all fit. Especially with Raiya at her side, moving the pieces on the board. "But Amestris fails to consider that I may be barren too," she added sadly.

"Don't be a fool," said Ayana, adding, "my lady," rather belatedly for the sake of the other servants who might still be listening, though they were all either dozing or chatting among themselves. "You have miscarried one child. Some women miscarry three or four, and still bear healthy sons. You can conceive, that much we know. Someday you will bear the king a child."

Esther was silent, thinking of Sarah, the wife of Abraham, who waited all her life for the promised son. She thought of Sarah's long barren years and how she'd finally laughed at God's promise—and then at 90 years of age held her newborn in her arms. Impossible! Yet the God she read of in the Books of Moses was the God of the impossible if He was anything at all.

A few days later, at Parsa, Esther saw Manya face to face for the first time since the girl's rise to favor. Both were crossing the central courtyard of the harem. Manya was with a maid, going toward the king's palace. At once Esther thought that Manya must have been summoned to the king. It was early evening, and she was dressed in an elegant but revealing gown. When she saw Esther her small pointed face flushed with what might have been triumph, or pride, but she dropped to the ground in a deep bow and said, "Your majesty."

Esther nodded politely. "Good evening, Lady Manya," she said, then went on toward her own quarters. She remembered Tamyris' words on the eve of her wedding to the king. She might fall from royal favor, but she would always be a queen. It was a little comfort, but not much, as she watched the other woman on her way to Xerxes' bedchamber.

More comfort was the growing sense of God's presence she felt as she made her way through the scroll of Moses. She had read about God's call to Abraham to sacrifice Isaac. Recalling her own pain at the loss of a child she had never seen or even held, she could not even imagine how a man could make such a sacrifice. *What if God had asked Sarah?* she wondered. Surely she could not have done it. But then, God had not asked Sarah. He had asked Abraham, and Abraham trusted God's promise so completely that he knew—he must have known—that his God would bring good out of this apparently evil thing.

Sarah had a few moments in the spotlight. Esther read with interest how a foreign king, the Egyptian pharaoh, had taken her into his harem. God had sent plagues on the pharaoh's household to save Sarah's honor. Esther looked up from her scrolls at the woven hangings and fine furniture around her, the trappings of a pagan king's harem. God had done nothing to save Esther from going to King Xerxes' bed. Sometimes it almost seemed God Himself had sent her there. Why was she so different from Sarah? She still did not understand.

Now she was reading about Joseph, great-grandson of Abraham. Another story of trust, of God bringing good out of terrible, incomprehensible evil. Esther felt strangely close to Joseph as she read his story. He too had found himself elevated to power at a pagan court, the confidant of a king. A man, of course, had more choices than a woman, but Joseph's first and most important choice seemed to be trust in God and obedience to Him. That, Esther thought, she could do as well, no matter how dark the circumstances.

After dark, alone, she read the Hebrew scroll, straining her eyesight by the yellow-orange light. In the afternoons and early evenings Lilaios read to her from the Persian scrolls, while Roxane practiced her oud and the baby cooed and gurgled in his cradle. Some of Esther's household came to listen too. She began inviting friends to visit again, as well—Tamyris, Leila, Phratima. Lilaios read with the same ease and grace that he recited:

"Hear with your ears the best things;
　Look upon them with clear-seeing thought,
　for decision between the two Beliefs,
　each man for himself before the Great Consummation,
　bethinking you that it be accomplished to our pleasure.

Now the two primal Spirits,
who reveal themselves in vision as Twins,
are the Better and the Bad, in thought and word and action.
And between these two the wise ones chose aright, the
    foolish not so.
And when these twain Spirits came together in the beginning,
they created Life and Not-Life,
and that at the last Worst Existence shall be to the followers
    of the Lie,
but the Best Existence to him that follows Right."

Esther remembered long ago in the harem—it seemed long ago—listening to Hegai talk about Ahura Mazda and Anghra Mainyu, and wondering how the powers of good and evil could be so evenly balanced from the very beginning of time, creating Good and Evil, Dark and Light, Truth and Lie. Certainly that wasn't the story of the Hebrew scroll. In there it was recorded that an eternal God, a God who was there "in the beginning," had created everything good and perfect. Evil came later, with the tempting serpent and the fall of Adam and Eve.

"Do you think that's true?" she suddenly asked those in the room when Lilaios paused. "I have learned that many different people tell different stories about how the world came to be. The—we Persians say the Ahura Mazda and Anghra Mainyu have been twins from the beginning, creating good and evil. Ayana, what do they say in Ethiopia?"

Ayana, curled quietly in a corner, sewing, looked up, a little surprised. This was an occasion when Esther had guests. She had, in fact, given a dinner for Lilaios and Roxane, Tamyris and Leila, and two women musicians whose skills she admired and who were going to perform with Roxane after the reading. In this company, Ayana did not expect to be called on to speak, but she said quietly, "In childhood I was told tales of the god Wak, who lifted the vault of the heavens above the earth and filled it with stars. He made a man and then asked the man to build his own coffin, and Wak buried him beneath the earth in it. Then he rained down fire from heaven for seven years and made the mountains of the earth. Then he unearthed the man and woke him. Man was lonely, so Wak took his blood and made a woman, a wife for the man. The man and woman had 30 children, but the man was ashamed to have so many and hid 15 of them. Then Wak was angry, and he made the hidden children into animals and demons. That's all I remember of the tale," she finished.

Tamyris and Leila were chuckling. "Why was the man ashamed of his 30 children?" Tamyris asked.

"Because then his god would know that he and his wife must be in bed all the time!" Leila chimed in.

"Is that anything to be ashamed of?" Tamyris countered, and everyone laughed. A few others offered legends they had heard of how the world began, and Lilaios quoted a well-known passage from the Babylonian tale of creation. Then he added, "My lady queen, the book of the Jews I found for you has a lovely tale of creation." With Esther's permission he took up a scroll and began to recite his own Persian translation of the Hebrew words:

"In the beginning God created the heavens and the earth.
Now the earth was formless and empty,
darkness was over the surface of the deep,
and the Spirit of God was hovering over the waters.
And God said, 'Let there be light,' and there was light."

He recited on through the story of the creation of man and the choice he made in the garden to disobey. Roxane picked up her oud again and began to weave music under the words. When Lilaios had finished, the women were quiet a moment, appreciating the story and its performance.

"Perhaps it really was that way," Leila said at last. "Maybe everything was perfect in the beginning, and it was not the gods, but man, who made things go wrong."

"Well, woman, actually," Lilaios couldn't resist pointing out, then had to cover his ears with his hands as all the women argued back with him. Soon the two other musicians joined Roxane in playing. They persuaded Esther to join them, and everyone settled down to hear the music.

When the evening had ended and the guests had gone home, Esther stood alone in her hall. She heard footsteps and looked up to see Hathakh entering the hall. He had just come from supervising the servants' cleanup of the kitchen, which properly ought not to be the steward's job, but Hathakh liked to check every detail in person.

"A good evening, my lady?" he greeted her.

"A very good evening, Hathakh," Esther said, somewhat surprised at herself. She turned to him, smiling. "It has been a long time since I laughed and played music and enjoyed myself."

"It has been a long time since I have seen you smile this way." He crossed the room to stand beside her, smiling down at her. "We have all mourned to see you mourn, my lady queen. Ayana and I most of all, for we have known you longest and best. You have always had the gift of happiness. I hated to see you robbed of it."

"Not robbed, only—misplaced, I suppose. It seems to be coming back, in spite of me," Esther said.

And it was. Throughout that spring at Parsa she could feel herself waking to life again, shaking off the long cold sorrow that imprisoned her since she'd left this place almost a year ago. She went back to music-making with a passion. She dived into learning poetry, religion, legend, both reading on her own and having Lilaios read and recite for her. She entertained—her own friends from the harem, the queens Irdabama and Parmys when they arrived at Parsa, musicians and poets she found in Parsa who were only too glad for a royal patron.

Through it all Manya continued to reign as court favorite, taking the place of honor beside the king at private dinners and on hunts, visiting his chambers regularly, though not exclusively. The harem was still kept busy. Esther appeared at the royal table at official banquets—including the king's birthday, at which no one made any unusual requests. Xerxes had not summoned her to his presence privately since they had arrived at Parsa.

Just past midsummer the summons came. It had been more than a year since Amestris' detestable request at last year's birthday feast. Amestris was on her own estates, as was Irdabama again now. One hot afternoon Esther came in from riding with Ayana—she rode for pleasure now, having acquired the taste—to find Hathakh waiting for her. "The king has asked for you," he said.

"When? Tonight?"

Esther felt irritated to discover that her heart had begun a little dance of its own. She would much rather be completely indifferent to Xerxes, both as a man and as a king, but neither, it seemed, was possible. As king her whole status in the harem and in the world depended upon him. As a man, her husband, she could not entirely cease to care about him, even though she often wished she could.

"Tonight, my lady. You are to join him for a private dinner. No other guests are invited, I am told." Hathakh bowed formally, but his eyes never left her face. Ayana, too, watched her closely.

Esther laughed, lifting the veil of their formality. "You are worried about me, not as my servants but as my friends. Do not worry. Yes, falling from the king's favor hurt me. But I knew it would happen someday, and also knew that eventually he would call me back again, if for no other reason than that a king must try to get sons on his queens. What other purpose have we? However tonight turns out, I will not come home and draw my curtains and weep for another month. But this is inconvenient; I had invited Lilaios and Roxane. Send a messenger to tell them to come tomorrow night instead. Ayana, come help me choose what to wear."

Reaching Xerxes' private chambers, she found him closeted with a few attendants. She waited outside till she'd been announced and received the invitation to come in. The noblemen with him bowed low when she entered. One was Artabazus, whom she'd seen little of lately, as he'd been away, putting out small fires of rebellion in Bactria. His face creased into smiles when their eyes met. Esther hoped they would have a chance to talk soon. Her mind quickly registered the other faces. Only one was a stranger to her, a small dark-haired man with narrow, sharp eyes.

She accepted the men's obeisance even as she sank to prostrate herself before the king, who reached out a hand to lift her to her feet. "My queen," he said. "We are honored with your presence. Gentlemen, you are dismissed."

And they were alone. Xerxes gestured for her to recline on a couch in front of which the table was already set for a meal. He summoned a servant to pour wine for them both, then lifted his goblet toward her. "My lady Esther. It has been too long."

For an instant Esther panicked. She could not think quickly of any response that would not sound like she was reproaching the king for failing to summon her, without suggesting that she did not regret the time apart. Finally she said, "My lord king, all your subjects know that the light of your presence is as the light of the sun, and any day without you is dark."

There was a moment's silence; then Xerxes burst into laughter. "And you said it with such a straight face, my Esther! What a mouthful of praise. It would be better suited to the lips of a poet than the lips of a wife. Tell Lilaios to work it into his next ode. Now that you've said that, you may, of course, scold me for failing to pay you enough attention. All my wives do."

Esther smiled up at him, but she was still treading cautiously. "All your wives know, my lord king, that you have many demands on your time. I am sure they are all grateful, as I am, for any opportunity to be in your gracious presence."

This time he did not laugh, but smiled and nodded, as if she had scored a point in some game whose rules were too complex to be written down. "I am pleased to be able to say you are looking well, Esther," he said after a moment.

"Thank you, my lord."

"The last time you came to my chambers, you were sad, and sadness robs a woman's beauty. I hear that you are busy now, that you have musicians coming to play at your court, that you are giving banquets and hiring poets to recite for you."

"All these things are true, my lord. I have ever had a great interest in music and poetry." A servant came and placed a plate before her: lamb, lentils, greens. Another servant refilled the king's goblet.

"I am glad to hear it. Your protégé, Lilaios, and his wife—the musician—are very gifted. I have had him perform for me several times lately, and he is composing a poem for me to be performed upon our return to Susa in the fall. You have excellent taste in poets."

"Thank you, my lord."

The conversation continued like that throughout the dinner. It was somewhat formal, awkward in places—though not unpleasant—skimming only the surface of the thoughts each was hiding. Esther steered the conversation away from herself through poetry and music, to the rise and fall of newly popular court musicians and poets, to artists and architects, and finally on to what was still the king's favorite subject, the ongoing expansion of the palace complex.

"Have you passed by the Gate of All Lands lately? The bulls are taking shape," Xerxes told her.

"I have not seen them since we entered Parsa in the spring, my lord, but I hear of their progress. They must be magnificent."

"They will be," Xerxes said, staring into his goblet as if he could see the sculptures reflected there. "Working in stone is a very different thing from commanding an army. The king chooses an artisan, the artisan begins his work, and it takes a lifetime to see the result take shape. In war the king gives an order, his generals carry it out, and by nightfall thousands of men are dead and a reputation is lost or won."

He looked up at her and said again, "It is a very different thing."

It is a better thing, Esther thought, thinking of the men dead on battlefields. Only a handful died in the building of a palace. A workman had fallen from a scaffold the week before last, but it was nothing compared to the losses in war. "It will last longer, too," was what she said aloud.

"You must see it all," he said suddenly. "Come ride with me tomorrow when I go to inspect the works."

Esther nodded her head in a slight bow. "I would be honored, my lord."

The evening slipped by. She learned many things, some of which she already knew from rumor. The king was depending heavily on Artabazus, seen by many as the second most powerful man in the kingdom. A new favorite adviser was a man named Haman—this was the small man she'd not recognized on entering the room. The rift between the king and his chief wife Amestris had widened since last summer's events. The king was as absorbed as ever with the building of Parsa, but had not entirely ceased to brood on his lost chance of glory in Greece, nor on his brother's failed rebellion. The king was drinking again, as steadily as he'd been when she first met him. By the time the meal was cleared and they stood next to the royal bed, she could tell he was on the very verge of drunkenness.

"It has been too long, too long since you have come to me," he said as he untied her sash and slipped her dress down her shoulders. Esther suppressed a smile. *As if it had been any choice of mine, one way or the other, to come or stay away.*

Yet in spite of everything she was glad to be here with him again inside the curtains of the bed that made a warm private world. He was her husband and her king, the only man she would ever know intimately, and he could be gentle, loving, and passionate. He was all those things tonight, and after a time when they lay together in each other's arms, he said, "You grieved deeply for the child you lost, my love."

"I did," she said. "They told me it was all part of the pattern of life—the other women, the midwife, even the magi. Children are born. Some die and some survive. We grieve and we move on. But it took me a long time to move on."

"I have . . . 15 children living, I think," Xerxes said after a pause. "How many dead—I don't even know. Maybe as many dead as living. Amestris lost a little girl once, when we were first married. A girl, they say, is little loss, but she would have been our firstborn."

"Fifteen children," Esther repeated, watching the shirting of the moon-drawn patterns on the canopied ceiling as the hangings lifted and swayed in the night breeze. "Which is your favorite?" she asked.

Xerxes laughed and sat up, looking down at her. "Is that a trick question, my lady? You know I am supposed to say Darius, my first-born son, my heir. But the truth is—sometimes I like Artaxerxes better. He is a good boy, though too gentle to be a king, I think. Parmys' boy is a clever lad. But I think that Amytis is my favorite."

Esther couldn't keep the surprise from her voice. "Amytis?"

"Indeed. A girl—you're surprised. I am too, but she was my first living child, and though she is strong-willed and too stubborn for a woman, I do love her. Why else would I have made Megabyzus take her back after she cuckolded him? She is like her mother, of course. But I loved Amestris too, when she was 17."

"I am 17," Esther said.

"And I love you," said Xerxes, leaning down to kiss her.

"As I love you, my lord," Esther replied, because there was nothing else she could say, whatever she might be thinking.

But Xerxes surprised her. Perhaps it was his ability to do so that kept her caring for him.

"What else can you say?" he said, almost sadly. "You are bound by law to love me, no matter how I treat you or neglect you. But I do love you, Esther. A few times in my life I have been with a woman—wife or a concubine—and wished I was a common man, without a king's worries or duties or privileges. I might be a better husband then. I have wished that, sometimes, when I have been with you."

"We are what we are made to be," Esther said. "You could not be other than the king."

"No—I could not. But you never set out to be a queen, did you? And here you are. I did grieve with you for the child you lost, though I had many other griefs at the time. I am . . . " he paused and cleared his throat. "I should have treated you better, I think."

"You need never apologize to me, my lord."

"No—because I am the king and you are my subject as well as my wife. You see what I mean? A common man might at least have to apologize to his wife sometimes."

The very air in the room seemed to hum, the moment was so heavy, so full of possibility. Xerxes took her hand. "I hope I have gotten you with child again tonight, my Esther. I want you to have a child for me, and not just because you are my queen. If not tonight, there will be other times. In six days I will go to our summer court at Ecbatana. Come with me."

"I will come, my lord," Esther said. Again, as if she had a choice. But she wanted to come, though part of her was sorry. She had just begun constructing a life that was ordered, pleasant, and manageable, with her friends and books and music, and now the king was crashing back into it, taking center stage again. But she would, of course, go to Ecbatana. She held to this moment of closeness, savoring it, until the king called through the curtains for a eunuch to bring him more wine.

Esther traveled to Ectabana in the king's carriage. She was the only queen going on this journey, and she was in a position of honor. Rumor had it that Manya was disgruntled at Esther's return to favor, but she herself had not lost her position as the king's favorite concubine. She was going to Ecbatana too, in her own carriage, as were a handful of other concubines. Esther rode along beside the king when he wanted to ride in the open air. He was once again eager for her company, but she understood that this was different from the heady days and nights of romance when they were first married. That had ended. She had her place, now, as his wife and queen—an honored but not an exclusive place.

Esther played with that thought for the rest of the summer, trying to understand her role exactly, what was expected of her, and what she could expect. She understood that Xerxes was a king, a man with many women at his disposal. Of course she'd always known that, but there was a time he had been madly in love with her, and that had colored her expectations of what life would hold, despite the things she knew about being part of a harem. Now she saw that Xerxes, like most men who had more than one wife, liked different women for different reasons.

"Amestris always comes first, of course," she said to Ayana one night as they relaxed on the balcony of the queen's quarters in Ecbatana. "She is chief wife and mother of the heir—nothing can change that. But she and the king do not like each other much."

"No, but they will always be united in one thing—the desire to secure the succession, to see young Darius on the throne," Ayana said, sipping her drink and fanning herself. Ecbatana was hot at this time of year. "Until Darius is a little older, anyway."

"You mean that when he's old enough, his mother will try to set him up as a rival to his father?" Esther said. It was hard to imagine anyone, even the formidable Amestris, defying Xerxes to that degree.

"It may happen. It wouldn't be unheard-of in royal families. But until then, yes, the succession unites them, and little else. They play their little power games."

"And he turns to Irdabama, of course, for advice on business and building," Esther said.

"That's right. She's a genius at managing properties and expanding her own buildings, so she's a good partner for the king in that way."

"He comes to me with the sketches and models and artists' designs when he plans a new wing of the palace or a new relief in the audience hall," Esther told her. "But then he goes to Irdabama to find out how many workers to hire and what to pay them. Of course he has men to take care of such matters, but he always values her advice above anyone else's." She smiled warmly. Queen Irdabama was a friend, someone she deeply respected. Whatever her role and Irdabama's were in the king's life, they did not interfere with each other.

"Queen Parmys—I'm not sure she plays any part at all," Ayana said.

"Yes she does," Esther put in quickly. "He talks to Parmys when he wants to hear someone say, 'Yes, my lord,' and tell him how wise he is. I mean, anyone will say that, of course, but that's all she *ever* says."

Ayana nodded. "A man needs that, I suppose," she laughed. A servant glided quietly onto the balcony. It was Talia, bringing a dish of grapes.

"Thank you, Talia," Esther said, taking the dish from her. She smiled at the small girl who bowed solemnly as she retreated. Talia had grown up. She was no longer the frightened little shadow of a girl who'd come to the harem straight from her family's ruin in Babylon. In Esther's service she had blossomed into a loyal maidservant, but she was still small, quiet, and shy.

"And then there are the concubines," Ayana said, picking up a handful of grapes and putting one into her mouth. "Their function is quite different, of course—they are to excite the king, to bring him pleasure. But different women please in different ways. Manya is sharp-tongued—she would not direct her wit at him, of course, but no doubt it pleases him to hear her gossip about others and make witty observations on court life. And no doubt she brings her fiery nature into the bedchamber."

"Enough said," said Esther sharply. She'd never grown used to the harem's practice of talking or freely speculating about what went on in the king's bedchamber. She knew about her own experiences there; she was in no hurry to imagine others'.

"And some of the girls are quite sweet and shy, and others exotic—especially the foreign ones, those who aren't Persian. Meteke, from my own homeland, is called upon from time to time, when the king wants a change. They all have their different skills to suit his different moods."

"He *is* a man of many moods," Esther said. She had spent the past two nights with him. Tonight he had not summoned her, but Ayana reported that Manya was at the baths preparing to go in to the king later in the evening. "But what about me, Ayana? I have a husband I must share with hundreds of other women—what makes me special? What does he value in me?"

"That is something you must discover for yourself," Ayana said. Her voice grew soft, almost tender. "Perhaps he sees what your friends see in you, Esther . . . something hard to put into words, but impossible to miss. You are so much—yourself, so vivid and alive."

"I didn't feel alive, not for a long time after I lost the baby," Esther said quietly, looking down into her glass.

"But that was part of it—you mourned. You mourned with all of your heart, just as you give all yourself to everything you do. I suppose the king loves you because you give all yourself to him when you are with him."

"Perhaps." Esther stared out at the unfamiliar landscape, so different from the Susa she knew so well, or Parsa which held its own bittersweet memories for her. "Lord Artabazus used to think I was placed in the palace to be a good influence on the king. I don't think I've done very well with that, but he spoke as though the gods had a plan and I was part of it." She laughed, and took another bunch of grapes.

"But you do believe your own god has a plan, don't you?" Ayana said seriously.

Esther had talked to Ayana a little about the God of her people. She had even read to her some of the scriptures Lilaios had found for her. "The God of Israel *does* have plans for his people," Esther said. "He leads people—such as He did Abraham, Joseph, and Moses— into the places He needs them to be. If they are willing to follow. But I don't read much about Him having a plan for a woman, except per- haps for Sarah, the wife of Abraham. Her role was to bear a child. Perhaps that's mine. Perhaps I'm to bear a child who will have some great part to play in the history of our people. Though it's hard to see how, since any child I bear will grow up in a Persian palace." She sighed. "I can't know my God's plans, Ayana, or even if I have a part in them. I just have to trust. But I'm learning to do that—slowly."

"He is a strange god, this God of yours," Ayana said. "He asks so much—that you worship Him alone, and no other. That is hard for me to imagine."

Esther just nodded. That one thing about Israel's God—the insis- tence that He was the only true God, the only one worthy of wor- ship—had been part of her world since she was born. She no longer questioned it, even when she went with her husband to sacrifice to Ahura Mazda, to Arta and Anahita, and the other gods of Persia, old and new. But so many other things, so many other ideas, were new to her, and she still groped toward understanding God's role in her life, just as she still struggled to understand her own role in her king's life.

After she'd dismissed Ayana Esther stayed back alone, watching the last rays of sunset paint the edges of the hills. A sudden sense of loneliness overwhelmed her, growing, she supposed, out of her con- versation. Her husband was a remote, difficult man she must share with scores of other women. Her closest friends were also her ser- vants, protected from her by walls of propriety and reserve. Her fam- ily was lost to her; even if she saw them again, they would be half strangers. There seemed no one in all the world she could ever be truly close to, ever love and give herself to without reserve. She re- membered that she had once felt deeply and acted impulsively; now every word, even every thought, was measured, guarded, calculated.

Without realizing it, Esther had slipped to her knees, and her thoughts had turned to prayer. "O my God, God of Israel, I know You see me and care for me here in this place far from Your land of promise. I am so alone, my God, and I see no chance of ever being less alone. I am not unhappy, but I need two things—a purpose for my life, and someone I can truly love and give myself to. If I turn to the king for either of those things, I fear I'll be destroyed. And so I turn to You, my God, God of Israel. I feel I hardly know You, but I have read the words of Your Law and tried to follow them." She drew a deep breath and looked out at the landscape. Above the dusky pink hills the sky was purple, the color of royalty.

"My God, here and now I make a vow to You. I choose to follow You, to give my life completely into Your hands. I do not know what my future holds, but it is Yours. I will try to be faithful, to live as a good Jew as much as I can in this place. And I will give my heart's love completely to You, for I cannot give it to anyone else. You, at least, will not let me down, as You did not let my fathers and mothers down in the days of old. My God, I am Yours, with all my heart."

She found that her face was wet with tears, but she did not wipe them away. She stayed on her knees a long time, unaware of the hard brick biting into her knees or the stiffness of her back. The feeling inside was hard to identify, though she could form pictures that mirrored it: a still pool; a bird at rest in the palm of her hand. If there was a word for it, it might be peace. Peace. An unaccustomed sensation.

On the journey back to Susa at summer's end, Artabazus joined them. Esther wasn't surprised when he found an opportunity to ride beside her one afternoon as she rode on horseback beside the carriages. The King had ridden on ahead. It had been a long time since she and the old soldier had talked.

"Have you come to chide me for not doing my job well, Lord Artabazus?" she asked him, glancing across at him with a hint of a grin.

"Your job, my lady queen?" He seemed genuinely puzzled. "From all I have heard you have been fulfilling the duties of a queen admirably."

"Forgive me, my lord—once or twice, long ago, you spoke to me as if you thought I had a duty to try to—" she hunted for words that would not sound brash.

"Ah, to save our lord the king from himself?" Artabazus grinned—the grin she remembered.

"Yes, that was it."

"Perhaps I placed too heavy a burden upon your shoulders, my lady. Yet the king is happier now than when he came back from Greece. He is well occupied with the building of Parsa and the running of his kingdom. He is planning a new campaign of conquest against the Dahae in the east, a small enemy we can easily conquer. He still drinks too much, and trusts men I would rather he didn't trust, but I no longer fear he is on the verge of destroying himself as I did then."

"I can hardly take much of the credit for that, I fear," Esther said.

Artabazus shrugged. "To want all the credit for saving a man—that seems a woman's problem to me. You do what you are able. So do I, so does everyone. We all do our part. Like an army, my lady—the thing I understand best. No victory is won by one man alone. Every soldier contributes his part. You are doing your part well."

That did nothing to answer Esther's question—what exactly was her part—yet she valued praise from Artabazus because she knew the hard-bitten soldier did not give praise lightly. "As you are doing yours well," she replied. "The king relies on you heavily, especially in Bactria."

"Ah, Bactria." Artabazus sighed. He had spent the last several months hunting down and fighting Prince Masistes' three half-grown sons and the small armies that had sprung up around them. "That was dirty work—especially the last young fellow, 13 years old, no more. But a ragged-tailed gang of bandits was ready to stick a crown on his head and call him King of Kings with the slightest encouragement—so he had to hang."

"That's terrible," Esther said with a shudder. She felt as if she'd just bitten into something sour.

Artabazus shot her a glance. "Terrible? I suppose it was. Nobody likes killing young boys. But I'll tell you something, my lady—something the king and I both know, and something you'd do well to remember. That boy may have known little and cared less about becoming king of Persia. He may have been a tool in other men's hands. But he knew that his uncle the king had killed his father the prince, and that his mother had died because the king allowed it—and *that's* more than enough to plant a seed of hate. Let that seed grow for five years, and it'd draw to it every discontented rebel in Bactria—and then we'd have had a full-scale revolt to put down. When you wipe out an enemy, my lady, you wipe out root, branch, seeds, and all, or you're just sowing problems you'll reap later. Women are too soft—and too short-sighted."

"I doubt anyone would call Queen Amestris soft," said Esther, almost in a whisper.

Artabazus laughed. "No, you're right there! But she's shrewd as well as tough, you know. There were plenty of rebels in Bactria long before poor Artaynte got her nose chopped off, you know. Plenty who wouldn't be sorry for an excuse to have put Masistes on the throne in place of his brother. Did you think that was all about Queen Amestris getting revenge on a woman her husband had bedded? She's jealous and vengeful as Anghra Mainyu himself, but she's no fool. Maybe she didn't know Masistes was behind the assassination plot, but she knew he had ambitions. If her little revenge gave her husband an excuse to cut off Masistes and stamp out any would-be rebellion, that's no accident. Remember, Xerxes' throne is young Darius' throne too, someday. Amestris does nothing on impulse."

Esther was silent, her head almost spinning. The complexity of the world in which she found herself still amazed her. She was so busy thinking through the implications of what Artabazus had said that she almost forgot she had another question. "What did you mean when you said the king trusted men you didn't think he should trust? Did you have anyone in mind?"

Artabazus snorted. "Oh, just this fool Haman he's taken up with lately. The man made himself useful in Bactria, and now he seems to be a regular at court. I've no real reason to suspect him—just seems like a mouse who believes he's a lion, that's all."

"The king is fortunate to be served by men as concerned for his welfare as you are, Lord Artabazus."

Artabazus smiled and bowed his head a little. "And that's not the only way he's fortunate, my lady. In case you missed it, that was my attempt at courtly flattery, so cherish it, won't you?" He cantered up ahead to join the king.

CHAPTER 13

Back at Susa in the autumn, life fell into a comfortable pattern. The king called for her two or three nights a week. They dined together—sometimes alone, sometimes with other guests. They talked; they went riding. He showed her the latest designs for carvings at Parsa or for the artwork the artisans were executing here at Susa, then she spent the night with him. On other nights he called other women. Manya had fallen from favor, but King Xerxes had other favorites, though Esther was commonly spoken of in the city, Roxane told her, as the "best-beloved queen."

Meanwhile Esther ran her own household, entertained guests, continued to patronize musicians and poets. An invitation to Queen Esther's quarters was becoming a prized thing among Susa's poets and musicians, for it often opened the door to the king's own court. Lilaios, her very first protégé, was now the most honored of the king's court poets, and his wife, Roxane, remained Esther's closest friend outside her own household. Roxane also performed at court, but again her music took second place now that she was expecting another child.

Esther's other close friends included Leila, Tamyris, and Phratima among the concubines, and Queen Irdabama, when she was in residence. But no one was closer than her own household, especially Ayana and Hathakh. It was to Ayana that she confided she thought she was pregnant again. It was to Hathakh that she confessed how much she wanted to see her cousin Mordecai once more.

"I am sure you can invite him to visit you now," Hathakh said. "Your position is well established. No one will think it strange if you have a guest from the city to visit you."

"But there must be some pretext, Hathakh," Esther said. "Other royal women have family members visit them as a matter of course, but my family are commoners, and have never been invited to court. It would seem odd if I brought in a man known only as a friend of my family, without bringing my own family."

"Then bring them," Hathakh suggested. "You have given the name of these relatives as your family. Invite them here, and invite Mordecai and his wife along with them, as friends of the family. Invite them to a dinner."

"That's a wonderful idea." Hathakh always had an answer. "You and Ayana decide when is the best time for me to have them," she said excitedly. "Is it too soon since our last dinner?"

Hathakh laughed. "Shaashgaz will grumble and complain about releasing the rations for another banquet, but what can he do? I have my ways, even if he gives us trouble. What would you like for entertainment?" He knew Esther's tastes; she was far more concerned about what music was played than what wine was served or what dishes were prepared.

"Ask Roxane and Lilaios to perform for us," she said quickly. "They'll do it, because it's for me, and it will be such an honor for my family to have the most popular poet at court perform for them."

Hathakh bowed, asked her permission to be excused, and turned to go. Then he paused, looking back over his shoulder. "Would you like to have the dinner on the twelfth day of Kislimu?"

Esther felt suddenly warmed, and not for the first time she thought, *I don't deserve to be as well served as I am.* "That would be very nice," she said softly. For the twelfth of Kislimu was her eighteenth birthday. Though many at court made a great fete of their birthdays, in her household she had never made mention of it or celebrated it in any particular way. Her sixteenth birthday had fallen just weeks before her first invitation to go before the king. Her seventeenth had come while she was still locked in mourning for her lost child. So since she'd come to the palace she'd not had a chance to celebrate, and only Hathakh, of all who knew her here, knew the date of her birth. But Mordecai and Rivka would know. They would be honored.

For the dinner she asked Lilaios to recite a portion of the Hebrew Scriptures he had found for her. She had read those scrolls so many times now that she knew them almost by heart, but in her public readings she only occasionally asked Lilaios to read them, along with the Avestas and the other texts he hunted down and brought to her at her request. She had finally let him into the secret of her birth, to explain her avid desire to read Jewish writings, and of course Lilaios had promised to guard her secret. He'd also responded by finding the entire Law of Moses, the other scrolls of Israel's history, and clay tablets holding some of the psalms and prophetic writings scattered about in different Jewish homes throughout the city.

It felt good to be reading again, learning, exercising her mind.

She felt as though she were stretching long-unused muscles and re-joiced that they still worked well. "Some of those who will be attending are Jewish," she told Lilaios cautiously. "They would be honored to hear the reading. Perhaps you could perform one of the poems they call psalms?"

"I know just the one," Lilaios said. "Leave it to me."

She did leave it to him, knowing that, of course, he would not choose the exiles' poem she had so loved to read as a girl, with its poignant longing for Jerusalem and its bitter hope that the captor's children might reap vengeance. No one would read, at the Persian court, a poem that suggested that any of the empire's citizens were anything less than delighted to be ruled by Xerxes, King of Kings.

Esther's guests gathered in her court on her birth night—friends and family whom she hadn't seen in more than three years. Rivka's cousin Salabas, his wife, and their son—now a grown man with a wife of his own—had often been guests at Mordecai's home when she was growing up. Rivka's mother had converted to the Jewish faith when she married Rivka's father, but the rest of her family, including these cousins, were as Persian as the king himself. These were the relatives who had pretended to be Esther's parents when the king's officials came inquiring into her lineage. Now they entered her hall where she was seated, and bowed before her. She raised them to their feet and embraced them warmly. But her eyes were already on the man and woman behind them, Rivka and Mordecai, who in their turn came forward and knelt down.

Tears sprang to Esther's eyes, and she almost stumbled in her haste to extend her hands and draw her foster parents to their feet. It seemed so wrong, so upside down, for them to be kneeling before her, yet that was protocol. That was required. What else could they do? She was a queen.

Mordecai kissed her warmly on the cheek. "It is so good, so very good to see you, Esther." But Rivka held back, looking almost frightened. When Esther drew her close enough for a kiss, she seemed awed. "Queen Esther," she whispered, absentmindedly holding the edge of a ruffle on the sleeve of Esther's gown and rubbing it between her fingers, as if she could not believe the fineness of the texture. When she glanced down and saw what she was doing, she dropped the fabric as if it were a burning brand and took a little step back. "Pardon me," she said, still in a whisper.

"Rivka, dear Aunt Rivka," Esther said. "Don't you see? It's me—your little Hadassah. I'm still here—somewhere, beneath all this finery. Don't forget me. I'm still the little girl you once feared you'd never make a lady out of." She smiled as gently as if she were trying to catch a timid bird. Rivka smiled back—a hesitant, nervous smile—and stepped into Mordecai's shadow as quickly as she could.

Esther led them into her dining hall, a small but elegant copy of the king's private dining hall. The room ran the whole width of her lower floor and was open on two sides. Pillared porticos led to the palace gardens on the north and the harem courtyard on the east. Esther saw Rivka's wide-eyed stare at the brilliantly colored linen hangings and the silver dishes on the table.

Despite Rivka's nervousness, the dinner went well. Everyone enjoyed the grilled fish surrounded by various vegetables and relishes. Esther described Parsa and Ecbatana and her life at those palaces to her guests. They, in turn, told stories about life in the city of Susa from which the women of the harem were generally isolated. When dinner was over, the musicians, who had played throughout the meal, stepped forward to perform a few more complicated pieces, then Lilaios took center stage.

Esther could see her guests were, indeed, impressed that such a high-ranking court poet was performing for them at this private dinner. Before he began Lilaios told Esther's guests that her explorations into the tablets and scrolls had inspired him to learn more of the poetry of other cultures, then he recited a series of lyrics drawn from many corners of the far-flung Persian empire. But for Esther and Mordecai, whose pleasure was clearly written on his face, the highlight of the evening came when Lilaios recited one of the Hebrew psalms. Esther knew it well. It was a poem so ancient it was believed to have been composed by the great leader of the Exodus, Moses himself:

"Lord, you have been our dwelling place throughout all
     generations.
Before the mountains were born or you brought forth the
     earth and the world,
from everlasting to everlasting you are God.
You turn men back to dust, saying,
'Return to dust, O sons of men.'

For a thousand years in your sight are like a day that has just
    gone by,
or like a watch in the night.
You sweep men away in the sleep of death;
they are like the new grass of the morning—
though in the morning it springs up new,
by evening it is dry and withered.
We are consumed by your anger and terrified by your
    indignation.
You have set our iniquities before you,
our secret sins in the light of your presence.
All our days pass away under your wrath;
we finish our years with a moan.
The length of our days is seventy years—
or eighty, if we have the strength;
yet their span is but trouble and sorrow,
for they quickly pass, and we fly away.
Who knows the power of your anger?
For your wrath is as great as the fear that is due you.
Teach us to number our days aright,
that we may gain a heart of wisdom.
Relent, O LORD! How long will it be?
Have compassion on your servants.
Satisfy us in the morning with your unfailing love,
that we may sing for joy and be glad all our days.
Make us glad for as many days as you have afflicted us,
for as many years as we have seen trouble.
May your deeds be shown to your servants,
your splendor to their children.
May the favor of the Lord our God rest upon us;
establish the work of our hands for us—
yes, establish the work of our hands."

"Establish the work of our hands," Mordecai echoed as Lilaios'
voice stilled and the music hushed beneath him. He smiled across the
table at Esther. "A fitting prayer for any man."

"Indeed, indeed," Salabas agreed.

For a moment Esther was still, caught up in the music and magic
of the poem. She had read it and heard it read before, but this was
the first time she'd heard it performed by a master poet, accompanied
by music that embodied the longing of the words. Wasn't this what

she had been asking God for—a sense of purpose to her life, a knowledge of why she'd been placed on this earth, in this position, for this short span of years? She would pray for God to establish the work of her hands, if only she knew what her work was supposed to be.

She tore her attention back to her guests who were applauding Lilaios and praising his skill. With the performances ended, drinks were refilled and the guests turned back to conversation. Esther's own most trusted household staff were the ones who served at her dinner, but even so, she did not openly acknowledge her link to Mordecai and Rivka. But shared stories and shared memories could be spoken openly, and just being able to do so for the first time in three years filled an empty place in Esther's heart.

The hours passed much too quickly for Esther. When her guests were ready to go, it was Rivka who came to her for an embrace. She still seemed wary, as if unsure how her hoyden girl had turned into this poised, elegant young queen, but she held Esther with a mother's fervor. "Mordecai told me when he heard you'd lost your baby," she whispered. "I wanted to be with you then. Next time you are expecting a child, get word to me. I want to be there with you, if I can do so at all."

"Thank you, dear Aunt Rivka," Esther murmured into her foster mother's hair. "Good night now, but you will come again. We will find a way to meet." She longed to tell Rivka that again she thought she was with child, but this was not the time or the place to make that secret public.

The joy of having seen her family sustained Esther for the next few weeks. And she needed it, for when she next went to the king he exploded at her in anger.

"More malcontents and rebels! Right here in Elam this time. Another plot to put one of my half-witted half-brothers on the throne!" he spat, throwing a handful of dispatches across the room. "My father had too many sons—*that* was his problem! Every royal concubine's brat thinks he has a chance to tear the crown from my head if only he can get enough disloyal discontents to back him up. Get that useless fool to bring me more wine," he added as an aside to Esther, apparently too distraught to deal with servants himself.

"The rebels cannot succeed, my lord. The whole empire is loyal to you. This is a futile attempt, nothing more," she said, beckoning the servant, who poured more drink. The king's agitation stilled a little now that his cup was once again full. He took a long draught, then questioned, "Do you know their latest complaint?"

"What is it, my lord?" Esther asked though she knew quite well, for rumors of discontent penetrated even the harem walls.

"Greece! They are mocking me for failing to conquer Greece. Saying we should make another attempt—pour thousands more lives into the Aegean Sea. Fools! Were any of them at Salamis? Did they stand on the battlefield at Plataea? Or even at Marathon! Darius couldn't take Greece. Have they forgotten that?"

Esther had had a brief visit just the day before from Artabazus, off to lead King Xerxes' armies in the east. "It's not about Greece at all, my lady," he'd informed her brusquely. "That's an excuse—something to rally the rabble, something to irritate the king. It's taxes. That's what they care about. Taxes have climbed every year since our king took the throne. First he poured them into his armies, and now he's pouring them into his palaces. People get uneasy when the king's hand closes too tightly around their wallets. And if he is going to spend their gold they want to see something for it—the banners of their enemies laid in the dust instead of a thousand workers chipping away at stones to a building that will take 20 years to complete."

"What should he do?" Esther had asked. "You were the one who thought building palaces was better than fighting battles, but that takes money."

"I said it was better than fighting *Greece*," Artabazus corrected. "An empire needs conquest now and then. We're pushing eastward, winning battles against the Sakae and the Dahae. We hold more of their land than ever before, but some fools think we should be conquering more, and faster." Then he sighed heavily. "Either way, it takes money. That's the real business of kingship—squeezing gold from stones. But he needs to give them a year or two of tax relief. He needs to give them a token, something to let them know he's listening."

Esther didn't know if Artabazus had expressed these views to the king. She suspected he sometimes said things to her in the hopes they would be passed on, though he himself had no trouble speaking bluntly. Either way, she was fairly sure Xerxes wouldn't listen. "I'm sending Artabazus back east with a larger force, and he has my orders to conscript these loose-tongued idiots and drag them into battle. Let's see how eager they are for conquest then! A firm hand—that's what they need. They need to be shown who's boss. As soon as a king—you mark my words, Esther—as soon as a king begins to show weakness, begins to let them think he's listening to their complaints, *that's* the beginning of the end. D'you know they want me to reduce their taxes, too?" he added, as though this were a startling new idea that had just hit him. "Ungrateful swine!"

He refilled his own glass this time. He was drinking hard again, and Esther's heart sank as she heard the slurring in his words, the unmistakable signs that he was traveling where reason and good sense could not reach him.

"D'you know what Haman says? Good man, Haman. Haman says—he says I should *raise* their taxes. To punish them for daring to mock me, for daring to say I'm no conqueror. Smart man, Haman. We need the tax money anyway. I've had to hire on two new crews of workers at Parsa this winter. They can't eat dust—be nice if they could, wouldn't it? Come here, girl! Come and serve your king!"

The rebellion continued to smolder; the king's mood darkened. Every few days he called for Esther. In between her visits a steady stream of concubines and new young virgins made their way to his quarters. Esther was almost relieved. She didn't think she could have borne the brunt of her husband's anger, his frustration, his despair, his drunkenness, night after night. But always he came back to her, asking her questions she knew she could not answer honestly. For she agreed with Artabazus: reducing taxes would be good sense. She tried to hint as much, obliquely, but it got her nowhere. And she could not confront him. A soldier like Artabazus, a man with a sword strapped to his side, a man who had gotten the army out of Greece and safely home—that man might just stand on his feet and defy the king's judgment. Barely. No woman could do it, not even Amestris, who was far away on her own estates during this crisis. Xerxes much preferred to surround himself with men like Lord Carshena and Lord Meres, and this newcomer, Lord Haman, who told him his every decision was wise and gave him the advice he wanted to hear. And when it came to women, he wanted a woman with enough spirit to be witty in conversation and exciting in bed, but certainly not enough to defy him.

Soon after midwinter, the midwife confirmed that Esther was expecting another child. The baby was due at midsummer. Privately, Esther tried to concoct excuses why she could not make the long trip to Parsa or Ecbatana. Susa was hotter and less comfortable, surely, but it was home. She felt safer there. She could not shake the uneasy feeling that something bad would happen to her at Parsa if she bore her child there.

But that problem was months away, and she had more than enough to deal with here and now. At sunset one evening Esther sat alone in the courtyard in front of her apartments holding one of the small fragments of Hebrew verse she'd copied out from Lilaios' tablets. She had been reading it over and over to herself. This had become the best hour in her day, alone with her God and His Word.

"God of Israel, it's me, Esther, daughter of Abihail, wife of King Xerxes, daughter of Israel," she began, as she so often began her prayers. It wasn't so much that she felt God needed to be reminded who she was—though with His eyes fixed on the land and people of Israel, surely He might need a little nudge to glance in the direction of the Persian king's harem. Mostly, she just needed to remind herself.

"I am still trying to do your will, O God, as much as I know. I still pray that you will establish the work of my hands, yet I still wonder why you have brought me to this place, to this position. Am I supposed to save the king? to be a good influence on him, to stop him from destroying himself and his kingdom? My lord Artabazus thinks so, but he is only a man, and he may be wrong. Perhaps the child I am carrying holds the key to my task in life. My God, I have pledged myself to follow You faithfully, but I know so little of what You ask me to do. I read the stories of your servant Joseph, a slave in a foreign land, yet faithful to You. I am no slave, but a queen—and this foreign land is my home, though not the land of my people. I will be faithful to You, too. I only wish I knew how."

No answer came to her from the darkening sky, yet she felt a tiny spark of certainty inside. What she was doing now was at least the right way to begin. To keep learning about her God, praying to her God, trying to seek Him and follow Him as best she could. It felt like walking in darkness with a hand-held lamp. She could see only a step or two ahead, and that must be enough.

It was on that night that she told the king she was expecting another child. Of late his moods had been so volatile she couldn't guess how he would react. Had he not just recently cursed his father for bearing too many sons? But he was exuberant; jubilant.

"At last!" He grabbed her and held her close. "My best-beloved queen will bear me a son! My finest, my best son yet!"

Esther was glad for his joy, but she hated to hear those last words. She wanted Xerxes to love and honor any child she bore him, but as soon as he said aloud that her child would be his "best son yet," he was signing the child's death warrant, for Amestris would brook no challenge to her son's supremacy. Nothing in Persian law guaranteed that the king's firstborn son would inherit the throne. Any son his father favored might be named heir, and in that possibility lay all the feuds and jealousies and plots of the harem and the palace beyond.

But in this moment the king thought nothing of that. So far tonight he was in the expansive and exuberant stage of drunkenness, and was already planning a celebration.

"Next month, is it not two years since we were wed? I will give a banquet—a banquet in honor of my most beautiful queen and the mother of our next prince. It will be the most splendid, the most glorious banquet Susa has ever seen. I must call a scribe—*Scribe!*—to write down even now. What would you like to feast on at your banquet, Queen Esther?"

Esther had to hide a smile. If he was going to make it the most splendid banquet ever held in Susa, he had quite a task ahead of him. The series of ongoing feasts he'd thrown for his nobles years ago, before the launch of his Greek enterprise, had gone on for fully six months. It was at one of those festivals that Queen Vashti had defied him and been deposed. Once the king had sobered up, this particular feast in honor of Esther's wedding anniversary and the unborn child would be trimmed to perhaps a week's worth of banqueting. Still, it was nice to have a diversion amid all the talk of war and rebellion.

The king left shortly after that to join Artabazus in the field. The cries that the king was an effete, luxury-loving coward had hit too close to home. The rebels were saying he sent his best general to fight a battle he himself would not face. When even his supporters in Susa began whispering that there was something to it, he had to go and show his face, to march at the head of his men in a few skirmishes. A few weeks later, with the army pressing ahead in the east and only a little "cleanup" left for Artabazus to do, Xerxes returned to Susa, and the banquet in celebration of his marriage to Esther became a banquet also honoring his return home and his victory against the Dahae people.

Esther found the week of festivities tiring. Her pregnancy was not far advanced, but she found it exhausting to recline in the same position at a table, on public display, for hours at a time. Many of the rich foods unsettled her stomach, and while with child she could not stand to drink wine at all. After the dinners, when the ladies of the court withdrew so the men could get seriously drunk while the dancing girls performed, it was required that Esther host the women in her own quarters. That meant extra work for her own staff and tedious late nights for her.

But the last night of the feast was enjoyable, if only because it was the last. Then, too, she had something special to look forward to. Lilaios would be reciting a new poem of his own composition, a tribute to womanly beauty and virtue dedicated to Queen Esther herself. It would be a little embarrassing, but she would be veiled, so no one would see her blush—and she did like Lilaios' original poetry. Roxane would be leading a troupe of musicians playing accompaniment to the new work. She'd been practicing steadily for weeks, even though her own pregnancy was fairly advanced and she was already in semiretirement until her baby came. "This is too important for me to miss," she told Esther, "even if the king had not commanded me." And the king had commanded—the best of everything was to be laid on for the final night of tribute to his queen.

Of the other queens, only Parmys was in residence at Susa. She attended each night of the banquet and seemed not to care that an entire week of feasting was devoted to celebrating her husband's attachment to another woman. But then, neither Parmys nor Irdabama had ever seen Esther as a rival. They viewed their roles differently, while Esther was still searching for hers. Presumably Parmys, who was Xerxes' half-sister as well as his wife, had never imagined herself in love with the king, nor he with her. She seemed to enjoy the banquets in a pallid way, sitting as alert as anyone on that final night when Lilaios rose to recite his new composition.

Despite embarrassment, Esther enjoyed the poem. Lilaios had cleverly woven in bits of the work of other poets, including a very short passage from a Hebrew poem as a private gift to her: "Who can find a virtuous woman? For her price is far above rubies." He wove in a longer passage Esther also knew to be borrowed from a Greek poet, though he replaced the king's name in the poem with the name of Xerxes:

"Her Xerxes made his wife,
and honored her as no other woman on earth is honored
of all those who in these days direct their households in
    subjugation to their husbands;
so heartily is she honored
and has ever been,
by her household and by Xerxes himself
and by the people,
who look upon her as a goddess,
and greet her as she goes through the city."

Then Lilaios moved back to his own words to pay tribute to Esther, and finally, and above all else, to the king whose court was graced by women of such beauty and virtue, because his own virtue surpassed all else.

Hearty applause filled the hall at Lilaios' last words. The women had been commanded to stay till the end of the banquet so the dancing was not as wild nor the drinking as unrestrained as usual. Esther was invited back to the king's chambers. She was pleased to find him still largely sober, but wished he was alone. She longed for rest, but a small group of courtiers were, as usual, hanging about him.

At least they were discussing things other than war and revolt. In fact, a good many of them were praising Lilaios and his poem. "He's a learned young fellow, that's for certain," Lord Meres was saying. "I tried to catch all his quotes from other poets—I recognized a few, but I'm sure there were some I missed. He's well read, I'll give him that."

The king laid a hand on Esther's hand. She was seated on a low chair beside him. "I'll wager any of you that the subject of the poem can identify all the lines. My queen is a learned woman, I'll have you know."

"Really?" That was Lord Haman. He raised a dark eyebrow her direction. It was clear he didn't consider this a compliment.

"Oh no, my lords," Esther demurred, dropping her eyes. "I can read a little, and Lilaios has shared some of the poetry of other lands with me at other performances. That is all." Sometime before she had revealed her ability to read and her interest in books to the king, and he had been surprised and a little bemused. She had not expected to be put on display.

"Perhaps the queen can tell us the source of some of the mystery lines, then," Lord Meres, who fancied himself a bit of a scholar, continued. "That line about a virtuous woman being worth more than rubies. It sounds common enough, but I can't place it."

Esther remained silent, but the king nudged her. "Come, my love, win my wager for me. Show Meres that you know where it comes from."

Esther could not refuse the king's command. A thought rose unbidden to her mind: *At least he's not asking me to dance naked in front of these men.* Still, she hesitated. "I believe I have heard that it is from a proverb of the Hebrews, the people of the land of Judah," she said.

"And that other piece, about the woman who goes through the streets like a goddess?" Meres pushed. Again, the king looked expectantly at Esther.

"The poet's words were too extravagant, my lord. I know nothing of that bard he quoted from, my lord, save that I once heard Lilaios say that those lines came from the Greek lands. That is all I know."

"Greek, is it? I'm not sure Greek poetry is what we need in the Persian court," Haman snapped.

"Well said, my lord Haman," the king agreed. "We have poets enough in Persia, have we not? And beautiful queens enough— which reminds me, I must be left alone now, to enjoy my own queen. Good night, gentlemen."

Toward morning, Esther's sleep was disturbed by voices in the chamber outside the bed. She rolled over to see that Xerxes was gone and heard him talking to the men outside. Still half asleep, she could not hear their words, but his tone told her he was upset with the news they brought.

A few moments later she heard the visitors leave and King Xerxes call for his servants to dress him. He parted the bed curtains briefly. "There is ill news from the city," he said. "I will be in my council chambers all day. You should return to your own quarters." Then as Esther got up, and he headed for the door, he looked back with a softer expression. "I am sorry our celebration has ended on such a sour note."

That was all. Two women slaves helped Esther dress and conducted her back through the palace grounds to her own quarters, where she sleepily ate a morning meal. Only later in the morning when Hathakh came to consult with her about household matters, did she learn what news had awakened the king before dawn.

"There was a great battle two weeks ago in the east among the Dahae, and Artabazus' forces were badly beaten. Many men killed. When word of the battle reached Susa, there was an uprising of rebel sympathizers here in the city—last night. They declared Phratares, the king's brother, their rightful sovereign and said that since King Xerxes was too weak to fight even against uncouth barbarians and effeminate Greeks, he did not deserve to hold the throne of Persia."

"What? Here in the city?"

"Yes. It was quickly put down, of course. It ended as quickly as it began, with Lord Haman commanding the force that quelled them. The rebel leaders were rounded up—there were about two score of them—and brought before the king this morning for trial. They will be hanged tonight at sunset."

"How horrible!" Esther gasped. She had seen men hanging from the gallows before. It was a common form of execution and the bodies were often left to decay on the gallows as a warning to others not to imitate their crimes. But she had never seen 40 men hanged at once, nor could she imagine rebels brazen enough to mock the king almost within the shadow of his palace.

That night, as Hathakh had said, the rebels were hanged, including the would-be usurper Phratares. The mood of both city and palace was dark. It was as if the seven days of feasting had never happened. The next two days saw dozens more arrests, many within the palace itself, as everyone from minor officials to distant members of the royal family itself were accused of disloyalty to the king. His councillors claimed they'd found evidence of an assassination plot, and a second group of plotters was sentenced to hang. The annual trip to Parsa for the New Years' festivities was canceled, for the king thought it unwise to leave Susa. While a fresh armed force marched east to aid Artabazus' decimated army, the energies of the king and his officials were directed toward stamping out all hints of rebellion in Susa and the palace.

Esther heard nothing from the king, nor did anyone in the harem. None of the concubines or wives were summoned to him, though she heard that messages had been send to Irdabama and Amestris demanding they return at once to Susa from their own estates. A half dozen times a day someone came to her with a new rumor, many of them false, a few chillingly true. But the worst blow for Esther came on the third day after her feast had ended when Ayana announced that Roxane was below waiting to see her.

Esther invited her friend up to her private chamber and was shocked at Roxane's appearance. She looked as if she'd been sleepless and weeping for a night and a day—which was the literal truth. Lowering her unwieldy body onto a couch at Esther's invitation, she looked at the queen with hollow, red-rimmed eyes.

"Have you heard about Lilaios?" were her first words.

"Heard what?" Esther had heard nothing. The poet's name had never been mentioned in all the fast-flying gossip she had heard.

"Yesterday noon the guards came for him. They told him he was being stripped of his position as poet to the king and thrown in prison for suspicion of inciting rebellion."

"What? Lilaios?" Esther knew there were poets who used the gift of words to stir up political passions among the people, but she had never suspected Lilaios of being anything but loyal to the king.

"It was the poem he composed for your banquet that put him under suspicion, Queen Esther. Because he used Greek verses in the poem someone accused him of sympathizing with the king's enemies. They're saying he was taunting the king over his failure to conquer Greece, and appealing to rebels. It's mad, Esther. Mad!" Tears streamed down her face. "It's a total lie. Who could believe it? Can you do anything to help?"

"Roxane, I'll do anything I can, of course—what folly! Could anyone really imagine that Lilaios meant to incite revolt by quoting a few lines of Greek poetry?"

She called for bread, cheese, and juice for her guest while her mind raced through the accusations and what had to be the reality. Lilaios was the victim of terrible misfortune. He had chosen to use those lines on the very night when revolt had erupted far too close to the king for comfort. As a result, anyone and anything that looked even remotely suspicious was the victim of the backlash.

Roxane calmed a little as she held a cup in her hands. "I haven't eaten," she said. "I left our little Lilaios with my mother. Thankfully, we still have family to go to. We were turned out of our quarters and told that our slaves were no longer ours. We could take none of our goods. Nothing! Everything we have was the gift of the king, and now it's all gone. We don't even have any rations. Lilaios' mother's family is living in a house I bought them with the king's gold. They were living on our extra rations. The king was generous to us, but, my lady, once his favor is withdrawn a person has *nothing*. And Lilaios is in prison. He might be hanged, just like those other men—"

"Those other men were wielding swords and chanting slogans against the king, Roxane," Esther reminded her. "The king can— he can be hasty in his wrath, and may even judge poorly at times. But even at a time of such danger he could not be convinced that Lilaios seriously intended any harm by his poem. It's a mistake, nothing more."

"Will you speak to him, then, and have Lilaios released?"

Esther was taken aback. She'd never realized before how great her power must seem to her friends and how slight it actually was. "I can only promise," she said slowly, "that I will speak for Lilaios as soon as I get a chance. I have not been called before the king since this all began, and am not likely to be until things become calmer. And, of course, I cannot go to him unless he calls me. But I can get word to some people who will give me news. I don't think Lilaios is in any immediate danger. He will probably just be kept in prison till the crisis has passed. If there is any threat that he will be tried, I will do everything I can to stop it, and when I have a chance to speak to King Xerxes, I will ask for his release."

Roxane hunched forward, hugging her belly. "Thank you," she whispered, wiping away tears.

"And Roxane? I will send Hathakh to your mother's home tonight. He will bring some food from my own stores, and some things to help you and your family through this time. None of you will starve. I will see to that." Esther hoped her generosity to the family of an accused man would not come to the attention of Shaashgaz or anyone else who might wish her ill, but it was a risk she would have to take.

She talked to Hathakh after Roxane had gone. He agreed to supply the extra rations for the poet's family, at least for the moment. "But you cannot do this secretly for long," he warned her. "Since you have no property of your own, everything you have comes to us from the harem's stores, and Shaashgaz will know of it. If you are supporting the family of a man with whom the king is displeased, believe me, the king may be displeased with you when he hears of it."

"I know, Hathakh," Esther said a little desperately. "I need to talk to someone about Lilaios, to see if he can be released from prison. But the only person I know with ready access to the king is Artabazus, and he's in the field."

"There's Hegai," Hathakh suggested.

"Hegai! Of course! Can you arrange an appointment for me with him tomorrow?"

The next day the lord of the harem came to see Esther in her apartments. He had not visited her chambers since she had become queen, and was suitably impressed. "The banquet in your honor was a great success, my lady," he said after his formal greetings were complete. "So sad that it had to be followed by such tragic events, but such are the times we live in. What can I do for you? Hathakh said you had a request for me."

"I do," Esther said. "It is a small thing, one I would not bring before the king myself lest he think it a greater matter than it is." She had thought long and hard about this. Even if she were called to the king, would it be safe to mention Lilaios? Her own loyalty might be called into question, especially if the king learned she was sending rations to Roxane.

Then, on the other hand, if she mentioned Lilaios, it might make the king think far too seriously about Lilaios' supposed crime. He might decide to try him, and a trial, in the current atmosphere, almost certainly meant a guilty verdict. Better that the request come through an intermediary, slipped in among other court business almost as an afterthought. "You know that the poet Lilaios has been imprisoned because he quoted a few verses from a Greek poem on the night of the banquet a few hours before the uprising?"

"I had heard, my lady," said Hegai, keeping his face composed. He looked about to say more, but waited. He had not yet gauged Esther's reaction to Lilaios's arrest.

"A trifle extreme, is it not?" Esther said. "I am sure the poet had no ties to the rebels."

Hegai's face cleared. He smiled openly. "Indeed it is extreme, my lady. I am as sure as you are that the poet was not connected to anyone who wished the king ill. The general feeling I have heard among those who heard the poem was that the Greek lines—and very few people even recognized their origin—were a poorly timed mistake, an accident of fate."

"I could not agree more," Esther said. "Now this poet and his wife, a musician, have been very loyal and good to me. I was their patron even before they rose in the king's favor. His wife is very distraught, as you can guess. There is a child, and another on the way. She begged me to do what I can to effect her husband's release."

Hegai smiled again, leaning back in the chair Esther had provided for him. "Ahhh . . . and you came to me. You have a subtle mind, Queen Esther, and you are learning the game of court politics well. Indeed, it might not be wise if such a request came directly from you. But I can speak to people who will speak to people. If we take care to be sure that it never appears more than a trifling, small matter—which it is—I am sure the poet can be released."

"I leave it all in your hands," Esther said, visibly relaxing. "Will you stay for a drink?"

She heard nothing more about Lilaios for the rest of the week though she continued to send food to Roxane's family. Several more conspirators were hanged, but no new arrests were made, and the palace began to breathe more easily. Good news came from the Dahae country. Artabazus, with the help of reinforcements, had conquered there. On his return journey he had met and engaged the troops of the king's half-brother. The would-be usurper and his supporters were being brought in chains to Susa. And with the renewed peace, Esther was summoned once again to the king's chambers.

She found him moody and preoccupied. Even after he dismissed the courtiers and officers who were demanding his time, he was still fretting about rebellion and conspiracy. "A king is never safe, *never*," he told her when they were alone in his chambers. "I dare not relax my vigilance for a moment."

"But this rebellion has been put down, and your justice was so swift and final that surely no one will dare defy you again," Esther said soothingly. She closed her eyes against the picture of the forest of gallows—trees with scores of bodies rotting in the sun. She would never—*never*—get used to such horror.

"I hope not. Those carcasses will hang there till the last morsel of flesh is picked off by birds. I want those fools to remember the cost of plotting against the King of Kings." Xerxes reached for his wine cup. "I've released a few poor wretches from prison, though—men who obviously had no real part in the plots. You'll be glad to hear your young poet was one of them."

Esther released a held breath. "I think that was wise, Your

Majesty," she said at last. "Lilaios' poem seemed harmless enough to me. I have always known him to be loyal to you."

"Loyal? Perhaps. But harmless, no. He was an impudent fool to go quoting Greek verses to me, and I never want to see his face or hear his voice again. A man that foolish could easily be the tool of rebels, even if he was innocent this time. But losing his position is punishment enough. He need not rot in prison. Enough others will do that. Let him work with his hands and find out what real labor feels like for once. Poets!" Xerxes spat the last word like a curse, but Esther felt relieved. Lilaios was free, perhaps home with Roxane and their family already.

She thought that was the end of it, but a fortnight later Roxane came to her door again, asking for an audience. Once again Esther was shocked at Roxane's appearance. She no longer looked grieved, but she looked impoverished and exhausted. Her gown was coarse and colorless. Her dark curls were pulled severely back under her headdress, and her cheeks hollow beneath her broad cheekbones. Roxane had grown up in the palace. In recent years, as she and Lilaios had risen in the king's favor, she'd had fine clothes and jewels. Esther had never seen her when she was not well dressed. Now she looked like a peasant woman, a tired, weary peasant woman, a few weeks away from bearing a child.

"We've lost everything, my lady," Roxane said. "The house, our rations, even the clothes on our backs. My mother's family, Lilaios' family—we all lived off the king's generosity, and now we are bereft. Lilaios has tried to find work as a scribe or a copyist, but no one will hire a man in disgrace, a man accused of disloyalty to the king. What will we do?"

"I don't know," Esther admitted. "I heard only that Lilaios had been released. I thought that was good news."

"Oh, it was! I didn't mean that. I'm sorry. Thank you so much. I haven't thanked you." Her hands unconsciously twisted the edge of her rough sleeve. Tears had sprung to her eyes. "But with the baby coming we need food and shelter."

"I can help you. I'll send more supplies. I'll give you some fabric for clothes for yourself and the children, and all the food I can spare," Esther promised. Even as she said the words she knew it was like dropping tiny pebbles into a huge crater. Two extended families had been living on the bounty Roxane and Lilaios had earned from the king. Roxane's mother had a small pension from her service to Queen Atossa, but even that, it appeared, had been cut off. They were destitute.

"My lady queen"—Roxanne leaned forward—"you must speak to the king again. Lilaios meant no harm. He has always been loyal. If only he could have his position back. Not his old position, perhaps, but any small position at court, anything that would put a roof over our heads and prove he's not still under suspicion. Can you ask the king on his behalf?"

"Roxane, do you know what you're asking? Lilaios was suspected of being disloyal to the king! He was released, it's true, but in the aftermath of an uprising any man who was suspected is lucky to have his life, much less his position back. Lilaios will have to find something else."

"There *is* nothing else!" Roxane's voice rose to a shrill cry as she covered her face with her hands. "Forgive me, my lady, I did not mean to speak so. But this is our life—our children's lives. Maybe . . . perhaps if Lilaios could have an audience with the king himself, to plead his case?"

"Perhaps," said Esther dubiously. She thought there was very little chance Lilaios would ever get an audience with the king or even with one of his officials. Even if he did, she thought it unlikely he'd get any position back. Xerxes was in no mood to be forgiving just now. But she said, "If he asks for an audience, and I have the opportunity, I will urge the king to listen to his case."

The small drama of Roxane and Lilaios continued to unfold as winter warmed into spring. Lilaios applied for an audience. He was ignored, and when he persisted, he was turned down and told to quit the palace and never be seen in the area again. Roxane sent more messages to Esther, asking her to plead for the king's favor. Only once the subject arose when Esther was with the king. He mentioned the poet as a minor irritant and Esther said, "Could you not listen to him? Or have someone hear his plea?"

Xerxes looked at her incredulously, as if she had suggested he eat an earthworm. "Why should I do that? The man was a fool. He may have been disloyal. He is still alive. What more does he want? If he wants me to change my mind and throw him back in prison, he's going the right way about it."

She tried putting a word in the ear of Artabazus, now returned in triumph and once again the king's closest adviser. They sat one day in the west portico of the throne hall while the king heard requests from those who had been granted audiences, and Esther asked, "Is the poet Lilaios still requesting audience with the king?"

Her words were casual, but Artabazus glanced at her sharply. "He is, and the king has little patience with fools who do not know when to give up. I have made sure the poet's latest requests have not come to his ears. I've done that much for your sake, but now you must give up championing these people. I know you've been sending food to them, and if I know it, everyone does. You may want to be kind, but you'll make trouble for yourself and for them. Drop it. It's over. People fall from favor, and their lives go on."

Esther nodded without reply. It was harsh, but it was true. The king shone on his subjects like the sun. When a shadow fell, it was fate and must be accepted.

Yet just a few weeks later another desperate plea came from Lilaios, this time asking for an audience with Esther herself. She agreed to see him in her hall. He, like Roxane, looked poor and desperate.

"The babe is born," he said bluntly. "Another little boy, weak and thin and sickly. Roxane is afraid her milk is not good enough to keep him alive, and of course there's no question of a wet nurse."

"Oh, I am sorry," said Esther. She had sent no food since Artabazus' warning; even receiving Lilaios here made her nervous. But she could not help remembering the very different visits after their first baby was born, the warmth of the family that had drawn her in and helped to heal her own grief. Impulsively she pulled off her earrings and bracelets and handed them to Lilaios. "Sell these," she said. "They will feed your family for a while."

He looked down at them sadly. "I will try, though everyone will think me a thief. But it will not keep us forever, my lady. I must have a position. If only I could talk to the king. If only he could see how loyal I am."

"It cannot be, Lilaios. He will not grant you an audience."

Lilaios' face hardened. "Then I must go to him without an audience."

"Don't be a fool, Lilaios. The guards will never let you in. Even if they did—and they won't—what would happen? You know the law says a man will die for entering the king's presence uninvited."

"How often has that penalty been imposed in King Xerxes'

time? Seldom if ever. I am sure he will see me, my lady. I know I can appeal to him to save me and my family. He must know that I was never a rebel. Never!"

"I know that, Lilaios. I will try to help you, but don't do anything foolhardy." She felt uneasy. Awkward. Helpless. "Give my love to Roxane and to the children."

"I will, my lady. You have always been good to us. Pray to your God for us. Will He see and care for one who is not of His people? I have lost faith in my own gods, but I remember yours."

Esther felt a knot in her stomach after that meeting. She took her troubles to God in her nightly prayer. "Should I do more for them, my God? But what can I do without endangering myself? Surely there's some other solution, some other position Lilaios can find. Please help him, my God, even though he is not one of Your chosen people. Help him for my sake, I pray." She bit her lip and swallowed a cry. "Dear God, I would not know Your words at all if Lilaios had not found them for me." At least here was one Sovereign she could petition on her friends' behalf, even if her husband's ears were closed.

The next day Esther was summoned to join the king in the audience hall. She saw her husband about once a week. With her baby due in just a few weeks she was no longer invited to his bedchamber, of course, nor could she go riding or hunting with him. But occasionally an invitation came to sit in the hall of audiences and join him afterward for a private dinner with a few courtiers. She found the audiences physically tiring, though interesting. The great throne room itself, with its 36 elaborately carved pillars rising up from the mosaic floor, spoke of the power and might of the King of Kings, demonstrating to any supplicant who entered exactly where he stood in the scheme of things.

Today's audience promised nothing unusual, except an envoy from the satrap of Hindush, the exotic, far-flung eastern outpost of the empire. Esther remembered that Hathakh had been born there and planned to remember the details of the envoy's dress and speech to share with him later.

As it happened, the Indian envoy never got to speak, and his appearance was the least memorable event of that day's audience. For on that warm spring afternoon, Lilaios the poet came seeking audience with the king.

Getting a royal audience was a long and tedious process. Those who wished to speak to the king were almost all turned down. If they were fortunate, their requests were eventually heard by some minor functionary. The people who actually appeared in the throne room were those Xerxes genuinely wished to have audiences with. The well-known-though-seldom-applied threat of death kept away the idly curious and the importunate. A pair of armed guards at the door helped, too.

But guards could be bribed. In fact, the two guards directly guarding the entrance to the audience hall that day were each found to be in possession of a valuable gold earring and were duly punished for accepting bribes. But all that came later.

An army officer was speaking with the king about a list of men he wanted honored for bravery in the recent battles in Babylon. Artabazus, the man's superior officer, sat near the throne, peeling an apple and looking bored. Haman also sat near the throne. Since the recent unrest in the city he had moved ever closer to the center of power. Esther, veiled, of course, sat discreetly off in the portico where she could catch any slight breeze that might drift in from the gardens. No other women were in attendance, except for slaves and musicians.

The commander was halfway through his list when a commotion near the door caught everyone's attention. A eunuch's voice was heard rising to a high pitch: "You can't! You simply cannot enter His Majesty's—" The voice, and the surrounding chatter of other voices, stopped abruptly. The king himself had heard, had seen.

Xerxes, who sat so regally erect on his throne that only those closest to him would know he was bored almost to the point of madness, leaned forward. Esther looked where everyone else was looking—toward the main entrance of the throne hall. Her heart leaped to her throat. Even before she saw, she suspected who it was.

"My lord king!" The voice that rang out clearly in the hall was one they all recognized. They'd heard it accompanied by flowing strains of music, chanting the praises of the king. It was the voice of Lilaios the poet. He strode into the hall apparently unafraid, unabashed, and stopped at the edge of the carpeted approach to the king's throne. For an instant he caught and held the king's eye, then sank to his knees and finally prostrated himself on the ground, doing the required obeisance.

Everyone's eyes shifted back to their ruler. As always during a formal audience he wore the Robe of Honor. A crown was on his head; a golden scepter lay across his lap. The scepter had an important role, for as a petitioner approached, the king held out the scepter. The petitioner would rise from his obeisance to come forward and touch the end of the scepter. On those rare occasions when someone came uninvited—occasions so rare that Esther had never spoken to anyone who actually remembered it happening—if the king accepted the person's presence he was supposed to hold out the royal scepter. That would indicate that he granted the intruder permission to speak. If the king kept the scepter in his lap . . . if the scepter was not held out . . .

King Xerxes' face was hard. His eyes darted around the room as if searching for the one who had helped this man, who had allowed him in. His gaze did not rest on Esther. She felt a breath of relief, glad she had not done more to promote Lilaios' cause.

Xerxes' hand never touched his scepter. It lay unregarded on his lap for the long moment he took to survey the room. At last his gaze returned to the poet prostrate before him.

"Guards, seize this man!"

Two soldiers stepped forward and gripped Lilaios by his two arms, dragging him to his feet. Even then, incredibly, his lovely voice burst out again. "My lord king! I beg you—!"

"SILENCE!"

The king's voice rocked the chamber. He half rose from his seat. Esther saw in his eyes and posture all of Xerxes' rage at those who defied him—the rebels, the plotters, the would-be assassins, everyone who failed to quake at his authority. He had exercised his royal prerogative to punish in full these past weeks. He had even shown some mercy. But now he'd been pushed a step beyond the breaking point.

"Lilaios, once poet at our court, hear my words. You were imprisoned and charged for defying us once, for mocking us and colluding with those who sought our overthrow. On our great mercy you were released and returned to your loved ones. Now you dare— you dare—to defy our orders and our expressed wishes, to enter our royal presence without invitation, without permission, without cause. Tell me, word-wielder, what penalty does our law lay down for those who thus approach the king and arouse his displeasure?"

There was only the barest of pauses, then Lilaios, still speaking loud and clear in that poet's voice, said, "Death, my lord king."

"And is it the king's right to pronounce this judgment? Are the king's laws fair and just?"

Esther drew a breath. Surely this interrogation was designed only to humiliate Lilaios, to make an example of him. Perhaps he would be imprisoned and released, though she couldn't imagine who would dare plead for him now.

"Your laws are right and just, my lord," said Lilaios.

"Then hear my words!" Xerxes called out. He was on his feet, in full royal command. Everyone seated in the chamber arose as he did, for no one remained sitting when the king stood. Esther, too, struggled to her feet to hear her husband's sentence. "I command you, guards, to take this man, Lilaios the poet, from my sight. Hang him at once on the gallows reserved for rebels and plotters."

His piercing eyes raked over his advisers. He seemed about to speak as he saw Artabazus, then focused on Haman instead. "My lord Haman, go with them to see that this sentence is carried out within the hour."

Haman stepped forward. "As the king has spoken, so it shall be done." He bowed. Everyone in the chamber bowed, except Lilaios, who hung white-faced in the grip of his guards. He made no further protest. The guards dragged him away from the throne, out of the audience chamber as Haman followed briskly behind.

The room was silent as a tomb. Esther willed herself to remain standing.

Xerxes did not resume his seat. Instead he looked at his chief minister, Lord Admatha, the shaking old man who seemed so unequal to the tasks of these perilous days. "Dismiss this audience," the king commanded, and strode down off the throne platform and out of the audience chamber. Guards, slaves, and attendants scrambled to take their places in his wake. Everyone else stood, still silent, in the chamber, unable to think what to do or say next.

CHAPTER 14

The world had narrowed to a small corridor of mind-numbing pain and fire. Through that corridor Esther hurtled, trying to hang on to some small fragment of herself, of who she was and what was happening. Far away she heard voices encouraging her, but she could make out none of their fragmented words. She was in a world alone, with an agony she had never imagined.

She'd been in labor since dawn; now it was dusk. Ayana stayed with her from the beginning; when the pains intensified a few hours before, the midwife and her assistants came too. Little more than an hour ago the midwife told her the baby was on its way and the women helped Esther to her feet then eased her down onto the birthing stool, clustering around her.

Through a red blur of pain Esther recalled that other women—mothers themselves—had tried to describe the experience of childbirth to her, but nothing could have prepared her for this. She wondered if she were dying. She felt as if this would never end, yet she'd heard no worry in the voices about her. Apparently this was exactly how things were supposed to proceed.

Then, with a final, violent push, she felt a change—the agony was gone, and in its place was a baby's cry. "Here's the head—ahh, here comes the rest," she heard the midwife say. "Once more push. Ahh, that's good. Here he is . . . here is . . . ," she paused, concentrating on catching the small, wet body. "Oh, a girl," she announced. "It's a daughter." She laid the small, squalling, bloody bundle in Esther's arms.

"A girl. A girl." The whispers echoed around her, and she heard the disappointment in their voices. Everyone knew that any baby born was just as likely to be a female child as a male, yet everyone hoped for a son, especially when the child was royal. When a queen was pregnant, all the talk was of the new prince who would be born. A princess, however often one occurred, required some adjustment.

But Esther was the fourth wife of a king who had many fine sons, after all, so the disappointment would pass quickly. A girl was fine; a daughter was a blessing from the gods. As for Esther, she felt no disappointment at all. Her tiny princess was rooting for her mother's breast, and, finding it, she latched on and began to suckle. Esther felt flooded with wonder and something that could only be love, though she had never felt it as fierce and intense as this.

"Look at her," the midwife said in awe. "Most newborns don't know how to suck like that. How strong she is. And how clever."

"The wet nurse is here, my lady," Ayana said. "Do you wish her to nurse the child?"

Esther looked up at the circle of faces above her. "Can I, can it wait? Can I nurse her myself this first time?" She never wanted the child out of her arms or away from her breast. Even more intense than the agony she'd felt a few moments before was the joy and delight that filled her from head to toes now. And of course, the women melted away and allowed her to be alone with her baby.

Later that night Esther lay exhausted but happy, thinking about the little daughter who slept in a cradle nearby. The last weeks of her pregnancy had not been easy. Lilaios' sudden execution had cast a pall over the palace just as the tension and fear of the uprising had begun to lift. And the fact that she had supported Lilaios—had asked the king to show mercy—made things difficult for her. When her earrings—for whose else could they be?—were found on the guards Lilaios had bribed, the king had questioned her stringently, then sent her away. He was clearly angry, even though she insisted that she'd urged Lilaios not to seek an audience and had never intended her gift to be used in that way. Xerxes told her sharply that she should not have interfered in the affairs of Lilaios and Roxane, and that it would go ill for her if she meddled again.

After that, the whole terrible business was not spoken of between them again. When Esther was called to the king's presence—during the daytime only, for in her condition she would not, of course, be invited to share his bed—an uneasy constraint stood between them. It was a constraint shaped by Xerxes' mild but freely expressed annoyance with Esther and her deep, unspoken anger at the thing he had done. They did not argue, but neither was there much warmth in their times together. Esther was relieved when at last Xerxes and his court departed for Ecbatana, leaving her behind to bear her child at Susa.

And then there was Roxane. The day after the execution she'd come distraught and weeping to Esther's apartments, and Esther could not bear to turn her away despite the cloud hovering over her because of her concern for the couple. But Roxanne's presence was painful because her grief took the form of accusation.

"You are the queen!" she'd wept. "You were Lilaios' patron. How could you not have stopped this terrible thing?"

"I did all I could to stop it, Roxane," Esther insisted. "I asked the king to reinstate him, and when it was clear he would not I begged Lilaios not to go before him. There would have been another choice, another solution, if he'd only waited. As difficult as it was for you both, he should have waited. He meant well, but he was rash."

"If my husband was rash, yours is a tyrant!" Roxane shouted. "No, don't try to hush me. What? Is it now a crime to speak a word against the king? Will he have me hung too?"

"I don't know," Esther cried. "How do I know what is a crime and what isn't? You call him a tyrant. He is king, Roxane. 'Tyrant' is the name that a king's enemies give him. His power is absolute. His word is life or death. Everyone knows that, and everyone wise abides by it." She lowered her voice. "Yes, I think he did wrong to kill Lilaios. I will say that much. But he had the right, if he chose to use it. And he did. He is the king, and I am only a queen—one of many wives. I did what I could." She sighed as she sank onto a couch. "And I will do what I can for you, even if I suffer for it, Roxane. Perhaps I could be allowed to give you a position here in my household as a musician. Do you want me to see about that?"

"A musician?" Roxane stared at Esther from dark, haunted eyes. "I will never touch the oud again, my lady. I'd rather scrub someone's dirty linen for my food than ever play again."

Roxane's baby died a few days after its father. Roxanne did not return to the palace. Esther was left alone to ponder the fact that despite incurring her husband's wrath she had not managed to save her friend from an untimely and horrible death. She wondered if anything would ever feel right again.

Now she lay on her bed worn out from childbirth, thinking of her precious sleeping child. Her world felt well and wonderful again. Troubles and cares were still there, but they were distant, like voices drifting up from the courtyard.

"Nurse," Esther said, and the nurse who lay dozing on a couch near the baby's cradle, stirred. "Yes, Your Majesty?"

"Bring me my daughter again. I wish to hold her."

The nurse hesitated. "She is sleeping now, my lady. It may not be wise to disturb her."

"I want my baby here now," Esther said again, and the nurse rose, bowed, and brought her the small bundle. The child did not awaken, but slept on, cuddled in her mother's arms. The ritual lamp that had been lit in the room at the baby's birth burned on, warding off evil. But Esther had her own rite to perform, though she knew no rituals among her people for the birth of a girl child. Soon the magus would come and consult astrology charts and advise the proper name for the baby. In 40 days she would be given haoma juice to drink, to confer health. Before any of that, Esther had to present this child, all alone, to her God.

"God of Israel," she whispered so softly not even the nurse across the room could have heard her words, "here am I, Esther, wife of King Xerxes, daughter of Abihail, child of Israel. And here is my daughter, newly born and nameless. Everyone says a son pleases the gods, but it has pleased You to give me a daughter and I thank You for her. I do not know what her future will hold, but I dedicate her to You, my God, as far as is possible for a Persian princess. I ask Your guidance as I teach her and care for her. Please, I pray, seal this child as Your own."

So many worries, so many fears, fell away as she looked at the sleeping child in her arms. Yes, she was still the wife of an unpredictable, sometimes violent man, living in violent and troubled times. This child would be raised in a harem full of gossip, politics, deceit, and plots. People would seek to influence and to use her all her life. Yet despite past tragedy and future uncertainty, Esther felt at peace. She felt encircled by God's arms as surely as the child lay circled in her own arms. And she felt blessed with a gift she had given up daring to hope for—here at last, resting against her breast, was one human being she could love completely, without caution, without reserve.

For 40 days Esther observed the ritual seclusion, seeing only the midwife, the nurse, a few of the women slaves, and Ayana. The nurse kept the baby in Esther's own chamber throughout that time, taking her to the adjoining nursery only when she was restless and Esther needed to sleep. The king sent gifts and a letter of congratulations from Ecbatana. Esther lifted his gifts from their box: a beautiful set of lapis lazuli jewelry for her, and the same set, in miniature, for his daughter. There was another present for Esther accompanied by a note, *For Queen Esther, mother of my daughter and my loveliest musician.* It was a gorgeously carved and ornamented oud. Esther cradled the oud, not plucking its strings, wondering if Xerxes had enough subtlety to appreciate what a bittersweet gift this was. Her happiest times playing had been with Roxane and Lilaios. Was some message she could not read embedded in this gift, or had the king only thought of something she would like, something to make her happy?

With the gifts came an official message. Together with the astrologers, Xerxes had decided that his daughter's name would be Damaspia. On the fortieth day after the birth Esther took the ritual bath, Baby Damaspia was formally given her name and her first taste of haoma, and Esther's new life—her life as a mother—began to find its shape.

As always, Susa in summertime was unbearably hot. The baby was sometimes cranky and restless in the heat, but Esther was still glad to be at home. When her confinement ended, Baby Damaspia and her nurse moved into the nearby rooms that had been set aside for the nursery. Some women chose to have their children's nurseries as far as possible from their own bedchambers, but even before Damaspia was born Esther knew she would not be that kind of mother. She was grateful for the services of the nurse, an excellent, kindly Ethiopian slave woman in her late 20s. Sofia was gentle and skilled and, unlike some nurses, did not resent the baby's mother as an intrusion. Indeed, she seemed both pleased and amused that a queen would so often want to visit the nursery to hold, rock, and play with her own baby.

Damaspia transformed the household. She was everyone's baby, not just Esther's. Ayana adored her, and loved to hold her and croon little lullabies to her. The slaves played with her and made little rag dolls and bracelets for her. And Hathakh held her as tenderly and proudly as if she were his own. Seeing him cradling her in his arms tore at Esther's heart for a complex web of reasons. It reminded her of Lilaios with his son and namesake. It reminded her that her own husband, the king, would have little time to be a father to this or any child she bore him. Most of all, it reminded her that Hathakh, so good and loving, could never father his own child, and she determined he would have every opportunity he wanted to love and play with Damaspia.

When the baby was almost 3 months old, King Xerxes returned to Susa and came for his first official visit with her. She could hold her head up and look around, bright-eyed and alert. She made cooing and gurgling noises that the nurse agreed were unusually advanced for a baby of her age. When Esther placed her in the king's arms, she reached for his beard, then wrapped a tiny fist around his finger. A smile crept onto his lips.

Later, when the baby had been returned to her nurse, Esther and the king were alone. Almost five months of distance lay between them, and Esther felt that everything important in her life had happened since the last time she had gone to his bedchamber as his lover and wife. She was no longer the same woman at all.

"You have borne me a fine daughter, Esther," Xerxes said, sitting across from her on a bench in the main hall of her apartment. "I am sorry she was born into such troubled times. But the rebellion is completely put down now. I have been victorious over the Dahae and the Sakae, and we can put uneasy memories behind us, can we not? A new life is cause for celebration."

"Indeed it is, my lord," Esther said smoothly. "I am honored to have given you a child."

"Next time, a son." The king paused. "I wish you had come to Parsa with me. The artists had just completed a fresco in the throne room that I wish you could have seen. They were painting it while we were there. Such color! It brings the whole scene to life. Well, you will see it next year, and a great deal more. When you come to my quarters I will show you the sketches I brought home with me. I would like you to dine with me tomorrow night," he added.

As if there had been no interruption, Esther's life with the king resumed. The loss of Lilaios' and Roxane's friendship left a gap, but she had other friends, and again she invited poets and musicians to entertain at her dinners. A scribe friend of Hathakh took over Lilaios' task of finding clay tablets and scrolls of poetry and history for her to read, though she dared not confide in a stranger her special interest in Hebrew writings. The following spring she moved with the court to Parsa, spent some weeks in Ecbatana, and returned to Susa in the autumn. Throughout those months the king summoned her to him once a week or so, to ride or hunt or dine, and to spend the night afterward. Other women met his needs on other nights. At the moment there was no clear favorite among the concubines, but knowing Xerxes' volatile nature and his penchant for falling madly in love, most observers were betting there would be one soon.

Esther moved through this world, ordering it, making her contributions, but the center of her life had shifted. Because of Damaspia everything was balanced differently. Her daughter was her new center, the thing that gave shape and purpose to her days. Watching her as she learned to sit up, then to creep, and finally to take her first tottering steps mattered more to Esther than anything in her everyday life could have done.

Another small joy warmed her heart. A few months after Damaspia's birth Roxane sent a message asking for an audience. Esther was glad to see her. It might not be wise to consort with her, but Esther's loneliness for her friend and her sorrow at Lilaios' death made the risk worthwhile. Roxane kept her eyes on Esther's feet throughout their conversation, but after a little small talk she said, "I've come to realize that I can't keep my family by the wages of a scrubbing woman. I have a skill and I must use it, whatever it costs me. You said once you'd take me on again as a musician?"

It was a risk, but Esther had failed to take a risk in the spring and Lilaios had died. Employing Roxane seemed the least she could do. Clearly Roxane was still deeply wounded, but Esther hoped that with time, friendship, and work she would move through her grief and begin to heal.

On her twentieth birthday Esther hosted her relatives at a dinner, as she'd done two years before. Hathakh had helped her find opportunities to invite Mordecai and Rivka for brief visits three or four times since Damaspia's birth. Watching Rivka cradle the baby, Esther saw clearly how different this was from what Rivka had hoped for. She'd dreamed of Esther someday marrying a neighbor, living nearby in a house where Rivka could help raise her foster-grandchildren. The king's palace was a higher destiny than Rivka could ever have hoped for for her adopted daughter, but it was also a destiny that placed her almost out of her family's reach.

The birthday dinner was a success. Along with Mordecai and Rivka, Salabas and his family, Esther invited a few other relatives. Damaspia, who was a few months past her first birthday and beginning to toddle about, was brought out for the guests to enjoy for a few minutes before her bedtime. Everyone enjoyed the performance of Esther's latest poet, who recited a long original poem. Then Esther herself took up the oud to join Roxane in a short performance, which brought warm applause from all the guests. As the last notes drifted away Esther glanced at Roxane and saw her eyes lit with a smile. It was the first smile she'd chanced in a long time, and Esther glimpsed in it a hope that their friendship, their partnership once woven in music, could be knitted again.

At dusk, when all the guests sat and talked in the gardens after dinner, Mordecai drew Esther aside.

"It makes me glad to see you so happy with your child," he told her. "This life . . . it has not always been easy for you, has it?"

Esther glanced around at the imposing buildings of the harem that walled them in. "Not always easy," she admitted. "But yes, I am very happy now, with my household and baby."

"Our God is watching over you," Mordecai said. "You know, Esther, there was a time when you were growing up when I did not think God was very concerned about us, about me. I thought He was distant." He shrugged. "I thought perhaps He lived in Jerusalem and had little time for those of His people who had chosen to stay behind here in Persia. But since you came to the palace, I have been driven to prayer and to study again. I believe God does see us, that He does care. That He has a plan."

"I believe it too, Uncle."

"Have you kept your promise, to tell no one here you are Jewish?" Mordecai probed.

Esther hesitated. "Some in my own household know," she admitted. "Ayana. Hathakh. A few of the servants. But no one outside. The king does not know."

"Keep it secret. I still fear for our people. There is a man who is rising fast in the king's favor who bears ill will toward the children of Israel. I am sure of it."

"Who is that?" At no time in the king's court or household had Esther ever heard anyone even mention Jews. They were such an insignificant minority among the empire's myriad races.

"His name is Haman. You know him, of course."

"Of course." Haman continued to be close in the king's councils, and Esther's first impression had never changed. She didn't like him; she didn't trust him. It was true that Artabazus' distrust of the man might have influenced her. She was still friendly with Artabazus and often accepted his judgment of people, but from what she herself saw and heard, she felt Haman was a bad influence on the king. His counsel often seemed to make situations worse instead of better. He played to the king's vanity in a way that seemed shameless even in the fawning atmosphere of a court. Most damning, however, in Esther's private judgment, was the fact that he especially urged the king to drink when he wanted Xerxes to listen to his opinions. In Esther's opinion a man who sought solace in wine as readily as Xerxes did needed no encouragement. But none of these things had anything to do with the Jews.

"He is an Agagite," Mordecai said. "Long before our exile his people were enemies of our people, and that remains so. From all I've heard of him, he carries on that enmity. He has been in conflict with a Jewish neighbor of his for years, and I have heard he refuses to employ Jews on his estates. He strikes me as a man who likes to have a good supply of enemies handy—as scapegoats, if nothing else. Watch him carefully. Does the king trust him?"

"Sadly, I think he does," Esther said. She smiled. "Do not make the mistake so many have done, Uncle, of overestimating my influence with the king. He does not listen to me as much as he does to Haman. I am only a woman, and one woman among many. I have my place, and he expects me to keep it."

"I know that," Mordecai said. "And you do well. All the same, watch Haman."

"I will," Esther promised. After that they talked no more of politics or court. She warmed Rivka's heart by turning the conversation to stories of baby Damaspia's cleverness and wit.

Winter drew near; the days grew cooler. Esther spent her time practicing new pieces of music. She finally brought herself to use the new oud, and was glad for it had a lovely tone. Her life was full— reading, entertaining guests, and playing with Damaspia. She looked forward to being able to teach her daughter to play the oud in a few years and hoped she would be gifted in that area. Still she went once a week, or a little more often, to the king. Their time together was companionable and pleasant. He talked about Parsa and his other building projects. He thought out loud about whatever political or military problem vexed him at the time. They made love and woke in the mornings to go about their separate lives. At dinner with him and a few of the nobles Esther usually stayed quiet unless her opinion was asked, but she was developing a reputation for being perceptive and quick-witted when she did offer a comment.

Artabazus appreciated her insights. He was still described by all as the king's right hand; officially he commanded the military, but unofficially he advised the king on matters of all kinds. He continued to be blunt and outspoken. He could get away with saying things to Xerxes that lesser men might have been imprisoned for.

That winter Artabazus fell into the habit of walking in the palace gardens just beyond the harem a few times each week. Esther's apartments opened onto the gardens, and she often saw Artabazus when she went out to walk. In the cool hour after the evening meal they fell into the habit of walking a little ways together. Like the king, Artabazus used the time to think out loud about vexing problems of government. Unlike the king, often he seemed to listen to Esther's replies.

"Can't think why the king doesn't make better use of you," he told her. "For years he used to listen to Amestris on matters of state. Doesn't now, of course, because she crosses him at every turn, but still you'd think it would be enough to teach him a woman could have sense."

"Perhaps that is why," Esther said. "Amestris. Maybe that experience taught him not to mix the bedchamber with the throne room."

Artabazus laughed. "Maybe you're right. He did love her once, and he never forgave her for turning against him."

"What was it? What made her turn?" Esther asked. She had often wondered this. She, Irdabama, and Parmys all had complicated relationships with their husband the king, relationships that included a good deal of distance, yet none of them was cold or hostile. Only Amestris, the chief wife, seemed to be constantly at odds with her husband.

"Oh, the usual thing—power. Amestris will always want more than she has, and as she's the most powerful woman in the land, the one person she has to lock horns with is the most powerful man. But as for a specific thing, well, I suppose it was jealousy. Like any queen, she knew her husband would have other women but when he put the crown on Vashti's head and made her—a commoner, a harem girl—into a queen, Amestris never forgave that betrayal. She made her feelings clear in a thousand ways. I guess that was what *he* couldn't forgive."

"Vashti," Esther echoed. So often she felt like Vashti's mirror image—the second commoner to be raised to the throne, the second concubine to become a queen. Was that why Vashti's fate haunted her so? She did not, of course, discuss this with Artabazus, who had already lost interest in the topic of queens and was railing about the king's advisors.

"This fellow Haman. Not only is he not very bright; he's petty. He thinks that now that he has the king's ear, he can use the king's power to carry on his own private feuds. He's had some dispute going for 10 years with a neighbor. It's some foolishness about a boundary line, an orchard both men think they own, and now, on some flimsy pretext, the neighbor is stripped of his estates and his land goes to Haman. There's not even a pretense of justice in it."

"That's terrible," Esther said, wondering if this was the Jewish neighbor of whom Mordecai had spoken. "Doesn't the king realize that if he goes along with this sort of thing, the other nobles will begin to resent Haman and that will reflect on him?"

Artabazus snorted. "Who knows what the king realizes? Haman's nothing more than a drinking buddy to him, a position Haman's quite happy to exploit. I'm sure His Majesty was well in his cups when he signed the papers robbing Haman's harmless neighbor of his property. Oh, and he's just given Haman a new house near the palace. It's property that belonged to Lord Memucan and should have gone to his nephew when he died. But no, suddenly it belongs to the king and the king can give it to his favorite minister. Haman has his mistress ensconced there in incredible luxury, while his wife rules the house outside the city. Neither woman seems to mind as long as she's well fed and dripping in jewels. Well, I must go," he said abruptly as their path turned toward Esther's apartments. He rarely came inside, only once or twice accepting an invitation to take a cup of wine on the garden terrace. Today, as usual, his duties called him.

Esther entered her hall feeling refreshed. A chat with Artabazus was a like a brisk outdoor wind blowing through her enclosed world of women, eunuchs, and poets. She liked his perspective, so different from what she generally heard.

Tonight she would have her share of feminine conversation. Her friend Leila was coming to dine. Esther enjoyed Leila's company, but Leila's life saddened her; it was the kind of life that might have been hers if she'd not been made a queen. Leila had been called to the king no more than three times in the five years since she'd joined the harem. She lived in a tiny apartment in the concubines' quarters where her small staff of maids seemed to be always on top of one another. She had, of course, no children, and nothing to do with the long hours of her days save go to the baths, have her hair and makeup done, and visit with the other concubines, exchanging gossip. Leila had once been acclaimed as a fine dancer. She confided to Esther that she wished she'd been chosen to join the king's dancers rather than becoming a concubine.

"At least I would have had something to *do*," she said fretfully, twisting one of her bracelets. "This is no kind of life for a woman. It's ridiculous—living with only one purpose, waiting month after month and year after year to be summoned by a man who doesn't even remember my existence."

Esther privately agreed that it was no life at all but only said, "Being noticed and remembered by the king has its own burdens."

"I know, Esther. I know your life hasn't always been easy, but you do have your baby now, and you have these lovely apartments. You have your own household—a whole life of your own. I wish I had something to do with my days, that's all."

"But you have your friends," Esther said. "Being a queen often sets me apart from the other women. It's only with a few such as you and Tamyris and Phratima—girls I knew before I became queen—that I can really be friendly. It's often lonely."

"Oh, yes, I have plenty of company," Leila sighed. She left her bracelet alone and began twiddling an earring. The meal was ended and the plates were taken away. Soft music filled the room. Roxane was playing softly in a corner, teasing an intricate melody out of her chang.

"The problem is, even the other concubines seem to have more interesting lives than mine," Leila complained. "I don't know what it is. Well, Phratima has a baby too, of course. That makes a great difference." Though Phratima had only enjoyed a few visits with the king one of those had resulted in her daughter being born a few months before Baby Damaspia. Leila's eyes widened. "And Tamyris! Have you heard?"

"No, what's there to hear about Tamyris?" Esther asked, secretly hoping her old friend had not become her husband's new favorite.

Leila glanced around the room dramatically, leaned closer to Esther, and whispered, "She has a *lover*."

"What?"

Leila nodded, putting a finger to her lips. "It's true. Nobody important, just a soldier, one of the palace guard. She's met him a half dozen times already. Once he smuggled himself into the harem disguised as a woman." She giggled. "He was veiled from head to toe."

"Leila, is Tamyris mad? Does she know what could happen—to herself and her lover—if she were found out?"

It was a rhetorical question; Leila—and Tamyris—knew as well as Esther did that unfaithfulness to the king was punishable by death. Rumors of love affairs were rife in the harem, although most of the women were rumored to be having affairs, of a sort, with eunuchs or even with other women. Stories of women who had actual lovers—real men, from outside—were rare, and usually turned out not to be true.

Leila shrugged. "Our lives aren't like yours, Esther. Nobody notices us. Yes, she may get caught someday, but she may not. Whatever happens, she will have had some excitement in her life. Perhaps she thinks it's worth the risk."

"It's not," Esther said sternly. "It couldn't be. And it's wrong." Their whole complex world existed because of a code everyone had to honor: the king was the law, and loyalty to him was everything.

"It's wrong," Leila repeated. She looked up and her eyes held Esther's gaze. "But is it? In all honesty, Esther, from the little I've seen of him I don't even like the king very much." At Esther's frown Leila lowered her voice, but went on. "He's rough. He's rude to women. He's a drunkard . . ." She dropped her voice even lower. "If he weren't the king no one would give him a second glance. And why is it so wrong for one woman in this whole anthill of concubines to take a lover? No one expects the king to be faithful to one woman. Isn't it a bit mad to expect 300 women all to be faithful to one man?"

"Leila, it's not the same thing, and you know it." But Esther couldn't fully explain why it wasn't the same, nor could she deny any of Leila's reasons for not liking the king. Liking him or not was irrelevant, and Esther could not have explained why—despite recognizing the same poor qualities Leila saw—she cared for him so much.

She touched Leila's hand. "Please tell Tamyris she's risking her life, and she ought not to do it. I'm afraid for her."

"I'm envious of her," Leila said simply. "And do you know who else I envy? Well, everyone, I suppose, except the slaves. But I envy the girls who didn't end up becoming concubines. Like Raiya. Remember how we hated her when we were all new girls together? And laughed at her later because she was never called to the king?"

Out of the corner of her eye Esther saw Roxane, still playing her chang in the corner of the room, glance up sharply at Raiya's name, then quickly look back down. Esther couldn't remember any conflict between Roxane and Raiya in the days when they were all young girls together. She wondered if they'd even met. Roxane had not lived in the harem and Raiya was not a musician. Yet obviously the name meant something to Roxane. Esther laid aside her curiosity; she could pursue it later.

"But look at Raiya now!" Leila went on. "An honored position in Queen Amestris' household and a lover she can flaunt as openly as she wants—because she's not one of the king's women. I suppose that if her lover wanted to take another wife, she could even be married. She'd need royal permission, but knowing her, she'd likely get it."

"Why, who is her lover?" Esther had heard rumors from her own maids that Raiya had been seen with a high-placed official, but this was her chance to tap into the kind of gossip that was meat and drink to most of the women in the harem.

Leila raised an eyebrow. "Why, Lord Haman; didn't you know? He already has one wife, Zeresh, and a couple of concubines. I don't know how many altogether, but I think he has 10 sons, so there must be a few women involved. The rumor is he's asked Raiya to join his household, but she doesn't want to leave Queen Amestris' service, which is why he's keeping her as a lover. She lives in his splendid new city house."

"I'd heard something about that," Esther admitted. "I just hadn't connected it with Raiya. Well, she certainly does seem to land on her feet, doesn't she?" It was no business of hers, really, but something made her uneasy. Perhaps the idea of an alliance between the two people she considered untrustworthy, two people who had no reason to like her, one of whom was closely tied to Amestris. Raiya had always been a schemer, and both Mordecai and Artabazus had warned her about Haman. A shiver tickled her skin. She shook it off and diverted Leila back into gossip.

After Leila's visit Esther kept her ears open for rumors about

Tamyris and her lover, but heard none. She invited Tamyris for a private dinner, but her friend did not offer any confidences. Perhaps she thought that Esther was too close to the king to be trusted with such a secret, or perhaps, Esther hoped, the whole thing was over by now.

Midwinter passed, and the days began, ever so slowly, to lengthen. Little changed in Esther's life. She spent a night or two each week with the king, who remained absorbed with plans for more building at Parsa. Damaspia was trying out new sounds, including the heartwarming "ma-ma."

One day Esther paused at the nursery door as she came to get Damaspia and take her for a walk in the gardens. Surprised to hear a male voice within, she hesitated. Instantly she recognized Hathakh's voice. But he was not conferring with Sofia, the nurse, about linens and other baby supplies. Far from it. He was threatening in a lilting, laughing tone, "I'll get you! Watch out. I'm coming to get you! You can't escape!" His playful words were punctuated by screams of little-girl laughter and the tread of tiny running feet.

Esther moved into the doorway where she could see inside. Hathakh, the austere and efficient steward so revered and feared by the younger staff, was chasing little Damaspia around the nursery, his fingers extended and waving as if he were about to tickle her. The delighted child was running in circles, shrieking and laughing. Her dark ringlets tumbled over her eyes. Her round cheeks dimpled with delight. Sofia watched, her arms folded, smiling, shaking her head as though this foolishness were a common occurrence in the nursery. Suddenly Damaspia stopped, let Hathakh "catch" her, and clung with her arms around his neck as he swooped her up. Amid her giggles, Esther clearly heard her daughter say, "Pa-pa."

Hathakh's back was toward Esther, but she saw how he stiffened and grew still. Esther's eyes met Sofia's, and echoed each other's sadness. Damaspia saw her father once every couple of months when Esther, accompanied by Sofia, dressed the child in her best gown and brought her to the king's quarters for a half-hour's visit. The only man the child saw on a daily basis, the only man she knew and loved was the eunuch who served her mother so faithfully. It was this man who held her as he would have held a child of his own, if it had been possible for him to have had one.

Hathakh must have seen that Sofia was looking at someone for he touched his lips to Damaspia's hair for the briefest instant then placed her in Sofia's arms. "Damaspia, this is Hathakh," the nurse said. "Ha-thakh. Say goodbye to Hathakh, now." The child waved and whispered, "Bye-bye," and Hathakh turned slowly to see Esther in the doorway. He bowed as he came toward her.

"My lady," he said quietly.

"Hathakh," Esther said just as softly, laying a hand on his arm. His face was shuttered with the closed, guarded look she knew so well.

His eyes met hers, respectful and yet never hesitant. "My lady, if I have offended, or been too familiar, I beg—"

"Beg nothing, Hathakh. This is your home. Nothing you do here can be seen as taking liberties. Do you understand?"

He bowed his head again. "I thank you, my lady. Now, if you will excuse me, I have a list of linens Sofia needs for the young princess—I must go." And he was gone, clutching his dignity as firmly as the clay tablet he picked up on the way out of the chamber.

Esther took her daughter from the nurse and carried her out into the gardens. Damaspia was energetic and giggly after her romp with Hathakh. Esther tried to match her mood, but she couldn't entirely shake the melancholy feeling left by that little scene. She played alone with Damaspia near the large shaded pool in the center of the courtyard. Soon Damaspia would be old enough to run off and play with the other children of the harem, but for now, she always wanted her mother or nurse close by. Esther loved watching her daughter try out her new skills. She was walking well now and beginning to run. As Esther watched Damaspia mastered—with a few tumbles—the difficult skill of bending down to pick up a bright stone from the ground without falling over. When she came toddling back with the stone clutched in her fist, Esther hugged her and said, "I'm so proud of you."

But it would be nice, Esther thought as Damaspia hurried off to another adventure, *to have someone to share it with.* She wished, impossibly, that King Xerxes might suddenly, casually, appear at her side by the pool and sit down next to her so they could spend an hour watching their daughter play. She wished she could share the joy of parenting with the king. Or that she could scoop Damaspia up and take her to Mordecai and Rivka's home and let her play there. Or even that Hathakh could have laid aside his reserve, the awareness of position, with her as he did with Damaspia, and come outside and play with them. *Like a real family,* Esther thought wistfully. *I suppose that's what I want.*

Instead of the king, or Rivka, or Hathakh, Ayana joined them a few moments later. She sat down next to Esther on the fountain's edge and said, "She is so determined. Look, even when she falls it doesn't bother her at all. She just picks herself up and goes on."

"I know. She's wonderful," Esther said, suddenly feeling better. Ayana was like a second mother to the child, and despite her status as lady-in-waiting she truly felt like the sister Esther never had. Esther searched for some way to explain to Ayana what she felt but the words never reached her lips, for Ayana spoke again.

"I came to find you because you are summoned to the king today," she said. "Not tonight. Today. Before the evening meal. He wishes to see you in his private chambers on a matter—so he says— of some importance."

"What could that be?" Esther wondered. In a few weeks it would be the fourth anniversary of their marriage, but he had not suggested any celebration. That was fine with her. Could he want to talk about that?

An hour later she left for the requested meeting. She wore a gown that was appropriate for dinner, should he asked her to stay and dine. She went happily, though not sure what to expect. Of late their relationship had settled into a warm routine, but she knew her husband was quickly swayed by extremes of passion. Who knew what he might consider "a matter of some importance"?

As soon as she was conducted into his private chamber she knew he'd not called her here to discuss a banquet in honor of their marriage or to invite her on a hunt or a journey. Nor was she likely to be staying for dinner, much less for the night.

Xerxes kept his seat as she entered. Though he was in his private chamber he sat on an ornate carved chair exactly as if he were on his throne in the audience hall. He wore the Robe of Honor, a wide, full gown arranged so that it fell in a series of ripples in front and back. His face was stern, his eyes hooded. One hand drummed impatiently on the arm of his chair. Behind him, his guards and personal attendants had stepped slightly back, but advisers stood on either side of him—Lord Haman and Lord Carshena. It was obvious that they were there as advisers, not friends. All three men stared at Esther with hard, narrowed eyes as she sank to the ground in obeisance.

The king was in no hurry to extend his scepter to Esther. Though he was not in the throne room, he grasped it with both hands—another bad sign. After keeping her bent to the floor for several long moments, he held out the scepter and she rose, waiting for him to speak.

His voice was cold. "Queen Esther, you have answered our royal summons."

"Yes, my lord king. It is my delight to do your bidding."

"A matter has come to our attention, Queen Esther. It concerns a letter Lord Haman received from Shaashgaz, keeper of the king's concubines—a letter whose contents Lord Haman properly relayed to me at once. This letter concerns you, my lady."

Esther's heart seemed to stop while her mind raced. What had she done that could possibly offend? Was the king angry that she'd employed Roxane again? She couldn't imagine anything else that could be taken as disloyal or dangerous, and surely, even for that misdemeanor, the king would understand her need to show pity on an old friend who had fallen so low.

Esther did not reply, waiting for King Xerxes to speak again.

Haman slapped a rolled parchment in the king's outstretched hand. He unrolled it, then slowly, deliberately read:

"I feel it is my duty to inform you as one who has the ear of the king, that one of the king's wives, the former concubine Esther, is carrying on an affair with one of the king's officers, a man held in the highest trust and position by His Majesty. They have been seen together on many occasions in her private quarters, and there are those in her household who can testify that she entertains him in secret and has given him tokens of love. It is important that this matter be investigated, for if the king is dishonored, we are all dishonored."

The room spun, reeled. Esther barely kept her balance. The final words of the letter were drowned out by a rushing, roaring sound that filled her head. This was—unthinkable. A dagger-thrust of pain tore at the pit of her stomach. For one of the king's women to be unfaithful meant—death. She had warned Leila of that about Tamyris.

Tamyris. Could this be connected to her? No, impossible. How could anyone make such a link, even if Tamyris' infidelity were known? And yet, where could such a rumor have begun? Except the few poets and musicians she invited to her banquets, Esther saw no one outside the harem unless she was in the king's presence. But this was no poet or musician she was accused of dallying with. It was "a man held in the highest trust and position." Who? What or who could Shaashgaz mean?

"Do you know to what this letter refers, my lady?" the king asked, his eyes as dark and impenetrable as the burial caves outside Parsa.

"My lord king, I know nothing! I swear to you I am innocent of any wrongdoing. I swear it on my life!" Even as she said the words, Esther knew how very literally they would be taken. Her life, indeed, would be surety for her pledge. "I have never, never been unfaithful to you, or even thought of it!"

"And you have had secret meetings with no man?"

"No, my lord, no secret meetings. I have hardly seen any man at all, except the eunuchs who serve me and who serve in the harem, and such men as I see when I attend you here in your court. At times musicians and poets come to perform for me, but I know none of them intimately." Her thoughts flew frantically, searching for an explanation. "Oh, and I sometimes have speech with Lord Artabazus when he is in the palace. He has come to talk to me briefly, but only to walk in the gardens. He has never visited me privately in my quarters."

The room spun again, and Esther feared that she would faint. She saw the look in both the king's eyes and Haman's when Artabazus' name was mentioned. *An officer of the king.* This was it, then.

"Indeed. Lord Artabazus." King Xerxes remained deadly calm. She knew that calm and feared it. "Shaashgaz did not name the man in his letter, but when Lord Haman questioned him, he admitted that one of your women had told him Lord Artabazus is a frequent visitor."

"Frequent?" She tried to keep the desperation from her voice. "My lord, he has spoken with me when we met in the gardens. We are in view where all may see us. There is nothing improper, nothing private in our conversation. Indeed, my lord, he talks to me only of you, of affairs of state . . . not of any personal concern."

"And does he visit in your private chambers?"

"No, my lord! *No!* Perhaps twice he came to my garden terrace to take a cup of wine. My servants and others were present. I have never had him—nor any man—into my private chamber. How could I? How would I? My lord king, I am your *wife!*"

Esther's whole body shook with fear and cold. The air in the usually stuffy chamber felt chilly. She dropped to her knees, holding her open hands toward the king. "You may question my household staff, my lord. They will confirm what I say."

"Yet one of your own people has given Shaashgaz this report, and confirmed it for us," the king said, leaning forward. "What is more, this woman told us that you had given Lord Artabazus a love token, a gift I myself had given you."

Esther could only shake her head. "I know not what you mean, my lord. I have given Lord Artabazus nothing. I would have no cause to give him a gift."

The king glanced briefly at Haman, who stepped forward, holding out a carved wooden box. "Do you recognize this, Queen Esther?" He lifted the lid on the box. "At our informant's suggestion we searched Artabazus' private quarters, and this was found there." Nestled on black cloth was the beautifully decorated oud given Esther from the king at Damaspia's birth.

Esther ignored Haman as she looked from the oud to the king. She took a deep breath and willed herself to meet Xerxes' eyes. "My lord, this is the instrument you gave me when our daughter, the Princess Damaspia, was born," she said. "I could not easily forget it, nor would I ever give it to another. I keep it with other musical instruments in my private chamber, in a locked cupboard." Unconsciously she clasped her hands at her waist as if in supplication. Would the king believe her? Would the truth be enough to save her?

"It is not the oud I play from day to day. I save it for special occasions, which is, perhaps, the reason I had not noticed its absence. No one can open that cupboard save myself, my steward, and the chief among my musicians." The conversation moved so swiftly that Esther felt she was running to keep pace. The truth unfolded in her understanding even as she spoke. The chief among my musicians. Her voice shook. "My lord, may I ask you who was the woman in my household who gave this information to Shaashgaz, and to you?"

"You may not," came his chill reply. "You may ask no boons, no favors, no considerations or kindnesses. You have had your say. You will be escorted from this place by my servants to your own quarters, where you will stay under guard. You will not go in or out until I have made my judgment. Your own household staff will be removed from you and brought here for questioning, as will Lord Artabazus and his staff, along with others who may have cause to know in this matter. When our decision is made, we will send for you."

Esther stood up, opened her mouth to speak, and shut it again. Begging and pleading had never endeared anyone to Xerxes. She bowed her head deeply. "I await my lord's judgment, knowing that it will be right and true," she said. "I would sooner die than be untrue to my lord the king." Two guardsmen stepped forward. Rather than allow them to lay hands on her she fell into step between them.

At her apartment she found that the king's men had been there ahead of her. All of her staff were gone. A handful of unfamiliar slaves remained to meet her basic needs. Hathakh, Ayana, Talia—all her faithful servants were being interrogated about her personal behavior. And one of them—one of those she most trusted—had betrayed her, had made up a malicious story and stolen her property to provide evidence. Which one was it? Esther was terribly afraid she knew.

But the loss of her staff, and even the guards outside her door, meant little in comparison to another loss. Heading straight for the nursery, she found it empty. Not only was Damaspia and her nurse gone, but many of the child's personal belongings had been taken.

"Where is my daughter?" Esther demanded desperately of the nearest eunuch. She'd expected to find Sofia taken with the other staff and Damaspia alone with a strange nurse. That was why she had come directly to the nursery. Finding her child gone clutched her heart like a cold hand.

"The princess has been taken into the king's care, my lady." Of course. A woman accused of adultery would never be entrusted with the king's daughter. The tears Esther had held back during this whole ordeal sprang to her eyes, and she turned away, hurrying as fast as she could to her own room before the floods burst. She lay on her bed and wept, utterly desolate.

Finally she rose, washed her face, and, ignoring the plate of food a servant had laid out for her, went out onto her balcony. The sun had set, and twilight painted the sky indigo. Esther knelt, burying her head in her folded arms. She thought of the experience of Joseph, unjustly accused of raping his master's wife. God had cared for the innocent Joseph, yet he had spent years in prison. What fate awaited her?

"O God of Israel," Esther prayed. "You promise to protect Your people, yet You never promise that the innocent won't suffer. You know, Lord God, that I am innocent, yet that will not guard me against the king's wrath. My friend Lilaios was innocent too. How

many others have been innocent, yet were sentenced to prison or death? Even Vashti . . ."

She'd thought of Vashti so many times in her years in the palace. That other wife, disgraced and cast aside. And all Vashti had done was refuse to appear at the king's command.

"My life is in Your hands, my God," Esther said, trying hard to believe it with all her heart.

Her seclusion lasted three days. She ate but little. She tried to pray and to read the Scripture tablets. She longed for Damaspia, worried about her fate. At last the king's guards came for her, formally saying they had orders to bring her before the king.

Again she was conducted to his council room. Six of his seven closest advisers were present. Lord Admatha, on his deathbed, was too ill to come to any meeting, but Lords Carshena, Shethar, Tarshish, Meres, Marsena, and, of course, Haman were all present. Led into the room, Esther prostrated herself before the king, who gestured for her to rise. Then guards led in yet another person. Artabazus. Esther looked at him, but his face was blank. Was he regretting the friendship he'd shown her?

"Queen Esther, Lord Artabazus, lords and councillors of this kingdom," Xerxes said in a strong, clear voice. "Accusations have been made against the queen and against Lord Artabazus, accusations of improper conduct and unfaithfulness to our royal person. None know of these accusations but those of you in this room and such servants as we have employed to find out the truth. We would not publish such a thing before the truth was known. Now you may know what we have learned: this accusation has been found to be entirely false, groundless, and malicious."

Esther lifted her head, meeting her husband's eyes for the first time. She could not read his expression. His gaze slipped quickly from hers to rest on Artabazus, then away again as he addressed the nobles. None of them looked surprised. They had been privy to the investigation, she supposed. Only she and Artabazus were shocked to hear their names cleared. Shocked, because in the king's court an accusation was often—usually—as good as condemnation. Even the whisper of scandal, in a case such as this, could condemn.

King Xerxes continued. "The accusation was made by a person who bore malice against my wife, Queen Esther, acting, perhaps, in concert with others who wished her ill. All her household, all Lord Artabazus' servants, all others questioned, denied any knowledge of any wrongdoing. We have judged that their testimony is true, and that the queen and Lord Artabazus have been falsely accused."

He turned to address Artabazus directly. "Artabazus, my loyal servant, I am glad to see any hint of scandal removed from your name. It is my decree that you remove at once to your satrapy of Phrygia, there to carry out your duties which your service to me has prevented you from fulfilling in recent months."

Artabazus bowed low. The king's message was clear. He was innocent of adultery with the queen, but even a hint of impropriety attached to his name required his disappearance from court, from Esther's circle of acquaintance, as swiftly as possible. He was not in disgrace, for he bore his lands and title as before, but the king wanted him out of sight.

Then it was Esther's turn. "My lady queen, we are glad to see your name cleared of the stain of this accusation. You will return to your quarters, where your own servants have been returned also, to resume your duties as before."

Esther wanted to bow her head and accept the king's pronouncement as simply as Artabazus had done, but a question cried out to be asked. "My lord king, what about my daughter? Is she back in my household?"

Xerxes' expression softened for the barest moment. "The Princess Damaspia will return to her nursery," he said. Esther's heart began beating again. If he had dared to think that a woman once accused of adultery was not fit to raise his daughter . . . she could not have imagined life going on after that moment. But now the sun, moon, and stars were back in the heavens. Life could go on. Esther accepted her dismissal and returned to her quarters.

Everyone was there already—Hathakh, Ayana, her servants. Hathakh and Ayana both embraced her. "It was terrible," Ayana said, "knowing you were going through all this alone, and we could not be beside you. You know who did this, of course."

"Shh—we will talk of that later," Esther said. Right now she cared for only one thing, and that one wish was granted almost immediately. The king's guards arrived with Sofia carrying Damaspia. Set down on the floor, the child ran at once for her mother's arms, and Esther held her as if she could never again let go.

Only later that night when Esther herself had put Damaspia to sleep, and eaten her first good meal in three days, did she and Ayana sit on the balcony outside her chamber and talk.

"It was Roxane, of course," Esther said. Even saying the name felt as painful as biting down on a rotten tooth.

"Of course," Ayana said. "Who else would have had access to your oud, and cause to want to hurt you so?"

"I didn't know," Esther marveled. "I didn't know she blamed me—at any rate, not so fiercely."

"She nursed her anger like a child," Ayana said. "Still, I doubt she acted alone. I think Amestris was behind this, as she is behind so many things. It would not be difficult for one of her people—Raiya, perhaps?—to guess that Roxane might still resent you and to make use of that resentment."

Esther thought of Roxane, Raiya, Haman, Amestris. Difficult, perhaps, to draw a clear line from one to the other, to say, "This is how this thing happened." But not hard to see that all were, in some way, her enemies. All had some reason to dislike her. For Raiya, their old enmity from their first days in the harem. For Roxane, anger at Lilaios' murder that Esther could not prevent. For Amestris, most powerful of all, hatred and suspicion of a rival. And Haman? Esther didn't like the king's latest minister, but she had never sensed in him any personal animosity toward her. Perhaps in this case he had just been caught in a web of women's intrigue. Yet she remembered Mordecai's warning, and shivered. At least Haman did not know she was Jewish. Who did know? Lilaios had known, she remembered. Roxane knew.

Roxane was arrested and imprisoned for spreading malicious rumors about a queen. Esther sent her no message, did not speak to the king on her behalf. When a messenger came from Roxane's mother asking if Esther might show pity, might send them something to help buy food for young Lilaios, Esther sent the messenger away. She remembered Artabazus' words about rebels: stamp out the enemy, root and branch. She had no desire to stamp out the rest of Roxane's family, but also no desire to help them. To care for them now would be like coddling a nest of snakes in her bosom. She tried to put out of her mind images of the friendship she had once shared with Roxane and Lilaios. Betrayal had made even the memories taste bitter.

And yet, nightly she wrestled it out on her knees before God. She could, perhaps, have done more to prevent Lilaios' death. Nothing excused Roxane's treachery, but had she done all she could? Or had she been too concerned for her own safety, her own position, to risk herself for friendship's sake?

There were no easy answers, but she had plenty of time to ponder them. For a fortnight Esther received no summons from the king. She had hoped he would call her. She needed to see him alone, to learn what mark this accusation had left on their marriage. But there was no summons.

Soon, though, there was news of another kind. Lord Admatha, chief of the king's ministers, had died. Rumors about his replacement had been flying for weeks, but the oddsmakers said there was no clear favorite. None of the other councillors.

"Artabazus was considered by many to be the likely choice," Ayana told Esther the evening after Admatha's death, bringing her up to date on gossip. "Even though Artabazus had no seat on the council many thought the king would give him Lord Admatha's place among the seven and promote him to chief minister. Everyone knows how heavily the king relies on Artabazus. But now Artabazus has been sent off to his satrapy to serve his king at a distance," she added, glancing up from her needlework. "The bets are now on Haman filling the chief minister's place, though some say he's too new in the king's service, or has made too many enemies, to serve well."

"I know one who will not be pleased if Haman becomes chief minister," put in Hathakh, who sat at the other end of the hall going over household accounts.

"Who is that?" Esther asked.

"Your kinsman, Mordecai. Among the eunuchs and those who serve at the palace gate, everyone knows of Mordecai's dislike for Haman. When Haman sweeps in with his retinue of servants and hangers-on, many already bow before him as if he already held power. Mordecai never does. And Haman cannot compel it, for he is not yet chief minister. But if he takes that position, he will certainly have no tolerance for disrespect."

"Mordecai is being foolish," Esther said, afraid for her foster father. "He ought not to defy anyone as powerful as Haman. But perhaps he is too unimportant for Haman to trouble with?"

Hathakh laughed. "Haman? A fly on his windowsill is not too

small an enemy if it annoys him. Everyone says the man has a petty mind. He will seek revenge on anyone who stands in his way, no matter how small."

The next day news came that Haman had, indeed, been given the use of the king's signet ring and all the power and position that came with the role of chief minister. Esther heard the tidings with regret. Haman was the worst possible influence on the king, and if his affair with Raiya meant he did have ties to Amestris—which was likely—he was in a position to make Esther's life difficult. And there was Mordecai to think of, too. If only he would have the sense to cloak his dislike for Haman.

The king threw a three-day banquet in Haman's honor. Esther, of course, attended each night and sat at the royal table, along with Amestris, Parmys, and Irdabama, and all the other members of the royal family present in Susa at the time. Haman might not have been well-liked, but he celebrated in fine style, giving lavish gifts to many of the nobles present to celebrate his new position. His wife, Zeresh, was there—a thin, tense-looking woman who seemed ill at ease in the presence of royalty. Raiya, of course, was not in evidence, but throughout the week she'd been seen parading about the women's quarters in especially fine new gowns and jewelry.

As Esther prepared to return home late at night on the final night of the banquet, a messenger from the king stopped her. "His Majesty requests that you come to him tomorrow at the time of the evening meal," he said.

Esther nodded. "I will do as His Majesty bids." She went home in the company of her own servant, feeling oddly nervous about the following night. It would be her first time alone with Xerxes since she'd been falsely accused. Innocent though she was, she knew that the accusation had changed things. He had sent Artabazus away. Not disgraced, but away. And he had not called for Esther herself in three weeks. The anniversary of their marriage had passed with no notice or mention. Now he wanted to see her.

She went to him the next evening dressed in a carefully chosen gown, wearing the silver and turquoise collar he'd given her soon after their marriage. She was conducted through his chambers and out into the small garden adjoining his bedchamber where she'd often joined him before. Once, early in their marriage, they had even made love out here in the garden, excited by the boldness of being outdoors, without all the usual constraints that surrounded a king's privacy. It had only been once, but she still thought of this small garden as a place of love, passion, tenderness.

She saw a table laid with a light meal for two. Xerxes stood a little away from the table, beside a tree. He was alone, except for the servants who blended imperceptibly into the background.

Esther sank to the ground. He came over and offered his hand to lift her to her feet. "I have missed you, Esther," he said, as he had once before when a long time had passed without his summoning her.

"It is gracious of you to say so, my lord," she said.

"Sit, and let us dine."

So Esther sat. Yellow and purple flowers nodded on one side of the garden. A fountain gurgled among artistically trimmed trees. It was a quiet meal. Neither of them spoke very much as they ate. When a servant came to offer more wine the king waved him away. "You will be pleased," he said to Esther. "I have taken no wine since noon. Tonight you have me exactly as I am, myself."

Esther looked at him. She had thought, over the years, that she had restrained her desire to criticize or worry when he drank too much. He was, after all, the king, and no matter how she cared for him, he had the right to do exactly as he pleased. But yes, it was true— and he obviously knew it—that she hated it when his drunkenness fell like a veil between them. She had long wanted to tear it aside and be with the man himself, alone. Tonight that was what he promised.

"I think you are wise, my lord," she said carefully. "I am honored to see you as you truly are."

"Are you? I wonder if anyone really wants that—me, as I really am, I mean," the king said, a little bemused. His eyes warmed, then cooled again. "You already know I am not always an easy man, Esther. There is a reason I often want to be drunk. If I do not want to be alone with myself, why should anyone else want to?"

Esther said nothing. There was nothing she could say that would not be disrespectful, nothing that would not deny the truth of what he said. He was a king, and beneath that royal veneer with all its trappings he was a complex, troubled, driven man. He was the man who'd murdered her friend Lilaios with a single word of command. And the reason she tried to think about that as little as possible was only partly because of grief for Lilaios. It was also, partly, horror at the kind of man she was married to. And yet she could not entirely stop caring about him. She remembered her first sight of him, hand-some and virile. She remembered thinking that she saw behind his eyes the shadow of what he might become in later years if he never recovered from his failure in Greece, if he always took solace in drink. She hated to admit the truth—that the man she saw tonight was far closer to that vision than he had been five years ago.

The moment passed. The king's mood seemed to lift, and he held out a hand to lead her away from the table. Hand in hand, they sat down on a low garden bench, and Xerxes took her face in his hand. "Take off your headdress and let down your hair," he said.

Esther took off the elaborate headcovering, unpinned her hair, and let it fall unbound. No one but her maidservants ever saw her with her hair down—except her husband, alone. From the first he'd loved her hair. He loved to run his hands through it as he did now, to take handfuls of it and draw her face up to kiss him.

"Ah, my Esther," he said. "You would think a man with hun-dreds of women in his harem would find it easy to forget one, wouldn't you? I always have . . . forgotten, that is. But not you. I have tried. How much easier it would have been if you could have been a queen only, a wife only, like the others—and not a lover." He kissed her again. When he was cold sober, like tonight, his words of passion had a rougher edge, sounded less polished than when he was slightly intoxicated. "But you keep coming back, Esther. You come into my mind and my heart. I don't know what your spell is, but I can't quite be rid of you."

"Would you want to be?" Esther asked, touching his face with her fingertips.

"No. I might pretend to wish it, but no."

In his bedchamber Xerxes held her at arm's length. "You are beau-tiful," he said. "Even more beautiful than the first time I saw you."

"I thank you, my lord."

"I should have called for you sooner," he told her, "but I could not bear to think—I knew it was a lie, but to think of Artabazus . . . of any man . . ."

"Hush." She put a finger to his lips. "As you have said, my lord, it was a lie."

"But such a damnable lie!"

He led her to the bed and reclined next to her, but she saw that he was agitated, that the tension building in him all evening was about to break. "It was calculated to strike where it would hurt me most—for loyalty is everything, Esther. You know that, don't you?"

"I do, my lord."

"I cannot stop thinking. No, I will put it from my mind!" He reached for her again, then pulled away. "But you were foolish. You should never have entertained him, never have talked with him. To allow even the appearance of impropriety—even the hint of a scandal. It should not have been done."

Esther raised an eyebrow at that. Was she never in her life to have another conversation with a man? How could she be any more secluded than she was in the harem? But she said only, "I had no thought of anything improper, my lord. But now that I know you would not have it so, I will be more cautious."

"Cautious?" His eyebrows drew together. "Caution is for deceivers!" He looked genuinely angry. Esther felt as confused as if the room had turned upside down.

"Lies! Deception!" he raged. "A stench in the nostrils of Ahura Mazda, the god of Truth." All the passion he had shown a few moments before had melted away. He was an enraged, deeply disturbed man. A few times before she had felt that the aura of kingship had fallen away, and she'd been with Xerxes only as a wife with her husband, but those had been good times, times of tenderness. Now she felt it again. He was not a king, simply a man, a jealous husband, a man tortured in ways she could not even understand. She had never felt so distant from him, so frightened both of him and for him.

"Would you deceive me, Esther? Are you such a fool?" He took her chin in his hand and pulled her face toward his, then thrust it away, with a rough motion that hurt her neck.

She lowered her head; would not meet his eyes. "I am no deceiver, my lord, and I have never been unfaithful to you in word, thought, or deed."

Xerxes was silent a moment, then burst out, "It's no good!"

He swung away from her, out of the bed, parting the curtains. "I thought I could forget, but I can't. *Harbona!*" She heard him calling for his body servant, pulling a cloak around him, striding away from the bed, out of the room. He said nothing more to her. She listened till she knew he had gone on down the corridor, to . . . who knew where? She was fairly sure he was going to find a place to get thoroughly drunk. Perhaps that was what he had wanted all along.

Esther lay back down on the bed, hugging herself like a small child, suddenly exhausted. She was in an odd position. The king did not seem likely to return, but he had not given her permission to depart. Without his permission she could not leave his chambers, at least not until morning. So she drew a cover over herself and tried to sleep. She felt too tired to analyze the past few hours. She only knew that something that had long been fragile was now shattered. Faces, images, worries chased each other around in her brain. She saw the king's face, in tenderness and in anger, as she'd seen both sides tonight. She saw Lilaios' and Roxane's tortured faces. She saw Mordecai and Rivka, and even Haman. Finally she reached for the one picture that could calm and soothe her troubled mind. Holding an image of Damaspia in her mind's eye, Esther fell asleep at last.

CHAPTER 15

Esther sat with Damaspia on her lap, crooning a lullaby to the almost-asleep little girl. Sofia stood nearby, waiting to take Damaspia back to the nursery. Two of the maids were cleaning away the plates from Esther's evening meal. Ayana sat in a corner, sewing. A musician played the chang, and Hathakh had just returned from a meeting with Shaashgaz to discuss the household's upcoming move to Ecbatana. This year the king and court would not be at Parsa in time for the new year. The month of Nisanu had begun, and the ceremonies surrounding the death of Lord Admatha and Haman's elevation in the court had delayed their departure until later in the spring. This year the satraps had sent their envoys to Susa with tribute, instead of to Parsa. But they'd been told that in a month or so they would go to keep the summer court at Ecbatana, and that always meant a great deal of extra work for Hathakh.

Tonight Hathakh paused, looking down at Damaspia in Esther's arms with undisguised fondness. "I heard news of Mordecai today," he told Esther.

Esther quickly glanced round the room. It had become habit to do so before talking openly of her family, but all here were trusted, longtime servants, and most of them knew that Mordecai was her foster father. "What news?" she asked, her heart sinking, for surely it would have something to do with his stubborn refusal to pay Haman the respect due to him.

"His refusal to bow to Lord Haman is the talk of the palace gate," Hathakh said. "He tells those who ask that he has no respect for Haman, that Haman is an enemy of his people, the Jews. He says that if he honored Haman he would dishonor his god."

Esther nodded slowly, and rose to give Damaspia to her nurse. When she sat down again, relieved of the warm burden of her sleeping child, she said, "I understand Mordecai's feelings, but not why he clings so stubbornly to this one thing. I have heard him say that our God—the God of Israel—is the only one we should worship, and that to do homage to another man is to raise him to the level of God. But even Mordecai himself does not observe that strictly; it would be impossible, working in the palace. If he came before the king himself he would certainly bow. He has bowed before others." She paused, thinking. "He distrusts Haman, I know."

"He's far from the only one who does," Ayana murmured.

"True, but no one else goes out of their way to antagonize Haman. He is a dangerous enemy." Esther fell silent again. If Haman was a dangerous enemy, she too had better be careful, for though she knew of no specific enmity between them, she also knew he had no reason to like her, and good reason to be allied with those who did not. That malice had already done enough harm.

Weeks had passed since Esther's last, ill-fated encounter with the king. That night had ended with Esther going back to her own apartments alone in the gray light of dawn. No word had since come from King Xerxes. Every night he summoned a different girl to his chambers. Not all of them were happy when they returned, for the king was rumored to be in a foul mood and drinking heavily. Haman was seldom far from his side. Esther was left with her last memories of Xerxes turning from her, not so much in disgust or even in anger, but in a kind of despair too dark to drown in love-making or in wine. She felt cut loose, adrift. It was a relief, in a way, not to have to journey into that darkness, but she had left a piece of herself there. She could never truly be indifferent to Xerxes or what happened to him, even if her life was easier when her husband was at a distance.

She concentrated on her own household, her friends, Damaspia—and now on this new worry about Mordecai. She hoped he would not get himself into any serious trouble. Perhaps Hathakh could arrange a visit so that she could counsel Mordecai to be more cautious, more diplomatic. As for herself, Esther had no desire to ever be involved in scandal again, or even to draw any attention to herself. If that meant not being called into the king's presence for the rest of her life, so be it. She was beginning to think that would be a price worth paying.

A fortnight passed before Hathakh again brought news of Mordecai. This time he asked to speak with Esther alone.

"What is it, Hathakh?" she asked.

"It is Mordecai, my lady. Since this morning he has been sitting down in front of the palace gates, clothed in sackcloth and ashes—mourning clothes—weeping and wailing."

"What? Why?"

"I could not learn with certainty, my lady. I heard the report this morning, and went out to see for myself. However, such a crowd had gathered around him that I was unable to speak with him. I have heard, though, that other Jews in Susa are also in mourning. They say that a terrible evil has befallen their people."

Esther's mind raced. For years Mordecai had warned her that being Jewish could bring trouble. Now, it seemed, he was right. But what kind of trouble, and from what source? "Hathakh, you must find out more," she told him. "And you must give Mordecai a message from me. Bring him a new suit of clothes and tell him that he must put off this mourning, cease this public display. Whatever has happened, he will only make it worse by behaving in such a fashion."

Hathakh bowed. "I will tell him, my lady. And I will find out what this is all about, I promise you."

He returned later in the day and found Esther sitting in the courtyard with a piece of needlework, a little removed from the groups of other women walking and chatting. She didn't feel like talking. She couldn't help worrying. What danger threatened her people in the city? And why was Mordecai determined to make such a spectacle of himself? She jumped up, eager to hear the news, when she saw Hathakh. His face was sober, and he carried a cloth bundle and a rolled-up parchment.

"I had speech with Mordecai," he said. "He sent the clothes back.

He says he will remain in mourning as long as this edict is in force."

"What edict?"

Hathakh handed her the scroll. "I heard it not just from Mordecai, but from others. Of course, to those who are not Jews it seems a small thing, though a strange one. But to the Jewish people it is a disaster, and one they cannot understand."

Esther scanned the scroll. It was an official document, bearing the king's seal. "Just this morning it was posted and cried aloud in Susa," Hathakh said quietly.

The decree was an order that all Jews living in the Persian Empire were under sentence of death.

Esther read it again, for she could not believe she had read it aright. But on second reading the sense was the same. Every Jewish man, woman, and child—in Susa and in all the provinces—was condemned to death. A date was given for the annihilation: the thirteenth day of Adaru.

"Adaru," Esther echoed, hardly knowing what she was saying. It was only Nisanu now. "That's nearly a year away. Why publish such a decree, so far in advance?"

"Mordecai told me a great deal more than what the text of the edict states," Hathakh said, bending closer. "He has learned Haman is behind this. It's Haman's grand scheme of revenge. He convinced the king to sign it—with the help of a payment of 10,000 talents into the royal treasury."

"Ten thousand talents! Well, I'm sure Haman could afford it, and the royal treasury needs it," Esther said. She had a sudden, vivid picture of King Xerxes and Haman, alone in the king's chambers late at night, empty wine jugs on the table, and a handful of glittering silver in Haman's hands with a promise of more to come.

She visualized the king's signet ring slipping from his finger, offered to Haman, giving permission for the king's most trusted minister to do exactly as he pleased with some obscure clan of enemies scattered throughout the empire. Haman would only have to suggest that the Jews might be troublesome, not conforming to the king's laws, refusing worship to Ahura Mazda in favor of their own god—a dark god, a daiva. Xerxes was growing increasingly zealous about the worship of Ahura Mazda and more eager to stamp out the worship of gods he believed were evil. It would have taken no more than that—along with the wine and the silver, of course.

Esther shivered. She could see it happening, very easily.

"Apparently Haman and some of his supporters—his friends and his sons—cooked up this scheme, then cast lots to determine the most auspicious day. The lot fell on the thirteenth of Adar. Haman is a superstitious man, so he would not tamper with the result of the lots. Besides, if anyone has a grudge against a Jewish neighbor, business partner, or employer, they can take their revenge as they please now that this edict is public. In the 11 months until then much of Haman's work may be done for him. This edict is as good as declaring that the king's protection has been removed from this group of people, and a crime against a Jew is no crime at all."

"You're right." Esther's words were barely audible. She looked up from the parchment, the enormity of it dawning on her.

"Mordecai sent you another message, my lady," Hathakh said, his face showing his reluctance to go on. "He said that you must—forgive me, these are his words. No one should presume to tell you what you must do, but Mordecai says you must go to the king and plead for the life of your people. Ask him to overturn the decree."

"Go to the king? Overturn the decree?" Esther echoed. Mordecai's command held so many impossibilities that she could barely begin to comprehend them all. The king's decrees weren't simply "overturned." The law was *law,* and to change it suggested weakness or vacillation, things no Persian king would admit to. As for going to the king! Mordecai knew nothing, of course, of the accusation made against her or of the estrangement between her and King Xerxes. Perhaps he assumed she still had ready access to the king every few days.

Even so. Even if they'd not been estranged . . . Her mind refused to go that far. To attempt to see him now—when their last meeting, more than a month ago, had ended so unhappily—would be a disaster. And as for simply appearing in his chambers, well, everyone knew what the law said about that. Since Lilaios had come unbidden before him and paid with his life, few doubted that Xerxes would apply the law, perhaps even to a queen.

"Of course you cannot do it, my lady," Hathakh said quickly. "Mordecai does not understand. He sees only his own grief and fear. If you send him a message explaining why you cannot go to the king, surely he will find another way to fight this edict."

Esther frowned, thinking. "Tell him . . . No, wait. I'll dictate a letter. I'll put it in writing so he can't doubt what I'm saying. This is terrible, Hathakh, but I can't become involved. The king doesn't even know I'm a Jew, and if he were to find out now that I'd lied to him about my family all these years, it would be the final blow."

Lies! Deceit! His words rang in her ears.

She dictated a brief message:

"All the king's officials and the people of the royal provinces know that for any man or woman who approaches the king in the inner court without being summoned, the king has but one law: that the person who so appears be put to death. The only exception to this is for the king to extend the gold scepter to the one who comes, thus sparing their life. But 30 days have passed since I was called to go to the king."

As Hathakh left with her letter in his hand Esther reached out and touched his arm. "Hathakh," she pleaded, you must find a way to make him see that no matter how much I care, I cannot do this thing."

"No, my lady. Of course you cannot." Hathakh's voice was firm and sure. He, at least, agreed that intervention was impossible. But he left without promising to try to convince Mordecai. Esther, remembering her uncle's strong will, had a feeling that would not be easy.

Moments later Ayana came and found her, and heard the whole story. "What are you going to do?" she asked.

"What can I do?" Esther replied. "I feel terrible for Mordecai and the rest of my people, but I've spent six years here in the harem hiding who I am. Following my uncle's advice, I've made every effort to conceal the fact that I'm a Jew just in case some danger should ever threaten the Jews. Now that danger has finally come, Mordecai—the very one who insisted I hide the truth—is urging me to unmask and reveal my heritage. What was the point of all those years of silence, of hiding?"

"Is there no possible way Haman could know you're Jewish?" Ayana asked. "Are you sure this is not directed at you?"

Esther picked up the needlework she'd laid aside and fretfully picked at it with her needle. "I don't see how. Haman has no reason to hate me, though he has plenty of reason to be angry with Mordecai for defying him. And of course there have always been people in Susa—and other places too, I suppose—who dislike and resent the Jews for being separate. The Jews worship a different god, and they don't follow many of the traditions and customs of Persia.

But me? I don't see how or why such a thing could be aimed at me."

Ayana nodded, turning to her own needlework. "Haman has his own reasons, I'm sure," she said. "This fits well with his history of feuds and revenge against anyone who crosses him. But . . . I'm not so sure you're not involved. Remember, Roxane knows you're Jewish. Roxane was involved in trying to discredit you before the king, and we think Amestris may have been behind it. Raiya is Haman's mistress. There's no way to be sure, but there could be a link. Even if Haman himself doesn't know you're Jewish, Amestris could be pulling strings behind the scene. It's what she does best, after all."

Esther said nothing. She felt like a tiny fly trapped in the glittering strands of a spider's web. Laying down her work, she crossed the room and looked out the window onto the lush springtime beauty of the harem courtyard. "Ayana, I cannot do this thing that Mordecai asks," she said at last. "The last time I went to the king . . ." Her voice trailed off. She bit her lip. "Do you know what happened?"

"Only that you came home at dawn weeping and refused to talk of it, and have not been called since."

"He rejected me, Ayana. I thought when I went to him that all was well between us. I never forget that I am only one of his many women, but sometimes still, I know that he loves me. And I thought he called for me because he wanted things to be good between us again, that he wanted to make love to me." Tears filled her eyes. "Then something happened, Ayana. He turned away from me as though I disgusted him. In some way he still blames me for Artabazus. Oh, not for being unfaithful"—she shuddered—"or else he'd have had me killed. But for being careless, I suppose. Careless enough to allow for gossip. Perhaps he can't bear to think of my name having been linked, even falsely, with that of another man."

"Perhaps," Ayana said very softly, "he is a very unhappy, troubled man who lashes out at those closest to him. Perhaps the trouble is not you at all, but something within his own heart."

"You may be right." Esther sat down again, unconsciously twisting the needlework in her hands. "What difference does it make, Ayana? Even if the problem is that the king himself is disturbed and unhappy, that will not stop him blaming me. If I request an audience now, he will say no. And if I simply stride uninvited into his presence . . . " The result could be too terrible to speak aloud.

Ayana said nothing. She was the best kind of listener, simply absorbing what was said, making comments but no judgments. After a moment Esther went on,

"But if I do nothing? If the plot includes me! If Haman knows I'm Jewish, or if it comes out . . . I may die anyway. And if I don't—if I'm spared—I could live the rest of my life knowing that my people were slaughtered and I did nothing to save them. I've felt guilty for so long because I didn't do more to save Lilaios, and he was just one man. He was a friend. How can I refuse to lift a finger to save an entire people—*my own people?* Oh, Ayana, I don't know what to do."

Ayana placed a hand on her shoulder. "You have said it clearly. You cannot go to the king, and yet you cannot refuse to go. You cannot think and plan your way out of this. Wait and see what answer Hathakh brings from Mordecai, and then talk to your God."

Esther waited in the courtyard until dusk when Hathakh returned from the city. His face was serious. He carried no letter. Mordecai's words were inscribed on his memory.

Hathakh bowed. "Forgive me, my lady. I give you the words of your kinsman Mordecai. They are not the words I would have wished he had spoken. But I report faithfully that Mordecai, who is still in mourning before the king's gate, says to you, 'Do not think that because you are in the palace, you alone of all the Jews will escape. If you remain silent at this time, relief and deliverance will come for the Jews from another place, but you and your father's house will perish. And who knows? Perhaps you became queen for just such a time as this.'"

Mordecai had always been her source of wisdom, of strength, of support. Now his words stung like a slap.

She asked Hathakh to repeat once more what Mordecai had said, so that she would not forget, and then dismissed Ayana and Hathakh. She told Ayana not to send a maid to help her dress for bed, and retreated to her bedchamber.

She went out onto the balcony from which she had so often spoken with her God. Just a few months before when she'd faced the false accusation of adultery, it had seemed the darkest time of her life. Now she knew that she stood at a far more important crossroads. Then, only her own fate had hung in the balance. Now the fate of an entire people might depend on her.

Or would it? Slowly, as if lifting jewels from a box, she took out Mordecai's hard, shining words and examined them, one by one. *Do not think you alone will escape. . . . You and your father's house will perish.* What did he mean? Did he, like Ayana, think that Haman—or someone aiding Haman, Amestris, perhaps?—knew of her Jewish background and meant this as an attack on her? Or was he just making a threat, trying to frighten her into doing what he obviously believed was the right thing? If Mordecai was right, what choice did she have? Go before the king, and risk death? Or remain silent, and risk death.

Deliverance will come for the Jews from another place. God, of course, had a thousand ways of working out His purposes. If one human vessel failed Him, He could choose another. Was Mordecai speaking as a prophet? Was he sure that God would provide another way out if Esther failed to do her duty? Or was that just Mordecai's fervent hope? Disaster had come to the Jews before, otherwise her family would not be here in Persia. Esther had read that in the times before the exile, the prophets had warned that Israel's and Judah's unfaithfulness to God would bring destruction. What if Esther's unfaithfulness brought destruction, too?

Who knows? Perhaps you became queen for just such a time as this. Here at last was the one thing in Mordecai's words that was not confusing, not double-edged. It was a clear challenge. For six years she had been asking God why He had brought her to this place, given her life this unexpected turn. She had almost become content with the answer that she had no special role to play in God's plan, that her becoming queen was a human accident, not a divine destiny. Now Mordecai had thrown that belief back in her face. She had wanted to know and understand her purpose here in the harem, and later as the wife of the king. Here was a purpose handed to her on a silver platter edged in blood.

Go to the king.

Risk death.

Save your people.

She looked up at the dark sky above the palace. Thousands of stars shone in the darkness—some in distinct patterns, others looking like diamonds spilled on a black cloth. But despite their beauty, the stars were silent.

Throughout the long night hours Esther prayed and thought. In the darkest hours between midnight and dawn, she went back into the house and down into the empty, echoing main hall. She stepped outside into the courtyard. Mist lay in low swirling veils, hiding the apartments on the other side of the court. She heard the ceaseless night noise of chirring insects and the faraway sounds of life—stray dogs barking—beyond the safely enclosing walls of the harem. But the safety of this place was an illusion, wasn't it? She was as much at risk here as anywhere.

She tried to imagine armed men bursting into homes, dragging out old men, children, women, slaughtering them for no other reason than that they were of Jewish blood. Shivering, she felt nauseated at the thought. Surely, in the civilized Persian kingdom where all peoples mingled together and all forms of worship were tolerated under the benevolent gaze of Ahura Mazda—surely such a thing could never happen here.

But it could. She thought of the things she had seen since coming to the palace. Artaynte, a princess of royal blood, horribly mutilated at a queen's command. Bodies hanging from gallows simply because they were *suspected* of conspiracy. A gifted young poet executed on the king's angry whim. Nothing was impossible.

She heard a sound; someone walking in the grass. She looked up. In the shadow of her apartments someone slipped through the mist toward her. A chill of fear raced over her skin. She put a hand over her mouth to keep from crying out. Then she saw it was Hathakh.

He saw her at the same moment. "My lady," he said. "Forgive me. I could not sleep. I came out to walk and . . . think."

"I too have been thinking all night." She gestured to the bench beside her. "Sit down, Hathakh."

He sat down next to her, but said nothing. After a silence Esther said, "Of course I have been awake praying, and thinking of what I am to do about this edict. But what has kept you from sleep?"

Hathakh looked at her a long moment as though he thought her question very strange. "Why, the same thing, of course. What you are going to do."

Tears sprang to Esther's eyes. "How good of you to think of my troubles," she said. "So . . . have you found an answer? What am I to do?"

Hathakh leaned forward and seized her hand, without, for once, a single apology about being too familiar. "My lady, Esther, you *must* not do this thing. You must not go before the king! He is already—fool enough—to hold you in his disfavor. If you push him—if you go to him, making demands, bringing this matter to his attention, telling him you have hidden the truth about your ancestry—he will be angry. I beg of you, my lady, do not unleash his anger upon you. You know what he is capable of!"

"Hathakh, hush!" Esther said in a piercing whisper. "You have already said enough to have yourself tried for treason, or near enough, speaking so rashly against the king." She was worried by what she saw in his eyes. His eyes held something more than concern for her difficult decision. He had real fear in his eyes, something close to panic.

"You need not fear, Hathakh," she added. "No matter what happens to me, I do not think the king will take his anger out on my household. You should not be in any danger."

Now Hathakh's expression changed to something like bewilderment, or annoyance. "Is that what you think? That I'm afraid for my own skin if something should happen to you?"

"Then what are you so afraid for?"

"For *you!*" The words burst from his soul as if he could contain them no longer. "Do you think it has been easy for me, all these years, standing by your side as you ran the risk of being disgraced, or divorced, or even killed anytime the king was displeased with you? He is a man of fierce passions, and not always a wise man. No, I don't care who hears me. He holds your life in his hands."

"All of our lives," Esther whispered.

"Yes, all of our lives, of course. But yours so much more, and you care for him. I suppose that was inevitable, but I did not expect it. It places you in his power. He can hurt you—has hurt you—in so many ways."

As Hathakh talked, something dawned on Esther, something she realized she should have known a long time ago. Hathakh was speaking as if it was something she had always known, but she had been blind to what was so obvious. The fear in his eyes tonight was more than the concern of a loyal servant or even a faithful friend. It was the fear of a man who loved her; who had, perhaps, loved her since they'd first met years before—a man who could never be her lover or her husband and yet was truer to her, perhaps, than husband or lover could ever be.

She found she was clasping his hand; she squeezed it. She had cherished his friendship, yet never recognized how deep it ran. The king had hurt her, but here was the unspoken echo. Esther had hurt Hathakh, and she could not have saved him from that hurt. There was so much to say, yet there was nothing to say—not now, not tonight. She was quite sure Hathakh would not want her to say anything more. He believed in leaving things unspoken; only great need had driven him to say as much as he did. Someday there might be time to sort out her feelings and see how this unexpected revelation fit into them. Before that could ever happen, she must decide what to do about the king and what to do about her people. Depending on what happened next, all friendships, all loves, might be quite irrelevant.

For years now she had felt set apart from everyone, even those she loved most. She had built wall after wall of protection around her heart, yet it seemed love could pierce even the most solid walls. She sat there hand in hand with Hathakh, so much more guarded and careful than even she had learned to be, and knew one thing surely—she was loved, greatly loved. Would it be a foolish gamble to throw away a life so dearly treasured? Or did love make her life the best, and only, gift she could give?

They sat like that for a while, neither speaking, until Esther said, "I must go." She rose and went back into the house. She retreated to her own chamber, this time not to pray but to lie on the bed and fall into a brief exhausted sleep. She had feared she might dream of violence and bloodshed, but she did not. She wasn't sure what she dreamed, though she awoke with an image in her mind: a small twig or branch afloat on a rushing stream that ran between high walls of stone, and a shaft of light from somewhere that touched the water, making the twig gleam like a jewel. Then, in the way of dreams, the picture slipped away, dissolving before she could grasp it.

She opened her eyes. Talia was in the room, laying out her combs, cosmetics, and clothes for the morning. "Ah, you are awake, my lady," Talia said. "I will go tell Kalinn. She will send you up some food and drink, then I'll come back to help you dress."

"Before you do, Talia, please call Ayana to me. I need to speak with her."

In morning light, things seemed clearer. She had knelt before her God once and made a vow, handing over her life like a gift. She had been allowed to keep holding that gift for a time. Now it was time to place it finally in God's hands. Her choice was not so difficult after all.

Ayana came a few moments later. She too looked as if she had slept poorly. "Have you decided what to do?" she asked almost immediately.

"I think I have," Esther said. "It's strange. I prayed and thought and worried all night, and went to bed with no sure idea of what was the right thing to do. I can only have slept a few hours, and I don't remember my dreams, yet when I awoke it was as if the answer was clear in my mind."

Ayana smiled. "Perhaps that is how your God answers."

"It may be," Esther said seriously, pausing to accept a drink and a piece of bread from Kalinn. "I do feel as if His hand is on me. Perhaps this is the first time in my life I've felt close to Him. I don't know. But I've decided to go to the king and plead with him to overturn the decree."

Ayana's smile faded, but she nodded slowly. "It's a terrible risk, Esther. Might it not be better just to send word to him, to ask for an audience?"

"I know how our last meeting ended, and I do not think he will grant me one. He dislikes for his women, even his wives, to ask for meetings. Irdabama has told me she has tried to ask for an audience, even to discuss matters of business, and he has kept her waiting for weeks. What might happen in weeks, or months, now that everyone in the empire knows that the Jews are no longer under the king's protection? Will people hesitate to hurt or kill a Jew a few months in advance of the decree date? I cannot take that risk."

"So you are going right away?"

"No," Esther said, taking a deep breath. "First I mean to ask Mordecai to gather all the Jews of Susa to fast and pray for me for three days. I am going to fast and pray too, and I am going to ask all my household to do the same. Even though we worship different gods, I trust you will all wish me well in this."

Ayana leaned forward and took Esther's hand in hers. "I do not even know that you and I worship different gods, my lady. I have long felt the gods of my childhood were distant and faraway. They stayed behind in Ethiopia, I think. But the more I hear about your God of Israel, the more I feel as you do, that perhaps there is only one true God after all. I will certainly fast and pray with you, as will all the rest of the household, I am sure."

Esther embraced her old friend. "Thank you, Ayana. You'll never know what that means to me. Now I must call Hathakh and give him a message to give Mordecai. He won't be pleased."

"Mordecai? I thought this was just what he wanted."

"Not Mordecai. Hathakh. He doesn't want me to go to the king."

"Hathakh." Ayana sighed. "He is blind with love, my lady." She hesitated. "You knew that, didn't you? I would not have spoken if—"

"It's all right. No, I didn't know, not until last night. I am the one who has been blind. But now that my eyes have been opened, I must shut them again. There is no time to think of this. What Hathakh feels for me—what anyone feels—cannot sway me."

"None of us wants you to risk your life, my lady," Ayana said, standing up. "But I know you must do what you believe is right, as we all must. And I admire you for it, whatever the cost. I'm sure that in the end, Hathakh will think the same. I'll go send for him now."

When Hathakh came in, he looked as he always did: perfectly groomed, completely efficient, a trifle remote. There was no hint here of the driven and desperate man who last night had pleaded with her not to risk her life. She gave him the message for Mordecai, finishing with, "Tell him that when the three-day fast has ended, I will go before the king, even though it is against the law. And if I die, then I die."

Hathakh listened, nodded, and said gravely, "I will endeavor to find him at once." He turned to go.

"Hathakh, wait." They were alone in the chamber; Esther reached out as if to pull him back. "Wait. I need for you to tell me. I know you think I am doing the wrong thing . . ."

For a moment he did not turn around, then slowly he faced her. "On the contrary, my lady, I am sure you are doing the right thing."

"You are? But last night you said—"

Hathakh interrupted quickly as if not wanting to be reminded of the words he'd spoken only hours before. "I spoke from my heart. I did not—I do not—want to see you risk your life. But I spoke as would the family of a man going to battle, who still wish to keep him alive and safe, even as they wave goodbye. I know what your duty is, and I would not have you do less than your duty. And yes, I will fast and pray with you. Some may pray to their own gods, but I will pray to yours." And with that, he was gone.

Hathakh's and Ayana's words sustained Esther through that difficult morning. A few hours later Hathakh returned. Mordecai had agreed to gather the Jews for a season of fasting, beginning at sunset that day. He would announce only that they were fasting and praying for deliverance from the death decree. No word of Esther's plan would be spoken publicly, but behind closed doors he would ask them to pray for Esther, daughter of Israel, wife of the king, that she might be God's instrument to save her people.

That afternoon she assembled the household in the hall. Twenty servants—mostly maids, a few eunuchs—looked curiously at her as she stood before them, Ayana at her right hand and Hathakh at her left. In the front of the group stood Sofia with Damaspia in her arms. Esther had thought long and hard about her daughter. Did she have the right to risk throwing away her life when a child depended on her? On the other hand, if she wanted to raise Damaspia to worship the God of Israel, how could Esther not give her own self, whole-heartedly, to her God's demands? Whatever happened, Damaspia would be too young to understand or even remember. Perhaps that was the hardest part.

Briefly, Esther told her servants about the decree against the Jews. Many of them had already heard about it, for the news had traveled around the palace, though a little more slowly than it had around the city. Only a small number of Jews served within the palace itself. She saw her servants listening, nodding, but many of them were still puzzled. Those closest to her, who had served her the longest, understood, but others didn't see the connection.

"Not all of you know that I am a Jew," Esther said, her voice stumbling a little over the words she had not spoken publicly in all her time in the harem. "But my family is Jewish. I am Jewish. this law affects me and those I love. I cannot stand by and say nothing, even if my position in the palace were enough to protect me from harm, which it is not. I am going to go to the king, uninvited, and ask him to overturn his decree. You know what that could mean.

"For three days, starting tonight at sunset, I will fast and pray to my God for His protection, guidance, and deliverance, both for me and for His people. I ask that all of you fast and pray with me, if you would. Hathakh my steward and Ayana my lady-in-waiting are standing here beside me because they have already pledged themselves to keep this fast with me, and add their prayers to mine. Will you do the same?"

"Of course we will!" Talia's soft voice burst out. Sofia echoed her; other voices joined the chorus. The women and eunuchs of the household clustered around Esther, expressing their fears for her safety, their admiration of her courage. She had always felt loved and cherished by her household, but never as much as she did at that moment. Not much time had passed since all of them had been hauled off and interrogated about her faithfulness to the king. They'd shown perfect loyalty then; they showed the same now.

Yet even as she took their hands and thanked them for their good wishes, she could not help thinking of Roxane. Who knew if her household might hide a hidden spy, someone who wished her ill? But it was too late now for caution. They must know all her plans, if they were to be a part.

"Two more things," Esther said. "If I can help it, I would not have all the palace, or even all the harem, know of my plans. If we can keep our fast secret, and tell no one of my plan to go before the king, I will have the advantage of surprise. And another thing"—at this she smiled—"while you are fasting, I must also ask you to plan for a banquet." Their eyes widened in surprise. "On the night after the fast ends—if my God spares my life—I will be giving the most lavish banquet I have ever hosted. No expense must be spared. I must have the finest of everything."

"How many guests, my lady queen?" asked the cook.

"Only two, besides myself," Esther said, and smiled again at the man's wrinkled brow. "Two guests, but one will be the king himself, so you see why everything must be of the best. I dismiss you to your duties now. Tonight at sunset we will meet here together again."

So began the strangest three days of Esther's life. For six years she had hidden her identity, pursued her worship of God and her search for the truth about Him in private. Now she met with her household at morning, noon, and night to lead them in prayers she read from her cherished collection of Hebrew scriptures. Many of them, she knew, were praying to their own gods on her behalf. She appreciated their intent, but she would no longer hide the fact that in her eyes there was only one true God, and it was in the service of this God that she was taking her life into her hands.

Hunger pains knotted her stomach—and thirst, for Esther had even extended her own fast to exclude drinking. But her mind became more sharply and clearly focussed on the thing she had to do.

Between her times of public prayer, she spent much of her time in private prayer and in reading the scrolls of God's Word. God had delivered His people miraculously in the past. He could do it again, if He chose to honor her in that way. But those who died in His service were honored too, she remembered.

The rest of her time, Esther spent with her daughter. Damaspia was far too young to understand what was going on, and of course no one expected her to fast. Esther played with her, told her stories, and held her until she fell asleep each night. How she treasured those hours! It was possible that after the three days were over, Damaspia might never see her mother again. Was she too young to retain even the faintest memory—a voice, a touch, a kiss?

After sunset on the third day, when Esther finished praying, she invited her servants to go to the kitchens and break their fast. Most went eagerly, after stopping to say a final goodbye to their mistress and promising she would be in their thoughts and prayers on the morrow. Esther went alone to her private chamber, but in the anteroom outside her bedchamber, she found Ayana and Hathakh both sitting there.

"I've brought something for you to drink," Ayana said, holding out a cup. Esther took it and drained it eagerly. She'd felt that her tongue was glued to the roof of her mouth. Reading through the prayers had been particularly difficult tonight.

"And will you take some food?" Hathakh asked, but Esther waved the proffered bowl of dates away.

"No, I will go on fasting until tomorrow after my deed is done," she said.

Hathakh nodded. "We thought as much," he said. "We too will fast with you until the morning."

"You don't need to do that!" Esther said, but Ayana chimed in, "We want to. If this is the last thing we can do for you, we will do it."

"Whatever happens, it's not the last thing," Esther said. "I need you both to promise me that if—if I really am put to death, you will look after Damaspia. Beg the king to allow one or both of you to serve in her household, where you can see who cares for her, what becomes of her." She fought back the tears. "If the decree goes ahead—surely, even if her mother is Jewish, the daughter of the king would not be put to death."

"Surely not," Ayana said quickly. "And of course, we will serve her if need be. But there will be no need, my lady. I cannot believe that the king would have you put to death."

Esther sighed. "Who knows what the king may do?" The three sat quietly for a long time, until finally Esther said, "I want to be alone for a little while. Ayana, at the hour the king goes to his audience chamber, come and help me dress."

She spent those last hours alone in prayer, though really there was nothing more to say, even to God. Finally she just rested, saying nothing more, not even thinking . . . simply waiting.

Ayana tapped lightly at the door. "Hathakh has gone to the palace. He says the king will be in the throne room shortly. It is time."

The day before, Esther had decided that she would wear the finest robes she possessed, those she'd worn when she was married and named queen. The robes were elegantly beautiful, edged with the purple, declaring her royal status. Even the royal tiara and her wedding jewelry would be brought out on this occasion. Xerxes must not underestimate the importance of the occasion, nor be given reason to forget who she was, and why he had raised her to such a position.

When she was washed, her hair done, her cosmetics applied, and her clothes donned, she looked at herself in her polished bronze mirror. The woman returning her gaze looked like she had been through a three-day fast accompanied by great anguish and fear. Her eyes were dark and hollow. Even with her eye paint the circles under them could not entirely be disguised. But she knew, too, that she looked lovely. Would beauty, which had once won Xerxes' heart, be enough to snare it today? Or was something more required?

Ayana, also gowned in her best, accompanied Esther out of the harem and through the king's private court, then through the corridors that led to the inner court—the center of the king's three courts guarded by powerful winged sphinxes. She turned north to pass between the sphinxes, up the columned walkway that led to the throne hall.

Heads turned as Esther passed. None of the royal women came out of the harem without being summoned by the king, and such a summons was usually common knowledge among those who served him. For one of the queens to appear unexpectedly—especially so richly dressed and ornamented—was an unexpected occurrence. With hesitant and cautious glances, courtiers and servants bowed to

Esther as she passed. They were not sure of her standing with the king, and thus unsure how much respect to show.

Finally she stood under the purple and white awnings, the pillared throne hall before her. The great bronze-plated doors were guarded but ajar. In that instant two pictures sprang to Esther's mind: Lilaios, dragged from this same room to his death, and Xerxes' cold, angry face the last time she'd seen it. "My lady . . ." one of the guards at the door stammered, knowing the law but unsure how to proceed. "We received no word . . . that you had an audience. Perhaps you . . . could you . . . it might be best if we informed the king."

"Inform the king of nothing," Esther said firmly. Just as firmly, she replaced the two mental images with two others: Mordecai sitting in sackcloth outside the palace, and thousands of Jews being slaughtered at King Xerxes' command.

I am in Your hands, God of Israel, she said as she stepped past the confused guards and into the throne hall.

CHAPTER 16

The buzz of talk that always hummed through the audience hall stilled as Esther walked through high, wide doors. Nobody missed her entrance, including the king.

Esther began the long, slow walk between the two central rows of pillars, between dozens of staring eyes. She did not glance at them, nor at the king, who sat enthroned at the far end of the room. She kept her eyes on the mosaic floor at her feet while each light footfall reverberated like a heartbeat in the absolute stillness of the echoing throne hall.

Just before she reached the steps of the throne, Esther sank onto the brilliant mosaic tile floor in a deep and graceful obeisance. Head bowed almost to the ground, eyes closed, she waited and listened. For a moment the only sound she heard was her own heartbeat. Then she heard what she had been waiting for, a barely audible "Aaahh," and then another. Around the throne room, men were letting out their held breath in small gasps of relief.

She allowed herself to lift her eyes.

The king's arm was upraised, holding out the golden scepter toward her. Esther rose slowly and walked forward, reaching out with her own hand to touch the tip of the scepter before again kneeling before the throne.

"Rise, Queen Esther," said King Xerxes. She heard no annoyance or anger in his voice, only surprise and curiosity. He knew, as did everyone in the room, that only something terribly important would cause a wife who was not in great favor to risk her life by appearing publicly in the king's audience chamber. "What do you wish?" A smile twitched behind his beard. "You may have whatever you want, up to half of my kingdom."

Esther allowed herself to feel encouraged by the grandiose words of royal favor. They were a sign that the king was intrigued rather than disturbed by her appearance. But she'd already decided that to state her request here and now would be a tactical mistake. Xerxes would be put on the spot, required unexpectedly to address a thorny question in full view of courtiers and soldiers. Esther had another plan.

"My request is simple, my lord king. I ask only that if I find favor in your eyes, if it pleases you to grant my request, you and my lord Haman should come today to a banquet in my quarters."

Again she heard the little ripple of noise that hurried around the massive square room; again she saw the bemused smile at the corners of her husband's mouth. Such a small request—an unusual one, perhaps, but at the same time trivial; something any servant could have delivered. Everyone in the room understood that Queen Esther had something important to say to the king, important enough for her to risk death, important enough for her to invite him to her quarters in this most public and attention-getting fashion.

Esther shot the briefest of glances at Haman, who was standing a few paces to the right of the throne. His eyes were fixed on the king. He, like Esther, was trying to read his royal master's expression. But she saw in the twitch of his lips how the honor of being included in a private dinner with the king and queen had elevated him a few notches in his own importance.

"It will be our pleasure to dine with you," the king said. He glanced at Haman. "We will change our previous plans. Make ready to accompany me to Queen Esther's quarters at the time of the evening meal."

Esther bowed again. "I thank you, my lord king," she said, and turned to take her leave. A ripple of questions and conjectures followed in her wake.

By midafternoon, Ayana told her, the story of her sudden appearance in the throne room had circulated throughout the palace. It was being talked about all over the harem.

"And no one connects it with the decree against the Jews?" Esther asked. She felt much better now, with the first and most dangerous part of her ordeal over. She relaxed in her private chamber, breaking her fast at last with the fruit, nuts, and sour milk Ayana had brought her.

"No, I have heard no one make that connection," Ayana said.

"Then my secret is still safe," Esther said with a sigh of relief. "Either no one knows or the ones who know are not telling." She bit into a pomegranate with pleasure. "I feel quite sure now that Haman doesn't know, and that he did not direct this against me personally. He seemed proud to have been included in the invitation. If he knew I was a Jew, I do not think he would count it such a mark of favor."

"That sounds reasonable," Ayana said, nodding.

"Of course, it's still quite possible that someone else who does know—perhaps Amestris—is working with or behind Haman on all this, encouraging him in his campaign against the Jews with the knowledge that it will harm me too. Who can say? I have made the first move. Let us see what happens tonight." Almost lighthearted, she gave her friend a sparkling smile. "Come, you must help me dress."

As the time for the evening meal drew near, Haman and the king, accompanied by a retinue of guards, entered the harem and arrived at Esther's chambers. Her staff, relieved to have the fast ended, had worked diligently all day to prepare the most delicious and attractive meal possible. Their mood was optimistic. If the king had consented to dine with Esther, surely nothing could go wrong, and her request would be successful. Of course, Esther knew that for most of her household only her own fate mattered. If their mistress was safe, they did not much care what became of those obscure Jewish people she claimed to be related to.

Esther knew she faced at least two major hurdles still to leap. As Haman and the king sampled the best wine and most elaborate food presentation Hathakh had been able to procure, and her best musicians wove a background of light, intricate melodies, Esther turned those two problems over in her mind as she'd been doing all day long.

First, in order to lay her case before the king, she must reveal that she was a Jew. That meant revealing that she had lied to him and his officials about her family background when she first came into the harem and, later, upon the occasion of her marriage. Esther knew Xerxes well enough to know that—in theory, at least—he was passionately devoted to the truth. A king must, of course, dissemble and stretch the truth for reasons of politics, but Xerxes regarded the Lie as the ultimate evil and the pursuit of Truth as the ultimate good. While he might not be rigorous in his own adherence to truth, he expected it unequivocally from everyone else. Esther, whose own God had said that lying lips were an abomination, did not at all look forward to making this revelation.

Second, supposing she ever got past the first problem, there remained the fact that she was asking the king to change his mind, to repeal a law that had already been made public. No king wanted to do such a serious thing. It would make him look weak, vacillating. If word got out that he'd repealed a law to grant someone a favor, that would make him look easily influenced. If it were known he'd done it under the influence of a woman, even one of his queens, that might make him a laughingstock. And Haman was here, right now gesturing with the thigh of a roast duck he held in his hand. Haman, who was very high in the king's favor—higher, indeed, than she. Yet he was a part of the plan. She could not place this request before the king without Haman's being present.

Despite pondering these difficult problems, Esther kept a flow of small talk going by sharing light palace news and asking questions of Haman and the king. The meal had ended. Esther and her guests sat back enjoying their wine. The moment could be put off no longer. Esther's husband, the king of Persia, leaned forward, obviously still intrigued.

"A lovely banquet, my queen. But I know you did not appear in my audience hall just to invite me and my chief minister to dinner. Tell me, what is it you wish? I will indeed grant you anything you ask, up to half my kingdom."

"My lord king, if it pleases you—" Esther began, and stopped. When she caught her breath she had changed her mind. "I would like to invite you and Haman to a second banquet here, tomorrow evening. At that time I will make my petition of you."

She found herself holding her breath.

For a moment the king looked almost irritated, as if this woman was wasting his time, and he might force her to reveal her request then and there. That might be disastrous. Then he checked himself, sat back and nodded, as if she had moved a piece on a game board. "Very well then," he said pleasantly. "Another banquet tomorrow night. But then you must tell me."

"I will, my lord."

The king did not linger long after Esther had issued the second invitation. When the men had gone, Esther sat alone in the dining pavilion looking out at the gardens beyond. She wondered if she had made a wise choice or simply been a fool. Delaying for another night was a tactic born of fear, but it had felt right, too. She sensed that the king would be that much more intrigued, and more convinced of the importance of her request when it finally came.

Esther slept better that night than she had since she'd first heard the news of the edict. In the morning she awoke and went to the baths, returned home and dressed, and then went to the nursery to visit and eat with Damaspia. Already the staff bustled around preparing for the next banquet. Esther had told Hathakh that everything— the food, wine, and entertainment—must be even more lavish than the night before. With almost no time to prepare, and no explanation as to why all this was necessary, Hathakh and his staff set to work with surprisingly good grace. Esther was surprised to see her steward appear in the nursery just as she and little Damaspia were finishing their meal.

"Is all well, Hathakh? Are there troubles in preparing for the banquet?"

Hathakh bowed slightly. "No troubles, my lady. It is a great deal of work, but as you know, I am an expert at creating much out of nothing." They both smiled. "But I came to tell you that there is news in the palace this morning. It seems that much has happened overnight."

"Really? What?" The quick note of concern in Esther's voice caught Damaspia's attention for the child looked up curiously though Hathakh delivered his news in a flat, unemotional tone as if to convince Damaspia that this was dull, grown-up news not worth the attention of a little girl almost 2 years old.

"First, construction workers have been at Haman's estate outside the city since before dawn. He is having something built—a great tall tower—no one knows for certain what it is, but it's being erected very hastily. Some say it will be a gallows."

"A gallows! Who would Haman have the authority to hang?"

Hathakh frowned. "Someone the king gave into his power."

"Not Mordecai—?"

"Perhaps that is Haman's intent, but I assure you Mordecai is in no danger today. That is the other, and stranger, piece of news. At noon today there will be a procession out through the gates of the palace and through the streets of the city. Mordecai has been brought from his place at the palace gate—apparently he is no longer wearing mourning, since he believes God will deliver the Jews through you, so there were no awkward questions about that—and he is to be dressed in royal robes and given the king's own horse to ride through the streets."

"Mordecai!" Esther repeated. Such a procession was given only to honor someone very high in the king's favor, someone who had performed a great service for the country. "Why? What is the reason for this?"

"Apparently the king could not sleep last night," Hathakh said, betraying another hint of a smile. "Perhaps something in the evening troubled or intrigued him or made him curious . . . we'll never know, I suppose. But whatever the cause, the king could not sleep, and he called one of his eunuchs to read to him from the royal chronicles."

"A good choice for someone who wants to be put to sleep," Esther said dryly. She wondered why the king hadn't chosen one of his more usual means to a good night's sleep—wine, or a concubine. No doubt he had his reasons.

"At any rate, dull as they may be, the chronicles brought up something the king had apparently forgotten. Five years ago there was an assassination attempt that was foiled when his new bride, Queen Esther, heard news of a plot from a man named Mordecai. You'll remember that two eunuchs were executed for their part in the plot."

"Bigthan and Teresh. I remember," said Esther.

"But the man who reported the plot, Mordecai, was never honored for his service to the king. He simply went on quietly doing his job, and asked for no reward."

"And just like that, King Xerxes decided to honor him so lavishly?" Esther asked. It seemed almost too much of a coincidence. Had the king asked to have the annals read at random? Or had he deliberately asked to hear about those months after his and Esther's marriage? Was there something in the past he was trying to recapture?

"Not quite as simple as that," said Hathakh. Damaspia began tugging on the edge of his tunic. "Up, up," she said, and Hathakh lifted her in his arms before continuing. "From what I hear, the king began brooding on how he should honor Mordecai, and asked one of his attendants, Zethar, if any of his advisers was about. As it was halfway between midnight and dawn, it seemed unlikely anyone would be about, but Haman—who certainly went home after your banquet last night—had returned to the palace already. He was due to meet with the king in the early morning, but perhaps he was having trouble sleeping too. At any rate, he was in the outer court, and the king summoned him and asked, 'What should I do for a man I wish to greatly honor?'"

Esther laughed as she saw the picture unfold. "You mean— Haman assumed the king was talking about him?"

"Of course. What else would a man like Haman think? Haman described with great detail the kind of procession given to conquering generals or others who have performed the greatest of feats. And the king, who is not without a sense of humor, promptly assigned him to prepare this exact parade in Mordecai's honor."

"The king knows, of course—"

"That Haman dislikes Mordecai? I'm sure he's heard rumors. I don't think, though, that he realized Mordecai is a Jew. Indeed, I don't think the king has given much thought to that decree since the day he signed it. Or even that he gave it much thought when he signed it."

"You think he was drunk at the time, don't you?" Esther said bluntly.

"That is what is said," Hathakh replied carefully. He swung Damaspia gently to the ground. "I must go. I have much to do."

"Wait, Hathakh. Can I add one more thing to your list of duties?"

"Of course, my lady."

"Can you arrange a litter and an escort for myself and Ayana this afternoon, at the time this parade will be held? I cannot miss seeing this."

Hathakh bowed briefly. "It shall be done, my lady."

At noon Esther and Ayana, both veiled, left the harem and walked for the second time in two days through the private court to the inner court, and beyond to the outer court, another place Esther had never seen. This was the bustling service court where servants, guards, and officials moved like insects swarming. Here, a litter was waiting. Esther and Ayana were helped into it, and the slaves hoisted it onto their shoulders. Beyond the closed curtains, Esther could hear the change in the pitch and intensity of sound as the litter moved, swaying and jolting, out of the palace proper into the open grounds between the palace and the king's gate. The noise swelled even more as they passed through the gate and out into the city streets. Voices were louder, children shouted, peddlers hawked their wares. They could tell by the sounds as they passed that the litter was attracting some attention, for any litter coming out of the palace was likely to contain one of the women of the royal house, but Hathakh had wisely arranged that neither the litter, its bearers, nor its guards should attract undue attention. No one would be likely to guess that one of the queens was inside. Nothing must draw attention away from Mordecai's procession.

In a shaded square not far from the king's gate the bearers stopped, leaving the litter to rest upon their shoulders as Esther and Ayana watched the parade. They kept the curtains closed until the noise of the crowd indicated that the procession was coming out through the king's gate and entering the square. Then Ayana drew the curtains aside so Esther could look out.

Through the fine fabric of her veil Esther could see armed men marching, the vanguard of the procession. Hangers-on followed in front, beside, and behind. At the center of the throng was a man mounted on a horse. It was Mordecai, dressed as a king in royal robes such as a prince of the blood might wear. But that wasn't the best part to Esther's view. Ahead of Mordecai ran a man in the garb of a herald, leading the reins of the royal stallion upon which Mordecai sat. The man was Haman, crying out loudly, "Behold! This is what the king does for the man he delights to honor!"

From the buzz of voices around them Esther sensed that the crowd hardly knew what to make of the spectacle. Almost no one recognized Mordecai or had any idea what he had done to deserve such honor. Many, however, knew Haman. Who was this man so exalted that even the king's greatest minister ran before him as his herald? To those in the palace itself who would have recognized both men and knew the bad blood between them, the irony would have been delicious.

But of course, in any such spectacle, the person really being honored was the king. The whole pageant, including Haman's cry, was designed to clearly send the message that Xerxes, the King of Kings, was a ruler so mighty that any man who pleased him, in however trivial a way, could wear royal robes and ride a royal horse. The king had glory enough and to spare.

As the horse drew closer, Esther lifted her veil for just an instant. She so wanted to catch a glimpse of both men's faces. Haman's was all she would have expected—angry and embarrassed. But Mordecai's face was a mystery. He must have been confused; he must have felt a chaos of conflicting emotions. He had just spent three days fasting and praying to be spared a death decree, only to find himself riding through Susa on the king's stallion, wearing the king's clothes. But nothing showed on his face. He was calm, impassive. He looked at no one in the crowd. It was almost as if he had retreated from the scene, leaving only his body behind, clad in the royal robes.

When the crowd had passed, Esther commanded the slaves to take her home. It was past time to get ready for the second banquet.

That night, as before, the king and Haman arrived together. As Hathakh had promised, the food, wine, and music surpassed even the previous night's offerings. The banquet room looked even more beautiful than it had the night before. Elaborate bouquets of flowers banked the tables. The dishes and flatware were polished mirrors. And the cook had outdone himself with unique garnishes for the meat and vegetables. It was a feast for all the senses, not just the mouth.

The king showed the same mixture of pleasure and curiosity he had on the previous night. Esther felt the same nervousness. But one guest was in a markedly different mood. Haman was almost surly. He barely spoke, but stared into his wine goblet and picked at his food. The day's events had humiliated and sobered him. Haman opened like a plant to the sunshine of royal favor, but the slightest hint of disfavor shut him up tight.

Once again the dinner was cleared, goblets were refilled, the musicians struck up a new song, and the king turned to Esther. He set down his wine—he was drinking with some restraint tonight, she was glad to see—and said, "Come now, my queen. For two nights you have feted us with the best your kitchens and cellars have to offer, but you refuse to tell me what you ask in return. I must know. Now—what is your request? I have already promised to grant all that you ask."

It was time to cast it all onto the table. "My lord king," Esther said, slipping from her couch to kneel before him, "if I have found any favor in your eyes, I have only one petition. Spare my life. And I have one request. Spare the lives of my people."

The king's face registered complete surprise. What was she talking about?

Esther rose from her knees and stood with her open, empty hands toward her husband. "My people have been sold, my lord— to be destroyed, slaughtered, and annihilated!"

"Your *people?*" the king echoed. "Your *family?*"

"Not merely my family, my lord, but my people, all the people of my race, all those whose blood I share. A decree has gone out saying that we are to be exterminated. My lord, if we had simply been sold into slavery I would not have begged you like this, for I know that your laws are carved in stone. No mere slavery or exile would have caused me to distress you in this way. But this is a decree of death, my lord! I must plead for my own life and the lives of my people!"

She had not rehearsed the speech. It came tumbling out without any planning, any restraint, but she saw that it had had an effect. A frown darkened the king's puzzled face.

"What are you talking of, my lady? Who would dare pass a death decree on my queen and her blood kin? Who would do such an evil thing?"

With a deep breath and a prayer Esther spun and pointed at Haman. "This man, my lord!"

She'd not even glanced at him before. Now she saw that he'd frozen—wide-eyed and openmouthed in horror. Her earlier guess had been right. He had not had the slightest idea that she was a Jew, much less related to Mordecai. This revelation coming on top of the afternoon's events, must have seemed like the end of his world. But Esther could show him no pity. "This wicked, vile man Haman is the enemy of my people, the Jews."

The king jumped up at the word Jews, and Esther knew that all the pieces had fallen into place. He must have finally remembered the decree over which he'd so lightly given Haman his seal. A minor matter to a wine-soaked king in the hands of a crafty, power-hungry minister with his own grudges to pursue. Without a word Xerxes turned and strode from the room, out through the north portico to the garden terrace and the palace gardens beyond.

Esther was alone at the table with Haman. Suddenly weak, she sank down on her couch. Around the room stood the guardsmen and a few of the upper servants, including Hathakh and the king's two eunuchs. One soldier had followed the king into the gardens. Everyone else stayed as they were.

Now with the lots cast and all revealed, Esther could guess a little of the emotions swirling through Xerxes' mind. He would be angry at Haman for making a fool of him, for tricking him into signing a decree whose full implications he had not understood. He would be angry at himself for allowing himself to be put in such a situation, angry that he was such a weak ruler that he gave away his seal without knowledge of what it actually meant. And somewhere in there, Esther thought, the realization was bound to dawn that he did not know Esther was Jewish. He thought she was Persian. Thus, she must have lied to him.

And it followed—Esther trembled at the thought—that he would be angry with her.

Her ears strained to hear the king, pacing and muttering in the courtyard. *What was he thinking? What was he saying? Just how angry was he with her?* As the questions swirled around her mind, she forgot about the man left in the room with her. No, she hadn't quite forgotten him, but Haman seemed almost insignificant. Everything hinged on the king. She closed her eyes, wordlessly begging God for mercy. Then suddenly she was aware of Haman, off his couch and kneeling before hers. She saw two guardsmen and Hathakh step forward in unison, the guardsmen with hands on their swords, but Haman was not kneeling by her couch in anger but in fear.

"My lady queen, you must forgive me," he stammered. "You must. You must tell the king that I knew nothing of this. I didn't know . . . I never guessed . . . you were a Jew. Believe me, lady, I meant you no harm. You must know that. It was only this one man—this evil, shameful man, a worm named Mordecai—"

Esther put out one hand as if to block his words. "Mordecai is my cousin. He is my foster father who raised me in his own home," she said coolly, just for the pleasure of watching Haman trip over his own tongue trying to take back his words.

"He is . . . ? Mordecai . . . your kinsmen? My lady, I beg you. I swear . . . I never . . . I will take it all back. There were others, I swear, it wasn't me alone. My friends, my sons, Raiya—she urged me on to ask the king for the decree, to attack all the Jews."

Esther laughed bitterly. "You hope to excuse yourself by claiming your lover influenced you? What a pathetic excuse for a man you are, Haman."

His face was purple; his eyes mad with fear. "My lady, quickly!" he choked out the words. "Before the king comes back, you must tell him—"

His hands desperately groped the air. He grabbed for Esther's hands, flinging himself on the couch. In the same instant, before she could react, she heard a roar.

"Venomous little worm! Will you attack my queen while I am here in her house?"

Silence. A long, deathly quiet filled the room. Not a movement. Not a sound. Even the guards held their breath.

Xerxes stood statue-still, staring at Haman. The little man had frozen, his hands locked on Esther's, his knees on the floor, his body half across her couch.

Without a glance or a word, two guards stepped forward and seized Haman, each with a hand on an arm. Their eyes turned to King Xerxes, who nodded. One of the guards took out a square of dark cloth and placed it over Haman's head.

It mattered not what had actually happened; the king had accused Haman of molesting the queen. And indeed, Haman had snatched the hands of the king's wife. He had flung himself on a woman who was, after all, the king's property. No further accusation, no trial, no sentence, was necessary.

A small whimper came from beneath the cloth. One of the guards jabbed Haman in the ribs with his spear, and the once-arrogant man said no more.

"Where shall we take him, my lord king?" asked the soldier.

In the brief pause before the king answered, his attendant Harbona stepped forward and bowed. The king gestured permission for him to speak.

"My lord king, on Haman's property there stands a great gallows, built just today. It is said that he built it to execute Mordecai the Jew."

The king smiled. The smile widened until his shoulders shook, and he threw back his head and laughed.

"Take Haman home," he commanded. "The gallows is prepared, and here is the body to swing from it. Hang him above his own house, in the sight of his wife and concubines and sons and servants, so that all may see what happens to the man who threatens the queen."

Hours later, when Esther tried to piece together the rest of the evening, it blurred in her memory. Haman was half dragged, half carried from the room. The king commanded Esther to accompany him back to his council room, where his remaining six councillors were summoned for an unexpected late-night meeting. As they waited in the long room, darkened by its heavy wall hangings, for the councillors to arrive, King Xerxes turned to Esther.

"Tell me of this man Mordecai," he said suddenly. He had not spoken to her since they'd left her quarters. "He is a treasury official, is he not? Someone of no importance save that he had some personal feud with Haman—as did many—and suddenly he is at the center of attention. Who is he?"

Esther bowed her head and took a deep breath, then gave the same answer she'd given to Haman. "Mordecai is my foster father," she said. "He once worked in your treasury, but now he is a keeper at the king's gate. He raised me as his own daughter. He and I are blood kin, though I am almost sure Haman did not know that. Whether Haman hated Mordecai because he hated all Jews, or whether he came to hate all Jews because of his hatred of Mordecai, I do not know."

"Nor does it matter much," he mused. "Haman had a nature given to hatred." The king was agitated, pacing the room. "And I indulged it. I trusted him too much. You said that, didn't you? You, and Artabazus, and a great many others."

He fell silent, brooding as he stared down at the signet ring he'd once given Haman. Within the seal of the ring—the king's official seal—lay the power to wipe out a whole race of people without even troubling to find out who they were or the nature of their crime. His eyes darkened and he unconsciously shook his head.

Esther saw his grim expression and caught her breath.

"You have no estates of your own, have you?" he said suddenly.

"No, my lord."

"Of course not. You told me your people were common merchants of Susa. But that was not quite true, was it?"

"No, my lord. When first I was brought to the palace, I chose to keep my lineage a secret. Mordecai had warned me once that it was sometimes dangerous to be Jewish. I did not believe it, for I knew of your tolerance toward all peoples, yet I thought it wise to hide. The family I claimed are distant relatives, by marriage only, without a drop of Jewish blood. My true family are all Jews, as am I."

She braced for a reprimand, but the king said only, "I think we can remedy that problem of your having no lands. I know a very nice property that will be vacant shortly, as soon as an unsightly gallows is taken down from it. And can this man Mordecai be summoned to our meeting tonight?"

"Yes, my lord," Esther said. "If no one else can get word to him quickly, send my steward Hathakh. He knows where Mordecai lives."

"We will summon him," the king said. "He wore my robe and crown today; let him be my adviser tonight."

Footsteps in the corridor indicated that some of the ministers had arrived. The king twisted his signet ring on his finger again. "Let us see now what we can do with this decree without making me look an utter fool, shall we?" He gave Esther a wry smile, and for an instant, covered her hand with his. Then the herald at the door announced that Lord Carshena had arrived.

▼ ▼ ▼

Eleven months later Esther sat again in the king's council chamber as he heard reports of what had happened on the thirteenth and fourteenth days of Adaru. So much had changed in the months since her life had turned upside down—again. Incredibly, it was now Mordecai who sat at the king's right hand, bearing his signet ring and all the symbols of authority. Xerxes had been so impressed with Mordecai in the aftermath of Haman's execution that several weeks later he'd appointed Mordecai to the council in Haman's place, with all the power and authority of the chief minister.

The move had, of course, caused consternation among the courtiers. For the second time in a few short years the king had raised up a newcomer from virtual obscurity and given him the second most powerful position in the land. The nobles were by no means pleased. It was seen as one more evidence of the king's growing instability, his susceptibility to outside influence.

But Mordecai himself won over many of his critics. He was a good, steady adviser to the king and a capable administrator who did not use his power to make himself rich or punish his personal enemies, as Haman had done. Though many still resented his sudden rise to power, they accorded him a grudging respect.

His main role, at first, had been to help the king and his councillors find a way out of the problem posed by Haman's edict. Most of the councillors had thought the original decree ill-advised and foolish, but not a major problem. No one knew or cared very much about the Jews, a scattered band of conquered foreigners left behind when their leaders returned to their homeland generations ago. But overturning a royal decree was a tricky business. Mordecai's proposed compromise—a decree that permitted the original attack, but also allowed the Jews to defend themselves—posed problems of its own.

Most of the people who might have originally sought to attack their Jewish neighbors would probably see in the death of Haman and the new decree good enough reason to abandon the attempt. But in areas where there was a strong anti-Jewish feeling—and once the council began to explore the matter, they discovered that such feelings did exist in parts of the empire—the edict amounted to permission for open warfare in the streets. Yet to overturn the king's decree would only add to the growing groundswell of feeling that the king was fickle, easily influenced, and untrustworthy. Of course this was an opinion that no one could voice out loud in council with the king, but one of which everyone present was keenly aware.

Mordecai's compromise was taken apart and put back together 20 different ways, and finally accepted. The new decree went out. Now the month of Adaru had arrived, and some Persians had indeed attacked their Jewish neighbors, particularly in cities and neighborhoods where large pockets of Jews were concentrated. Jewish people had taken up arms in their own defense. Today Esther sat with the king's council as they heard reports of the slaughter. In some place—including Susa—the death toll was high, though almost exclusively among the enemies of the Jews. The Jewish defenders had shown unusual restraint, however, in not plundering the property of their defeated foes. Fighting had gone into a second day in some places, but finally all was quiet.

Among the dead in Susa were Haman's 10 sons. Esther remembered something Artabazus had told her long ago—root out the entire family of your enemy, or you breed a new enemy. If she had urged the king and Mordecai to follow that policy immediately after Haman's death much of this slaughter could have been avoided. Haman's sons had absorbed their father's hatred of the Jews, and when the king executed their father and dispossessed them, their anger, understandably, flared hotter. They'd been the leading instigators among those who still wished to attack the Jews—and all 10 of them died in the fighting.

Esther voiced one request. She asked that the bodies of those 10 men be hanged on a gallows in front of the palace gates, as a clear reminder to everyone that the king showed no tolerance for those who would attack and wipe out an entire race of people.

Privately, though, Esther knew the victory of the Jews had little to do with the king, and everything to do with Israel's God. Xerxes had lashed out at Haman because he saw a threat to his queen and a challenge to his own sovereignty. Without Mordecai at the helm and Esther encouraging him, Xerxes would have quickly lost interest in the Jewish people. But Xerxes needed a strong leader, if only to preserve the appearance that he himself was a strong leader. He relied more and more on Mordecai, as he had once done on Haman. Esther wished her husband was a different kind of king—the king he had once dreamed of being, perhaps—strong and bold and resolute. But if he could be nothing but weak and irresolute and dependent on his councillors, then she thanked God that a man as good and wise as her cousin Mordecai was chief among those councillors.

The Jews in Susa and throughout the empire would celebrate today, and on this day each year, their deliverance from the enemy. Mordecai and Esther together had met with leaders in the Jewish community and agreed that this date should be proclaimed as a festival.

"For so long," a young scribe named Ezra had told Mordecai and Esther just the day before, "our people here in Susa have felt almost abandoned by God. We felt that those who returned to rebuild Jerusalem were close to the heart of our God, while we were forgotten."

"And now?" Mordecai probed gently.

The young man's face shone. He was a few years younger than Esther, one of the brightest and best of the new Jewish scholars of the Law, a boy of common birth who showed no nervousness or awe at being called to meet with the queen and the king's chief minister. "Now, my lord Mordecai," he said, "because of you, and because of our lady Queen Esther, we have seen that the God of our fathers is with us still, even here, far from the homeland. All around the city I see Jewish people returning to the observance of our faith, seeking out the writings of the Law and the Prophets, wanting to walk in the ways of their fathers. And scores of Persians are coming to us to be taught what it means to be a Jew. They ask how they can learn our ways and join themselves to us." He looked from Mordecai to Esther with burning eyes. "It is a wonderful time to be a Jew," he said fervently.

Many others shared Ezra's enthusiasm. Hope, optimism, and a renewed dedication to God swept the Jews of Susa and the provinces as they celebrated what they had begun to call the feast of Purim—named for the *pur,* the lot, that Haman had cast to pick the date of their destruction.

As the councillors droned on, reading the reports and discussing them, Esther sat back in her chair and tried to find a comfortable position. She was in the sixth month of her pregnancy. Once again secure in her role as the best-beloved queen, she had been told that the portents pointed toward this baby being a boy, the son that would gladden Xerxes' heart. For herself, she wasn't sure. She looked forward to bringing another life into the world and was delighted that she, herself, would have another child, but the thought of a son gave her the usual misgivings. Amestris was no fonder of Esther than she'd ever been. Now that Esther's kinsman had been catapulted to prominence, the balances of power were shifting yet again. Esther was still sure that Amestris, perhaps through Raiya, had urged Haman on in his vengeful scheme. Who knew what the queen might do if Esther bore a son to threaten her beloved Darius?

Yet today she pushed such thoughts aside. All was well in the empire, in Susa, in the palace, and in Esther's own life—at least for this small space in time. She would rest content in that, for now.

CHAPTER 17

The chant rose from the next room where the men were gathered. A sonorous, melodious voice intoned, "May the great name of God be exalted and sanctified."

"Amen," the men's voices responded as one.

"Throughout the world,
which he has created according to his will,
may his Kingship be established in your lifetime and
in your days,
and in the lifetime of the entire household of Israel,
swiftly and in the near future;
and say, Amen."

Again the voices swelled in response, "May his great name be blessed, forever and ever."

The voice that led the prayer was that of the scribe Ezra. The man they were mourning had sired no son to recite prayers after his death, but the man had grown to love this young scholar as a son, and perhaps it was fitting. The person most fitting could not, of course, lead the prayer or even participate, for she was a woman. But Esther, queen of Persia, wife of Xerxes the King of Kings, sat on the floor of her house in her torn and dirty mourning garment. Her aching, hollow heart was strangely filled by the voices coming from the adjacent room as she said her private prayer to God for her foster father, Mordecai, dead and buried for almost a week now.

Rivka sat nearby, looking wretched. The support that held her life in place had been knocked from under her. Mordecai's death had been swift and sudden; a lingering illness might at least have given her time to get used to the idea. In the past five years Rivka had had to adjust from her familiar role as the wife of a minor palace official with a comfortable city home and a well-worn routine, to the wife of the king's chief minister, with lodgings in the palace, ceremonies to attend, and rituals to learn. She'd never grown accustomed to it, nor to the fact that she was now known publicly as a kinswoman of Xerxes' favorite queen. In fact, Rivka had gone so far as to suggest that Mordecai should take another wife, someone younger, more sophisticated, who would fit better into the glittering new world in which he moved. She would, she told him, be quite happy to slip into retirement. But Mordecai, of course, would have none of that. Rivka remained his only wife, which was both a tribute and a burden as she coped with the unfamiliar world into which she'd been thrust.

Now Mordecai was gone. Esther had never imagined her aunt looking so alone and abandoned.

The one bright note in the house of mourners was 7-year-old Damaspia, who sat clothed like the others, in drab torn garments and who was quite genuinely sad at the loss of the great-uncle she loved so much. Even in mourning, Damaspia had a beauty and vivacity that could not be extinguished. It was partly the light of childhood, but partly something uniquely her own. Or not, perhaps, unique. Rivka often commented, "How like our little Hadassah she is!" Esther supposed that the past few years must have entirely erased Rivka's memory of how headstrong and boyish little Hadassah had often been. However, Damaspia did resemble her mother. Her face was Esther's, as were her height and her long dark hair, but Damaspia was a far more suitable little lady than her mother had ever been. Still, knowing how Rivka adored Damaspia's sweetness, her brilliance, and her beauty, Esther took the comparison as high praise.

The three women, other female relatives, and servants sat on the floor of Esther's house, the home outside the city in which she spent more and more time as the years went by. Five years Mordecai had served as the king's chief minister, and much had changed in those five years. The Jews of the empire, particularly those in Susa, had flourished under Mordecai's and Esther's patronage. Many were given the means to return to the homeland and help with the building of Jerusalem, but the many who stayed had a renewed spirit, and the patronage that enabled them to build meetinghouses and to spend time and resources collecting and transcribing the writings their ancestors had brought with them into exile, as well as the writings done by faithful Jews here in Persia. Many, many Jewish people in Susa had cause to be grateful to Mordecai, and most of them had passed through this house at some point in the past week, coming to mourn a beloved leader.

Many who were not Jews came as well, for Mordecai had won

the respect—the grudging respect, in some cases—of most of Xerxes' subjects. He was a fair administrator, and those close to Xerxes could see that Mordecai exerted a good influence over the king, reining in some of the worst of Xerxes' excesses. The grand building schemes at Susa and especially at Parsa had gone ahead, but Mordecai had encouraged the king to find ways of doing this that would not be a constant drain on the royal treasury, increasing the citizens' taxes year after year. It was Esther who suggested enlisting Queen Irdabama's help in doing this. No one in all Persia knew better how to get the best value out of workers than Irdabama. Xerxes had always valued her advice. Once she was given a completely free hand with the works at Parsa she was able to hire men who could find cheaper sources of materials and more efficient ways to use labor, so that the massive buildings, sculptures, reliefs, and carvings plunged ahead while the demand for new taxes slowed—much to the relief of the populace.

In all, Esther thought, as the men's chanting came to an end, they had been five good years. Good years for her, too, though not without pain. The baby boy she carried during that first Purim lived only a few days after his birth. The birth itself had been such a painful, harrowing ordeal that she almost felt relieved when the midwife told her that the damage to her womb was so great she would probably never carry another child. She had a daughter who, it now seemed, would be her only child, but Damaspia was surely enough for any mother's heart.

A low murmur of conversation went round the room as the men returned from their prayers. Though family and close friends were observing the seven days of mourning, even in Mordecai's absence life went on. In the snatches of conversation Esther heard talk about affairs of interest to the Jews—the latest reports from a traveler who had been to Jerusalem—and the business of the court, where Lord Carshena had already been named to fill Mordecai's role as chief councillor.

"Carshena has waited seven years for this," Esther overheard Ezra say. Now a court scribe, Ezra was familiar with the intrigues of the palace. "Ever since Lord Admatha died he has expected to be first among the councillors, but first that snake whose name I will not speak held the office, and then our lord Mordecai. Now, at last, Carshena's time has come."

"That leaves only one question, then," another man said in

equally low tones. "Who will be the real power behind the throne? Lord Carshena is not one to influence the king to any great degree."

"Another will arise," said someone else.

As a woman and as Xerxes' queen, Esther was barred from this conversation as effectively as she was from the prayers, but she agreed with the last two speakers. She knew the king well by now. More and more as the years went by, he looked for someone strong to lean on—someone with a clear vision of what the kingdom should be and what the king should do. Sadly, it seemed he had no such vision beyond erecting ever greater monuments to himself and his royal house. In recent years he'd become immersed in the study of Zarathustra's teachings, and Esther knew there were some among the magi who hoped to exercise greater power by influencing the king. As long as Mordecai was alive and held office no one usurped his role as the king's closest adviser. Now the field was once again open.

As for the king's bedchamber, that too was an area where influence was highly prized. No one now contested Esther's place as Xerxes' favorite wife; she was as secure in that role as Amestris was in her role as mother of the heir. Queen Parmys was dead; a fever had taken her two years ago. Irdabama concerned herself more and more with the business of her own estates, and, except for overseeing the building projects, she kept apart from the business of court. During the past five years Esther had had little cause to complain of her marriage to the king—as royal marriages went, it was a good one. She was in her husband's company and his bed once or twice each week. He enjoyed being with her and sometimes even listened to her opinions. The fact that she and Mordecai shared the same goals had helped keep things running smoothly these past years, for the man at Xerxes' right hand and the woman behind his throne worked in concert.

But for all that, Esther cherished no illusions about her husband's devotion. Xerxes craved novelty and excitement, and as he grew older it seemed he craved it ever more. He still found most of his stimulation in wine, but he kept his harem busy too. Every few months another new favorite arose among the concubines, and the identity of the newest one and the fate of the previous one kept tongues wagging behind and beyond the harem walls. These young women exercised what power they could during their short reigns. It was not uncommon for a concubine to go about draped in new jewels and fine gowns boasting of positions in the palace for her relatives and the promise of good marriages for her children. But that was as far as their influence ever extended. None ever rose to a position of real power; none lasted long enough. Esther understood that she was a constant in Xerxes' life, and that he needed a constant exactly as much as he needed variety.

But now everything would change. She felt change in the air, and fear, too. When the balances of power shifted, some people were inevitably left at the bottom of the heap. Here in her house where so many of the influential Jews of Susa had gathered, she sensed the fear of those who had, for a short time, been protected by power and now found themselves powerless. They looked to her now as a protector, but they all understood the ways in which a queen's power was more limited than that of a minister of the king.

Ayana came to the doorway of the room where Esther and the other mourners sat, and beckoned to her. Ayana wore the attire of mourning, as did all Esther's household. The queen followed Ayana to the outer courtyard, where a small commotion among the servants indicated that the latest visitor come to offer condolences was someone important indeed. A moment later Queen Irdabama stepped down from a litter.

The two queens sketched very slight, graceful bows toward one another, neither superior in rank or status, then moved together to embrace like the good friends they were. "I am sorry for your grief, Queen Esther," Irdabama said. "All the nation mourns. Mordecai was a good man."

"I thank you," Esther said. "I am sitting with my family and our people in the inner chamber. Will you come and join us there?"

Irdabama and her attendants followed Esther into the chamber. Everyone bowed as the queens entered. A servant brought low stools for the two women to sit on. Esther had been sitting on the floor, but would not, of course, expect Irdabama to do the same.

Irdabama sat in silence for a while, as custom dictated, but her small bright eyes flickered everywhere, taking in everything she could see of the room, the adjoining rooms, the wall hangings and reliefs, the servants moving unobtrusively in the background with trays of food and pitchers of drink. Finally Esther smiled and said, "Thank you for coming to mourn with me, my friend, but I can tell you are wondering how long you must sit before you can get up and take a tour of the house and grounds."

Irdabama smiled too. If she'd not been in a house of mourning Esther would have heard her sharp, explosive snort of a laugh. "It's true I'm very curious," she admitted. "How long since I visited you here? Two, three years?"

"Almost three years," Esther said. In those first couple of years after Haman's death, Esther had not particularly wanted to visit the estate she had inherited from the enemy of her people. She had placed Mordecai in charge of hiring a steward for the estate, dismissing Haman's people and hiring her own people to staff it, but she had never wanted to live there. It was Irdabama who had changed her mind.

"Don't be a fool, Esther," she had said in her blunt way when they dined together one night in the palace at Susa. "Do you know what I have, what Parmys has, what Amestris has, that you don't? Land of our own, in our own names. Inherited from our families or granted to us by the king. Our own estates. It's no small thing. If poor Vashti had had land of her own, she might have been saved. The king might have divorced her and stripped her of her title but allowed her to retain her properties, and she would have had someplace to go."

"I hadn't thought of that," Esther said. It was true that she alone among the queens—like Vashti before her—lived entirely on the king's bounty, her only home the harem. In that way she was more like a concubine than a queen.

"Income of your own makes a difference," Irdabama had pressed. "If you manage your own estates well, you're not dependent on whatever rations are assigned to you by the palace. You have your own resources. Even if you always remain high in the king's favor, no man lives forever. Who knows what will become of his queens when Darius takes his father's throne? Or what if there is a coup, a revolution, and someone entirely different seizes power? It's been known to happen. Nothing is secure, of course, but a woman with her own land is far more secure than one entirely dependent on her husband, even—or especially—if her husband is a king."

"But the very idea of living in Haman's house, sleeping in Haman's bed, makes my flesh crawl," Esther had burst out in disgust.

That time Irdabama actually had snorted. "Don't be superstitious. The man is dead and gone. His family and servants are dead or scattered. If you don't want to live in Haman's house, make it over so that it's not Haman's house. Admittedly, you don't have the resources to build on the scale that our lord husband does, but you can certainly tear down a tower and put in a partition here and there. Make the place your own. And have a look at the accounts. Haman was a notoriously poor manager—he was a gambler, of course, always selling to pay his gaming debts. I'm sure you could have a handsome income if the waste and mismanagement is cleared up. Those lands will produce well."

"But I know nothing about managing an estate!" Esther had protested.

"Ah, but I do."

And that was how Queen Irdabama had come to be invited to Queen Esther's private estates one autumn at harvesttime, to oversee the innovations and improvements and give shrewd advice on the hiring of workers and managers, the choice of crops, the quality of the artisans' product, and many other subjects that would never have entered Esther's head. Mordecai, busy with the king's affairs, was more than happy to turn over management of the estate. It was Hathakh who watched and learned from Irdabama. By the time the visit was finished Esther did indeed feel that the estate was her home, and over the years it had become her favorite place—a place where she felt at home as she never had in Susa, Parsa, or any of her husband's other homes. Mordecai and especially Rivka made it their home too. The king visited her there, and though she still maintained a residence and a staff at the palace, many of her household preferred to live on the estate.

Hathakh, particularly, had risen to the challenge of managing a large estate more quickly than she could have imagined. "I love this work," he confided in her. "It pleases me greatly to be free of the politics, the maneuvering, the hundred petty battles a steward faces running a household within the palace—especially within the harem. This is honest work."

Esther still remembered the happiness in his voice when he said that. It was a happiness that was evident as he strode around the house and farms, speaking with the overseers, checking the books, tallying the harvests. She was glad he had found work that suited his talents so well. Over the past five years she had thought many times of the night she realized that Hathakh loved her. She had always imagined that sometime she would speak to him of it, but that time had never come. He was warm, kind, friendly, but reserved as always. On that one night he had opened a door to his heart and shut it again quite firmly afterward. Perhaps it was best for them both. Esther knew as she watched him carrying out his duties, playing with Damapsia, caring for her in a thousand small ways, that Hathakh was part of the life she might have had, if she had married an ordinary man who might have grown to love her. But even to look at him so, even to think that—despite the impossibility of it all, despite the fact that he was a eunuch—surely to cherish such thoughts was to be unfaithful in some way to the king.

No, it was better not to speak of such things. On Hathakh's recommendation, she had found another eunuch to manage her apartments at the palace, while he stayed mostly on the estate, managing things with a skill that gave her exactly what Irdabama had promised—resources of her own and a degree of security.

When the seven days of mourning were finished, Esther was summoned to return to the palace and attend upon her husband. She brought Damaspia with her. The little girl also preferred the estate with its open grounds and far more relaxed discipline, but Esther brought her to court as often as possible, for it was essential that a princess be schooled in the etiquette and expectations of her father's court.

Bringing Damaspia was the right choice. Mother and daughter were invited to dine with the king on the evening after Esther's arrival back at court. "I am deeply grieved for your loss," he said as they entered his chambers. "Mordecai was a good man. There are few like him."

"I thank you, my lord," Esther said. She shot a glance at Damaspia who echoed, "Thank you, my lord father," and bowed neatly toward him. A smile flitted across his face.

It was just the three of them dining together. They sat at a table in the small interior garden where Esther often joined the king for private meals. This was the first time Damaspia had been invited to eat in her father's presence, except for formal court banquets where she sat next to her mother at the high table while the king kept to his private table. Esther recognized Damaspia's nervousness as she glanced at her plate and cup, probably hoping not to spill anything. She reached under the table and quickly squeezed Damaspia's hand to reassure her.

"I suppose Lord Carshena is busy with his new duties?" Esther asked.

"He is caught up right now with planning for the new year's ceremony at Parsa. Princess Damaspia," he added, addressing her directly for the first time during the meal, "it is our royal command that you accompany us to Parsa this year."

"Yes, my lord," the girl whispered.

"It is my custom to bring the princess and her nurse with me when I accompany your lordship to Parsa," Esther said. In fact, she had never left Damaspia behind on one of these journeys, and she wondered why the king made a point of mentioning it this time. Perhaps it was to make his daughter feel important.

After dinner they retired to the king's chambers. Some courtiers were admitted to discuss business, Lord Carshena among them. Their talk centered mostly on the newest military threat from the west—the ambitious Athenian general Cimon was said to be readying his forces for an attack in Pamphylia. Xerxes was already outfitting a force to join the Phoenicians in fighting Cimon and he had appointed Tithraustes, son of one of his older concubines, as one of his commanders. Tithraustes was about the same age as Prince Darius, who, it was rumored, had asked to be allowed to go west as a commander. Xerxes had refused, telling Darius he was needed at court. Esther wondered whether that meant Xerxes expected to lose this battle, and did not want to risk his heir. She could not imagine how another defeat against the Greeks would affect the mood of either the king or the country.

Rumors of war ricocheted throughout the room. As the men talked strategy Esther turned to Prince Artaxerxes, whom she was pleasantly surprised to see there. The tall, slender young man came to greet her and said at once how sorry he was for the loss of Mordecai. Then he asked, "Are you still playing the oud?"

"When I can," Esther said. "And you?"

"The education of a prince leaves little time for music," Artaxerxes said. He was about 16 now, and said to be a bright lad. "I seem to spend all my time riding and shooting, or else being taught politics, history, religion, and military strategy. It occupies my time— but I have been known to pull out the oud in a spare moment and try a tune or two. I have not forgotten our lessons." Involuntarily Esther glanced at his hands, and he followed her gaze with a laugh, holding up the oddly long, tapered fingers for her inspection.

"Yes, I still have a musician's hands," he said. "The fellows call me Long Hands, and Darius still says I'd have been better born into a family of musicians." There must have been a sting in Darius' voice when he said that. Prince Darius said nothing lightly, and was known to have little respect for his brother. But something in Artaxerxes' easy, humorous manner drew away the sting. Esther found herself glad that this pleasant young man would not be burdened with a throne. He seemed unlikely to be drawn into intrigues against his brother once Darius came to rule. Perhaps this would be one prince who could enjoy a smooth and untroubled career, with a little time to play the oud now and then.

"I might have been better in a family of musicians myself," Esther said, smiling. "I have always loved playing, and I loved the times I used to teach you and the other children." A stab of pain accompanied that memory—the memory of Roxane, who'd joined her in giving those lessons. But she put it aside and kept the part of the memory that gave pleasure. "Nowadays I tutor only the princess Damaspia, but she is quickly growing beyond what I can teach her and needs a proper music master."

"Ah yes, the little princess." Artaxerxes turned to Damaspia, who sat very still and quiet in her mother's shadow, her dark eyes and ears taking in everything. She looked sleepy, though, and Esther hoped she would be excused soon. "So you like to play, do you, my lady?" Artaxerxes asked.

"I love it," Damaspia she told him. Artaxerxes was the first person to speak directly to her all evening—except for her father, whom she held in such awe that it was painful to reply—and her words tumbled out as if they'd been locked in prison. "I've been learning some folk tunes on the oud, and Hathakh—he's our steward—has been teaching me to play the nay, and the singing master says I have a good singing voice. I'm learning to dance, too."

"How very talented you are!" Artaxerxes said, smiling at her as he turned away. It was a small encounter that obviously pleased the child. Esther herself might have forgotten it altogether, had it not been for what happened later that evening.

The courtiers had gone. Damaspia had been sent home in the company of her nurse and a eunuch guard. The servants had withdrawn, and Esther was alone with the king. He motioned for her to sit beside him on his couch, and she settled down next to him with the ease and familiarity of a long-married couple. It had been nearly two weeks since she'd seen him. He wanted to know all about the mourning period for Mordecai and even asked about Rivka, which Esther thought was nice of him to do.

Xerxes' mood was quiet but pleasant. He'd been drinking steadily, but not heavily, since dinner, and Esther was relieved to see that he was not angry, nor elated, nor sunk in despair. "Darius' marriage will be celebrated while we are at Parsa," he said after they'd sat together in comfortable silence for a few moments. "Amestris has the entire occasion planned with great splendor. The feasting, I am told, will continue for 30 days."

"I suppose that is reasonable," Esther said, leaning back against his chest. "There hasn't been another such wedding—the wedding of a crown prince—since you married Amestris."

"Indeed." Xerxes reached for an orange from a bowl on the nearby table and began peeling it as he spoke. "Given the current state of affairs between us, one wonders why Amestris would be anxious to recall that particular celebration, but, of course, she thinks nothing is too good for Darius."

He pulled the peeled orange into sections and handed one to Esther, who sucked the juice and slowly ate it before saying, "I wonder how Artaynta feels about having her wedding planned by the woman who murdered her mother."

"I am sure the queen would prefer the term *executed* to *murdered,*" said Xerxes, in a tone so quietly neutral Esther was not sure if he was chiding her for using the word *murder* or simply exercising the same caution everyone did in speaking of Amestris. The spy network of this queen was legendary, presumed to extend even to the king's private chambers. "It was so long ago, and the girl was so young," he continued. "After all, she was raised in Amestris' household. Perhaps she thinks of Amestris as her true mother." He sounded troubled, and Esther immediately wished she had not raised the spectre of Artaynte and Masistes.

Yet how could the memory of those terrifying, heartbreaking weeks be laid to rest when the daughter was marrying the heir to the throne? That entire family had been obliterated in the course of their blood feud with Xerxes and Amestris, yet their daughter Artaynta, a child of 6 at the time, had been allowed to live. Not only that, but— strangely, Esther thought—Artaynta's childhood betrothal to Prince Darius had been honored. In a short time they would be wed.

Over the intervening years Esther had met the girl very few times. Amestris kept her quite cloistered, living mostly away from court. Perhaps Amestris wanted to restrict the life experiences of the girl who would be her son's bride, or perhaps she wanted Artaynta to hear as little gossip as possible about her parents and brothers and the fate they had met. It was impossible to know, or even to guess, what this 15-year-old girl might feel about marrying her cousin Darius, or about her future in-laws, the king and queen.

"She's 15," Esther said aloud. "The age I was when I came here."

"The perfect age," Xerxes said. His hand, still sticky with the orange juice, idly caressed her hair. "Ripe as a ripe fruit. How old is Damaspia?"

The question alarmed Esther. She could not imagine Damaspia being talked of in the same sentence as brides, harem girls, and ripe fruit. "She is only 7!" Esther said a little sharply.

"Still, not too young to think of a betrothal. I have been giving thought to the matter."

"Have you?" Esther was glad Damaspia was much on his mind. A king's daughter was, of course, a valuable commodity in the marriage market, and Esther prayed every day that Xerxes would make a match in which Damaspia would have at least a hope of finding some happiness, although she knew that would be far from his first concern. "Whom are you thinking of?"

He chuckled. "Hadn't you guessed? The most obvious choice—Artaxerxes."

"Artaxerxes?" Esther saw the young man in her mind's eye as clearly as she had seen him an hour before in this chamber. In truth, he was a perfectly sensible choice for Damaspia. It was just that the idea of her marrying at all was so unexpected that Esther thought that no matter what name Xerxes had said, she would have repeated it stupidly. "Artaxerxes," she said again, running it off her tongue, testing the name as if she were testing the man—or boy—himself. "But she's so young, my lord," she reminded her husband.

"Not too young for a betrothal," he repeated. "They would be well matched, and by the time she is old enough to wed—another six or seven years—Artaxerxes will be well ready for a bride. She would be his first wife, of course," he added. Marriages between half brothers and half sisters were very common among the Achaemenids. Xerxes himself had married Parmys, who had not even the honor of being first wife, but then her mother had been a very minor wife of the first Darius. A match between the king's second son by his chief wife, and his daughter by his best-loved wife, would be fitting. However, it would draw Damaspia inevitably into Amestris' sphere of influence, which was unfortunate. Esther wondered whether Artaxerxes, in seven years, would be a strong enough man to protect his wife from his mother.

"Are you settled on this? What does Amestris say?"

"I have not yet informed her," the king said, offering Esther another slice of orange. "I doubt she will protest much. Artaxerxes is extra baggage to her." It was true. Amestris had focused her ambitions, her dreams, and her love on Darius to an overwhelming degree. "I have asked a few of my councillors. Carshena and Meres think it's a good match—oh, and Artapanos approves, I'm glad to say."

Esther did not miss the pleasure in the king's voice as he imparted that last piece of information. Artapanos was becoming quite the favorite lately. That was Xerxes' way. A man's rise to prominence might have little to do with the office he held or even with his skills. It was personal qualities that drew Xerxes to a man, and the confident, lively young guard captain had the sort of personality that made the king listen to his opinions. Esther wondered whether she distrusted the man just because he was likely to replace Mordecai as the king's favorite adviser, or whether her distrust was an instinct she should listen to.

Damaspia was pleased enough when Esther had told her the news. Her eyes widened. Obviously, she'd given no thought to the idea of being married. That was a good thing, in a way. Girls closer to marriageable age occasionally cherished either romantic or rebellious notions on the subject of bridegrooms. Damaspia was as high-spirited and vivacious as Esther herself had been as a child, but she had been raised in an atmosphere that made it unlikely she would even think of questioning her royal father's choice of husband, time of marriage, or anything else.

When Esther finished telling her, Damaspia said, "I like Artaxerxes. He seems—kind."

Esther nodded. It was exactly what he seemed, and the main reason she felt at ease with the king's choice. Kindness, of course, was a quality in a 16-year-old boy that might not survive the rigorous journey to manhood, especially in a royal house, but she did not burden Damaspia with that knowledge. At least Artaxerxes was not heir to the throne. He might be permitted a quieter, gentler life, as might his wives. Esther was grateful Damaspia would not be a queen. It was no easy role.

"It won't be—for a long time yet, will it? Till I'm grown up?"

"Not till you're 13 or 14 at the very least," Esther reassured her.

"And will I—I mean, will I have to live at court more? I won't—I won't have to go stay with Queen Amestris, will I, like Artaynta does?"

"No!" Esther said firmly, as firmly as she had made this very point with the king. "You will remain right here, with me, in my household. You will go to court when I do and retire here to our estates when I do. Nothing about your life will change for many, many years, except that you will know that someday you are to marry Prince Artaxerxes. It will be a fine match," she had added, drawing her daughter into her arms and pressing her lips into the girl's shining black hair.

"Mother, will you please . . . ? Is there a prayer you could say for me?" Damaspia asked. Her unexpected question tore Esther's heart open and brought tears, finally, to her eyes. She had held nothing back in teaching Damaspia the Jewish faith. The girl would learn about Persian beliefs and other religions of the empire, but Esther had taught her to practice the religion of her own family. Esther was touched to see that in this moment of hope and fear, Damaspia turned to her mother's God, the God of Israel.

Esther knew no prayers from Hebrew Scripture appropriate to telling a young girl she was betrothed to her half brother, but she pulled the child even closer and recited words she'd recently learned from a scroll of the prophet Isaiah that Ezra had copied for her, words that had winged at once into her heart.

"Do not fear, for I am with you;
    do not be dismayed, for I am your God.
I will strengthen you and help you;
    I will uphold you with my righteous right hand."

Then she added her own petition, in her own words: "O God of Israel, God of Abraham, Isaac, and Jacob. You who were also God of Sarah, Rebekah, and Rachel, hear the petition of your handmaid

Damaspia, daughter of Esther. If it be Your will, bless the match that has been made between her and the prince Artaxerxes, and guard her always and guide her steps."

▼ ▼ ▼

While the court was in the midst of its monthlong journey to Parsa, couriers brought word of the battle at the river Eurymedon. The 200 ships of the Athenian fleet had decisively defeated the much larger Persian fleet, after which the Athenian army had soundly defeated Xerxes' forces on land. A double defeat—on water and on land—meant that Persia's power in the west was severely limited. It meant even more doubts and whispers about the king's abilities, his fitness to rule. And it meant that the king grew even more often drunk, angry, and short-tempered.

Despite the ill news, festivities at Parsa went ahead. The new year was celebrated in grand style, and then began final preparations for the lavish wedding banquet—30 days' feasting to mark Prince Darius' marriage to Princess Artaynta.

Esther was exhausted by the end of the festivities. The many nights of banqueting interspersed with the days of riding and hunting ran together into a blur. The newlywed couple were very much the center of all attention. Darius, now a young man of 21, was as handsome and strapping as his father had ever been, confident in speech and full of opinions. Harem gossip said he was quite taken with one of his concubines who had already borne him a son, but he seemed pleased enough with his bride—the quiet, rather shy, young Artaynta.

Artaynta's wedding was her first court appearance for many years, and Esther was not the only one in the hall who caught a breath of surprise when she saw the girl for the first time. Grown up now, decked out in her most beautiful gown, Artaynta was in every image and feature the exact copy of the unfortunate mother whose name she bore. Esther remembered so well that dark glossy hair curling loose, the large brown eyes looking even larger when rimmed with kohl, the small nose, and the tiny red bud of a mouth. The elder Artaynte had had a calm self-possession that her daughter lacked, but it was early yet. If Darius treated the girl at all decently, she might well develop a manner like her mother's as well as a face that was the mirror image of hers. Esther noticed the king's face as he got his first good look at his son's bride, and she remembered that Xerxes had once been madly in love with this girl's mother.

Of course, another young girl was far more prominent in Esther's thoughts than was Darius' bride. Damaspia sat beside her mother on the final night of the feast with Artaxerxes seated on her other side. He made several attempts to start conversation with her, but Damaspia, who had been warmly and openly friendly with him before she knew of the planned betrothal, almost visibly shrank into herself and replied in whispers whenever he spoke.

She'd been required to appear at a few official functions during the wedding celebrations, more than would commonly be expected for a girl of her age and status. Rumor had already begun to link her name with that of Artaxerxes, and tonight's placement at his side meant that this evening's announcement would come as little surprise to most of the guests.

Esther remembered the words of the prayer she had prayed for Damaspia when she told her of this betrothal. Now, Esther prayed them silently for herself. It had taken her years to learn to truly believe that God cared for her destiny, to truly trust His guidance in her life. Could Damaspia's faith bloom so early, and take firm root? Who knew what her future might hold?

Servants had taken away the dishes for the final course and were pouring more wine. The musicians brought the music to a finale. Speeches in honor of the bride and groom had already been made. Now Lord Carshena rose to speak.

"Before the ladies leave our presence, it is my honor as the king's mouthpiece to thank each of you for coming to celebrate the wedding of the king's most glorious son and heir, Darius." Carshena was very good at the fulsome, overbearing praise expected of the king's spokesman, and he continued for several minutes about Darius' fine qualities, making sure, of course, that they were clearly presented as only reflections of the far greater qualities of his father Xerxes.

Esther looked around the high table. Darius looked openly bored and darted glances of unconcealed desire at his young wife; apparently the marriage was going well so far. Artaxerxes looked tense and nervous, as did Damaspia, who suddenly reached over to clutch Esther's hand. Amestris, who had been looking smoothly pleased all through the wedding festivities, now tapped her fingers on the tabletop while a tiny frown wrinkled her white-marble fore-head. Princess Amytis leaned over to say something to her husband, Megabyzus, and they both smirked.

"And, as a conclusion to this grand festivity," Lord Carshena was saying, "it is the king's greatest pleasure to announce that another royal marriage has been contracted and the betrothal is to be made public this evening. It is the marriage of Prince Artaxerxes, second son of his gracious majesty King Xerxes and his noble wife Queen Amestris, to the princess Damaspia, his sister, the daughter of his gracious majesty King Xerxes and his beloved wife Queen Esther."

The guests burst into applause as Artaxerxes and Damaspia, at a graceful signal from Carshena, rose. Artaxerxes took Damaspia's hand in his and held it up a little, a small salute to the crowd. Esther saw him dart a quick smile down at her. It looked as if he might even have squeezed her hand. *She's such a little girl,* Esther thought, and then, looking at the new bride Artaynta, she thought, *Artaynta was a little girl—it seems like yesterday.* Late last night Esther had gone into the nursery and sat watching Damaspia sleep. Sofia, her nurse, sat softly down beside her. "How quickly seven years have gone," Esther said.

"Not nearly as quickly as the next seven will," Sofia had replied.

It will seem no time before she's old enough to be a bride. Slow down the years, O God—give me enough time with her. Enough time for what, Esther wasn't sure—but that did nothing to lessen the fervor of her prayer.

CHAPTER 18

The musicians played a wild melody with a fiercely insistent beat. The room was hot, the air still, and the women's voices grew loud and their laughter shrill. Esther stood by a pillar looking across the courtyard to the king's almost-completed palace here at Parsa. Xerxes' birthday feast had been celebrated just a few hours earlier, men and women together dining in the banquet hall. Now the women were dismissed to Amestris' quarters, where she was hosting them while their husbands, entertained by dancers, concubines, and slave girls, drank themselves insensible. Esther leaned her head against the pillar, momentarily grateful for its cool stone.

In place of drinking and debauchery the women enjoyed gossip and small, petty cruelties. These were in full swing around Esther as small knots of royal and noble ladies stood together in Amestris' hall or strolled through the courtyards. Esther wondered idly how many such evenings she had endured since her marriage to the king. Far more than she could remember or count, for on most great occasions the women either dined separately from the men, or retired to women's quarters once the dining was done. She herself had been the host at many such events. But when Amestris was in the palace, *she* was the host. She always laid a good table, served fine wines, and hired the most expensive musicians, though not always those whose performance was to Esther's taste.

The princess Amytis passed by, her arm circling the waist of her young sister-in-law Artaynta. A year had passed since Artaynta's marriage, and rumors already circulated that the match was not a happy one. Lady Carshena, wife of the king's chief minister, came quietly up beside Esther and frowned as she watched the other two women pass. Esther liked Carshena's wife. She was modest and unassuming and, occasionally, quite shrewd.

"Don't they look a cozy pair," she murmured softly. "Anyone would think they were the best of friends."

"Anyone who didn't know Amytis," Esther replied, just as quietly. Amestris' daughter had all her mother's venom—distilled, if that were possible, to make the sting stronger. She'd become notorious for an extramarital affair when she was barely 15, and, though still married to Megabyzus, she continued to set tongues wagging even now in her late 20s. As she passed they could hear her saying to Artaynta, "Of course, husbands can be so insensible at times. I truly wonder if men have any feelings at all. But then, they have so many other outlets for their feelings, while we have so few . . . "

"That's a dangerous conversation," Esther said when Amytis and Artaynta were out of earshot.

Lady Carshena nodded. "Indeed it is. It sounds as though Princess Amytis is about three moves away from advising Princess Artaynta that a neglected wife may find other consolations if her husband's bed is cold."

"Artaynta would probably welcome that advice right now," Esther said.

"And she may not be wise enough to realize how dangerous it is."

"I do pity her, though," Esther said. "Darius has been a complete fool over that concubine of his."

At the time of his marriage Prince Darius had already had a small harem of a half dozen girls, one of whom—an Assyrian slave named Zenobia—had already borne him a child. Apparently Darius was madly in love with Zenobia and treated her as Artaynta's equal, if not her superior, in every way. He had given her the best apartments he could procure and showered her with jewels and gifts. He'd even contrived to arrange the same rations for the two women.

"She has cause for grievance, there's no doubt," Lady Carshena said. "Did you know they say that the slave woman spends 10 nights in his chamber for every one night Artaynta spends there? And he's been heard to boast that he plans to free Zenobia and marry her."

"Ah," said Esther. There was little she could say about this particular indiscretion. Xerxes had, after all, done virtually the same thing with herself and with Vashti, though neither of them had been slave-born. In fact, over every discussion of Darius' misdemeanors hung the unspoken assumption that a king ought to school his son better in the management of his wives and concubines, but Xerxes was not considered to be a particularly good source of fatherly wisdom on that score. No one, of course, ever said that aloud, at least not in public and surely not in front of Esther.

Still watching Amytis and Artaynta, Esther said, "The problem with Artaynta is that she may just be young enough—or unhappy enough—to believe that because Amytis got away with cuckolding her husband, she can do the same. That would be a terrible miscalculation."

"Indeed," agreed Lady Carshena. "A king's daughter may be forgiven for being unfaithful to her husband if he is a mere general. The daughter of a dead rebel would never be forgiven for being unfaithful to the king's son and heir. Is Artaynta bright enough to understand that? And what is this business that Amytis is about? She's usually hand in glove with her mother, but surely Queen Amestris would never approve of anything that might trouble her precious Darius." Amestris had turned a blind eye to Darius' obsession with his concubine. In her eyes he could do no wrong.

"I think Amytis is just stirring up trouble. Doing what she does best," Esther said. She wished they could talk of something else; she wished she were home in her own quarters telling stories to Damaspia, playing her oud, reading, or talking with Ayana—talking about anything but harem intrigue and gossip. She liked Lady Carshena, but she was very tired of this conversation.

"Oh, and there's that woman, you know—Amestris' woman— the red-haired one," the vizier's wife said, pouncing on a new subject for gossip like a cat pouncing on a skittish mouse. "I hear she's been seen a great deal lately in the company of Artapanos."

"Really?" Esther glanced through the weaving mass of bodies at Raiya who was sipping a cup of wine and watching Amestris' face very closely as the queen talked. This was one piece of gossip that *did* pique Esther's interest. She had little contact with Raiya, but she was still intrigued by her old rival, who managed to squeeze an incredible amount of contempt into a very proper bow whenever she did encounter Esther. She had emerged unscathed from Haman's disgrace despite her entanglement with him, but had kept a low profile in recent years.

Esther was a little surprised to hear of her involvement with Artapanos, for Raiya was the same age as she—a few years short of 30—and it seemed more likely that Artapanos would be interested in a younger woman. Women nearing 30 were seldom involved in dangerous or scandalous romances. They were more likely to do as Amytis was doing, and position themselves as counselors to younger girls.

Lady Carshena's voice turned sour as she spoke Artapanos' name, and Esther wasn't surprised. "His power continues to grow, doesn't it?" Esther said.

"I am afraid the king would far sooner listen to his captain of the guard than to his chief minister," Lady Carshena said, a little bitterly.

Esther knew well how heavily Xerxes leaned on Artapanos, how deeply he trusted the man. He considered Lord Carshena to be a mere figurehead, a man with no authority and no vision. Esther tended to agree, but she disagreed—privately, of course—with the idea that Artapanos made a good substitute adviser. He was arrogant, self-seeking, and not, she thought, terribly bright. "In many ways, he is another Haman," she said to the chief minister's wife—the comparison was made freely throughout court circles. "Bent only on his own advancement, with no thought of the kingdom's good."

"That is exactly what my husband says!" Lady Carshena looked as if she were about to say more, then stopped. Esther knew the unspoken, unspeakable question: *Why does our king allow himself to be ruled so readily, especially by men so unworthy?*

The chief minister's wife could not ask the question, and Esther could not answer it, though the answer was absolutely clear. Xerxes, who had never been a strong man or a strong king, had grown weaker as the years went by, feeding his own weaknesses instead of his strengths, and finding others to feed them. That was another reason Esther disliked Artapanos. He was Haman all over again in his willingness to be the king's best and merriest drinking companion, then leave his sovereign in a drunken stupor in his chambers and go out to speak to councillors and petitioners in the king's name.

"I can do nothing about it," Esther said, more to herself than to her companion. Nothing about Artapanos, nothing about Xerxes. She had enjoyed an illusion of power for five years while Mordecai ruled as chief minister, but that was only because a man she trusted and agreed with had become, however briefly, the king's prop. That was a testament to Mordecai's own strength of character, for he did not pander to the king's vanity or ply him with wine as so many others did. But he had clearly seen his ruler's flaws.

A moment came back to Esther, one she'd never forgotten in all the long months since her foster father's death. Mordecai had not known he was dying. The attack that stopped his heart had been sudden. So it must have been God's mercy that had given him a little time, a few weeks before his death, to walk with Esther in the gardens on her estate and tell her, "Hadassah, my daughter, this life is very uncertain. No one save our God knows what the future may hold. Today I am high in the king's favor; tomorrow I may fall—or die. But you are bound to him for life. I must warn you of one thing, my child. You must stop trying to save this man from himself, or you will be destroyed."

Esther could still see the severe expression on Mordecai's face as he spoke. For 10 years Esther had ruled her life by the belief that she could in some way influence or help her husband, that this might even be God's plan for her. Now Mordecai told her this was impossible.

"You can help him in some ways, if he will allow you," Mordecai had continued. "But you cannot save him. He is bent, I sometimes think, on destroying himself, and no one but God can stop a man from such a course once he is determined on it."

"But God can use His servants," Esther said.

"Yes—as He used you to save His people. But we Jews wanted to be saved, Esther. We cried out to God, and He sent you to plead for us. But I think not even God will force a man to be saved if he does not choose to be. And it is the worst of pride—what is that Greek word you said their poets use?—the worst kind of pride to think we can do what even God would not."

"*Hubris,*" Esther said. "They call it hubris. It means the pride of those who would set themselves above the gods."

"We have only one God," Mordecai had reminded her, "and we are subject to Him. But He allows us our free will, even when we choose to destroy ourselves. Israel and Judah did that in the days before the exile. They ignored the prophets' warnings and continued their unholy, destructive behavior." He paused, pondering his next words. "Your husband, I think, will continue his self-destructive ways, too. I would not see you break yourself trying to save a man who will not be helped."

The words were harsh, and if Mordecai had not died so soon afterward Esther might have tried to erase them. As it was, she could not forget. She had tried to do as her uncle urged, though it was difficult because she still cared deeply for Xerxes, even as he became less and less the man she had wed 10 years ago.

Lady Carshena excused herself, and Esther stood alone again, watching the room, thinking about the patterns of power and politics being played out here among these women. Amytis and Artaynta were still in close conversation, Artaynta now bright-eyed and giggling. She'd had too much wine, no doubt. And then, as Esther went looking for a servant to summon Ayana to escort her home, she crossed paths with Raiya.

As usual, Raiya gave her a bold haughty glance dropping her eyes and sinking to a low curtsy. "Your majesty," she said.

Esther nodded acceptance of Raiya's bow and was about to pass on when she had a thought. Raiya was a lady in waiting in Amestris' household. Technically, her rank was the same as Ayana's rank in Esther's household, though Raiya had none of Ayana's modesty and had always styled herself more as a companion than a servant to her queen. Her appearance in such a prominent role here among Amestris' guests was proof of that. Yet there was no reason in all the world why Esther could not say to her, as she now did, "Raiya, can you send someone to find Ayana for me? I am retiring to my own quarters, and wish her to escort me home."

The other woman's face flushed. She understood precisely that she was being used as a servant, but there was nothing she could do about it. After a moment's silence she said, "I will do as your ladyship requires," and sketching another bow she turned to go.

"Raiya! Wait." Esther had not planned to speak, but something in Raiya's green eyes made her put out a hand to beckon her back, even though she was unsure what she wanted to say.

"Yes, my lady?" This time Raiya allowed anger to touch the edge of her voice.

Esther had no idea what made her suddenly so reckless. She herself had had very little to drink, so she had no excuse. Suddenly something wild stirred in her. Just as a moment ago she'd needed to wound Raiya, now she felt a need to make contact, to try to speak honestly.

"You have always disliked me, haven't you, Raiya?"

Raiya looked straight ahead. The words she spoke were deferential; her tone was not. "It is not the place of a humble lady in waiting to dislike one of the king's wives. I respect you, as I do all the royal family."

"Since we were girls," Esther went on, ignoring what she'd just said. "I know you started the story, years ago, that I was having an affair with Artabazus. I know you incited poor Roxane to lie about that. And you were Haman's lover. Did you tell him I was Jewish? Or just fan the flame of his hatred for the Jews, knowing that I too might get burned?"

Raiya was silent, though her eyes glittered and her cheeks flushed. She would neither confirm nor deny any of Esther's accusations.

"But why, Raiya?" Esther said after a minute. "There were rivalries in the harem when we were all young girls, of course, and you and I didn't like each other, but why would you carry such a grudge through life when I can't even remember whether it was based on anything at all?" The accusing note was gone from her voice. She was genuinely curious, for this was something she truly wanted to know. "Why would you make a lifelong vendetta out of it? Why do you still resent me, and for what?"

"You don't know?" Raiya said in a hoarse whisper. Her voice

raised a shade louder. "You honestly don't, do you? Could you possibly be so blind that you don't see?"

"See what?"

"That your good fortune was everyone else's ill fortune," Raiya said, forming each word like a slap. "That when *you* became queen, everyone who came behind you was barred from winning that contest. How did you think the rest of us would feel?"

"The rest of us? But who, Raiya? Of course we all knew, always, it would be a contest with only one winner. But the rest of the girls from our time are still in the harem, and many are my friends—Leila, Tamyris, Phratima. No one else has spent her whole life hating me for that. Why you?"

Now Raiya drew herself up so that she looked straight into Esther's eyes—both she and Esther were uncommonly tall for women—and flared like a flame. "Because it would have been mine. *I* was the favorite before you came! Hegai talked of me; they all talked of how I would catch the king's eye. *You took what should have been mine!*"

For one brief second—on the word "king"—Raiya's voice had risen. She reined it in as a head or two turned their way, finishing the sentence in a fierce whisper. Turning away from Esther, both women saw that Queen Amestris was watching them from the other side of the room with a small smile on her face.

Raiya spun, walking away, then turned back to say in a voice that sounded as if she were swallowing knives, "I will find your servant for you."

"No, Raiya," Esther said, and realized that her own voice was roughened by something that caught her about the throat—or the heart. "I will find her myself. You do not need to serve me." It was a tiny gesture, just taking back that earlier pettiness, but it was all she could do.

She thought at first that she would not repeat the conversation to anyone, but she told it to Ayana almost as soon as they were clear of Amestris' apartments. "Is it true, Ayana?" Esther asked. "You and she were both there before me—was she really such a favorite?"

"*A* favorite, perhaps, but not *the* favorite. There were many girls talked about, though I think you quickly became the front runner." Ayana looked puzzled, trying to remember the world they'd lived in so many years ago.

"But she believed herself the favorite," Esther said. "I remember how you told me back then that Raiya was a slave girl and had no family, no nothing. All she had were her hopes, her ambitions. She must have come here really believing she was going to be queen."

"And she still believes you robbed her of that destiny," Ayana mused. "How strange to live with such a passion for so many years. Most people would move forward and find something else to build their lives upon. But not Raiya."

"Not Raiya," Esther echoed. They went into Esther's own apartments, smaller and less comfortable than her quarters at Susa. The main hall, empty and dark, echoed with their voices. Talia came out of the shadows to lead them to their chambers.

"But she is a candle whose wick has burned low," Ayana said. "Too many years have gone by. You have nothing to fear from her now."

"Perhaps not," Esther said, but she thought of the rumor that Raiya was the lover of Artapanos, and wondered.

A fortnight later the court went hunting. Esther was informed that she was to join the party, which she was glad to do, as she enjoyed a day's riding in the open air. Royal women were not always invited to the hunt; sometimes the men preferred to bring their concubines along. But when the party assembled outside the Gate of All Lands—where Xerxes' winged bulls now stood in massive splendor—Esther saw that she was the only woman from the king's harem who'd been invited. She smiled to see Artaxerxes there too. This was good, for she welcomed every opportunity to speak with the young man her daughter would marry. Perhaps they might ride together and talk about music.

She also saw Darius, accompanied by Artaynta, who rode a pretty white mare and looked sad. There was no need to guess the cause of her unhappiness. At once Darius left her side to join his concubine Zenobia, mounted on a gray horse. The girl might have been a slave, but she had the proud carriage of a queen. Darius remained at her side all through the morning, leaving Artaynta to ride alone.

Esther thought of befriending the poor girl, but before she could ride alongside her, Artaxerxes rode up. "May I ride along with my mother-in-law-to-be?" he asked, laughing. Artaxerxes was about 10 years younger than Esther herself. She gave him a wry smile.

"You may, if you try not to make me feel so very old," she said.

"We have seen little of you this summer."

"I have been at Ecbatana, practicing statecraft, but not very well, I gather," he said, not seeming much daunted. "I am 17 this summer, the same age Hystaspes was when the king gave him Bactria, but I do not look for a satrapy anytime soon."

Hystaspes was Xerxes' son by Queen Parmys. He was between Darius and Artaxerxes in age and was by all accounts a clever, steady young fellow. Most likely he would be the one named heir if anything were ever to happen to Darius, for he seemed to rule his satrapy well. Esther knew him but little. What interested her here was the total lack of resentment in Artaxerxes' voice.

"Sometimes I think—and I mean no disrespect, prince—that your brother is right, and you might have been happiest born into a family of musicians." She hoped not to wound him but to learn more about him, and she succeeded.

"Happier? Oh yes," Artaxerxes said without hesitation. "A family of oud players, a family of weavers—the hands would come in handy there, too—anything but a family of princes, I believe."

Esther paused to admire as he steered his horse neatly over a rough patch in the road, then turned back to watch her to make sure she came through it all right. "Yet you ride beautifully," she said, "and I hear that you shoot well, too. And you are cleverer at your lessons than you give yourself credit for. The king is not dissatisfied with you."

"I know," Artaxerxes shrugged. "I am good at everything—not brilliant, but good enough, which is all that's required of a third son. The only thing I can't manage is really caring very much about it all. Whereas music, or anything beautiful—now that, I do care for. My father seems to have spent his whole life caring that he couldn't be as great a conqueror as *his* father. My brother will spend his whole reign trying to prove he's better than either. Maybe he'll throw his armies into Greece again; I wouldn't put it past him. And the only thing my father's ever done that I would care to imitate is what he's built here at Parsa. A few of the sculptures, a few of the buildings—I'd be happy to have my name attached to those. But, of course, my name won't be attached to anything, so all in all I might have done better in the weaver's family."

Esther smiled. "I want to say that you don't give yourself enough credit, but that's not it exactly, is it?"

"No," said Artaxerxes. "My problem is a little different. It's that I'm too honest."

She thought about that after he'd ridden ahead to join the other men, who were now on the trail of the boar. He wished he had not been born a prince, because he cared too little for the business of ruling. But his father had cared, if anything, too much. As a young man he had, and even when Esther first married him she recognized that Xerxes cared passionately for statecraft, for conquest, for kingship. And all that had burned out now. In many ways Xerxes cared less than if he'd been born into a family of minstrels or weavers. Perhaps there was something about greatness, or the quest for it, that by its nature could not last long. Perhaps Artaxerxes, if given a quiet little satrapy to rule, might live longer and fare better than either his father or his brother. Yet surely it was not so with all kings. She thought of the tales of King David of Israel, who had by all accounts ruled both long and gloriously. Had he cared for his kingdom as much at the end as he had at the beginning? The tablets did not say. Could love of God somehow preserve that spark of fire in a man? But Xerxes loved his god, so perhaps the love itself was not enough.

Tangled in such thoughts, Esther forgot to pay attention to the road beneath her feet, which was unfortunate because her inattention caused her horse to stumble, almost throwing her. In a half dozen heartbeats Hathakh was at her side. He rode with the other attendants at a respectful distance, but was always watchful.

"Are you all right, my lady?"

"Fine, I'm fine, but I think my horse may be lame." The mare seemed reluctant to put her foot down and shied back nervously when Esther tried to urge her forward.

Hathakh dismounted neatly and held out a hand to her. "If you will allow, my lady, I will lead her back and bring you a fresh mount. It will take only a moment."

Esther stood by the edge of the wooded trail, waiting for Hathakh to return with a new mount. A few of the riders—mostly noblewomen, now that the men were hot on the trail—paused to ask what the trouble was, then rode on. In a moment she saw a threesome ride up—Princess Amytis, Princess Artaynta, and Raiya. She had seen Raiya earlier in the company of Artapanos. Now that her lover had ridden ahead with the king and the other huntsmen, she seemed quite intimate with the two princesses. Artaynta, who had looked so desolate earlier, seemed much more cheerful in the company of the two older women, and Esther wondered what they were telling her to lift her spirits. Esther did not like this alliance; it made her uncomfortable. In some vague way she could not name, it seemed to bode evil.

It was late afternoon before she found a name for the thing that was troubling her—the premonition of danger.

The men had chased the boar since late morning. In the early afternoon, while the women sat in a grassy field eating a meal laid out by the servants, several of the older men came riding back. Somewhat to Esther's surprise, the king was among them. His horse, too, had been lamed. Esther suspected that gave him and several of his men a convenient excuse to give up the chase, while the younger men continued it. Lord Carshena and some of the other councillors were with him. Darius, Artaxerxes, Artapanos, and several other younger men had stayed with the chase, pursuing the boar.

"Leave glory to the young men!" the king announced, dismounting. His servants hurried to bring a wooden stool to serve as his throne. Food and wine were placed before him. "I must be growing old," he said as he raised his goblet. "Once I loved to chase the boar and risk death, but now I think that this is the best part of the hunt—a meal served in the open air, good wine, good music, and the company of lovely ladies. To the ladies!"

The women smiled and murmured polite thanks. Esther wondered if the king would summon her to his side, but he did not. It crossed her mind, in fact, to wonder why he'd invited her at all, since he had not spoken more than a few words to her all day. Probably, since the noblewomen were joining their husbands for the hunt, he required the presence of one of his queens, and he found hers more congenial than Amestris. Esther did not much mind. She finished her meal and walked down to the river with Lady Carshena, talking about the reliefs that were being done in the new audience hall and the poet Esther had just discovered and hired to perform at an upcoming banquet. Before she left, Esther noticed that the trio of Amytis, Artaynta, and Raiya had converged upon the king but, after all, there was nothing odd in him seeking the company of his favorite daughter.

More than an hour later Esther and Carshena's wife returned to find most of the company scattered—walking about, riding, or resting. Except for the servants who lingered in small groups to see to any needs that might arise and the guardsmen who guarded the king, the only people left on the grass were the lords Carshena and Meres, deep in conversation, and the king with the same three women surrounding him. This time, however, the scene was different. Raiya was serving as the king's cupbearer, pouring his wine, of which he'd obviously been drinking freely. His daughter Amytis still sat at his feet, apparently engaging him in conversation, but his daughter-in-law Artaynta sat on his lap, herself quite drunk, giggling and pink-cheeked as the king lazily caressed her with the hand not holding his cup.

Esther stopped in her tracks, hardly able to believe her eyes. In a marriage such as hers, the sight of her husband with another woman on his lap was certainly no shock, but the woman's identity was a very bad shock.

"Oh, no," Esther breathed. *"No!"*

Lady Carshena, who'd turned toward her husband, looked back and saw the king. "Oh, no indeed," she echoed in astonishment. "No! He cannot be such a fool."

She drew a quick breath, adding, "Pardon me, my lady."

But Esther still watched the king, who was glancing first at his daughter with apparent interest in her conversation, and then at his daughter-in-law with a hunger he did not—or could not—bother to disguise. She felt frozen to the ground, her heart like stone. "You need no pardon," she told the other woman almost absently, "not for calling the king a fool. If he can do this . . . " Her voice trailed off.

She stood watching the little tableau for a while, then went off alone toward the servants in search of Hathakh. He came to her quickly, asking how she felt and if she needed to rest.

"What I want is to go back home," she said, "but I don't think I can. Perhaps I should go for another walk. You will accompany me, won't you?" As they passed nearby the king, Esther turned away. "I cannot look," she said. "It sickens me."

"My lady." Hathakh's voice was rough. He took a long breath and did not speak again till they were within cover of the woods. "Though the king is our lord and master, I cannot bear to see him do this dishonor to you in the sight of all. Please, let me make some excuse on your behalf, and I will take you home."

"No, please don't. Thank you, but it truly isn't the shame, not for myself. No, of course he should not do this—not even with one of his own concubines—in the plain sight of his wife. And yes, I suppose it shames me, but that's not what bothers me. It's the king himself, that he could sink to such a level, to toy with his son's wife like that before the eyes of all. And what will happen when Darius hears of it?"

Just then they heard the blare of horns far off in the woods. The hunters were returning, the hunt successful. Esther and Hathakh trailed back into the clearing on the heels of the triumphant party. Darius himself had slain the boar, and he was exultant and full of himself. His concubine Zenobia was by his side, so she must have ridden out to meet him. It was she whom he embraced as he celebrated his victory. He paid no attention to his wife, who by that time was sitting on the ground at the king's feet. Darius never came close enough to see his father's fingers playing in the girl's hair.

"She's so like her mother," Esther said to Hathakh, remembering the first Artaynte. "He was foolish then, too—dallying with his brother's wife—but this thing seems much more shameful."

"They say there is no fool like an old fool," Hathakh said. There was a certain bitter satisfaction in his voice; perhaps it was just the relief of knowing he could finally call the king a fool out loud. She knew by now what an iron lock Hathakh kept on his emotions. Only once in a great while did he allow her a glimpse of what he hid so carefully. But today she read easily enough, in the set of his firm jaw and the dull glow of his dark eyes, his anger at the man who cast her aside for a pretty, tipsy young girl. Hathakh was more deeply offended on her behalf than she was on her own. She laid a hand on his arm, as if she needed support. She could do no more.

The king's dalliance with Artaynta was not to be a single indiscretion born of a lazy, drunken afternoon in the woods. Rumor was rife in the harem within a week. Artaynta had been summoned into the king's presence, invited to dine alone with him, sent costly gifts. The girl who had gone about for a year with her eyes lowered because of the shame of her husband's preference for his slave woman, now went about with her head high, the light of new love glowing in her eyes.

Of course Darius found out. Xerxes and Artaynta made little effort to keep the affair secret. Once Darius discovered what was going on, the wife to whom he had paid so little attention became a valuable piece of property—property his own father was trying to steal.

"I haven't seen Artaynta about at all in the past several days," Esther's friend Leila said as they sat in the baths one day having their hair washed. "Do you think it's true that Prince Darius has her locked up so she can't leave her quarters?"

"That's what I've heard," Esther confirmed. But later that evening, Artaynta was seen walking from the harem to the king's quarters with two maidservants and a eunuch.

"The king set her free," said Ayana, who had been to the storerooms and heard the latest news. "He sent a squadron of guards to inform Darius that the princess was under his protection and that Darius had no right to hold her."

A confrontation between the king and his heir was inevitable, and the expectation of it hung like a threatened summer storm in the still air of Parsa. Artaynta had been given quarters in Xerxes' own new palace, smaller than those she had enjoyed as wife of the crown prince but entirely independent of Darius. The girl seemed not to care about the loss of status involved in being counted as the king's concubine; by all accounts she acted like a girl dizzy with love.

The king was no better. "He has not behaved as foolishly in 10 years—no, not since he first married you," Ayana judged as she and Esther sat sewing in the courtyard.

"That was folly, was it?" Esther challenged, but with a smile. The passionate devotion her husband had once felt for her—and she for him, perhaps?—was now a slightly bittersweet memory. She could almost have been detached from his new romance if it were not that it boded such terrible disaster and upheaval, and showed so clearly the level to which he had fallen.

"No, it was passion, which is much the same thing," said Ayana, stabbing her needlework decisively. "But it was passion for a woman who was legally his own, which one can understand. I suppose as king he owns every woman, child, and man in the land, but law and decency should prohibit him from taking his own son's wife! She is in his chambers day and night, they say, and he treats her more like a concubine than like a woman of royal blood—kissing and caressing her in full sight of his courtiers and jesting about her skills in the bedchamber. It's nothing short of disgusting."

Darius, meanwhile, had left the palace and was staying on lands of his own nearby, with Zenobia of course. His true love might be for his concubine, but he was not the kind of young man to let his pride be so wounded and his wife be publicly bedded by another man—least of all his own father.

"This has been coming for a while," Ayana said. "Do you remember I told you once, long ago, that once Darius was a grown man he would not stay forever in his father's shadow—nor would his mother wish it."

"But Amestris can have had nothing to do with the king's passion for Artaynta," Esther said. "That dishonors both her and Darius. Why would she encourage it?"

"I don't say that she does," Ayana said, "but let us recall that the girl is very close to Amytis, and also to Raiya. Amytis does little without consulting her mother, and Raiya has ever been Queen Amestris' devoted servant. None of those women care anything for poor little Artaynta herself. Might they not use her as bait to draw the king and force a confrontation between him and Darius? If the prince and the king battled over this cause, how many would support the king?"

Esther was silent. She knew the answer. Darius was seen by most Persians as a handsome, capable young king in waiting. Xerxes was perceived as an aging, drunken fool, at the mercy of his women and his courtiers, consumed with trivialities and unconcerned for his kingdom. If this shameful affair were the catalyst for a confrontation, surely many people would support the wronged young prince.

The weeks of the king's infatuation with Artaynta stretched into months, and during this time Esther seldom saw her husband. Neither Esther nor any other wife or concubine was summoned to the royal chambers. At every public event where women were present, Artaynta sat by the king's side. The court returned to Susa, and the situation continued unchanged. No one in either palace or city could talk of anything but the scandal, unless they talked of the support Darius was said to be gathering. Still he had not confronted his father. Most people guessed he was waiting till he had enough strength—not for a mere confrontation, but for outright rebellion.

"Everyone in Persia thinks that the king is mad and that he has wronged his son," Hathakh said matter-of-factly one evening as he, Ayana, and Esther sat in the courtyard talking in the cool of the evening. "But that doesn't mean Darius is having an easy time raising support for a revolt."

"I heard hundreds of men were declaring allegiance to him," Esther said.

"You heard that because you are here, in the harem, where Amestris' people control what news comes in and out," Hathakh said. "It's not true. A few army officers have sworn loyalty to Prince Darius, that's all. Most of the army agree—as most of the people do—that Darius would make the better king, but few are willing to go to war over what happens in the king's bedchamber. They may laugh at the king, but to overthrow him? Over a woman? It won't be as easy as Darius thinks."

They were all silent. There was really nothing more to say.

"It's so strange," Esther told them. "This is my husband we are talking of, yet I feel like a bystander, as though all this has nothing to do with me."

"Really?" Ayana asked.

"For the most part, yes. I think I felt some jealousy at first—I knew the king had other women, of course, but I did not ever expect him to be so—so consumed by anyone. I suppose I was disappointed that he could forget me so completely. But now . . . I don't know. It's very hard to explain."

Her friends did not press her, as she knew they would not. They were much more friends than servants. That they respected her privacy so completely had less to do with their positions in her household than with the people they were, which was probably why, of all the people she had been close to over the years, Ayana and Hathakh were her two closest friends, the two she trusted the most.

Others were not so reticent. Her friends among the concubines liked to gossip endlessly about Artaynta and what she must be doing to have the king so bewitched. "Bewitched it is," Tamyris said. "I hear she uses love potions, charms, and spells to bind him to her."

"That's folly," Esther said at once. "If that were the case, it would have been she who wooed him. I cannot imagine that she did—a girl so young and untried with a man so experienced, so . . ."

"So lustful," Phratima said promptly. To the other women's laughter, she protested, "He is. He always has been. Of course they say that no man can be satisfied with one woman alone, but the king has hundreds, and still he wants more!"

"Amazing, at his age," Leila said.

"Perhaps that's part of it," Esther suggested. "He is 50 years old. No doubt at that age a man begins to fear old age and death. Perhaps because Artaynta is so young he feels like he is hanging on to some of his own youth."

"Well, I must say you're very cool about it," Leila said. "I mean, what is the king to me, after all? I've been summoned to him perhaps four or five times in my whole life, and it's the same for most of us. You have a child by him, Phratima—"

"But even so, I have been with him no more than half a dozen times and all of them years ago," Phratima said. "I couldn't say I really know the man, or feel anything for him. But you, Esther. I thought he really loved you, and you him."

Esther shrugged. If she could not explain herself to Ayana and Hathakh, who knew and understood her so well and whom she trusted so deeply, she would not even attempt it with these women. Better they should think her shallow and uncaring. Perhaps she was.

Hardest of all for Esther to deal with was her aunt Rivka. She'd been back on Esther's estate all the while the court was at Parsa and had heard rumors about the king and Artaynta filtered through the most lurid of gossip. She was incensed on Esther's behalf. Unlike those who lived in the harem, she had never really understood what marriage to a king meant.

"How dare he disgrace you so, in everyone's eyes?" she demanded hotly.

"He hasn't disgraced me, Auntie," Esther said, sitting down beside her aunt on the balcony outside her rooms on the estate. She picked up a bowl of pears and offered one to Rivka. "The one person who has been truly disgraced in this is Prince Darius, for it's his wife the king has taken. In a strange way, it has nothing at all to do with me."

Rivka looked keenly at Esther. It was one of those moments when Esther missed Mordecai so much she could have wept. She'd never had the same intimacy with her aunt, yet she suddenly found she needed a confidant after all.

"Yet it does have much to do with you," Rivka said.

Esther stood up and walked to the rail, leaning over to look at the neat, well-manicured gardens below. Rivka herself oversaw the gardeners. Here on Esther's estate she had the kind of grounds that gave her imagination free rein.

"So many people have asked me this," Esther said, "and all I can tell you is that from the day I was taken from your house to the palace I felt like a leaf floating on a stream—as though I had no control over what happened to me. For years I thought that my life, my destiny, was in the hands of others. Sometimes I felt that this feeling of helplessness was what it was like to have my life in the hands of God, that I'd simply drift along, making no choices, accepting what came to me.

"I was taken to the harem against my will. I married the king when I had no true desire to. All these things were my fate, I believed. My destiny. But something changed me."

"What do you mean?"

"When Haman made his decree—when I had to choose whether to risk my life by going unbidden before the king, or remain silent—for the first time in my life my fate was in my hands."

Holding her open hands before Rivka, she continued. "And it was not just my fate, but the fate of others. That's when I found that allowing God to guide my life did not mean drifting like a leaf on the current. It meant making a choice—sometimes a hard choice. My part was to choose. God's part was to give me courage for the choice and to see to the outcome. I don't think I've ever been the same. I'm stronger somehow. Things don't just happen to me anymore. I can't explain it any better than that," she said to Rivka's puzzled face. "It's just that there is something inside me now that isn't touched by anything the king can do for me, or to me."

She looked at Rivka. "I don't think I'm saying this very well."

"I think I see, though," Rivka said. "I think Mordecai would have seen, and would have been glad for you. Glad and proud."

Little changed through the winter months. The king and his lover were inseparable. Darius did not return to court, but neither did the smoldering rumors of rebellion flare into flame. Then, not long after midwinter, something happened.

"I heard news at the baths today," Tamyris said, meeting Esther in the courtyard of the harem.

"What news?"

"The Princess Artaynta is with child."

"*Is* she?" Esther's mind leaped back through the years to when she had told the king she was pregnant with Damaspia. For a moment she felt the pull of their web of intimacy as they celebrated the child they would have together. She felt a sharp pang of loss, then curiosity. "What will happen now, I wonder?"

What happened was that the king's ardor for Artaynta cooled almost as rapidly as it had begun. She was unceremoniously moved back into the women's quarters. Then in a new development Xerxes sent a squadron of men to his son Darius' estates to summon Darius to the palace. Gossip said that the king wanted Darius to take Artaynta back.

"This is madness," Esther said when Ayana told her the latest news. "Who is counseling him? What is behind this?"

"I have no idea what's behind this," Ayana said. "Can anyone answer that question where the king is concerned? But as for who is counseling him, that's easy: Artapanos. Artapanos has been entirely supportive of the whole affair with Artaynta. He is almost the only one of the king's counselors who supported him in his foolishness. Now, they say, he is urging the king to send her away. And all the women of Amestris' household—even Queen Amestris herself—who have been so friendly with Artaynta, are now giving her the cold shoulder. They snub her when they see her at the baths or in the courtyard. They refuse her invitations and are not inviting her to their quarters."

Esther thought back to the first time she'd seen the king and Artaynta together. The scene was burned into her memory—the young girl on his lap, her flirting, and rippling laughter. And there with her—as if they'd set it up—were Amytis and Raiya. "It's almost as if there was a conspiracy all along to bring them together—though why, I couldn't imagine," Esther said. "Now the same conspiracy wants to be rid of Artaynta."

"Perhaps. If Queen Amestris has any part of that, she will certainly not want to see a son born of the union."

"I truly don't understand what's going on here," Esther said, "but there is more to this than just the king's passions. They are real enough, but a man as much at the mercy of his passions as is the king is an easy tool for anyone who wants to play on him. Someone is at play here."

Whatever plots might have been going on behind the scenes, Darius did indeed come to Susa, escorted by his father's soldiers, to meet with his father. It was no private meeting. Xerxes would see Darius only in his throne room. Sitting on his throne, crowned, robed, in the full majesty of his position, Xerxes held out his golden scepter as his son and heir entered the room and bowed to the floor before him.

Esther, like most of the court women, sat under the porticos, watching. Only one woman was in the room itself. Artaynta, visibly pregnant now, unveiled, and standing with downcast eyes, stood a few feet away from the king's throne where she'd obviously been commanded to stand. The sweet prettiness that had always characterized her face had faded. She'd put on weight. Her face looked swollen. The glossy sheen was gone from her dark curls. She looked years older, weary, and saddened.

Esther thought of the description she'd given Rivka of herself at Artaynta's age: a leaf carried by a stream. *That's what she is,* Esther thought. Whoever was plotting and scheming in this situation, it certainly was not this sad, defeated girl. Her life was at the mercy of those around her.

Darius rose at his father's gesture and faced Xerxes, his eyes hard, his expression impassive. Everyone in the room knew his rage against the king, his justified contempt. What no one knew was whether he would dare express it here in this room where every garment, every piece of furniture, every ornament shouted that Xerxes the Great was King of Kings.

"Our son and heir, Darius," the king said, his voice as clear and ringing as it had ever been. "You have been too long absent from our domains. We welcome you."

Silence. Darius' eyes were hard, his face flushed. At last, in a voice that sounded as if he were being strangled, he spoke. "It is my pleasure to appear before you, my lord king."

The king smiled. "Before we rejoice in our reunion, there is a small matter that must be cared for." Xerxes waved a hand almost casually toward Artaynta. "Your wife has been resident in our court these many months. She is with child. It is not seemly that she should be living apart from you at such a time. Our pleasure is that you take her to your home, live with her as man and wife, and provide for your child."

A ripple of gasps ran through the watching women as well as quite a few of the men around the throne. No one had expected the king to be quite so blunt, so audacious.

"My lord king," Darius said, choosing his words with care. "My wife and I have not lived together since midsummer. The child she carries is not mine."

"Is that so?" The king's tone was smooth and confident. He had every step planned and seemed completely in control. Esther wondered how many people noticed what she saw—the king's eyes slid quickly toward Artapanos for a heartbeat before he spoke, and Artapanos gave an all but imperceptible nod. "This is a serious accusation you make, Prince Darius," Xerxes went on. "Who is the man you would dare accuse of dishonoring your wife and fathering a child on her?"

Dare. The word was well chosen, for Darius would have to be daring indeed to make any such accusation against his father, here in the throne room with Xerxes' guards all around. Esther wondered what had become of the soldiers who were supposed to have been loyal to Darius. Had they followed him here to the city, perhaps? At any rate, they were not in this room. Darius stood alone before his father. To accuse the king publicly of doing what everyone present knew he had done would certainly result in his arrest and perhaps even his death.

The silence grew long. Esther found herself biting her lip. Finally Darius spoke. "No man, my lord king. There is no man I would accuse of this deed."

"Then the woman is yours, and the child is yours," the king said, waving his hand again. "Take her away."

For the first time, Darius turned to look at his wife. He had never loved her. Everyone knew that, yet in his eyes there was no anger, no contempt, no judgment. Perhaps all those emotions were too finely focused on his father to be spared for anyone else. If anything, Esther thought, there was a touch of pity in the way Darius gravely extended his hand to Artaynta.

She looked up at last, darting a glance at the king. That one glance said everything about her feelings. No matter how ill-used she had been, she adored Xerxes and longed for him to call her back to his side. But his face was hard. He looked away.

Artaynta put her hand in Darius' hand, and he led her from the room.

Darius had no intention of staying for the father-son reunion the king had so mockingly spoken of. He prepared to leave Susa and return to his own estates that same day. He was prevented by a small force of the king's soldiers who detained him on his way and informed him that it was the king's pleasure that he and his wife remain in the citadel of Susa. Darius and Artaynta returned to his quarters in the palace, unused for almost a year. That same night, a small band of armed men traveling toward Susa on the road Darius would have taken home was apprehended, imprisoned, and hanged as brigands.

Life in the palace was unbearably tense that winter and spring. Darius was virtually his father's prisoner. He still maintained all the trappings and honors of an heir to the throne, yet he was not free to leave and go to his own estates or travel about the kingdom. Meanwhile, Artapanos, captain of the guard, became more and more firmly entrenched as the king's right hand.

As for women, no one from the harem was called to Xerxes for several weeks after he sent Artaynta away. Then he summoned Esther.

The evening did not go well. She came to the king's chamber after the evening meal and found him alone, drinking, and already quite drunk. She understood quickly that this was a night when he wanted her to listen as he poured out his troubles, his anger, his griefs. Every word tonight was about Darius. Not Darius his father, as it had been when they first married, but Darius his son. He paced around the room. He shouted, swore, and threw things as he said that Darius was ungrateful, disrespectful, rebellious, and unfit to rule. He talked about making Hystaspes or Artaxerxes his heir instead. Never did he mentioned Artaynta's name, or suggest that anything he had done might have caused Darius' rebellion.

"Why have the gods cursed me with such a son?" he begged of Esther, kneeling on the floor at her feet. Tears streamed down his face. "I am a just man, Esther; you know this. You know how I worship Ahura Mazda, how I live my life in pursuit of the truth and reject lies—all lies. You know this, don't you? Yet I have been cursed—cursed in my family, cursed in my councillors, and now cursed in my sons. Not one of them is fit to rule! Artaxerxes is an idiot. Hystaspes cannot think for himself. And Darius—my Darius, the one I had pinned all my hopes on—he hates me! He is unworthy! And why?"

Esther felt an overwhelming mixture of pity, contempt, even a little revulsion. Yet she took his head in her hands and eased it onto her lap. Stroking his face, she let him rave on. Nothing she could say would bring him to any sort of reality. He was lost in a world of his own. She let him talk and drink and weep and rage until his eyes finally closed. He had paced and raved and shouted, and now lay stretched out on her couch, his head in her lap. She sat there a long

time, stroking his graying hair and remembering their first night together when he had been drunk, and angry, and had fallen asleep. So
much had changed, and so little.

She looked at his face, slack now in sleep. It seemed to her the ruin
of a fine, noble, kingly face, and she mourned for the loss of what had
been, and what might have been. But even while her tears fell she remembered Mordecai's words. It had never been within her power to
save Xerxes, to make him other than what he had chosen to be. At
last she too fell asleep, even in that uncomfortable position. When she
awoke in the spilled light of morning, the king was gone.

CHAPTER 19

A few weeks later the court moved to Parsa, Esther and
Damaspia included, along with the rest. Darius and Artaynta
remained at Susa with their household, and in midsummer Artaynta
gave birth to her father-in-law's child. It was a boy. He was given
the name of Cyrus. Her husband claimed the child as his own. What
else could he do?

In the fall, Lord Carshena, the king's chief minister, died.

"Carshena?" Esther said when she heard the news. "That is a
shock. He was about the king's age or a little older, but he always
seemed so hale and lively."

Ayana, who had delivered the news, raised an eyebrow. "That is
what many people are saying. What a shock, how sudden. And how
smoothly Lord Artapanos is poised to take over Carshena's position
and power."

"You can't mean—are they suggesting Carshena was murdered?" Esther dropped her voice, though she and Ayana were alone
in her bedchamber in the palace at Susa. The habit of speaking cautiously about those in power was deeply ingrained, and wise, for
spies were everywhere.

"Nobody is suggesting that," Ayana said. "Not aloud, at any
rate. But everyone thinks it very strange."

Strange or not, Artapanos took his seat on the council four days after Lord Carshena's death. Now the power he'd been exercising for years was backed up by law. The king rarely bothered even to appear in council anymore, and formal audiences were rare. Artapanos spoke in the king's name.

As soon as she decently could after Carshena's death, Esther removed to her estate. For several months she'd been called to the king about once a week when she was in the palace; occasionally she went to his bed, but more often she simply kept him company, listening to him talk. When he was sober, or nearly so—for she found him never fully sober, anymore—they had some pleasant times together. She did not attempt to give him advice or counsel. He disliked that.

Artapanos' first act upon taking office was a surprise to no one. For several years he'd been married to a woman from a good military family, somewhat superior in rank to his own. She had already borne him two sons who were halfway to manhood. Immediately after becoming chief minister, Artapanos took as a second wife Raiya, servant to Queen Amestris. Since Raiya was a woman with no family background and was past her best years for child-bearing, this might have been a surprise, save for two well-known facts: Raiya came extremely well dowered by the queen, and she had been Artapanos' lover for at least two years.

Hearing the news. Esther wondered whether Raiya was content at last. She had never become queen, but she had married the man closest to the king in power and position. Was that enough for her?

Esther spent even more time than before with her daughter, who was getting old enough now to sometimes ask awkward questions. As the years slipped by she was keenly aware of the need to educate Damaspia in things her tutors could not teach.

One day, several months after Lord Carshena's death, Damaspia said, "Mama, why does Prince Darius hate our father the king so much?"

"Where did you hear that?" Esther asked. They were riding horses on the estate. Damaspia was a good rider and loved to hunt when she had the chance.

"I hear it all the time from the servants. Even Hathakh says it's true, but he won't tell me why."

Esther looked at her daughter, now almost 10 years old. The court, the harem, the palace intrigue, was the world in which she'd grown up—the world in which she would live out her life. For an instant Esther felt awash with sorrow for the simple life Damaspia would never have. "Prince Darius has many reasons for not liking the king," Esther told her. "I suppose he wishes that he were king himself. He will be someday."

"But what does Princess Artaynta have to do with it?"

Esther sighed, wishing she had a magic potion that would give her all the right answers for a curious young girl. "Princess Artaynta is Darius' wife, as you know, but once, a few years ago, the king—well, she was the king's concubine." She paused, looking her daughter in the eyes. "While she was still married to Darius."

"But that's not right!" Damaspia protested.

"No, it's not. The king did something wrong, and Darius was angry at him for it."

"Why would the king do something wrong?"

That question stopped Esther in her tracks. Somehow it made her realize the enormity of the girl's innocence. It was not so much that she idolized her father; she barely knew him. It was simply hard for her to imagine how someone so great could knowingly do wrong.

"Damaspia, have you ever taken something that was not yours, something you were not allowed to have?"

Damaspia's cheeks colored. "I'm sorry, Mama! I didn't think anyone would notice," she stammered. "It was such a small thing, and Hathakh hardly even plays any of his flutes, but they're such nice ones. And it wasn't like I really took his nay. I just borrowed it to keep in my room and play sometimes, but I'll give it back to him, really I will. How did you find out?"

Esther struggled to hide her laughter. She had meant only to draw a comparison, not to elicit a confession. She'd had no idea about Hathakh's nay. "Damaspia, you must return the nay tonight, and tell Hathakh the truth about it. It is always wrong to take what belongs to another. But you didn't think of that, did you? You only thought of what you wanted." Damaspia nodded, not meeting her mother's eyes. "You see, it is the same with grown people, even with the king. Sometimes a person just takes something he wants, even if that belongs to someone else—just because he's selfish and doesn't think of the other person, or about what's right or wrong. We start by doing it with small things, like a piece of fruit or a toy—or a nay—but if we do not check that urge to be selfish, we will continue doing it even in big things, as the king did."

"Oh, Mama, I am sorry! I don't want to be selfish in big things when I'm grown up. And—oh! It's just like the commandment." Damaspia lifted her head and gave her horse's reins a brisk little shake, galloping on ahead.

"Which commandment?" Esther asked, trotting to catch up.

"You shall not covet your neighbor's house, or his wife. See, God even thought of someone doing that—or his ox, or his ass, or anything that is your neighbor's," Damaspia recited, obviously pleased with herself.

"That's right. And what does the other commandment say, the one about stealing?"

"You shall not steal. It's the same thing, isn't it, Mama? God doesn't want us to take things, but He doesn't want us even to *want* other people's things, because that's being selfish, and we might end up taking something. Just like I coveted Hathakh's nay."

Despite discovering her daughter's small crime, Esther was proud. The girl's mind was quick, and she not only knew the Hebrew scriptures, she was already a follower of Israel's God. Her tutors had taught her the teachings of Zarathustra, the religion of her father's people, and she understood it and respected it. But not long ago she had asked Esther, "Mama, can I be Jewish like you are, even though my father is the king of Persia?"

Again Esther assured her that if her mother was Jewish, she was indeed Jewish, and if she chose in her heart to follow the God of Israel, He would welcome her with open arms. Esther's own heart was warmed. Despite living in a Persian world, she'd longed to raise her daughter to know and worship the true God. It seemed, at least for now, that she had succeeded.

Esther's farms yielded poorly that year, but that was little surprise. All over Persia crops had failed again as rain still refused to fall. The year before had been poor; this year was a disaster. Hathakh was such a skilled manager that Esther's household felt few hunger pangs; their stores were well filled and carefully rationed. But not everyone fared so well. The royal storehouses, opened last year to provide for the shortages, were almost empty this year as the famine grew worse instead of better. In the markets, the price of grain shot up to seven times its usual cost.

In Susa, there was unrest, and rioting in the streets. "The king will have to do something," Hathakh told Esther one day upon coming in from the city. "Artapanos' archers are shooting into the crowds to control them, but soon not even the threat of death will stop hungry people from demanding food. They are claiming that the king's ministers have mismanaged the storehouses and left the people to starve."

When Esther next visited court, she found Xerxes quite unconcerned about the famine and the protests. She sat in his private chamber, listening as Artapanos and his men discussed the subject over and around him. When they were gone and she was alone with him, he made no reference to the anger and unrest in both the city and the countryside. His mood was dark. He was drunk and still drinking. His step grew more unsteady and his speech more slurred as he recited the list of his troubles and the people who had disappointed and betrayed him. By now the list included almost all of his courtiers and most of his family.

That made Aratapanos' next move easy. A few days after that summons to court, Esther's servants told her about the proclamation being shouted in the city streets. Scores of the king's ministers and palace officials, from the very highest officers to the most menial, had been dismissed. In all, almost 100 men had lost their positions, with new men appointed to replace them.

"The people are all out cheering in the streets," Hathakh reported.

"Why?" Esther asked. "What good does it do them? They're as hungry as ever."

"Yes, but they believe that the king has heard their pleas and is punishing those who have failed to help them. So of course they believe things will get better."

"Who of the council is gone?"

"You should ask, 'Who is left?' All the old men—Marsena, Tarshish, all the councillors," Hathakh said. "Vashush is gone as treasurer. Countless more have been dismissed, and others will follow. Almost all are men who have served a long time in their positions."

"And the new men are Artapanos' friends and allies, aren't they?" Esther guessed. "I wonder if the king even realizes what's happening? What a splendid opportunity for Artapanos to clear the field of his rivals while looking like a hero."

She'd guessed right. New men, loyal to the chief minister, filled the council and most of the important palace posts. They could do nothing, of course, about the famine, but the illusion of change helped pacify the rioters for a few weeks, anyway.

Esther spent most of that winter on the estate, though from time to time she was still summoned to attend King Xerxes. She kept her court visits as brief as possible, for she disliked the atmosphere of the palace these days. At times she studied Xerxes as he sat in the midst of the ambitious younger men who now surrounded him, and thought that he seemed lost, unable to grasp how things had changed so quickly and why he was no longer able to rule these men as he'd ruled others. He did not even seem to understand why or how so many men—men whom he'd once trusted—had been let go so quickly, and replaced. In fact, it often seemed that he forgot about the famine, which, of course, did not affect his own table. Esther felt pained to see his helplessness, for she acutely felt her own lack of power to help him. She much preferred to be on her own estate, closeted with Hathakh and the understewards, trying to figure out how to make their carefully hoarded supplies stretch as far as possible, for they fed not only their own household but scores of hungry Jews who came looking for help.

Meanwhile, the crown prince Darius, who in any normal reign would have been his father's second in command, still fretted and paced like a young eagle with clipped wings. He remained in his quarters in Susa and was given no role in government. However much Artapanos might dominate the king, he had no intentions of allowing Darius to gain any power. Darius was surrounded by a network of spies and men loyal to his father—or rather, loyal to his father's chief minister—unable, it seemed, to strike a blow.

The following spring, as crops ripened in the fields with hope of a marginally better harvest, as usual the court moved to Parsa for the new year. This year the new year's celebrations and the arrival of the satraps and embassies to pay tribute would be the most elaborate ever. This year marked Xerxes' twentieth as king. Esther, herself, marked a milestone also, for at her autumn birthday she would be 30 years old.

Esther at 30. Xerxes in the twentieth year of his reign. Esther stood in front of her polished brass mirror and studied the lines around her eyes. Though she used the best creams available, the years and the Persian sun had done their damage. *Where,* she wondered, *have the past 15 years gone?*

King Xerxes was deeply and happily immersed in planning the New Year's celebrations. When Esther came to his suite he drew her into discussions about the musicians, the poets, the robes, and the gifts with an eagerness that held some small hint of his old energy. She listened and shared in the planning but felt sad, wondering if he had any understanding that this was the only small corner of his kingdom in which his chief minister allowed him a part to play.

Outside the closed doors of his chamber, people in the towns and cities angrily protested the rising price of food and their increasing taxes. From the far-flung satrapies, especially Egypt, came rumors of revolt. But nothing troubled the king. Artapanos allowed him to know only a small, controlled portion of the news from outside his narrow world, and that news was highly colored.

Esther worried about him and the whole situation, so tried to help him see the truth. "My lord, when the satraps come to bring tribute, will you hold council with them?" she asked him. "Everyone is saying that this will be another famine year, both here and in many of the provinces. The satraps will want to know what arrangements are being made to feed their people."

Xerxes looked up from the tablet he was perusing, surprised and a little annoyed. "Why would you worry about such a thing, my lovely queen? Artapanos assures me that all is well under control. I'm sure he will arrange these things with them."

He traced some letters on the tablet with a absentminded gesture. "Ah, did I tell you about the wine that the merchant found for me near Parsa? He brings his wares from the farthest reaches of the west, and it's a vintage to gladden the heart. His prices are reasonable, and he's agreed to supply the new year's banquet for a fraction of what we paid in the past, or so Artapanos tells me."

Esther sighed. "I'm sure it will be a banquet to delight all your guests, my lord." She felt weary, frustrated. She hated pretending to her husband-king that all was well, but there was no other way. She tried to make her voice bright. "Your choice of music is excellent, I must say."

That year's tribute ceremony at Parsa was, indeed, splendid. The entire royal family was in attendance. Darius stood behind his father's throne looking proud and regal, as the heir should, except for the glare of rage in his eyes. Artaxerxes was in the background, handsome and quiet, taking in every detail. Queen Amestris, resplendent in her jewels and royal gowns, sat at her husband's right hand. Her marble face had not aged or become careworn one whit that anyone could see. Queen Irdabama, as plain and plainspoken as ever, eyed the satraps as if she was calculating what each gift had cost. Queen Esther was very quiet, very watchful. She noticed how confident and commanding Xerxes managed to appear in this public ceremony where no decisions were required of him, where nothing outside the scripted, precise litany ever happened. *Surely,* she thought, *no one looking at him would know how shaky is his grasp on the reins of power.*

The satraps themselves were a splendid sight, robed and gowned in the fashion of their satrapies, bearing their tribute gifts. The satrap of Hindush, in his glorious robes and jewels, led in a double column of 40 girl slaves and 40 boy slaves—all barefoot and clad in white, exotically beautiful children of India. Esther looked at the little boys, eunuchs already, and thought of Hathakh, brought from that same far-off land so many years ago. Among her friends—and even her enemies—in the palace and the harem, so many had come against their will, sold as slaves or handed over as tribute. Yet many had found better, more comfortable lives than they'd have ever known in their homelands. People said the ways of the gods were strange. Esther, believing in no God but her own, had to concede that His ways were sometimes strange, too.

Many times the satraps sent representatives rather than coming themselves to pay tribute, but despite the famine, this year—in honor of the king's twentieth year of reign—they'd all come. Esther had forgotten, until he was announced, who was satrap of Phrygia. That is, she had not forgotten Artabazus—one of her first friends at the king's court—but in recent years memory of him had slipped to the back of her mind. She had not connected him with the name of his satrapy for a long time. When he marched—like the old soldier he was—into the audience hall to pay tribute, her heart warmed at the sight of him. He had been a good, true friend, though the memory of that friendship still felt sullied by the terrible accusations made against them both. Now his hair and beard were not merely grizzled, but white. White hair better suited his ruddy face, she decided. His face was deeply lined; the slight limp he used to have was more pronounced, but the keen small eyes seemed as sharp as ever. As he approached the throne, his eyes darted over the king's family and lit on

Esther's face. At that, he gave the faintest nod.

Esther and he did not have opportunity to speak until the following afternoon. The banquet had continued late into the previous night, with another banquet planned for the next evening. The king had requested that Esther share the midday meal with him, but he was poor company, recovering from the previous night's drinking. She sat quietly at his private table in company with his son Hystaspes and Hystaspes' wife, two other visiting satraps, and Artapanos, who fortunately had neither of his wives with him on this occasion. One of the satraps was Artabazus. His wife, Barsine, had remained behind in Phrygia with their children. She did not, Artabazus told the company, enjoy travel.

"My wife hates to travel, and I like my wife, so I've traveled but little these late years," he said. "Except what must be done in the line of duty, of course. But I'm fortunate in that way. Phrygia is quiet, and mostly loyal, for all its proximity to Greece."

"I would have thought, my lord Artabazus, that you would have had enough journeying in your younger days to last a lifetime," Prince Hystaspes said.

Artabazus laughed. "Indeed! My lord king," he said, turning to Xerxes, "if I never have to trace that ride back from the fields of Plataea again, I'll be a happy man. I got saddle sores then that still trouble me today!" Seeing that the king did not respond—apparently he'd not been following the conversation—Artabazus turned back to the table and earned a laugh from them.

Esther, veiled and eating quietly, wondered why she had been summoned. Almost 10 years had passed since she'd been accused of being unfaithful to the king, but she clearly remembered his anger. Why would he go out of his way to throw her into Artabazus' presence now? Unless—could it be that the old scandal had ceased to matter to him? Perhaps so much had happened since that time that he no longer remembered or cared.

Esther very much wanted to talk to her old friend, but when all had finished the meal and retreated to the courtyard to sit and talk, she placed herself a distance from him. She suspected that Artapanos, at the very least, knew of that long-ago slander and would be watching.

But Artabazus approached her with a deep respectful bow. She noticed that he moved stiffly when he tried to rise from his knees.

The joint illness that troubled so many older men, especially old soldiers, must be bothering him, too.

"My lady queen, how good to see you," he said with a gentle smile.

"And you, Lord Artabazus. I trust your family is well?"

"They are. Amazing how well I've adapted to marriage and family life. I never thought myself the type, but I find I'm quite devoted now. Couldn't fathom life without them. And you—you have just your daughter?"

"Just my daughter, but she is a joy to me. She is betrothed to Prince Artaxerxes, as I'm sure you've heard."

"Good for her. Good fellow, Artaxerxes. He'll come to no harm. Now the other one, Darius—" Artabazus broke off, glanced about him. No one was near enough to hear, but no one was very far away, either. Artabazus spat a soldier's curse, then apologized. "It's just that I'd like in the worst way to have a chat with you alone, but I guess we don't dare—all that foolish old business from eons ago. I wouldn't put you to the shame of having that dragged out again. Sorry it ever had to happen to you at all. I should have been more discreet even in those days, but discretion doesn't come natural to me."

"I understand," Esther said, "but no, we cannot talk alone."

"You understand, of course." Artabazus turned, if possible, even a little more red and shifted his weight uncomfortably from one foot to the other. "Of course, my lady, when I say I want to talk alone, I don't mean any such thing—anything improper. Only that you have good sense, and I always felt we understood each other. There are things I'd like to know, and like to get said. Never did mean anything more than that by it—though of course," he added, looking at her straight on now, "you were always a great beauty. Still are, in fact, and if I ever aimed high enough or was fool enough to trifle with one of the king's women, it would have been you, of course." He delivered his compliment as gruffly and matter-of-factly as if he were telling his groom that his horse had thrown a shoe, then it was back to business. Esther smiled and wished she could laugh aloud.

"But this folly with Darius and with Darius' wife—what's been going on here? Has the king gone mad, or the whole palace? And who is this new minister of his? I don't hear much good about him. What can you tell me?"

Esther grew serious again at once. "Only this, my old friend—I failed in the task you set for me so many years ago. You told me I might be the one to save the king, to keep him from destroying himself in his grief over losing Greece. But I could not do that. Everything is as you saw it long ago—his despair, his drinking, his love affairs. He is pulling it all down around his head, and I don't think he even cares anymore."

Artabazus nodded slowly. "Much as I thought. Don't blame yourself, girl—my lady. You did as well as anyone could. Might have all happened sooner if not for you. We all have our own lives to live. I liked the last chief minister, by the way—your kinsman, wasn't he? Good man. Not like old Haman. Not like this new fellow. But it shouldn't matter. Good man, bad man—it should be the king at the helm. And it's not, is it?"

Esther only shook her head. She saw Prince Hystaspes and his wife strolling their direction and gave them a glance of welcome. It would be dangerous to spend any more time in private conversation with Artabazus. "You said you had things you wanted to say. I presume you mean to the king," she said quietly to him as the others approached. "You will not find it easy to meet with him alone if Artapanos does not wish you to. If you do not have the chance, tell me, and I'll see what I can do. But I doubt he will listen."

"Perhaps there's nothing left to say after all," said Artabazus, grimly staring into his cup of wine.

The prince and princess came closer, and Esther stepped forward to begin talking with them. Out of the corner of her eye she saw Artabazus' gaze drift toward the king. He sat with Artapanos in close conversation, though Artapanos seemed to be doing all the talking. Artabazus had been a friend of the king's youth, she remembered, and her heart hurt for the hurt *he* must be feeling. She did not see him in private or speak with him again before the celebrations ended and he returned to Phrygia.

The satraps left, the celebrations ended, and the king returned to the only work he still cared for, the work on Parsa. Along with construction on the great hall of pillars and the new reliefs, he was having inscriptions made. They were an echo—in some places, a direct copy—of the great inscriptions his father Darius had left, chiseling the record of his reign—his own picture of who he was and how he wanted to be remembered—into stone. In the places where Xerxes' inscriptions differed from his father's, he hired one poet after another to fine-tune the words, sometimes rejecting one wording after the workers had already begun with their chisels. It mattered a great deal to him, Esther saw, to be remembered by posterity. And as always, his father was the measure against which he stood.

Xerxes, dwarfed by his father's tall shadow.

One hot night late in the month of Abu, the king summoned Esther to his bedchamber after the evening meal. She found him surrounded by sketches and designs left with him by the artisans. She was relieved to see him interested in the plans and drawings, even though she knew that what had once been his grand ambition had turned into an obsession. But it was better than finding him staring into the fire, brooding about everyone who had ever disappointed or betrayed him.

"They are finishing work on the inscription to go above the throne room portal," Xerxes said, looking up from clay tablets and scrolls with fever-bright eyes. "This is the wording I am going to give them to carve. I have been over it with the poets and with Artapanos. It's final now. Listen."

Esther nodded and smiled, touching his hand lightly with two fingers. "This is what you've been waiting for, is it not? Yes, I do want to hear it."

Xerxes straightened with pride and read, "You who may live hereafter, if you should think 'Happy may I be when living, and when dead may I be blessed,' have respect for that law that Ahura Mazda has established. Worship Ahura Mazda at the proper time and in the proper manner. The man who has respect for that law that Ahura Mazda has established and worships Ahura Mazda at the proper time and in the proper manner, he both becomes happy while alive and becomes blessed when dead."

The king looked at Esther for her reaction. Despite the sadness these words made her feel, she nodded her approval. Clearing his throat, he continued, "Proclaims Xerxes the king: Me may Ahura Mazda protect from harm, and my house, and this land. This I ask of Ahura Mazda. This may Ahura Mazda give to me."

Esther closed her eyes, picturing the last words carved in stone. When he finished reading she told him, "It is very well said."

He smiled, an echo of his old smile. "You still cling to your own god, your God of the Jews, do you not? But that is all right. Ahura

Mazda will not blame you for worshiping a god who is so good, a god of the light, not a demon like the gods of Babylon. I destroyed them, you know—their temples, their statues, everything. All for the glory of Ahura Mazda."

All for the glory—and security—of your throne, Esther thought. In recent years Xerxes, always interested in religion, had become intensely devout, and tended to interpret his past acts in terms of religious fervor rather than the political motives that had driven him for most of his life. Yet had Ahura Mazda rewarded him for his loyalty? *Happy while alive and blessed while dead.* Perhaps he still believed he would be blessed while dead. Esther could hardly imagine Xerxes thought of himself as happy while alive, but then she knew so little of what went on inside his mind.

She had tried to speak to him, in the years when Mordecai was alive, about the God of Israel. He conceded that Israel's God looked after His own people, but well beyond that he had no great interest in this tribal god of a small, powerless people. Now Esther said only, "Yes, I do cling to my God," and thought that she had spoken few words in the king's presence as true as those.

Xerxes stood up and walked to a window, leaning his arms on the broad sill—the depth of the wall—that helped insulate the house from summer's sun. "You will celebrate an important birthday this autumn," he said, looking at her with a smile.

Esther's eyes lit with surprise. Even in the early days of their marriage he'd taken little notice of her birthdays. "We must plan a great feast," he said.

She laughed, tickled that he remembered. "Yes, I am an old woman now. I'll be 30."

"Thirty seems young to me. When I was 30 I had not yet taken the throne." He shook his head as if to clear the memories, then crossed the room back to his work. Picking up a sketch, he said, "Life passes too swiftly, Esther. But you are not old, and you are beautiful still." One finger traced a line of inscription engraved with a stylus in the clay tablet. "You have been a good wife, a loyal and true wife to me." He closed his eyes and for a long moment seemed lost in thought.

"Better than the others," he concluded almost to himself. He reached a hand across the table to clasp hers, and she entwined her fingers through his. Somehow she found herself seeing things differently tonight, as if in more and sharper detail. She felt the pressure of the king's hand against her palm, felt each of his fingers side by side with hers. She saw each curled black hair on his fingers and the deep wrinkles across his knuckles. The grasp of his hand around hers broke her heart.

They made love that night, though they rarely did anymore, since the king was usually too weary or too ill or simply too drunk to want to take a woman to his bed. Lying beside him in the warm darkness, she felt more tenderness than passion. Though they lay in the bed's dim curtained tent, in her mind she clearly saw him. He had begun to look like an old man. His long dark hair was streaked with silver. His square-cut beard was gray, threaded with black. His chest hair was gray, and the skin below it was wrinkled and translucent. Too clearly his breastbone showed through his skin. Yet she felt something very much like love as she held him long into the night, something that in the end she could only feel as an acknowledgment that their lives were bound together, for good or ill, till they would be parted by death.

A week later Esther awoke to the sound of shrieks in the courtyard, and running feet. She sat upright in bed, a knot of fear twisting in her stomach, for little disturbed the nighttime silence of the harem. Esther remembered suddenly her first visit to Parsa, remembered not with her mind but with her body those summer weeks when Amestris had had Artaynte arrested and mutilated, and she herself had lost the baby she was carrying. Something of that old horror and fear came flooding back now as she waited in the dark for Ayana, who came running from her adjoining chamber, as Esther knew she would.

"Have you heard anything?" Esther gasped.

"Only shouts, and people running," Ayana said. "I awakened just now. Wait here, I will go down to find out more."

"No, hand me a cloak. I'll go with you. I don't want to be alone here. I fear this is something bad." The screams outside had diffused into a number of voices, all shouting incoherently. Within the harem walls she heard the high-pitched shrieks of frightened women, but there was something more. The low rumble of men's voices played a sober counterpart to the women's cries. Were they soldiers? What was happening?

Then as Ayana and Esther crept down the dark, narrow stairs toward the lower portion of Esther's apartments, one voice rose clear above the others with a sudden anguished cry: "The gods have mercy on us! The king is dead!"

Esther stopped in midstep. Ayana, a few stairs below her, turned back and put out a hand to steady her as if she'd known the queen would stumble before Esther's own feet knew it had happened. Esther lurched into her friend's arms, and together the two women staggered awkwardly down the last few steps until they stood, reeling a little, at the bottom.

"Are you all right?" Ayana said. Esther knew she was not talking about tripping on the stairs.

"I think so. I suppose it's true?"

"It may be. A rumor can be powerful, but rarely powerful enough to wake the palace at midnight."

Esther took a deep breath, trying to steady herself. "It had to come." She caught her breath. "It's a terrible shock, but . . . truly, I'm not surprised. Ayana, he was failing." She clutched her longtime friend. "Everyone saw it. Even though he had no particular illness the physicians could have named, I knew it would come before long."

Hathakh appeared out of the shadows. "My lady, you speak as if the king died naturally, in his sleep," he said kindly. "But is that likely?"

Esther looked at him with wild, wide eyes. "Why, yes, what—?"

"It's not been said that the king was ill, and even a man who is sickly and failing rarely slips away so suddenly—unless his heart fails. But this commotion, this running and shouting!" He shook his head, biting his lip. His hands were trembling. "To me it speaks of violence, my lady, and I have set an extra guard on the doors. Let no one in. I am going out to find news." He paused again, as if in thought. "My dear lady, I think it best if you both returned to the upper chamber."

"I am sure you are right," Esther whispered, struggling to comprehend the idea of violence and possible bloodshed. She turned back to the stairs. "Hathakh, bring us news as soon as you have it."

He returned in less than an hour. Ayana and Esther had spent the time in Esther's private chamber, speaking little, straining to make sense of the muffled voices that rose and fell outside their walls. Other servants crept in to join them, till most of the household crowded in the room. Esther was thankful that Damaspia, who slept very soundly, had not awakened. Sofia remained with her.

"Mur-DER!" came the muffled cry from beyond their walls. "Murder!" they heard, repeated over and over. "Treason!"

"It seems that Hathakh is not the only one who fears violence," Ayana murmured to the queen.

Then Hathakh was standing in the doorway, looking around the room packed with women robed in their nightwear. His eyes fell on Esther. He stepped toward her, then dropped to one knee. "My lady," he said, "our grief is great."

Esther stood up, feeling it better to hear the news on her feet. "Rise, and tell us what you have learned, Hathakh."

"It is true indeed. The king is dead. I have spoken with those who have seen his body. Sometime after midnight he was stabbed to death in his own chamber. The eunuch who attended him tonight—a new man named Spamitres—has disappeared. Other servants and guards have been arrested, and Artapanos has taken control of the palace and of the investigation into the king's death."

He paused, glanced round at all of them, then looked at Esther with tenderness. "My lady queen, your loss is our loss. Our king is dead."

The words whirled in Esther's brain. *Murdered . . . stabbed . . . Spamitres . . . arrested . . . Artapanos . . . control . . .*

None of it made any sense, but at the center was a picture she could clearly see—Xerxes in his bedchamber, asleep on his bed where she'd last seen him. The curtain hastily pulled aside, his chest stabbed and slashed, his blood puddled onto the bedcoverings. She shuddered, and closed her eyes. Too late. Too late for so many things.

Her people gathered round to comfort and support her, but they were locked in their own loss and fear. The king, for good or ill, had been the center of all their lives. What would happen now? Who had killed him, and why? Who was in control? Artapanos, of course, but Darius was still the heir, however much he and his father had hated each other. Xerxes had named no other heir. Surely Darius must be crowned. He must seize power, and soon.

Morning in the palace was a confused cacophony of people coming and going, trading rumors and speculations. At noon a messenger came to announce that the king's body was laid in the audience hall, and that Queen Esther and Princess Damaspia were to go there to attend his funeral rites. Already, despite violence and confusion, the machinery of death was spinning. Ayana had called for a seamstress to prepare new mourning clothes for Esther and all her household. For today's funeral, they would have to make do with white garments already in their wardrobes. Esther and Damaspia, dressed in their simplest white gowns, made their way out of the harem and toward the audience chamber.

The king's bier, covered in its white shroud, rested in the center of the room. White-clad courtiers and family members gathered around it, all in deep silence. Esther watched Amestris arrive, flanked by Artaxerxes and Amytis with Amytis' husband, Megabyzus, and their children. Irdabama and her youngest daughter took their places. There was, conspicuously, no sign of Darius.

Esther and Damaspia found their places on the floor, the required distance away from the unclean corpse. The magi entered. One lit a lamp; another, incense. Then the priests began their hymn:

> "May the bounteous miraculous power and glory of Ahura
>   Mazda the lord increase.
> May this prayer reach Sourosh, the righteous, the vigorous,
> whose body is the command, having a hard weapon, powerful
>   of weapon,
> the lord of the creations of Ahura Mazda.
> I am contrite for all sins and I desist from them,
> from all bad thoughts, bad words, and bad acts
> that I have thought, spoken or done in the world,
> or that have happened through me, or have originated with me.
> For those sins of thinking, speaking, and acting,
> of body and soul, worldly or spiritual,
> O Ahura Mazda! I am contrite, I renounce them."

Sitting on the hard stone floor, listening to the chanted hymns, Esther remembered sitting in mourning for Mordecai. Then, too, she had sat on the floor and listened to hymns and prayers. She had felt great sorrow then, deep loss, and yet a certainty that Mordecai was now in the care and keeping of the good God he had served all his days. Her people, unlike the Persians, did not talk much of a life after death. Zarathustra's followers had many stories about the weighing of the soul after death, about the bridge the dead must cross to the land of glory that awaited them, and the fate that met those who did not cross successfully, but fell off the bridge into darkness below. She had found no such stories in the Hebrew tablets, and she had heard both Mordecai and Ezra say that they did not know what would happen after death. "But God is good," Ezra had assured her after Mordecai died. "Whatever is after this life, we are in His keeping. What more should we ask?"

Even with that unknowing, at Mordecai's death she'd felt a peace that was lacking today. Xerxes had been a fervent follower of his god, but Esther did not believe Ahura Mazda had the power to guide any souls to a paradise after death, and even if such a paradise existed, how would Xerxes' soul fare in the balances? She was only glad she was not God, to judge a man's soul, to look back at the record of his life and see what was good and what was evil. Surely no human could fairly judge another.

She looked at the faces around her, impassive in their mourning. Who here truly wept for Xerxes? Did Artaxerxes and Amytis mourn their father? Damaspia looked troubled, but she had scarcely known Xerxes. Amestris, Irdabama . . . herself . . . who had truly loved the man? Who had known his soul? Yet all their lives would be scarred by his death, and all the more by its violent manner and the uncertainty that followed it.

In a break between the prayers she saw Artapanos, clad in mourning white like the rest, rise and leave the room. What hurried conferences, what trials, what executions, even, were going on outside this room? Amestris glanced toward the doors, agitated. Artaxerxes broke the silence to lean forward and murmur something to her. Death was in the room, commanding their attention, yet life swirled on, dragging them with it.

As the ceremony ended and the long hours of the three-day mourning period began, Esther remained seated, declining offers of food and drink. Others came and went. Servants carried in baskets of spices and dried flowers, packing them around the softening body of the king. Even these could not mask the odor of decay in the hot, airless room. Esther accepted the stench as she did her hunger pangs: a necessary part of keeping vigil for the dead. She tried to give herself wholly to the task of mourning her husband. The tangled knot of emotions she felt was far too complicated for the single word "grief." Perhaps "loss" was better. She had lost him. He was gone, and she wanted these three days to remember, to sift through her images of him.

Xerxes the king, virile and arrogant as she'd seen him the first night she'd been brought to his chamber. Then obsessed with her, unable to get enough of having her close; passionate and tender when he held her in his arms. In her mind she saw him lashed by anger and despair, as he'd been so often. Sitting on his throne, remote and powerful, as he was on the day Lilaios was executed and the terrible hour she spent before him and pleaded for the lives of her people. Confused, broken and lost, as she'd so often seen him these past few years. Growing old, growing weak. A victim of his own follies, yet pitiable in spite of that . . . perhaps because of that. She had no prayers for Ahura Mazda, and what could she say to her own God about this man? Yet she wanted to pray all the same, and the only words that came to her mind were those of that psalm so ancient it was said to have come from the patriarch Moses himself:

> "You turn men back to dust, saying,
> 'Return to dust, O sons of men . . .'
> You sweep men away in the sleep of death;
> they are like the new grass of the morning—
> though in the morning it springs up new,
> by evening it is dry and withered . . .
> The length of our days is seventy years—
> or eighty, if we have the strength;
> yet their span is but trouble and sorrow,
> for they quickly pass, and we fly away . . .
> Teach us to number our days aright,
> that we may gain a heart of wisdom."

The hours blurred into days. Esther continued her fast, her deliberate mourning, though on the first evening she sent Damaspia back to their quarters and told her to eat a good meal. On the third day the king's body would be carried to Naqsh-i-Rustam where his father, Darius, was buried. His tomb had long awaited him. Until then, Esther stayed, the one constant in an ever-rotating room of mourners.

She knew that confusing things were happening outside, but in the room where the king's body lay, nobody spoke. She could only guess—and she did guess, from those who came and went. Artapanos was rarely present, and always looked tense and preoccupied. After a few hours on the first day Artaxerxes left, and did not return. Amestris left, and did return the next day, her face drawn and anguished. Something in the interval had touched her far more deeply than her husband's death. When next she left the room again, she did not return.

Darius did not come at all. Not once.

Esther learned nothing until the third day when she joined the procession that bore her husband's body out of the audience hall, out of the palace, out of the city. Dogs attended the magi who walked beside the bier. Dogs at a time of death were sacred to the Persians, symbolizing the two dogs who would await the king's spirit as it crossed the bridge from this world to the next.

At the head of the procession, still robed in mourning white but wearing a circlet on his head, walked Artaxerxes. Not Darius. Artaxerxes.

Damaspia, walking hand in hand with her mother, pulled on Esther's hand and gestured toward Artaxerxes.

"What does it mean?" Esther asked when the procession had begun to move, when the sounds of people walking and priests chanting could drown out a little talk. "What has been happening?"

"I don't know," Damaspia whispered back. "I have kept to the nursery in our quarters. Hathakh and Ayana told me not to go out, and Sofia kept watch to make sure I didn't. None of them would tell me anything!"

"Shh. We will all know soon enough."

Soon it was Irdabama who left her place in the procession and fell back to walk alongside Esther. "You have been very faithful in your mourning," the other queen said.

"It was something I felt I owed him."

"I am glad someone felt that. But do you truly know nothing of what has happened?"

"Nothing."

"Darius is under arrest. He will be tried after his father is buried. The eunuch who murdered the king, Spamitres, had been a servant of Darius' before. He is still not found, but the trail points to Darius. Artaxerxes has been declared king and will be crowned when the funeral and Darius' trial are done."

Amid a swirl of emotions, Esther saw one thing clearly: the sudden pallor of her daughter's face. She reached for Damaspia's hand again. With one tragic act, Artaxerxes was thrust from the quiet role of a king's younger son to the very center of power. What would it mean for his intended bride?

That night, when the burial rites had ended, Esther returned to her own quarters. She was accompanied, as always, by two eunuch guards from her own household, but she was surprised to see that the guards at her door were strangers.

"New guard detail, Your Majesty," one said. "Posted today by Lord Artapanos. For all the private apartments, not just yours."

Esther ushered Damaspia into the house ahead of her, and went at once in search of Hathakh. "What is happening?"

Hathakh turned toward her a face as bleak as she'd ever seen on him. She was reminded sharply of how much he preferred being back on the estate, running her affairs, and how glad she was he had come to Parsa with her despite that preference.

"All over the harem, all over the palace, my lady. Guards are being changed, even servants are being pulled out of one household and assigned to another. Everything is in turmoil. Artapanos is in control, and he trusts no one and wants everyone off balance."

"But hasn't Artaxerxes been named king?"

"Yes, my lady. Named king. Prince Artaxerxes is a boy of 19— still more boy than man, I think—whose father has been murdered, and whose brother has been accused of plotting the murder. He is entirely confused, and Artapanos is firmly in control."

"So . . . Artaxerxes may be, in his way, as much a prisoner as Darius?"

"It may be, my lady."

The next few days proved Hathakh's analysis true. Darius was hastily tried for the murder of his father, and it was Artaxerxes who sat on the throne in the audience chamber and read the sentence of death upon his older brother. But nobody doubted that Artapanos— who stood by his side, who had led the investigation into the king's death—was the real power, barely hidden behind the throne. Artaxerxes' voice shook as he ordered the guards to take Darius out and hang him before the Gate of All Lands, where Xerxes' massive winged bulls proclaimed a power and might far more fragile than the stone in which they were carved.

CHAPTER 20

S oon after Xerxes' burial the court returned to Susa. Life in the palace was a virtual siege, with every member of the royal household tightly controlled and closely watched. Esther asked permission to remove to her own estate; permission was denied. Amestris and Irdabama were also required to remain in the harem.

Artapanos held total control. Artaxerxes, king in name, was rarely seen. No ceremony of coronation was held for him. He rarely appeared in the public audience chamber and never in private audiences. Artapanos issued decrees in the king's name; he ran the council meetings and held audiences, even sitting on the royal throne in the audience hall. Rumor had it that Artaxerxes was confined in his rooms almost as a prisoner, paraded out on a few public occasions to satisfy the people that a member of the royal family was still in control.

The fall harvest was a little better than it had been in the past few years. Artapanos made a great show of celebrating the harvest and giving extra rations of grain to people in the areas hardest hit by famine. People who'd been protesting against Xerxes the year before now spoke of Artapanos as their savior, the favorite of the gods.

Life in the closed community of the harem was especially tense. Immediately after Darius' execution his favorite concubine, Zenobia, and her children were executed, as was his wife Artaynta and her son, the 3-year-old Cyrus born of her affair with Xerxes. The rest of Darius' own concubines—a dozen or so childless young women— were brought from his private estates to the palace. They were now Artaxerxes' property, as were all of Xerxes' concubines. Most of the harem's older women were moved from their quarters into smaller, less comfortable rooms to make space for the new arrivals and the other, younger women who were told they'd be needed for the new king's harem. Confusion, bitterness, and resentment reigned. Shaashgaz, who'd been promoted to chief eunuch of the harem upon Hegai's death several years before, managed the changes with as little tact and consideration as possible—or so Esther felt.

One day in the baths Esther met a young girl, no more than 15, weeping piteously as a slave poured scented water over her shoulders.

"What is the matter?" Esther asked as she and the girl, now

robed, sat alone on the steps of the baths a short time later.

The girl looked wretched. "I don't understand what is happening! I was brought here from Babylon three years ago, when I was just 12, and given to Prince Darius to be his concubine. I met him only once. Then he came here to the palace and never returned. A few weeks ago we were all told to come here, that we'd be in the harem of King Artaxerxes. I have never seen him, but they say he is young, and kind, and handsome. But today I received a summons, and I'm to be taken to the Lord Artapanos instead of going to the king!" The girl's tears flowed afresh. "I don't know whom I belong to."

Looking into her eyes, Esther remembered her own fears and confusion in the harem, so many years before. "What is your name?" she asked kindly.

"Cosmartidine, my lady."

"Cosmartidine, I am going to tell you something you may not believe, something you will not often hear in this place. I was brought here when I was your age, though I did not have to suffer the confusion and upheaval you've had these past months." Esther put an arm around her and led her into the gardens. She was not much older than Damaspia, and Esther felt so sorry for her that she wanted to put into words something she'd only vaguely begun to understand herself.

"When I came here, everyone told me that now I belonged to the king, and in a sense it was true. By law the king had the right to use my body and I owed him my loyalty. The same is true of you. Whatever man you are sent to tonight, he has rights over you by law. But you said you do not know to whom you belong. Cosmartidine, you belong to *yourself*. Above and beyond any man, you belong to yourself. There is a God in the heavens who created you, and to God you ultimately belong. But He has not given you as a toy or a prize to any man. He has given you your own life and your own dignity. He's put something inside you that cannot be crushed or taken away."

Esther knew that when she spoke of a god, Cosmartidine would think of Bel or Marduk, the gods of her Babylonian homeland. For now it was enough that the young woman turn her eyes away from her present darkness and recognize that she herself had a value greater than any concubine-price paid for her in any marketplace. It had taken Esther years, and great cost, and much help to learn that.

Perhaps it was too much to hope that this Babylonian girl could see through her grief to grasp that truth. But she looked up at Esther with her great teary eyes full of hope and light.

"Oh, my lady, you are so very kind! I will remember that, truly I will, when I go tonight. And say a prayer for me, will you?"

Esther did say a prayer for her that night, not to the gods of Babylon but to her own true God. She prayed for the bewildered Babylonian girl, Cosmartidine, for all the women in the harem whose lives were being turned upside down, even for Queen Amestris, who had lost the son most dear to her. She prayed for Artaxerxes with his hollow crown and for the people dearest to her: Damaspia, Ayana, Hathakh, her household, and Rivka, who she could only hope was safe on the estate. And finally, she prayed for herself in her own words, which she had become more and more comfortable framing to address the Maker of the heavens.

"O God of my fathers and mothers, what would You have me to do here? Surely any task I ever had to do in this place is finished. I fear for my very life and all the more for the life of my daughter. Yet if there is some way I can still serve You, show me the way, O God of Israel, and I will do it. I place myself in Your hands."

Esther neither heard nor felt any answer to her prayers throughout the long months of a drab, dull winter. Gossip and rumor abounded, but no one challenged Artapanos' rule. Esther often saw Raiya walking through the courtyard of the harem, gowned like a queen. Once they met and both women paused, neither willing to offer obeisance. Esther was the wife of a dead king; Raiya, the wife of a commoner who held power as if he were a king. Finally Raiya bowed, very slightly and stiffly, and passed on with a smile on her face.

"You know how this will end," Esther said one day to Ayana, as they sat sewing in Esther's chamber.

"Of course," Ayana said, lowering her voice. "It will end as it must, with King Artaxerxes' death and with the deaths of however many more of the royal family it will take before Artapanos is secure enough to take the throne in his own name."

"I fear for Damaspia," Esther said. "A daughter poses little threat, but she is betrothed to Artaxerxes, and that might be enough reason to get rid of her. Artapanos has no intent ever to allow Artaxerxes to rule in his own right."

"No, and no matter how closely guarded, he is too dangerous to keep alive, especially now that he has the name of king. But who is powerful enough to help him? Even Megabyzus is allied with Artapanos now."

Megabyzus was the husband of Princess Amytis. He was brother-in-law to both Darius and Artaxerxes, but his relationship with his wife's family had ever been stormy. No doubt it had seemed best to him to cast his lot with the man who held power.

Esther looked at the back side of her needlework, at the tangled threads that knotted and wove in no discernible pattern, until the linen was turned over and seen right side up. "How far back do these webs of intrigue go, I wonder?" she said. "How long has Artapanos been plotting this?"

Ayana sighed. "We may never know. I am sure Artaynta's affair with King Xerxes was all part of a plot, though one that got out of hand for the plotters. I think Amestris' women pushed her into the king's arms because they knew it would drive a wedge between Darius and Xerxes. Amestris wanted to see Darius on the throne as soon as he reached manhood, and I think she thought Artaynta was a very small thing to sacrifice if it would give Darius an excuse to rebel against his father."

Esther nodded. "But Artapanos must have decided to use that to his own advantage—to keep Xerxes strong for a while, and Darius weak, so that when Xerxes finally was murdered, everyone would believe Darius had done it. Then Artapanos could step in and have Darius executed, and put Artaxerxes on the throne—young, frightened, unprepared. Another weak king for Artapanos to manipulate, but a young king with no heir. A perfect situation." The scope of Artapanos' cunning and evil—if that was really how it had happened—was staggering.

Winter ended, and the order came to prepare to travel—first to Parsa for the new year's celebrations then to Ectabana where the court would spend much of the summer. Esther found it hard to imagine this new year's tribute, a sharp contrast to last year's. Though Xerxes had been inwardly crumbling a year ago, he had looked the part of a king with power still firmly in his hands. Who would sit on the throne this spring and receive the tribute from the satraps? Would it be Artaxerxes? Or Artapanos?

Artapanos had begun adding titles to his name—not "King of Kings" yet, of course, but he was being called "Mighty One" by his palace supporters. Esther heard no news from outside the palace, for she was sealed off as effectively as if she'd been buried beside Xerxes in his tomb. She wondered how well the rest of the city and the empire were taking to Artapanos' leadership. Were they all ready, so quickly, to put aside Artaxerxes and his legitimate claim to the throne, in favor of the pretender?

But she was never to know how Artapanos might have ruled that new year's, for events took an unexpected turn. As the horses and wagons, carriages, and columns of foot-travelers prepared to leave Susa, a commotion broke out. Esther, waiting in her carriage with Damaspia and their women, heard shouts and running feet and gestured to Talia to see what was happening. Talia leaped down from the carriage, returning a few moments later red-faced and out of breath. "People are running toward the head of the procession," she cried. "King Artaxerxes has drawn his sword on Lord Artapanos!"

From where they were the women could see nothing, not even after they climbed down from the carriage and stood out on the road. But in the distance they could hear men's voices, the whinnying of horses, and the clash of swords. By now everyone in the procession had dismounted or gotten down from the carriages and wagons and stood on the road, craning to see, straining to hear. Every few minutes several small slave boys came running back from the scene of battle to where the women and servants stood, bringing news. All the armed men had raced to join the conflict already, but nobody knew who'd fight for Artaxerxes and who would fight for Artapanos.

"What could have happened?" Esther wondered aloud. "Did Artaxerxes simply take the opportunity of travel to break loose from his guards and challenge Artapanos?"

The words of a nearby concubine tumbled excitedly from her mouth. "I heard that Lord Artapanos had plotted to kill the king while he traveled, but someone warned him and he found men who would fight for him so that he could confront Lord Artapanos."

"Who?" someone asked. "Who was able to warn the king?"

Several people said they didn't know, but one eunuch said, "I believe it was Lord Megabyzus. He's been unhappy in his alliance with Lord Artapanos of late. Perhaps he decided the time was ripe to change sides."

Far away from the front of the column came a huge shout that could be interpreted only as a cheer. Esther and the others looked at each other, wondering. The outcome would decide their fate. Some of the women were crying. Others chewed a fingernail or paced up and down the road. To Esther it seemed that time stood still. She waited hand in hand with her daughter, her heart in her throat, for one of the slave boys to come back with news.

Then suddenly she heard the pound of hoofbeats and an armed man on horseback thundered down the road, waving his sword in the air.

"Long live King Artaxerxes!" he shouted. "The usurper is overthrown! Long live King Artaxerxes!"

A cheer rose up around Esther, and it burst from her own lips also. Beside her, Damaspia's face was flushed red, her eyes bright, clapping and cheering, shouting the name of her betrothed. She had picked a handful of dusty flowers by the roadside and now threw them in the air.

"Artaxerxes! Artaxerxes!" The name resounded throughout the ranks of his men, his women, his eunuchs, and his slaves.

A quarter of an hour later the cheers swelled as Artaxerxes himself rode down the long column of travelers. He sat tall and proud atop his stallion. The look of fear and cowering that he'd worn since his father's death was gone from his eyes. He rode slowly, and his people fell to their knees as he passed. Esther saw him stop near his mother's carriage and hold out a hand to Queen Amestris, raising her to her feet, briefly saluting her. What turmoil must she feel, to see this son she had never valued now taking hold of his father's throne?

Then Artaxerxes drew nearer, past the ranks of the concubines and the eunuchs, close to where Esther and her household knelt in the dust before him. Again he reined in his horse, again he held out his hand—this time to both Esther and to Damaspia—bidding them rise. Damaspia stood for an instant, then stepped toward him, clutching one last flower in her hand. She pressed it into her betrothed's hand, and he raised it to his lips as he rode on. All around, the crowd cheered and called his name.

And so Artaxerxes, son of Xerxes, became king of Persia, after seven months of ruling in name only. The court continued their trip to Parsa, and at new year's all the satraps and their representatives, along with the council members and the military officers, swore allegiance to Artaxerxes. He was crowned at Pasargadae. The women, as well as the men of the court, watched in the temple of Anahita as Artaxerxes entered, clad in the simple white robe that Cyrus the Great himself was said to have worn. The Robe of Honor was placed around his shoulders, and the crown was on his head when Damaspia reached for Esther's hand. Damaspia had had little to say since their arrival at Parsa, except that she was glad Artaxerxes was finally free and ruling them, as was right and good. But when Damaspia squeezed her hand, Esther knew that it was not until this moment that her daughter grasped that Artaxerxes was truly a king, and that she herself would someday be his queen.

One satrap was conspicuously absent from the new year's festivities and the coronation, one who did not send an envoy to represent him. Artaxerxes' older half brother Hystaspes, satrap of Bactria, did not come or send tribute. During the months of Artapanos' rule Hystaspes had kept quiet, though many wondered if he would rise up to take the throne from the usurper. Apparently he had been biding his time. Now, his absence from the ceremonies sent a message no one could miss. Succession to the throne was not bound by any clear law. With the death of Darius, the named heir, one could argue that Artaxerxes, the next son of Xerxes' chief wife, should succeed. But another could as easily argue that the second son Hystaspes, also legitimately born of a royal wife, might inherit the throne. Artaxerxes was triumphant today, but his throne was still shaky, as everyone at court well knew.

One of the best props for a shaky throne was punishment, and Artaxerxes had plenty of opportunity to mete that out in his first weeks of true kingship. Artapanos was dead by the king's own hand. His coconspirator, Spamitres, was found and hanged, as were Artapanos' sons and several others believed to have been involved in the king's murder.

Esther still hated the almost casualness with which the court treated human life, though she knew that in truth the executions were necessary to secure the throne. That was the way it was done. Anything else would be perceived as weakness, and the new king would be even more vulnerable to challenge. And yes, it was of utmost importance that Artaxerxes remain on the throne. She believed in him, in his inherent sense of fairness and his gentle soul. But also, and desperately important to her, the life of her daughter was also at stake. She wondered what the king would do with the women belonging to Artapanos. Then Ayana had some news.

"Have you heard what the king has decreed regarding the wives and daughters of Artapanos?" she asked Esther one evening.

"No, but I hope he does not have them put to death. It does him no honor to take vengeance on women and children."

"Apparently he agrees with you, for their lives are to be spared. Artapanos' first wife is going to be given to old Lord Meres. It's a way of keeping her in prison, of course, but it may be a kindly prison, for Meres is not a bad old fellow and will doubtless treat her well. As for the children and the concubines—and the Lady Raiya—they will be sold as slaves."

Esther shook her head with a sigh. It was a harsh fate for the women and girls, but not unexpected. She remembered again the advice she'd heard many years ago from Artabazus about rooting out the family of your foe. Did that apply to women and young girls, too? In a case as serious as the murder of a king, it generally did. Artapanos' womenfolk might well reflect that they were getting off lightly.

But lying in bed that night, Esther thought of Raiya. A woman of middle years now, childless, discarded. Certainly Queen Amestris would want nothing more to do with her. Esther remembered the proud tilt of Raiya's head, the flash of her odd green eyes. How fiercely, in girlhood, she had fought to distance herself from the slave market. She had begun her life on the auction block, and now she would end up there again, where any fate at all might await her.

Esther tossed fitfully. She couldn't sleep, for her mind wrestled with a thought that would not give her peace. In among her other mischiefs and meddling, over the years Raiya had done all she could to hurt Esther. Here, if anywhere, Artabazus' advice would surely apply. It was good that the harem *and* the palace would be rid of Raiya once and for all.

In spite of that, Esther quietly called Hathakh to her the next morning. "Find out what price is being asked for the Lady Raiya in the slave markets," she said. "Work through an agent, but arrange to pay the price, and issue papers granting her her freedom. I do not want her to know who has bought her, only that she is being bought to be set free."

Hathakh frowned, as Esther knew he would. "Is that wise, my

lady?" he said, in a voice that held so little question he might as well have said, *That is not wise.*

"No, it is not," she agreed. "But it is what I must do."

"If you feel so, then do not do it under cover. Let her know who grants her freedom, so that she will owe a debt of gratitude to you. Surely even she has enough honor to recognize that."

"No," Esther said. "Absolutely not." She could imagine how Raiya would feel if she knew Esther had purchased her liberty. "I would not do that to her. It would embarrass and shame her. Besides, the king would hear of it and disapprove. It must be done quietly, working through third parties. It might be best to let the traders buy her with the rest, then find an agent in the market in whatever city she is sold in. Place as much distance between us as possible."

Hathakh stood in silence, his arms crossed. Esther shrugged, and her voice faltered. "I cannot explain why I have to do this," she said. "I only know it is right."

Hathakh bowed. "It will be done, my lady."

It was done. Some weeks later Esther received word that Raiya had been taken to a slave market in Ecbatana and there bought by Esther's agent and given her freedom. What happened to her after that, Esther did not know and did not wish to know. But when Hathakh brought her the news, Esther went to her room alone.

"I have paid a debt, my God," she said. "I have sinned against her and against You by cherishing that old hatred and bitterness so long—and to say that she cherished it longer is no excuse. I cannot save her, but I have set her free to find her own fate. She is in Your hands, O God." And Esther's own hands—so long clutching that grudge, that unwillingness to forgive—lay open on the bed before her. If she lived long enough, would she find the grace to forgive and set free every old enemy? Only God knew.

For now, Esther had other business. She asked for an audience with Artaxerxes a month after his coronation, and was received in his private council chamber.

It was her first close glimpse of him since his father's funeral, and she saw at once how greatly he had changed from the boy who'd once teased that he would rather have been born into a family of musicians. He was as handsome and fine-featured as ever, but there was new steel in his eyes. He wore the clothes of his position well.

He sat straight and tall, his long, graceful hands clasped before him on the table. The turmoil of the past months had made him wary and cautious. The king, especially a king who waded through a river of blood to his throne, could never again be as open as the prince had been.

Yet his face lightened with a smile when she entered and did obeisance before him. "Rise, my lady, Queen Esther," he said with a lilt in his voice. "It brings me joy to see you here. What petition can I grant you? Anything, even to half my kingdom, shall be yours."

Now it was Esther's turn to smile at the traditional and meaningless words she'd so often heard his father speak. "I do not want half of your kingdom or any part of it, except one little piece, my lord king," she said. "You know I hold land and a house near Susa. I have not been on my own property in more than a year, and my kinsfolk and servants are still dwelling there. I have had no word of what has befallen them, or my estate. I humbly beg your leave to go home, that I may see to my affairs."

Artaxerxes frowned. "I have had many such requests," he said. "It is only natural, after months when everyone has been kept to the palace, unable to move or communicate. Yet what will happen if I let everyone go at once? I do not even know yet who is loyal to me, and who may be going home to foment rebellion. Not that I suspect you of rebellion," he added quickly. "But I must take care."

"I understand that, my lord," Esther said. If it was only her fruit trees and stables, she could have waited till summer's end. But she thought of Rivka, alone there and frightened. She'd been there an entire year, trying to provide leadership to a household without a mistress. Was she even still alive? Had Artapanos left the property untouched and Esther's people unharmed? She could send a courier for news, but she would never rest until she saw Rivka and her people in the flesh. "My old foster mother is there, my kinswoman," she told Artaxerxes, "and I fear for her safety and her health. I would see her again, as soon as your gracious pleasure may allow."

Artaxerxes leaned forward, suddenly decisive. "I will let you go," he said. "But there is one condition."

"Name it, my lord, and I will do your bidding."

"You must allow the Princess Damaspia to remain here."

Silence. Esther looked into Artaxerxes' clear brown eyes, and read there that he knew exactly how great a thing he was asking, but that he would not back down. It would be easier by far for her to give in and postpone her journey home. Except for Rivka.

Rivka there; Damaspia here.

She felt torn in two.

"I am sorry," the young king said firmly, "but I must have it known in the court and the empire that I have your allegiance and that the princess is still my betrothed." His voice softened. "At a time when it mattered little, I promised my father that the princess Damaspia would be my first wife, my chief wife. Now it matters much. The sooner I have a wife and an heir, the better, and I would marry her tomorrow if I could, but she is a child of 12. I cannot get an heir on her now, and it would be monstrous for me to take her as my wife so young. I *will* marry her, as soon as it is proper—but in the meantime, go where you will. She must remain at my court. I cannot compromise on this, my lady," he added, his last words almost an apology, sounding like the Artaxerxes she remembered.

"I understand, my lord."

"If you choose to go, the princess can be given her own household, or she might be placed in the household of another of the royal women until your return," the king said.

A wave of weakness passed through Esther at his words, fearing that he was about to propose that Damaspia be taken to his mother's household. That was the expected thing for a child bride—and how could she say plainly to Artaxerxes that she would not trust her daughter in his mother's hands? But he was quicker. Leaning slightly forward, he said, "Queen Irdabama has agreed to remain here for the summer, though she itches to be overseeing her overseers again. Perhaps the princess could go into her household while you are away?"

"Perhaps." Esther nodded slowly, thinking. "I will need time to decide. I will have to speak to my daughter."

"Come to me again at this hour three days hence and tell me your decision. If you go, you may take an armed escort, carriage, and horses with you."

In the end Esther decided to go. Damaspia urged her to. "I'll be all right here. Queen Irdabama will look after me, and I know the king won't let any harm come to me. And besides, God is watching, isn't He?"

Esther laid a hand on her daughter's cheek. "Yes, of course, precious child. God will take care of you. I wish I had trusted Him as much when I was your age."

Taking with her Ayana and Hathakh and a handful of her other most trusted servants, she traveled home as rapidly as she could. A courier had been sent on ahead to announce her arrival. When she reached Susa and rode beyond the city to her own lands, a knot filled her throat. So much had happened since she'd left here. Her estate, already weakened by famine the last time she'd been there, might have crumbled entirely without her or Hathakh to oversee it. Even as her head pounded with anxiety, her heart longed to arrived.

At last, coming through the gates, she saw that the house and the grounds had the proud air of a place well cared for. Her eunuch Atobar opened the doors for her, Ayana, and Hathakh, and ushered them into the great hall. Grooms and menservants came scurrying to care for their horses and carriage.

"We rejoice to see you again, my lady queen!" said Atobar, bending the knee to her. Eben and her ladyship will be here to welcome you in a moment."

Eben was the understeward Hathakh had left in charge a year ago, expecting his duties to last only a few short months. Now Eben entered the hall looking hale and confident, bowing before Esther and taking her hands in his.

Behind him came "her ladyship," Rivka. Esther could almost have laughed aloud when she saw her foster mother. Instead she hurried toward her and folded Rivka in an embrace. She had feared to find her aged and feeble, perhaps even dead. Instead, she saw a well-dressed, strong-looking woman who reminded Esther far less of the grieving, frightened widow she'd left behind than of the vigorous, strong-willed woman who had raised her. The hesitancy and timidity that had dogged Rivka ever since Mordecai's rise to power and had grown even worse since his death had fallen away like a cast-off cloak. It was obvious that in the year of Esther's absence she had risen to the challenge of managing the estate through troubled times, and clearly it had done her good.

Rivka was full of talk. She wanted to know all about Damaspia and how she was, of course. She clucked her tongue in disapproval at the news that Damaspia had been left behind, but nodded knowingly when Esther explained why it had had to be so. She wanted a full description of the coronation, but first she wanted Eben to drag out the household accounts so that Esther and Hathakh could see exactly how the estate was faring. "The cattle suffered badly last summer and autumn," she said, anxious to get the bad news out of the way, "but the crops yielded well last year, and we planted two new fields this spring."

"Perhaps the accounts could wait till this evening," Esther suggested. "After we dine?"

"If you wish. The cooks have been preparing your welcome feast for days now. They are roasting goose—did you know I was keeping geese now? But of course, you know so little of what has gone on. We lived in such fear all those months that that terrible man was in power."

However terrible the fear had been, nothing of it showed in her face or voice as she directed Eben to ready the accounts for a viewing later, and send to the kitchens to tell them the exact hour at which dinner must be ready. "Ezra and the others have been such a support, of course."

"Ezra and the others?" Esther assumed Rivka must mean that her Jewish friends in the city had been helpful, but Rivka meant more than that.

"Yes. Oh, you must come see. You see, without you here, we had no use for the banqueting hall, so Ezra asked, and it made good sense, as we have so much space here—come, I'll show you."

Rivka's unexpected return to her younger self had the curious effect of making Esther feel like a child again. She walked through her own house in her aunt's wake, expecting at any moment to be scolded for having untidy hair or stains on her gown. Then suddenly she stopped short at the archway opening into her banqueting hall. The walls were brilliant with the glorious painted reliefs she'd had done by one of the king's own artisans. That much was the same, but only that. All around the great banqueting table were piles of clay tablets, scrolls, blank parchment, writing instruments, ink, and four or five young Jewish men. Some were sitting, some reading, some writing or copying.

"Gentlemen, our queen has returned," Rivka announced, and the men looked up from their work and dropped to their knees in Esther's honor.

"Rise," said Esther, almost absently, as she began walking through the room. The half-buried scholar inside her quickened with excitement as she realized what was being done in this beautiful room.

Rivka kept pace with her, her bright eyes fastened on Esther's face. "You see, so many scribes and scholars were working in so many different cities, copying bits of this and that, having to travel across the city or even to other places to share copies with each other and discuss which version was the best," explained Rivka—who could not read, Esther remembered—"that Ezra thought it would be best if they had a central place. It would be good if there was a place they could all come, a place where the tablets and scrolls could be kept and studied and copied. A sort of library, or a school."

"A library . . . a school. Here, in my house?" Esther said in wonder. She stopped at a table where a scroll lay open to the laws of Moses. God's law, the Torah, here on her banqueting table. She bent over the scroll, studying the words without speaking.

At last Rivka spoke, with the first trace of hesitance or deference Esther had heard since her arrival.

"I told them, of course, that when you returned you might wish something different done. It was only, in the interval—"

Esther whirled to face her aunt. "Dear, dear Aunt Rivka, I couldn't be happier! This is a treasure trove—better than the jewels and gold the Babylonians carried off from the Temple. This is the true treasure of Israel—right here—and I could think of no higher honor for my dining hall. Tell Ezra that as long as I am alive his scribes may come here and bring others." She felt exultant, suddenly fully alive for the first time since Xerxes' death or perhaps even since Mordecai's. She was alight with a sense of purpose, an understanding of what she was meant to do, why she had come to this position and this power. Her usefulness was not, after all, at an end.

Over dinner Rivka brought her up to date about the fever among the cattle, the new cows she'd bought to replace those that died, the crops that had failed and the crops that had flourished, which servants had left and who had been hired in their place, until Esther clapped her hands over her ears. "Aunt Rivka, you have convinced me I could find no better manager than you. And I hope you don't intend to give up your role. I will have to be at court much, at least until Damaspia is married, for Artaxerxes intends to keep her close, and I don't wish to be parted from her for long. I want you to keep running everything, exactly as you have been doing. I know

Hathakh is longing to return to his role as steward, though Eben seems to have been filling it admirably. I hope there is no power struggle between them."

"Oh, there shouldn't be. There's more than work enough for two stewards here, though one would have to be superior in name at least, and that ought to be Hathakh, for he's senior, as I'm sure Eben would understand. But the management of the farm is enough for one man, and then there's the household itself to see to. I am sure they could divide the labors fairly."

"Then we shall tell them to do so," Esther said, raising her cup to her aunt. "It is wonderful, Aunt Rivka, to see you so—" She paused, not wanting to say anything that would imply she had ever seen Rivka as feeble or frail. "So happy," she concluded. "You are happy, aren't you?"

Rivka looked down at her plate. "I grieved for Mordecai till I thought my bones would wither. And then when you were gone and the king was murdered, I worried over you and Damaspia until I couldn't sleep and could hardly eat. But I knew the only thing left that I could do was to keep this place alive for you until you returned. I think God gave me that task to do, to keep me alive, to keep me from being eaten up with grief and worry. And yes, in spite of it all—I am happy." She raised her cup too, and the two women smiled at each other.

The months that followed were peaceful and untroubled ones for Esther, though not for the kingdom as a whole. Hystaspes rose in revolt against Artaxerxes, and after two clashes between their armies, Hystaspes was killed. Rumors began to spread that Tithraustes, Xerxes' son by one of his concubines, was also planning to challenge Artaxerxes for the throne. Tithraustes was several years older than Artaxerxes and an experienced military commander. Though he gathered no army and gave no sign of planning revolt, he was assassinated by Artaxerxes' soldiers only a few months after Hystaspes was defeated.

From the safety of her apartments in the palace or the comfort of her own estate, Esther followed all these developments with interest. She thought most of their effect on Damaspia, now 13 and keenly interested in the fate of the king who would be her husband. For several days after the news came of Tithraustes' death, the girl was quiet and withdrawn. At first Esther thought Damaspia was just experiencing the ebb and flow of moods that girls her age were prone to, but finally she made the effort to seek out her daughter and talk with her.

"I just don't see how he could do such a thing!" Damaspia burst out as Esther gently probed to discover what was troubling her.

"Who? Artaxerxes?"

"Yes, of course, him! I mean, I understand that he was pressured into having Darius executed, and he had to fight Hystaspes, of course: but in a little more than a year he's killed three of his brothers, and one of them hadn't done anything wrong. What will he do next, start killing off the little boys in the harem, his little half brothers, just in case they might grow up to be a threat to him?"

Her voice choked; she was crying. "Mama, I thought he was a good man!" she wailed, launching herself into Esther's arms.

Esther held her daughter, stroked her thick, dark hair, and wished there were words that would make this easier. But she must tell the truth. "Damaspia, I think you are right, and I pray that you are. I believe that Artaxerxes is a good man, and that he will be a good husband to you. But he is a king, and you will never be able to forget that, or pretend you are living with an ordinary man. Kings do things—things they feel they must do—to win battles or to hold on to power. Some of those things are wrong, but a king does not look at right and wrong as ordinary men do."

"Does that mean I can never find fault with anything he does? Were you that way with my father?" the girl demanded.

"I thought many of the things your father did were wrong," Esther said honestly. "But it was not my place to criticize him. I hope Artaxerxes will make many choices better than those his father made, but you will have to stand by his side no matter what he chooses. Just remember that though he is your husband, your king, and your lord, he is not you. You stand alone before your God, who is not his god. You are responsible for your own right and wrong."

She recalled the words she'd spoken to the young Babylonian concubine—who was already sleeping with Damaspia's future husband: *You belong to yourself.* How much more important it was to make her daughter understand that—to see that though her life would be tied to that of her husband and king, she need not be like a man lashed to the deck of a sinking ship. If Mordecai had not been able to help Esther see that, she might have plunged with Xerxes into the despair that plagued him during his final years. She prayed Damaspia would never have to know such darkness with Artaxerxes, but she could not lie to her and tell her that being a queen was an easy role to play.

It was in the winter of the following year, with his throne at last somewhat stable, that Artaxerxes asked for a private audience with Esther. She saw him often when she was at court, at official functions and smaller gatherings, and he sometimes asked her advice on matters relating to music and poetry, things of which she had some knowledge. Once he had even asked about handling a dispute between a Jewish citizen and his neighbor. She had referred him to Ezra, who was an expert in Jewish law. But she had never been called for a private audience with the king, and she knew this must have to do with Damaspia.

"My lady queen," he said, gesturing for her to rise from the floor and sit on a couch across from his. They were in a private chamber adjoining his bedchamber, with only two eunuch servants in attendance. "I am sure you have guessed I wish to speak with you about my marriage to the princess Damaspia."

"She is not yet 14, my lord," Esther said.

Artaxerxes sighed. "I know it, and for her sake I would wait, even till she is 15. That would be more fitting. But I cannot wait, my lady. You must see this. All my councillors are pressing me to marry and provide a legitimate heir, yet I want to honor my father's wishes—and honor Damaspia herself—by taking her as my first wife. How much longer can I wait? Already two of my concubines have borne me sons. Believe me, it will not be wise for my crown prince to have half brothers much older than himself. I do not wish that on him."

His voice was tight, his fist clenched at his side. Esther saw again, even more clearly, how heavy kingship weighed on this essentially gentle man. His beard was full now, and he had a man's profile, a man's depth to his voice, a man's breadth to his chest. He had, too, a man's burdens on his shoulders. "I understand your need, my lord," she said. "Can you wait till summer? Till she is 14?"

"We could be married at Parsa," Artaxerxes said. "I would like that." He seemed to be thinking, then smiled. Esther thought it was the first genuine smile she'd seen on his face since he'd been crowned. "Yes, let us plan for this summer, about the time of her birthday." He paused, then said hesitantly, "She is not—unwilling, is she?"

The mask of kingship had slipped a little. The boy was still there behind it, a little anxious. Harem gossip did not yet speak of any great love affairs between the young king and any of his women. He had no favorite, and Esther guessed that he held high hopes for his marriage to her daughter. "No, my lord, she is not unwilling," she said, and saw the relief in his eyes. "She holds you in high esteem, as she always has, and it is more my caution than her own that holds her back from being married so young."

Then, perhaps because of that one glimpse of the boy she had known, or perhaps because she was now an older woman without the allure of a young one, but able to wield a different kind of power, she said words she would never have dared say to his father.

"My lord, if I may be so bold, there is something that troubles my daughter's heart." Esther leaned forward a little, and Artaxerxes gestured to his servants. They withdrew behind the curtained arches. If they listened, they would still hear the conversation, but there was, at least, the illusion of privacy.

"The princess Damaspia was much disturbed by the death of Lord Tithraustes. Not, of course, because she knew him personally or had any great care for his fate, but because she cares greatly for you, my lord, and wishes to believe you are a good man, one who would not shed blood needlessly. She was not raised to think she would marry a king, and has a great fear of finding herself wedded to a tyrant."

Those were daring words, and they seemed to hang in the still air between Esther and the king. She held her breath. Artaxerxes did not speak. She felt her heartbeat in her temples and her wrists. She did not look at the king, fearing to see anger on his face. But when she looked up at last, she saw something quite different. The king's mask was gone entirely; no one was there but the boy she had taught the oud to, the boy who had not cared enough about being king. He was not yet 21, she remembered. He looked away from her, in profile, and his eyes, like Damaspia's when she had spoken of him, filled with tears.

"*I* was not raised to think I would be king," he said at last, in the voice of a man drowning, "and I have a great fear of finding that I have become a tyrant."

The king's person was sacred and not to be approached lightly, but Esther could not restrain herself from putting her hand on the table, palm up. Artaxerxes grasped it like that same drowning man grasping a rope, and she remembered vividly how little his own mother had cared for him, how she'd lavished all her love and efforts on Darius. Esther was not old enough to truly be a mother to him, but she held the long, elegant hand studded with the rings of power, and prayed that God would give her the words to help this boy, this man.

"They all told me it had to be done," he said in an anguished sob. "I wanted to resist. After those awful months with Artapanos, I wanted to prove I was no one's man but my own—but on this I knew they were right." He coughed. "Or I thought they were right. How can one man ever know when it's right to kill another? How can you make such a judgment? And yet—if I'd not had Tithraustes executed, what next? Would I be the one to wake up one night and find a dagger stabbing toward me? My father—you know, he must have woken up, he must have seen—and that is what I live with too. It might not be my brother. It might be anyone. Megabyzus, my sister's husband, he turned sides, and betrayed Artapanos to me. But he's changeable. He could turn again. Growing up, Darius was my hero, and Hystaspes was always good to me. *And I had them both killed. I had to!* I'd rather be any fool in the kingdom than be king!"

And yet, that could not be true. If it were true, why had he not just laid down his arms before Hystaspes and given his brother the throne? Esther did not say that. She knew too well the tangled play of motives that made up a king. She remembered vividly a night when Xerxes had come to her chamber, weeping because he had killed his brother. Did any man escape his father's fate?

But Artaxerxes sat here in his elegant, well-appointed room, telling her this, seeing himself and his deeds clearly in the light of a clear mind, not through a prism of drink and despair. He was still young, and open, and seeking a right path. Esther did not have any answers for him, nor could she offer him forgiveness for his brothers' deaths. But she had to say something.

"Life has not given you an easy role to play, Artaxerxes," she said, not even noticing that she had dropped formality and called him by name. "If I were speaking truly from my heart—and I am trying to—I would have to say that God has not given you an easy role. You know a little about the God of my people?"

"Not much," Artaxerxes said.

"I have come to believe that He is the God of all people, though especially of the Jews," Esther said, "and I believe He has a part for all of us to play. You worship different gods, yet I believe my God—who is also Damaspia's God—has His hand on you. I don't tell you that because I think it will make your life any easier, for believing that God had a purpose for me made my life a good deal harder at one time. It may be no comfort at all. Even the kings of my people who worshiped our God have had to make the same kind of hard choices you have to make—and often, they chose wrong, even the best of them."

Artaxerxes furtively wiped his eyes with the back of his hand, but left his other hand resting in Esther's. "Then what good is your God, any more than Ahura Mazda or any of the rest?"

"A good question," Esther said. "I cannot say for sure, except that He seems closer to His people than any of the other gods I've heard of. He walks with us through the dark valleys, though He does not take us out of them."

She paused, gathering her thoughts. "You have it in you to be a better king than your father was, Artaxerxes," she added, almost in a whisper. He looked surprised, but nodded.

"I did love my father," he said after a moment, "but by the time I was old enough to know him, he seemed—as if his heart was gone."

"He let that happen to himself, Artaxerxes," Esther said. "I was there, and I know. A king's role is difficult, but it does not have to destroy a man. That power is in your own hands. You can do better. I pray to my God for you every day. And Damaspia does too."

"Thank you," he murmured, withdrawing his hand from hers at last. "I value your prayers, and a good deal more than, say, my mother's." He made a wry face. "Her latest excess—other than hatching plots, which she seems to do in her sleep these days—is finding new gods to worship. Rather unsavory ones, I'm afraid. What the magi would call daivas. She is fascinated by darkness, even by human sacrifice. She needs close watching, or I don't know what she might do."

"That's a sorrow," Esther said. "She should be lightening your burden, not adding to it." After daring to speak so bluntly to the king, criticizing Amestris seemed almost an afterthought.

"Lightening burdens has never been her speciality, I'm afraid."

Artaxerxes stood. There was no trace of tears in his eyes. The king was back in place, hiding the frightened young man. But his eyes were warm as they held Esther's. "You may return to Princess Damaspia and tell her she is to be married at midsummer. And tell her—tell her that I truly am trying to be a good man, and that she must keep praying to her God for me."

"I will tell her all that, my lord."

▼ ▼ ▼

Damaspia became Artaxerxes' wife and queen at Parsa that summer, just after her fourteenth birthday. The wedding feast went on for 30 days. It was the first royal wedding since the ill-fated marriage of Darius and Artaynta seven years earlier, and Esther prayed fervently that this would be a happier union.

When the wedding celebration was finally over, the court moved to Ecbatana. There Esther asked for another audience with Artaxerxes. "I have a favor to ask," she told him frankly.

"For the mother of my queen? Anything," Artaxerxes declared. He was looking very happy these days.

"I beg your leave to retire from court and live permanently at my estate near Susa," she said. "I wish to end my public life, and live as a private person."

"Are you sure, my lady? As the mother of the queen you will always have an honored place in the harem and a seat of honor at our feasts and banquets."

"Thank you, my lord king, but I am decided on this. It was not by my own choice that I came to the palace nearly 20 years ago. My God had plans for me that I could not see then, and I rejoice that He brought me here. But now I believe He leads me in another direction. Will you allow me to leave court?"

"If that is your desire, Queen Esther, I grant it," Artaxerxes promised.

Esther took Ayana and Hathakh with her back to the palace at Susa to go through the belongings in her apartments there and see which should be moved to her house and which could be given away. She did not want to be burdened by too many possessions, too many memories. Without the help of slaves the three of them worked together quietly, sorting, packing, carrying, remembering.

In the heat of the afternoon when they stopped to rest, Esther went walking down through the courtyard to where the concubines gathered listless under shade trees in the blistering midday sun. She found Leila and Tamyris sitting together, picking halfheartedly at needlework. They were among the women left behind here at Susa, too old to be wanted for the new king's harem.

"Queen Esther!" Leila said. "We heard you had returned from court. What brings you to Susa at this ridiculous time of year?"

"I am going home," Esther told them, sitting down on a nearby bench. "I'm going to live permanently on my estates. I will not be keeping my apartments here in the palace. I think that my daughter will use them when the court is in residence here at Susa.."

Leila and Tamyris exchanged glances. Their faces looked drawn and weary in the heat, and sad, too. "This will be goodbye, then," Tamyris said. "You won't be coming back here."

"No, probably not, unless once in a while to visit Damaspia. But I have had enough of this place." Even as she spoke, Esther wished the words unsaid. Who among the women, especially the older ones, had *not* had enough of this place? But leaving was not a choice for most of them.

"Come home with me," she said impulsively. "I'll ask the king for permission. You can come live on my estates—or at least visit me there for a while. Phratima, too, if she wishes. We need not say goodbye."

Again, a glance between the other two women. "You're very kind to suggest it," Leila said after a long pause. "I can't speak for Tamyris or Phratima, of course. Sometimes I feel like a caged bird here—" She glanced around at the buildings that ringed the harem court, the boundaries of their world ever since they'd all been young girls. "But I can't imagine leaving, living someplace else."

"Neither can I," Tamyris said with a sigh. "Even if the king were to permit it, my life is here, all my friends—everything familiar . . ." Her voice trailed off. "What would there be for us to do on your estate, Esther, any more than there is here? We'd be useless there, and I know I'd feel strange, being out of the harem. I could never get used to it."

"Nor I," Leila said.

Esther bade them goodbye a little later, holding them both in a long embrace. She felt sorry for these friends, as she so often had. They had their own small pleasures and sorrows, but their lives had grown so narrow with the years she felt there was little room there for her anymore. It wasn't their fault, not really—or not entirely.

She returned to her own apartments, where Hathakh and Ayana had resumed work. There was little else to do. A few trinkets and some clothes were gathered up to be given as goodbye gifts to Esther's friends in the harem. By dusk the carriage was packed, ready to take Esther back to her home.

Esther, Ayana, and Hathakh sat together in the harem courtyard just outside the entrance to her apartments. There were too many shared memories to need words. All three of them had come to this place within a few months of each other, at the same time in their lives, and their lives had been bound together and shaped by all that had happened here.

"Again," Esther said, "if either of you wishes to remain at court, you know—"

Ayana put up her hand—that old commanding gesture Esther knew so well. "Do not speak of it, my lady. We go with you, as long as you will have us."

"And when you will not, we will sit in the dust outside your door and beg for scraps from your kitchen," Hathakh said. He smiled at her. His flashes of humor were rare but all the more treasured—glimpses of the warmth that lay beneath his serious and composed manner.

"There will be no begging, and no scraps, either," Esther said. "Before we go home, I have something to say to both of you. I could have asked my God for no better lady in waiting to serve me, for no better steward to manage my affairs. You know that. But as of today, I am dismissing you both. Talia will be my lady in waiting, and Eben my chief steward." She looked at their shocked faces, and smiled. "I do not want your service, my friends. We have been through so much together, and now I am free to do as I please. I am tired of knowing that my dearest friends are mine only because I pay them to be. I want your friendship. You are dismissed from service."

There was a silence. "Then . . . you are changing the terms of our agreement," Ayana said, a smile on her dark face too.

"I am. I told you long ago, Ayana, that you are the sister of my heart. Live with me as my sister, if you choose—unless you wish to leave altogether, to journey home to Ethiopia. I would not hold you back. I love you too much for that."

"I have no wish to travel anywhere, my—my sister," Ayana said, reaching for Esther's hand.

She turned then to Hathakh, who still looked troubled. Of course, this was far more difficult for him. No word as simple as "sister"—certainly not "brother"—could give him a place in Esther's new life. She could not cut through all the cords that bound them, but one thing she could do, and had done. She had even spoken with Ezra, who was a court scribe, to be sure she had the legal right. For Hathakh's case was not the same as Ayana's, who had been brought to the king's harem as Esther had. Hathakh had been bought and sold, so many years ago. He had been King Xerxes' property all these years, and was now Esther's.

"Hathakh, I have the tablet here," she said, reaching into one of the packing boxes. "Drawn up and legal. I have freed you. You are no longer a slave, no longer bound."

The fact of Hathakh's slavery had been unimportant to Esther, something she'd never even thought of until a few weeks before when she'd begun planning how to reorder her household after leaving court. She should have guessed, though, that it was no small matter to him, no minor detail. He grabbed at the clay tablet she drew out with an eagerness entirely at odds with his usual caution. He read it, then traced the letters with his fingertips.

"I am free," he said. "Thank you, my lady."

"I only wanted to say all this here, before we went home," Esther said, rising. "I was greatly blessed to have found such friends as you both in this place. Come, let us go home—the drivers are waiting for us."

And so they went home, riding out in the evening twilight beyond the palace walls, beyond the city of Susa, north along the river to Esther's estate, which buzzed and hummed with life and welcomed them in. Esther's heart was light. She had left the palace and harem behind. She had spoken her heart to her two friends. The rest of her life was her own.

She knew there was further business to be finished, but she did not think it would be spoken of at once. It had, after all, lain dormant for so many years, unspoken. But that night Talia came and said, "My lady, Hathakh is here asking to see you. He asks if you will come walk with him in the gardens."

Esther rose and followed Talia out, her heart beating a little faster. Hathakh was waiting at the entrance to the antechamber. She saw a difference at once in the way he carried himself, in the angle of his shoulders and head. Who would have guessed a few words on a clay tablet could make such a difference?

"I have been speaking with Eben," he said as she fell into step beside him. "He is frantically worried that he will tread on my toes if he permits you to give him the title of chief steward. I said it bothered me not at all, as long as he left me my little corners of authority, allowed me to keep on doing the jobs I like doing best, and give him all the unpleasant ones." He laughed, and even his laughter seemed freer.

"I knew you would manage to work out an arrangement that would benefit you," Esther said. They left the house behind and walked through the courtyard, out into the gardens.

"And so, my lady," Hathakh said, and put up a hand as she tried to correct him. "No matter what, you are still a queen, and I a commoner—it is right I should call you 'my lady.'"

Esther wanted to protest, but did not, knowing there was more to settle than the question of what title he should call her by. Silence filled the space between them. Finally, under a tree, Hathakh stopped and turned toward her. She looked up into his face. He had always been a handsome man despite the beardless cheek and slight frame that clearly marked him as a eunuch. He was handsome still. No grey touched his black hair. There was a light in his dark eyes that she had not seen since they were both very young.

"My lady, Esther. Your husband the king has been dead for a year."

"Yes." Her time of mourning was over.

"And you have freed me. I am no longer a slave."

This time Esther just nodded. Hathakh took her hand, turned it over in his, and looked at it as if memorizing it. A great deal did not have to be said at all. They had both lived in the harem long enough to have heard every strange tale possible of men and women and the choices they might make. Rich widows had freed slave stewards and married them, though no king's widow would ever be permitted to do such a scandalous thing. Women they knew had married eunuchs, both willing, perhaps, to accept a marriage that was less than normal, for the sake of love. People did many strange things in the name of love, but the strangest of all, Esther thought, might be to keep silent, and keep loving, no matter what. Lifelong friendship was something different from what most men and women thought they wanted or needed—but who was to say it was less, or more cheaply bought?

Hathakh broke the silence this time. "And yet . . . we are still who we are. There are many things we can never give each other."

"But so much we *can* give, and have given," Esther said suddenly. "Why dwell on what cannot be? You've never told me in words how you feel, Hathakh, and even now you don't ask me how I feel. If you were to ask, I would have to tell you that what I felt for my husband the king, and what I have always felt for you, were two things both so powerful, and so different, that I don't know how they could both be called by the name of love—yet what other word do I have for them? And for that matter, what else could I call my feeling for Ayana, for Rivka, for Mordecai, for Damaspia? There are as many kinds of love as there are people. Our lives are our own, now, more than they have ever been. Why waste time worrying about what we cannot have? You are free now to go wherever in the wide world you wish, but I hope you will stay here with me."

Hathakh looked as if he were about to say more, then an easy smile lit his face, crinkling the corners of his eyes. "Nowhere else in all the world," he said, holding her hand another moment before he let it go. "I am staying right here."

CHAPTER 21

News! News from Jerusalem!"

Ezra strode through the forecourt of Esther's house, a scroll raised high in his right hand, shouting that news had come from the Jews in the homeland. By the time he reached the great hall, a score of people had gathered to hear him read from the scroll.

Esther, who had been tending her flowers in the inner courtyard when Ezra arrived, heard the commotion and went to see what it meant. From all around her home people were rushing to the great hall to hear Ezra's news. The earnest young scribes copying the books of the Law in what had once been the banqueting hall were almost running. Their wives and children hurried in from other parts of the estate. Many of these had moved almost permanently into Esther's house. Esther's own household came, too. Many of her newer servants were Jewish, and of the rest, most of them followed their mistress in her allegiance to the God of Israel. News from Jerusalem was news that concerned everyone in the house.

Ezra read the letter aloud, pausing often to add his own comments. Esther watched and listened from the comfort of a bench against the wall. Ezra was the acknowledged leader of Susa's Jewish community, just as Esther was its patroness and her home was its hub. Although Ezra still held a position as a scribe at King Artaxerxes' court, he was more and more involved with the life of his people. Recognized by all as an expert in the Scriptures and the laws, he spearheaded the regular collections of gold, silver, and goods to be sent to the struggling community back in Jerusalem. Their fortunes rose and fell based on the favor of the Persian king, the strength and commitment of their own leaders, and the opposition they faced from their neighbors—other settlers in the homeland. And the Jews in Susa, safer and wealthier than their kinsmen in Jerusalem, listened eagerly to any news that came from the land of God's promise.

Esther worked closely with Ezra, a task she did not always find easy. He was a single-minded and strong-willed man, not easily given to compromise. But she admired him for that, even though her own way was different. She had learned that God always found the right person for the task He needed done. For rekindling the fires of devotion and dedication in the Jews of Susa, for collecting and transcribing the ancient and newer writings of the Jewish people, Ezra was the right man. She herself had given much time, much gold, and all of her home to the same task, but without a man of vision the work could not be done.

After the evening meal, Ezra led the Jewish men of the household in worship, while the gentiles, the women, and the children listened from their seats at the back of the hall. His ringing voice reading from the Torah then leading the men in their prayers easily carried to where they sat. The large room took on the glow with the golden light of sunset and Esther silently praised God for making this house—once the house of the bitterest enemy of God's people—into a holy place, a house where His presence could in some degree be sensed.

"Most of our people here will never see Jerusalem," Ezra said later that night, as he sat talking to Esther and Rivka in the gardens. "I wish more would feel God's call to move back home, but some are just so settled, so comfortable, in their lives here."

"It is hard to uproot an entire life," Rivka said gently. She was among the last of the generation who'd been young when the first proclamation came from Cyrus freeing the Jews to return to their homeland. Her own father had married a Persian and would not think of leaving, and she knew of many who had faced that choice and elected to stay.

"Perhaps, but the ways of God are often hard," Ezra said. "More men are needed there to help with the work of the Temple—the physical labor of rebuilding it, but also the work of sacrifice, of singing, of learning and teaching our laws. We need priests and Levites and teachers to go back there. And we need women, too, for the abomination of the men of Israel mixing their blood with pagan women continues into another generation."

Esther and Rivka exchanged glances. This was one subject upon which Ezra was inflexible.

"I mean no offense to you, my lady queen," he said quickly. "You had no choice in marrying the king, of course. But when these men choose heathen wives, wives of another race who know little of our ways but carry on their idol worship and their pagan ways, we threaten all that is Jewish." His eyes blazed in the faint lamplight. "Few, very few, are ever converted to the true God. It's bad enough that our people here must live surrounded by pagans on all sides, fighting to remember what it means to be a Jew. But to bring such confusion into our homeland—well, they can see what results if they only look to the north of them."

Esther knew what he meant. Beyond Jerusalem lived the Samaritans, a mixed-race people descended from Israelites left behind after the Assyrian conquest and Assyrians who had been settled there. "Their religion is an unholy mix of the true worship of God and the worst pagan idolatry," Ezra continued. " That cannot be allowed to happen in the land of Judah."

"Yet even here we can still remember what it means to be Jews," Rivka said. "Our people have not forgotten."

"Some never forgot," Ezra said, leaning toward her. "Many did forget, but they are remembering. They are waking up to the knowledge that they must hold on to our ways, our laws, or lose them forever. Men are studying the Torah again, and women are keeping their kitchens pure, cooking only the clean meats. People are gathering to observe Shabbat—not only here but in many cities of the empire. You both have done much to help our people here," he added, which was as close as Ezra ever came to paying tribute to another person's efforts. "Someone needs to do the same for our people back in the homeland. I will go—I must go. I am counting the days."

He stood, adjusting his robe around him. When he had gone, Rivka said to Esther, "I worry about that boy. He's so intense."

"He is devoted to God's cause and God's people," Esther said, "but he frightens people because he only sees black and white, no shades of gray. A fanatic, I suppose some might call him."

"But there are times, I suppose, when a fanatic is what God needs," Rivka added with a sigh. "I used to think Mordecai was mad when he refused to bow to Haman. He'd never been so deeply devoted to being a Jew, and then, just because this man was an enemy of our people, he would not bend the knee to him? You and he saved us from Haman's plan, but if Mordecai had simply bowed to Haman perhaps there would have never been a need to be saved. And yet, if not for that, then all this"—she waved her hand to indicate the house, the grounds, the thriving Jewish community learning and growing under Esther's roof—"might never have happened. The ways of God are strange."

"Indeed they are," Esther said, pulling her feet up on the bench, relaxing as she could not have done in Ezra's presence. "Strange, but trustworthy."

"Damaspia will be here tomorrow?" Rivka asked, turning her thoughts away from Ezra and toward the more welcome subject of family.

"Yes. She's bringing the children." Damaspia, now six years married, had a 4-year-old son named Xerxes and a baby girl just beginning to walk. Esther still worried about her daughter, caught up in the maelstrom of court and harem, but in general Damaspia seemed to be happy.

Almost from the day he ascended the throne Artaxerxes had been busy quelling rebellion and fighting battles. He'd been embroiled in conflict with Egyptian rebels for several years now, with no end to the conflict in sight. Yet for the most part he seemed to be a good husband to Damaspia, Esther mused to herself. A better husband, perhaps, than King Xerxes had been, though a weaker king than his father had been in his early years. The empire was pressed on all sides, rebellion from within and threats of conquest from without. Esther did not envy the gentle-spirited Artaxerxes the task of holding it all together.

The next day Esther, Damaspia, and Rivka strolled through the courtyard, watching the children play in the spray of a fountain. Young Xerxes was fearless, running through the arching water with his eyes and mouth wide open. By contrast, the baby stood at the edge of the spray where the droplets just reached her outstretched hands. Xerxes was soaked, but his clothes would dry quickly in the hot, dry air, and Esther laughed with him at the joy of being a child.

"Let's sit down here," Rivka suggested. "The spray from the fountain adds a little coolness to the air."

"Yes, but let's go under the shelter," Esther suggested. "We'll still be near the children and the fountain, and the roof will give us a little shelter from the sun." The women sat down on carved wooden benches and Esther asked a question she'd been mulling over in her mind for the past several minutes. "Damaspia, does Artaxerxes look favorably upon our people back in Jerusalem?"

Damaspia smiled. "He has little time to think of them, with his troubles in Egypt and other places, but I make sure that any thoughts he does have about Jerusalem are good ones. Why?"

"Ezra longs to return to Jerusalem. He believes God is calling him to go there and teach the law, establish the old ways of worship, and encourage the rebuilding of the temple. But he does not want to go as a solitary pilgrim. He wants to lead an entourage, almost a second return from exile, I think. To do all he wants to do will require royal patronage. Is this something the king can do, or will do?"

Damaspia looked thoughtful. "I believe he will if he can," she said at last. "He does not share my worship of Israel's God, but I think that he respects and honors our God above the gods of his own people. I believe he would honor God if he could, but he is a king; and as you told me long ago, Mama, a king makes different choices than a common man makes. Artaxerxes would not pour his resources into such an expedition at a time like this if he could not see that it would benefit his throne, his kingdom, in some way."

"The colony of settlers in Judah will be very loyal subjects of the king if they know that he has been generous to them," her mother said. She paused, calling her wandering granddaughter back to where her brother played. "If they know that he supports the building of their Temple and the worship of their God, yes, they will be loyal."

Damaspia nodded. "Then I'll put it to him in that way. Tell Ezra he should prepare a formal request for the king, telling exactly what he wants to do and what he will need. To send so many people away from here to Jerusalem at such an unsettled time will be a huge undertaking. But I will see what I can do." She glanced over at Rivka. "What do you think, Auntie? Is it wise, this plan of Ezra's?"

Rivka gave herself a little shake. She'd been dozing in the shade. This year, at last, she had started to feel her age. She was well over 70 now, a great age. "Ezra?" she said. "Clever fellow. Whatever he does will prosper, I think."

Esther winked at Damaspia, who returned it with a smile, and they let Rivka go back to her rest. A slight breeze rustled the leaves overhead. From a short distance away they could hear music. In her dedication to the service of God, Esther had not forgotten her love for music, and poets and musicians still came to her home and sought her patronage as freely as did Jewish scribes and scholars. Just then Xerxes ran to his mother with his fist clenched and opened it to reveal a struggling insect. His little sister fell down, got up, and fell down again. Esther, too, closed her eyes, enjoying the afternoon.

Damaspia did as she had promised, and soon Ezra was granted an audience with the king. He came back elated.

"My lady," he told Esther, "he has promised me everything I hoped for! I can bring as large a party as I wish. The king will give us an armed escort, and he will give me gold and silver, wheat and wine, oil and salt—and letters for the rulers of the provinces authorizing me to collect gold, silver, and goods from the Jews in their provinces as I pass. And he has specifically given me a letter stating that I have authority to teach and to enforce the laws of our Scriptures in our land. We are to purchase animals for burnt offerings and see that sacrifices are carried out in the temple. It is everything I had hoped for, and more!"

It was more than Esther had hoped for too, and her heart warmed toward Artaxerxes for his generosity. She prayed for him often, both in his role as king of Persia and as the husband of her only child. Activity around her home became even more frantic as Ezra began choosing and preparing those who would travel with him.

One afternoon as preparations continued, Esther sat with Ayana in her bedchamber sorting through jewels she had been given as queen. "I can send most of these with Ezra," she mused. "They are of no value to me now, and they will be able to do much good for the people and for the Temple in Jerusalem."

Ayana lifted a lovely set of sapphire earrings, with a collar and bracelets to match. "This is most generous. Have you told Ezra of your intent?"

"No. I think I will give a coffer of jewels to him at the last minute, just before he leaves. If I tell him of it sooner he will begin to think I should give him every gem I own!" The two friends laughed, then Esther grew serious again. "I would gladly give all I have for the glory of God, to do His work, but my life is not over yet, and I do not know what needs I might yet be called on to meet. Someday there may be a need even greater than that which Ezra goes to fill, and I would like to hoard a few jewels against that day. Is that wrong?"

"You will have to ask God, not me," Ayana said. "I am sure He admires your good sense, but what do I know?"

"You speak these days of our God as if He is your God too."

Ayana trickled a strand of pearls between her fingers. "I remember so little of the gods of my own people. Do you remember me telling you that I once thought those gods were tied to our land so that when I left Ethiopia, I left our gods too? Yet your God came with your people into exile. For 20 years I have heard you pray to the God of Israel, talk of Him, read the words of His scripture. He has grown into my heart, I think. I find it hard to believe in any other god, and the older I get, the more I believe I need a god. If I am to worship, I must worship the God of Israel—and so I do."

Esther grasped both of Ayana's hands. "Oh, it makes me glad to hear that, Ayana. As a child I was taught that we Jews are God's chosen people—and I believe that still. It is both an honor and a responsibility. But as the years have passed I have come to believe that our God accepts people of all races who turn to Him and seek His ways."

"That is what Hathakh says too," Ayana said quietly.

"Yes, I have heard him say that," Esther said. She held a polished rose colored gem in her hand, appreciating its cool weight. "I am not sure Ezra would approve," she added, "but it was Hathakh who pointed out to me that God promised Abraham that in his seed all nations of the earth would be blessed." She and Hathakh talked freely about God now and their faith in Him, as they did about everything else, too, making up in long evenings and afternoons of conversation for all the years of silence and restraint.

"You knew he spoke to Ezra about becoming a convert?"

"No, I didn't know that." Esther was surprised. It was not the kind of thing she would have expected Hathakh to keep from her.

"Yes, but Ezra told him the Law says that no eunuch can become part of the people of Israel."

"Is that true?" Esther dropped the stone and stood up, crossing the room to the open window. "I knew that a eunuch could not be a priest, but . . ." She had read much of the Scriptures but had to admit that she tended to read the stories and poetry, and to skip more lightly over the long passages of laws and genealogies. But that was the stuff on which Ezra thrived. She sighed. *He* would know. She understood, too, why Hathakh might not have wanted to tell her this.

"Yes, some of our people were talking to Ezra one day about becoming converts. He told them the men would have to be circumcised, unless they were eunuchs, in which case they could study the laws of Israel and worship God in their hearts, but they could never become full Israelites. He said, too, that if they went to Jerusalem, they could not enter the Temple. Hathakh spoke to him privately later on, and Ezra told him the same thing. He even showed him the place where it was written in the Law."

"It seems harsh."

Ayana sighed. "But it is not uncommon. In all lands eunuchs are always seen as less than other men."

"But I've never thought of Hathakh that way, as less than other men. In so many ways I have always thought of him as more."

Ayana smiled. In all the years since Xerxes' death she had never asked Esther to explain her friendship with Hathakh. She simply accepted their closeness, as she seemed to accept all things about her dearest friends. Now she moved decisively, scooping up the jewels in her lap and dumping them back in the coffer with a decisive gesture. "He is devoted to you, that is all that matters. As we all are. And these jewels here are going to Jerusalem. Choose a handful to keep, and let's not take all day over it."

"Sometimes I wish I were going to Jerusalem," Esther said, the words surprising even her.

Ayana looked up sharply. "You? Go to Jerusalem?"

"I know, it's impossible. I doubt Artaxerxes would ever give me leave to travel there, and what would I do? I can be more use here, and I would not want to go so far from Damaspia and her children. And yet . . . when I think of seeing the Temple, the city of our people, the land God gave us . . . Yes, I wish I could see it with my own eyes before I die."

"You will not die for a long time yet," Ayana told her. "Who knows what God may have planned for you."

"Not Jerusalem, I think," Esther said. "But I am willing to wait and see. I used to think I was a leaf carried on the current, but now I think that following our God is more like being carried in the arms of a loving father."

"Ah, yes," Ayana said. "Amen."

Both women looked toward the door where a servant stood quietly. "Queen Esther, Ezra sent me to ask if you would come to the library. There are men there he wishes you to meet."

Esther picked up the box of jewels and carefully put down the lid and the latch. She would not show it to Ezra—not yet. She followed the boy downstairs.

Ezra was in the library, surrounded by scrolls, talking to two young men. One looked very Jewish and very young. His beard was scanty and his body boyishly slender. He was not yet 20, she judged. The other was a little older, but not by much, and he looked like a native of Susa.

"My lady queen, how good of you to come," Ezra said, his brisk manner sliding right over the deferential words. "I thought you would be interested to meet these two young fellows who have just come to study in our library. This is Nehemiah, son of Hacaliah. He is a good scholar, though perhaps more interested in affairs of government and court. He is seeking a position at the king's court, though I think he ought to come to Jerusalem with me. Be that as it may, I told him he should speak to you."

Esther extended a hand to the young Jew, who bent the knee before her. As he rose, she said, "Ezra does not always agree that we need more than just scholars in this world. I have little influence at court these days, but many of our people are in the king's employ, and it should not be difficult to find you a position, if you are hardworking."

"I will do anything, my lady," Nehemiah said. "It's true, I'm torn by Ezra's offer to go to Jerusalem. I want so much to be there, to see our land, to help with the rebuilding—yet my mother is a widow, and as my brother is going with Ezra, I am her only support. She could not bear to see me go, not yet anyway. And there is so much I could learn at court!"

His brown eyes sparkled. He had a natural exuberance that obviously drew people to him, and Esther liked him at once. She was generally wary of people, even Jews, who wanted her to use her influence at court, but she silently promised herself she would see what she could do for this Nehemiah.

She turned to the other young man. He was clearly of Persian stock, an exceptionally handsome young man. There was something hauntingly familiar about his eyes and mouth. "Ah yes," Ezra said, "and this is Lilaios, one of our converts. He and Nehemiah were childhood friends, and he began studying our laws and expressed a desire to join our people. Now he is the real scholar—a great student, and a poet himself." He glanced at the young man. "Is that not right?" he asked. "Lilaios fairly leaped at me when I told him of the library of scrolls we have collected here, and insisted he must see them."

Esther could not stop staring at the young man. "What did you say your name was?"

"Lilaios, my lady. And yes, I am who you think I am." He smiled, but his eyes and voice were very serious.

Esther felt as if the world had stopped turning. Everything around her focused on this one man—a face and voice from her past. "Lilaios," she echoed. Then, regaining a little composure, she said, "Lilaios, I think you will come walk with me in the gardens. Ezra, Nehemiah, excuse us for a few moments. I knew Lilaios' parents long ago, and I would speak with him in private."

He walked a careful step behind her as they left the library and went into the courtyard. Once outside, she led him toward the tree-lined walks, and waited till they were in shade before she spoke. It was hard to think what to say first.

"So you are the son of Lilaios and Roxane," she said at last.

"Yes, the very one."

"I remember you as a baby."

"My mother told me she used to bring me with her when she

would visit and play for you—before my father died."

Esther stopped walking and turned to face him. "Your mother. Is she still living?"

"No, she died two years ago."

"Ah." Esther felt a little pain twist inside her. "I would have loved to see her again. But perhaps—she would not have liked to see me?"

Lilaios looked down at the paving stones. "My mother cherished her bitterness, my lady. I will not hide the truth from you. She blamed you for my father's death, almost as much as she blamed the old king. She thought you could have saved him. She spent a year in prison herself—she told me when I was young that she was unjustly accused, but my grandmother, who saw things more clearly, told me it was you who had been unjustly accused—that that was how my mother sought her revenge. She never forgave, though at the end when she was very ill, she told me that I should not waste my life trying to avenge my father's death. That I should go forward, forget the past. That was the closest she could come to laying her own anger to rest, I suppose."

"She had reason to be angry." Esther gestured to a nearby bench and sat down, inviting young Lilaios to sit with her. "King Xerxes did a terrible thing to your father, a thing that should never have been done. There was a law, and your father broke the law. But that does not always justify the harshest penalty. The king killed a man who was no enemy, who merely annoyed him, as one might swat a bothersome fly. And I have often wondered, over the years, whether I could have done more to prevent it. Your mother may have been right. Perhaps I could have. For a while I felt I owed a debt to your family, but then, when your mother made that accusation against me, I thought the debt was settled. In later years I have come to think differently, but then other concerns crowded out the memory. To my shame, I have not thought much about your family for many years."

"Time passes, my lady, and our lives flow on. My mother's tragedy was that she would not let her life flow on. It is all long gone now, and now that I see you, I find I cannot blame you. My grandmother encouraged me in my father's love of words and books. She told me, among other things, how he used to collect the writings of the Hebrew scrolls for you. I went to find some for myself and fell in love with them—and eventually, with their God. I knew Nehemiah, of course, and some other Jews. I wanted to be one of

God's people, though I was not born of Israel."

"So will you too go to Jerusalem?"

"Not now," Lilaios said. "I have more learning to do, more poems to make, here. But someday I will go. When my friend Nehemiah goes, perhaps. I don't know what use they will have there for a poet, but there may be some place for a scholar, anyway."

"Then do you, like Nehemiah, seek a position at court? King Artaxerxes is not like his father. If you have half your father's gift, you would be welcome there."

Lilaios shook his head. "No, I will work for no king. I try not to cherish grudges, but I am sure you can see why I will not put my livelihood and my life in the hands of a king."

"Yes, I can see it," Esther said. "But you are welcome in my house at any time, Lilaios. Come and make free use of my scrolls."

"I thank you, my lady."

Not long after those meetings, Ezra and his followers prepared to leave on their long journey. They took a coffer of Esther's jewels with them, as well as many other gifts from her household and from all the Jews of Susa.

Soon afterward Rivka took to her bed. She faded quickly, slipping back from speech and consciousness as Esther sat by her bed and held her hand. After a fortnight in bed she died in her sleep, just a few days before word came from Ezra of his successful arrival in Jerusalem. Esther mourned for the full mourning period for Rivka, the only mother she had ever known. She was glad to have had these last years of closeness to Rivka, as they managed the household and worked for the good of God's people together, for they had grown close in a way they had never been in Esther's girlhood. God had given her the gift of Rivka at the time she needed it most.

With Rivka gone, the balances of Esther's life shifted subtly, but there were no great changes. The years rolled by. Ezra wrote back about the struggles and victories of the Jews in the homeland. The library of scrolls continued to grow, as did the number of scholars who came to study and copy them. Nehemiah found a position in the king's household. Artaxerxes continued to fight rebels in Egypt and in other corners of his kingdom. Damaspia had two more daughters, and lost a second son. She worried that her Xerxes was growing up too wild, too undisciplined. Esther saw in him the wilful self-indulgence of his grandfather and the lenience of his father. A poor combination, she thought, for the boy loved his own pleasures, and no great ambition drove him to master them. However, she did not say this to Damaspia. She only watched and prayed for her daughter and her grandchildren, as she did for all those she loved.

In the sixteenth year of Artaxerxes' reign, Ayana came to Esther one morning to say that a beggar had arrived at the door and was unwilling to leave without seeing Queen Esther.

"How odd," Esther said. "Is he a Jew?"

"Not a Jew, and not 'he' either. It is a woman, and she is obviously destitute. The kitchen staff gave her food and a cloak, but she says she must see Queen Esther, and will not leave."

"An old woman?"

"Older than we are," said Ayana. She was three years short of her fiftieth birthday, with Esther another year behind. "And sick, I think."

"How very strange," Esther said, getting up.

"You're going to see her?"

"I suppose I must. What if she never leaves?"

The beggar woman was sitting in the forecourt. She did indeed look elderly and sick, with graying hair straggling around a face that must once have been very pretty. Ayana had not mentioned that the tattered rags she wore were dyed in gaudy colors that proclaimed that in her better days the woman must have been a prostitute. But that was hardly surprising. Many of the old women beggars in the streets had come from that profession, for what place was there for them once they were old?

Seeing Esther, the woman struggled into a kneeling position, but she did not keep her eyes downcast. Instead, she fixed them almost greedily on Esther's face.

Esther extended a hand to give her permission to rise. The beggar grabbed it, her hands surprisingly smooth to the touch. She stood up, much shorter than Esther and a little hunched over as well.

"What brings you here?" Esther asked as gently as she could. "I was told you wished to see me."

"I did. I do. I came because this was more than a fine house where I might get food." Her speech was far more cultured than Esther would have expected. "I came because this was your house, the house of the famous queen Esther, best-beloved wife of King Xerxes."

"That is what they called me."

The woman caught and kept Esther's eye, giving her a gap-toothed smile.

"And me," said the woman.

Esther felt caught again in the moment years before when she had met the young Lilaios, a sense of being dragged unwillingly back to the past. But this was far stranger. Someone she had never thought to meet, had presumed—if she thought of her at all—dead.

Yet she said the name, making it a question. "Vashti? Not . . . Vashti."

The woman's face split into a grin, and she nodded. "Vashti. You'd find it hard to believe now, wouldn't you? But I was once as you were, queen in Susa."

Esther turned to the nearest servant. "Bring this woman to a bedchamber, and bring a meal for her," she commanded. Turning to the woman, she said softly, "I will come to speak with you later."

When Hathakh heard about her he pointed out, not unreasonably, that the woman might well not be Vashti at all. "No one knows what became of her," he said. "Any old woman might claim she was Vashti."

Esther nodded, for she knew it was true. But somehow she sensed that her life was coming full circle. That God was giving her a chance, not to right a wrong, but to minister to one who'd been wronged so many years before. "You're right. She might," Esther said. "But I am taking her in all the same. If there is a thousandth part of a chance that she is telling the truth, then I cannot turn her away."

She visited the woman's chamber that night. The woman who called herself Vashti sat on the bed in a spacious, polished room, clad in a clean skirt and tunic. Her hair had been washed and arranged. She looked even smaller and frailer without the gaudy rags and the dirt.

"I am dying," Vashti said matter-of-factly. There was no self-pity in her voice. "I had nowhere to go, and I have always wanted to see you, so I decided to come here and throw myself on your mercy. I didn't expect it to turn out this well."

Esther smiled. "Life has a way of surprising us." Though Hathakh's words were perfectly reasonable, she did not for a moment doubt that the woman was who she claimed to be. "I have wondered about you so often. There were so many things I wanted to ask you."

Vashti looked out the window, away from Esther. Stars shone in the night sky. "Now that it's almost over, there's little to tell in my life. I came from a merchant family. I was taken to the harem. The king fell in love with me and married me. He gave me fine garments and jewels, and he made me a queen. One day I said no when he summoned me, and I was divorced and cast away like . . . like a dog who wandered inside and wet on the floor. I had no place to go, so I went to the streets. What other way had I of making a living?" Short gasps punctuated her story. Breath did not come easily.

"I didn't stay in Susa, of course. I traveled around." A racking cough shook her body, and she covered her mouth with a thin hand. "Some men were excited by a woman who'd once belonged to the king, though others didn't believe I was who I said I was. Other girls had had the same idea, used the same trick, in those years. But for me it was true. I was Vashti, the one who had been queen. When I got older, I kept a house for a while, teaching other girls the tricks of my trade."

She tossed back her head with a loud cackle, then doubled over with coughing. As she gasped for breath Esther picked up a pitcher and poured water into a cup. "Here. Drink this slowly. I'll see that you get something for that cough before you go to bed."

Once the woman gained control, she continued with a laugh. "Some women get rich that way, but I had no knack for business. I lost it all, and then I got old and ugly, and then sick. And now I've come here to die."

"Why did you say no to the king?" Esther asked. "I risked my life once to face him, but I don't think I could ever have done what you did."

Vashti shrugged. "You do what seems right at the time. It wasn't pride, or modesty. It was—I felt cheated. I never thought he would ask me to display myself before other men. I thought he prized me more highly than that. You know that poem, "Zariadres and Odatis"? He used to recite it for me, called me his Odatis. When he summoned me that night, I felt worthless, as if he'd already cast me aside. I was so angry." She coughed, a long racking series of coughs, and Esther held the cup of water to her cracked lips so she could drink again.

"But you know, a few hours, a few weeks later—and all my life after—I would have given anything to have those moments back, to say yes and go dance for him. What did the other men matter? I'd have done anything for him, anything to keep what I had. Not the crown, but the man." She looked up at Esther at last, bleak haunted gray eyes in a gray face. "When I heard of his death, I cried for a week."

"You . . . you loved him," Esther said, almost in wonder. "You truly did."

"I loved him with all my soul."

Esther was silent. She would not tell Vashti that Xerxes had recited "Zariadres and Odatis" for her, too—and for a half dozen other women. Vashti had, perhaps, just been another of his brief, consuming passions—just as Amestris was for a time, just as Esther herself. Other names floated through her mind—Artaynte the mother, and Artaynta the daughter. But of all those women, all the wives, all the concubines, had anyone ever loved him like this? Esther had cared deeply for the king. She grieved for his sorrows, enjoyed the good times with him. But she had never given her heart away—her *soul*, Vashti had said—in this way.

Only to her God, never to any man. She could not imagine such unbridled passion spent on any human creature, and was glad she could not.

She kept Vashti in her home, tended by her servants, for the month it took the older woman to die. Esther visited her several times. Sometimes they spoke little, but toward the end Vashti, heartbreakingly, began to beg Esther to talk of Xerxes. It was hard to choose what to tell her—stories that would not highlight his feeling for Esther, but that would not show the weakness and degradation to which he had fallen—but Esther tried. She wove stories of the kingdom, of his honor among the nation, of the statues that became his passion. Her voice was soothing—to her as well as to the woman he had spurned—and often Esther talked of him late into the night until Vashti fell asleep at the sound of her voice. Only then would Esther go to her own room, burdened by another woman's memories.

When at last Vashti slipped into death, Esther commanded that she be buried on the estate. It was a strange last chapter to the life of the woman who'd always haunted Esther. For years, back in the harem, she had thought that Vashti was her shadow self, the woman whose fate so closely mirrored her own. But at the most crucial moments, their paths had diverged. Their choices had been different, and Esther could not help thanking God.

That summer brought bad news from the palace. Megabyzus, Amytis' husband, had served Artaxerxes uneasily for many years, helping put down the rebellion in Egypt. Neither man could ever forget that Megabyzus had helped place Artaxerxes on the throne, after first conspiring with the usurper Artapanos. Their relationship was never an easy one, and now Megabyzus had risen in revolt. Damaspia said that Artaxerxes was deeply troubled by this new threat to his throne. Never a man who found decisions easy, he swayed back and forth on how best to deal with his rebel brother-in-law, and any choice he made seemed to make him angry at himself and at everyone around him.

The news from Jerusalem was bad too. After the rebuilding of the Temple the Samaritans were growing violent in their opposition to Jewish resettlement. They had sent a letter to Artaxerxes asking to have work stopped on the Temple, and Artaxerxes had supported their request. The land of Israel fell within Megabyzus' satrapy, and the Samaritans had convinced the king that they were loyal to him, while the Jews supported Megabyzus.

"I could do nothing to sway him, Mama," Damaspia reported on her next visit. Tears were in her eyes; the strain of these months was telling on her. "He barely listened to me. When I reminded him how much he had done for the Jews in the past, he only said that perhaps he'd done enough for them and asked me whom I was loyal to. He is not often harsh with me like that, but lately . . ."

Esther reached for her daughter's hand. Damaspia was a woman grown now, nearing 30, with her children growing up around her. Esther was grateful she had never outgrown her need for a mother. "I know, Damaspia. Being married to a king is not easy. It wasn't for me."

"I'm afraid for so many things, Mama. I want to have peace, but there never seems to be any. Artaxerxes is a good man when things are peaceful, but they so seldom are."

"We do not live in peaceful times," Esther said with a sigh. "Do you still pray, Damaspia? All I can tell you is to seek God. That is all I've been able to do, all these years. God's ways are not always clear to us, but He does not leave us alone."

Months slipped into years. Artaxerxes and Megabyzus made an

uneasy peace, but other battles dragged on, with peace nowhere in sight. One day Nehemiah and his friend Lilaios came to Esther's quarters to talk with her.

"I had a letter from my brother Hanani a few days ago," Nehemiah said. "All is going badly in Jerusalem. The gates of the city have been burned and the Temple wall destroyed. I wish I could go there! They need a man who can take charge, who can inspire them to fight on and finish the work."

"And you think *you* are that man?" Esther asked.

Nehemiah's seriousness turned to a sudden grin. "I sound prideful, don't I? But I feel called by God. Not called like a prophet. I have no mystical visions or dreams. It's just that I know I can do what needs to be done. I should have gone long ago, when my mother died and I was no longer needed here."

"Can you speak to the king? Ask him for leave to go?"

"I hardly think he will send me off with wagons of gifts, as he sent Ezra," Nehemiah said. "I believe he regrets siding with the Samaritans in this last conflict, for his sympathies are naturally with the Jews. But Jerusalem is far from his greatest concern these days."

Esther shifted uncomfortably on her couch. For several days now she had been in pain, deep inside her belly. It was a gnawing, high-pitched pain that would not go away no matter whether she ate or fasted, slept on her back or on her side, walked or stayed still. She tried, mostly, to ignore it. "I believe the king knows in his heart that Israel's God is the true lord of the nations," she said, "but he cannot always afford to listen to his heart. I know from what Damaspia says that he does, indeed, regret halting work on the Temple. But you are right. It is the least of his concerns. Yet if you were to bring it to his attention, he might listen. You are his cupbearer, Nehemiah, a valued servant and adviser. Speak to him."

"Perhaps I will. I can't get it off my mind that Jerusalem, God's city, should be in such a state." Nehemiah's face changed then, and his usual bright smile returned. "But how wonderful to think that God placed you in the palace, and your daughter the queen after you, just so that a heathen king would know and honor our God!"

Lilaios, silent until now, leaned forward eagerly. "But isn't this God's plan? To use the people of Israel to bless all the nations, just as He told Abraham He would do? 'In your seed shall all the nations of the earth be blessed,'" he recited.

"I found something wonderful a little while ago—so exciting, yet I've kept it to myself until now, for you were the two I wanted to share it with." He pulled a scroll from a fold in his garments. Lilaios had achieved quite a reputation as a poet and performer, but his avid interest in the Hebrew scriptures and his pursuit of their hidden treasures had never abated. He looked like a child with a new toy as he said, "I found this in a little house in Babylon. It's the house of an old Jew whose grandfather had been carried out in the exile. He had hundreds of pieces of writing there—some ancient, some very new, written by the Jews of Babylon today. But this one, he thought, was an old one. He thought it might have come from the great prophet Isaiah himself. I suppose I noticed it all the more because I am a convert, a foreigner within the gates of Israel, but listen! This is wonderful!" He stood up as he read:

> "Maintain justice and do what is right,
>   for my salvation is close at hand
>   and my righteousness will soon be revealed.
>   Blessed is the man who does this,
>   the man who holds it fast,
>   who keeps the Sabbath without desecrating it,
>   and keeps his hand from doing any evil."
> Let no foreigner who has bound himself to the Lord say,
> 'The Lord will surely exclude me from his people.'"

Lilaios looked up, excited by the words. The poetry was beautifully crafted, but the meaning beneath it was what thrilled Esther and what had surely thrilled Lilaios. He read on through the next verses, to the climax of the poem.

> "And foreigners who bind themselves to the Lord to serve him,
>   to love the name of the Lord, and to worship him,
>   all who keep the Sabbath without desecrating it
>   and who hold fast to my covenant—
>   these I will bring to my holy mountain
>   and give them joy in my house of prayer.
>   Their burnt offerings and sacrifices will be accepted on my altar;
>   for my house will be called a house of prayer for all nations."

"For all nations," Nehemiah repeated, his face glowing with excitement. Joy came so readily to him, even in the midst of trouble. "Yes! That's it. That's what we're building in Jerusalem. A house of prayer for all nations! *That's* why the king must let me go."

Esther laughed, caught up in his exuberance, though laughter made her wince with pain. "Lilaios, can you make two copies of that poem for me?" she asked. "One complete, for myself, and one of just these lines"—she indicated a few lines in the middle of the poem—"that I want to give to someone."

Lilaios bowed. "Anything in the service of my queen, my lady. I will have them for you tomorrow."

Nehemiah spoke to the king a few days later, and Damaspia relayed what she knew of the conversation to Esther. Artaxerxes had noticed that his usually cheerful cupbearer looked troubled and preoccupied, and had asked the reason. When he heard what was on Nehemiah's mind, he had seen the opportunity to reverse the wrong he'd done in stopping work on the Temple. He realized that he had the power to continue what he'd begun 13 years before with Ezra. And so he gave Nehemiah authority to go back to Jerusalem as its governor and oversee the rebuilding of the Temple and the city walls.

By the time Esther got the news, she was spending most of each day in bed. Hathakh had insisted on calling a physician, but after examining her the doctor shook his head. "I can give you herbs for the pain, that is all," he told her. He gave her the herbs; she tried to use them as little as possible. She wasn't sure why, only that she felt that even pain came from God's hand, and she must try to bear it as best she could. Even ill, she wanted to walk the path He had given her for as long as she could.

One afternoon, feeling a little better, she sat on the balcony outside her chamber in the warm sunshine. Ayana and Hathakh sat with her. For so many years all three of them had been so busy. Though Hathakh had not borne the title of steward for many years, nor Ayana that of lady in waiting, out of love and long habit they still served Esther and the household. Now the years were catching up with them all. Younger hands did most of the work, and there was time to sit in the sun.

Esther often encouraged them to come sit with her, to lay aside other duties. However, she had kept to herself what the doctor said. In fact, she'd told no one, not even Damaspia. That knowledge was between her and God. But they knew she was in pain and could see she was losing strength. Ayana tried to coax her to eat, but she coaxed gently, as if knowing it was almost too much to ask. Hathakh did not coax her at all—not to sit up, nor to eat, nor even to talk. He talked little himself when they were together; simply being together was enough. Either he or Ayana, or both of them, were with Esther almost all the time now.

"Nehemiah is leaving within the week," Ayana told Esther. "He came today while you were sleeping."

Esther nodded. She found it hard to talk. A hand seemed to have closed over her throat. "My jewels," she said. "Remember—I said—years ago when I gave so many to Ezra—I said there would be a need."

"All of them?" Hathakh said.

"You must keep one set for—" Ayana paused. "For your own need." She would not say "one set to be buried in," but Esther understood, and nodded.

"My wedding jewels," Esther said. "I'll keep—them. All the rest"—it was difficult to find enough breath for speech—"to Jerusalem. I'll never see it—now," she added.

Ayana rose to go get the coffer of jewels. Hathakh was silent a moment, then he leaned forward, looking not at Esther but down at his hands. "The followers of Zarathustra talk of a bridge between the land of the living and the land of the dead," he said almost to himself. "I've searched our Scriptures time and again, looking to see if we have any such bridge, looking to find what's on the other side. Our prophets say so little about what comes after death, but the sage Daniel writes of a time at the end of time, when he says 'Multitudes who sleep in the dust of the earth will awake . . . those who are wise will shine like the stars forever and ever.'

"I don't know what that time will be, or what it means to shine like the stars, but I know that whatever is beyond this life must be good, because God is there."

Esther smiled. "Perhaps I *will* see Jerusalem, then," she said. "At the last." Hathakh looked up then, into her eyes. Not everyone could speak of death and the world beyond it, to a dying woman, though there was little else now that she wanted to speak of. But Hathakh knew that, and was not afraid to speak the words. His faith helped her hold onto God when the pain grew too great. *How strange,* she thought, *that Hathakh should be the one to fix my eyes on the God of Israel—the God whose Temple would not accept his imperfect body, yet who had wholly won his heart's allegiance.*

That reminded her of something, but she need not strain to speak, for Ayana would have found it by now. It was with the jewels. And indeed Ayana came out carrying the beautifully carved coffer with its few remaining treasures. A rolled scroll balanced on top. "What is this?" she asked.

Too tired to reach for it, Esther nodded at Hathakh, and Ayana gave it to him. "For Hathakh," Esther whispered. Her last, and perhaps her best, gift.

She sat there watching them as Hathakh read the words on the scroll, whispering them to himself. She had found no dearer friends in life than these two. She was glad these last years had given them leisure to spend time together, to speak at least some of what was hidden in their hearts. She had dreamed, once, that they would all grow old together, but she had not imagined that—for her, at least— it would happen so soon. So many things left to do, so many problems left unsolved. But they were in God's hands. She pictured them now, the hands of her God, strong and scarred with hard work, yet gentle as a mother's cradling her child.

"Read it aloud," Ayana said to Hathakh.

And so Hathakh read the prophecy of Isaiah, the poem Lilaios had found and loved.

> *"Let no foreigner who has bound himself to the Lord say,*
> *'The Lord will surely exclude me from his people.'*
> *And let not any eunuch complain,*
> *"I am only a dry tree."*
> *For this is what the Lord says:*
> *'To the eunuchs who keep my Sabbaths,*
> *who choose what pleases me and hold fast to my covenant—*
> *to them I will give within my temple and its walls*
> *a memorial and a name better than sons and daughters;*
> *I will give them an everlasting name that will not be cut off.*
> *And foreigners who bind themselves to the Lord to serve him,*
> *to love the name of the Lord, and to worship him,*
> *all who keep the Sabbath without desecrating it*
> *and who hold fast to my covenant—*

> *these I will bring to my holy mountain*
> *and give them joy in my house of prayer.*
> *Their burnt offerings and sacrifices will be accepted on my altar;*
> *for my house will be called a house of prayer for all nations.' "*

The three sat in silence. Tears glistened in Hathakh's eyes. At last he rolled up the scroll and tucked it into the pocket of his robe. "Thank you, my lady," he said.

"Thank you," Esther murmured—to Hathakh, to Anaya. To God.

Esther lay her head back against the warm wall, enjoying the sun's golden glow through her eyelids. Opening her eyes, she memorized the dear, familiar faces of her friends. The sun was warm on her arms, her neck, her face.

She closed her eyes and did not open them again.

EPILOGUE

The two processions, each led by musicians and singers, marched along newly built city walls. Cymbals, harps, and lyres mingled with trained voices, filling the air with the praises of the God of Israel. In the streets below, throngs of people dressed in their holiday best mingled, echoing the singers, clapping their hands, and waving palm branches high in the air.

Among the crowds in Jerusalem that day were many who had traveled far to see this celebration as the walls of the old city, so long in rebuilding, were finally dedicated. Most of the travelers were Jews from different corners of the far-flung Persian Empire; a few were foreigners, friendly to the God and people of Israel or perhaps just curious, who stood here and there among the crowd.

Two of those foreigners stood near the East Gate, where they could see the Temple rising in its splendor. It too had been rebuilt, mostly because of the untiring labors of the man leading one of the two processions. "Look, there he is—it's Nehemiah," the woman said, nudging the man, pointing at him as the choir marched past. She was an elderly woman, tall and angular. Her hair might have been white or gray, but there was no telling, as it was covered by her head covering. Her skin was darker than that of most in the crowd, and she had bright eyes that seemed to miss nothing.

The man with her was slightly stooped with age. His hair was iron-gray; he was beardless, which was enough of an oddity in this crowd that everyone who saw him knew he must be a eunuch. He nodded as the woman pointed out the lord Nehemiah, and smiled a little.

Few in the crowd paid any attention to the elderly pair. When the two choirs and their following of musicians, priests, and Levites met and began the march into the Temple, the great mass of people flowed toward the Temple, too. Not all could get inside, of course, but everyone could hear the triumphant singing that echoed from its courtyards and walls.

The foreign man and woman did not even try to get near the Temple, for they knew that neither of them would have found a place inside. Yet they looked glad to be in this place on this day. A passerby might have seen the woman brush away a tear, with a gesture that suggested she did not often do this. They waited and watched, talking little, easy in each other's company. They were standing in a spot where they'd agreed to meet someone, and long afterward, when the singing in the Temple had stopped and the smoke of the sacrifices was curling lazily up into the sky, when the crowds were busy with their own celebrating, a man robed in the gown of a Temple singer came across the square and met them there.

He pressed both their hands to his lips, and bowed, though he was clearly a man of higher station in life than either of them. He too looked like a foreigner, though he had just come from the Temple itself.

"Lilaios," the woman said. "How long it's been since we saw you."

He smiled. "I do not use that name here anymore, Ayana. I took a good Jewish name, Shemaiah, along with my good Jewish wife and children. It is not an easy time for outsiders here. Those who know me know that I am a true convert. I have been circumcised and joined the people of Israel, but not everyone accepts me in spite of that."

"Yet you have chosen to remain here," the older man said.

"I have. Where else should a follower of Israel's God be, when His city is finally rebuilt and His Temple rings with His praises? Hathakh, Ayana, I am so glad you were able to come, both of you, though the journey is so long."

"I hope the people are not too unwelcoming to strangers," Hathakh said, "for we will not make this journey a second time. What days we have, we will have to live out here in Jerusalem."

"You are welcome in my home," said Lilaios—now Shemaiah. "And you are friends of Nehemiah, even of Ezra, who is more strict than anyone about keeping Israel pure. One can understand their concern, after all the long years of exile and the struggle to rebuild this land. And yet . . . I dream of a day when these doors will be open to people of all lands, that all may come and learn of Israel's God, the God of all the earth."

"A house of prayer for all nations," Ayana echoed.

"She loved those words," Hathakh said. "They were on a scroll you had copied for her. It was the last gift she gave me, before she died." Esther, queen of Persia, dead many years now, was on all their minds, though no one had yet spoken her name.

"She dreamed of coming here," Ayana said. "It was truly for her that we made this journey, though we both longed to see Jerusalem."

"She earned the right to see it, if anyone ever did," Shemaiah said. "The ways of God are strange, but He holds all in His hands, even our beloved dead." All three were silent a moment, remembering. The noise of the crowd shifted a little. People were moving away, back to their own homes to continue celebrating.

"Come," said Shemaiah. "I will take you both to Nehemiah. He will rejoice to see you again."

Ayana followed him at once. Hathakh remained behind for just a moment, looking down at the Temple shining in the sunset. He shielded his eyes against the brilliant light. How it reminded him of Xerxes' great palace at Parsa, for it too had shone like the sun itself when the golden rays slanted against the stone.

"To them I will give within my temple and its walls a memorial and a name better than sons and daughters; I will give them an everlasting name that will not be cut off," he slowly repeated. He bowed his head briefly, then turned away to follow Shemaiah.

AFTERWORD

As an avid reader of historical narratives and a lover of history, I always enjoy it when the author of a piece of historical fiction puts a note at the end of his or her book telling which details were actually drawn from history and which were the product of the writer's imagination. Since this book weaves together a Bible story with secular history and imagination, I wanted to offer those readers who are interested in this kind of thing the answers to just a few questions.

I have an undergraduate degree in history, which, as I've often told people, is just enough education to know what a historian does and to recognize that I'm not one. When sifting through the evidence for the stories of ancient history, the historian has a challenging task: to fit together scanty and often conflicting pieces of evidence to discover what is most likely to have actually happened. The creative writer who writes a historical story, like this one, has a much easier task. We follow in the footsteps of the historian, examine the evidence, and choose the pieces that fit together to make a believable and enjoyable story, without contradicting any known facts.

When I began researching the historical background of the book of Esther, I was struck by the fact that almost all scholars, except the most conservative of Christian and Jewish writers, treated the story as a romance, a piece of fiction. The argument generally made goes something like this: the book of Esther was written by someone very familiar with Achaemenid Persia and particularly with the reign of Xerxes (whom almost everyone agrees was the biblical Ahasuerus) and his palace at Susa, but none of the story's details can be confirmed historically and some contradict known facts. Particularly, it is often claimed that neither Haman nor Mordecai are ever mentioned in Persian records as viziers or prime ministers in the reign of Xerxes, and that Esther could not have been Xerxes' queen since: (1) Achaemenid kings married only within seven noble Persian families, and (2) Xerxes had only one wife, and her name was Amestris. Thus, the book of Esther must be fiction.

In fact, these arguments are convincing only to someone who has spent no time studying the period. Primary sources for Achaemenid history are notoriously scarce, except for the thousands of treasury tablets, many of which have yet to be read and translated. The Persian sources do not record the name of *any* "vizier" or "prime minister" in the reign of Xerxes; it is not even clear that the position existed under that name. The Persians either did a poor job of writing their own history or (more likely) lost it when they were conquered by the Greeks under Alexander the Great. For accounts of the reign of Xerxes we are dependent on the Greek author Herodotus, who has the advantage of being a contemporary, but the disadvantage of being the only person to record many of the events he writes about. We have no way of checking his reliability, and his presentation is often slanted to promote his pro-Greek bias. Historians generally discount many of Herodotus' stories as fiction, but whenever he contradicts the Bible, Herodotus is held up as the standard of truth, since so many scholars have so little respect for the Bible as a source of historical truth—or so it seems to me, coming to the subject as a well-read layperson.

So, for example, the argument goes that Xerxes had only one wife, and her name was Amestris. In fact, Persian sources tell us nothing about any wife of Xerxes. Herodotus mentions Xerxes' queen Amestris in two places; he doesn't tell us whether Xerxes had any other wives. Xerxes' father, Darius, had at least six wives; there is no reason to assume Xerxes suddenly decided to introduce the practice of monogamy. Furthermore, there is very little clarity about the meaning of the words translated as "wife," "queen," and "concubine," and almost no clear evidence about what the roles and status of different royal women were at that time. The statement that kings married only within seven noble families is also based on Herodotus, and is not supported in other sources—in fact, there is plenty of evidence that this rule, if it ever existed, was not strictly followed.

Some biblical scholars have done an excellent job of arguing that Herodotus' "Amestris" and the Bible's "Vashti" were actually the same woman. While I respect the scholarship that supports this argument, I don't think it's the most likely explanation: if Herodotus' stories have any truth at all, they seem unlikely to apply to a woman who was discredited and possibly divorced before Xerxes ever attacked Greece. Without further historical evidence we can't know the absolute truth of this. I built my story around the hypothesis that Xerxes had several wives, three of whom were Vashti, Esther, and Amestris. I invented Xerxes' other two wives, Parmys and Irdabama. Irdabama deserves a very small note of her own: I had already created the character of Xerxes' plain and practical second wife when I read about the records in the Persian tablets of a woman connected with the royal family by the name of Irdabama, who was apparently an excellent business manager with large estates to rule. While there's absolutely no evidence that this Irdabama was one of Xerxes' wives or even that she lived during his time, I thought it fair to give that name to the queen I had already invented.

Damaspia, Artaxerxes' wife, deserves a note of her own too. We know from a reference in another classical historian that King Artaxerxes had a wife named Damaspia, the mother of his son Xerxes. Absolutely nothing else is known about Damaspia, which left me quite free to invent the possibility that Artaxerxes had followed the common Achaemenid custom of marrying a half sister, and that Damaspia was the daughter of Esther. Again, there is of course no evidence to support this. But if we accept the Bible as God's inspired Word and a source of historical truth, then Esther really was Xerxes' wife, and probably bore him children, and unless she died young both she and her children must have continued to exert an influence at Artaxerxes' court. The kindness Artaxerxes showed to both Ezra and Nehemiah, and his support of the rebuilding of Jerusalem, stimulated my thinking on this area. Could there have been a family connection that made Artaxerxes predisposed to like and support Jews? Sharp readers will also notice that the Bible mentions the presence of Artaxerxes' queen when Nehemiah speaks of his desire to go to Jerusalem.

In constructing this story, I have tried as far as possible never to contradict anything we know from the Bible or from reliable historical sources—and the fact that the two fit together so well suggests to me that the story of Esther has a strong basis in history (for example, the period between Vashti's dismissal and the king's marriage to Esther corresponds almost exactly with the period during which Xerxes was away fighting in Greece). Only one major historical event in the story is completely fabricated: the rebellion that leads to the execution of the poet Lilaios.

When historical records give two or more versions of an event, two or more possible dates, or two or more names for the same individual, I unabashedly chose whichever fit my story better. And, since no one has ever suggested that Herodotus was divinely inspired, I felt free to modify the details of some of his more fantastic tales, particularly the story of Xerxes, Artaynte, and Amestris, to fit the needs of my own story.

Every writer of historical narratives fears the anachronism worse than almost any monster, and I'm quite sure that despite the best efforts of myself and my editors, a few have crawled into this text. Only one has been allowed in knowingly: the Kaddish, used today as the Jewish prayer for the dead, dates from a much later period. Since we do not know exactly how the Jews of the Persian exile mourned their dead, I have used the words of the Kaddish in Chapter 17, feeling they were appropriate though not historically accurate.

As well as consulting many historical sources, I also read a number of theological works on the book of Esther. The character of Esther, and her story, has been interpreted in so many different ways by Jews and Christians over the years, and the biblical account really tells us very little about Esther as a person: what she believed and what motivated her. Of course, the book of Esther is famous for being the only book in the Bible that doesn't mention the name of God, and this absence has been much commented upon. From out of the many "theories of Esther" I read, I felt most convinced by those writers who believed that Esther and Mordecai and the other Jews of the exile at that time were probably fairly "secular" Jews, assimilated into the Persian culture around them, and that Esther's faith in God grew throughout her experiences in the king's palace to the point where she was finally able to risk her life to save God's people. Larry Lichtenwalter's book *Behind the Seen* was an important influence on my thinking about Esther.

It would be impossible (and tedious!) to list all the books and articles I read in preparing this novel, but those readers who are interested in the story of Esther or in this period in history may refer to the list below for just a few of my favorites.

Researching and writing this story has done many things for me, but above all it has strengthened my faith in the historicity of the Bible, as well as in the God who moves in history. I hope that reading it has done the same for you.

SELECTED RESOURCES

Maria Brosius, *Women in Ancient Persia*, Oxford University Press, 1996.

J. M. Cook, *The Persian Empire*, Schocken, 1983.

Alev Lytle Croutier, *Harem: The World Behind the Veil*, Abbeville Press, 1998.

Richard Frye, *The Heritage of Persia*, Mazda Publishing, 1993.

Larry Lichtenwalter, *Behind the Seen: God's Hand in Esther's Life . . . and Yours*, Review and Herald Pub. Assn., 2001.

A. T. Olmstead, *History of the Persian Empire*, University of Chicago, 1959.

Gerald Wheeler, *Footsteps of God*, Review and Herald Pub. Assn., 1987.

D. N. Wilber, *Persepolis: The Archaeology of Parsa*, Darwin Press, 1989.

Edwin Yamauchi, *Persia and the Bible*, Baker Book House, 1997.